WINSTON'S KINGDOM

Winston Trilogy, Book III

A necessary sequel to
One Just Man
and
Elohim—Masters and Minions

A novel by
Stan I.S. Law

INHOUSEPRESS
Montreal—Canada

Contents

ACKNOWLEDGMENTS

By the same author

ALEC (Alexander Trilogy, Book I)
ALEXANDER (Alexander Trilogy, Book II)
SACHA—The Way Back (Alexander Trilogy, Book III)
YESHUA—Personal Memoir of the Missing Years of Jesus
PETER AND PAUL (An intuitive sequel to Yeshûa)
ONE JUST MAN (Winston Trilogy Book I)
ELOHIM (Winston Trilogy Book II)
WINSTON'S KINGDOM (Winston Trilogy Book III)
THE AVATAR SYNDROME (Prequel to Headless World)
HEADLESS WORLD—The Vatican Incident
(Sequel to *The Avatar Syndrome*)
MARVIN CLARK–In Search of Freedom
THE GATE—Things My Mother Told Me
NOW—Being and Becoming
GIFT OF GAMMAN
THE PRINCESS
ENIGMA of the Second Coming
WALL—Love, Sex, and Immortality (Aquarius Trilogy Book I)
PLUTO EFFECT [Aquarius Trilogy Book II]
OLYMPUS—Of Gods and Men [Aquarius Trilogy Book III]

Short stories

THE JEWEL & OTHER STORIES
CATS AND DOGS
Sci-Fi Series 1
Sci-Fi Series 2

Non-fiction Books by Stanislaw Kapuscinski

VISUALIZATION—Creating Your Own Universe
KEY TO IMMORTALITY
[Commentary on the Gospel of Thomas]
BEYOND RELIGION: Volumes I, II and III
[Collections of essays on perception of Reality]
DICTIONARY OF BIBLICAL SYMBOLISM
DELUSIONS—Pragmatic Realism

Poetry in Polish
[with illustrations by Bozena Happach]
KILKA SŁÓW I TROCHĘ GLINY
WIĘCEJ SŁÓW I WIĘCEJ GLINY

INHOUSEPRESS, MONTREAL, CANADA
http://inhousepress.ca

Part One

DREAMS

*"...Strominger and Vafa advocated 'designer' black holes...
...systematically constructed... but carefully, slowly, and
meticulously weaving together a precise combination of the
branes that emerged from the second superstring revolution."*

The Elegant Universe
Brian Greene

1

Back to Square One

The place looked sterile. It smelled of antiseptic. There was a feeling of everything having been freshly scrubbed. The lackluster thermoplastic tiles extended far into the distance. They were matched with equally spaced fluorescent fixtures, set flush with the ceiling. The walls converged on each other, the top and bottom corners of the floor and ceiling meeting somewhere, well ahead, at a single point.

Too far to see…

He walked briskly, his rubber soles making no sound. His white coat, opened in front, seemed to give him wings, adding to the lightness of his step. The inevitable stethoscope hung loosely around his neck.

He pushed the first door on the right. His eyebrows went up when he saw that the room was empty. He shrugged, turned around, and pushed the door on the left of the corridor. Same result. Two beds, neatly made up, only the patients were missing. He quickened his pace, pushing the doors to his left and right. The place was deserted. He started jogging. He had to get to the end of the corridor to finish his rounds. Only a mile to go. A mile? Perhaps a little more. The horizon continued to recede. New doors seemed to have punctured the pale green walls even as he reeled between them with mounting desperation.

I need a patient, he thought.

I need a patient!

Now running, hardly slowing down as he kicked at the doors, until he slammed one with his fist as though trying to get inside the room before the patient had a chance to disappear.

His fist landed on the headboard. It hurt. Badly. It woke him up. He wiped sweat from his forehead.

It was well past midnight when Cathy came out of the bedroom. She loved this time of the night. Some of the best ideas came to her in those idle moments of silence that was almost palpable. Sometimes she thought that the gentle buzz she heard in her head were atoms whirling, arranging themselves in an orderly fashion. Silently she approached the floor-to-ceiling windows. Forty-nine floors below, she could just see occasional lampposts, like tiny pocket torches. Or they could have been porch-lights, reaching her from the few villas dotting the lower slopes of Mount Royal—blinking, whimsically, between autumn leaves, as though trying hard to go to sleep also. Only the Cross, at the east end of the mountain, seemed frozen in time.

Perhaps it was. Aren't all crosses frozen in time?

She was still motionless when she felt Peter's hand stroking her hair. The thick carpet must have muted his steps. They were both naked. At this elevation, surrounding buildings were not high enough to invade their intimacy. It was their private Eden, high up in the sky—as perhaps Eden should be—where even a single leaf didn't camouflage Cathy's beauty. There was a strange innocence that imbued the love they had for each other. Innocence engulfing only those people who chose to live in Paradise. It was the innocence that had distinguished both Adam and Eve before that single apple from the tree of knowledge stirred their senses of sensual desire.

"Not even a bit…" Peter mused, without breaking the silence. He, too, was thinking of that fateful apple.

"What, darling?" She still didn't move, but a knowing smile played at the corners of her mouth.

His thoughts shifted.

"You had that dream, again," she whispered. It seemed proper to whisper in the middle of the night, even when they were alone.

He nodded. "They seem to come more often lately."

"It probably means something. Did you talk to Winston?"

"Aren't we supposed to be grownups by now?"

Cathy smiled. "Today is the first day of the rest of our existence. We're very, very young…"

"…considering we're immortal."

They both smiled. There was assurance in their faces, but the smile also trembled on the edge of uncertainty. The sort that is born in the unknown.

Peter regarded Cathy's hazy reflection, shimmering in the dark window. His thoughts drifted to old memories. She hasn't changed one bit, he thought, again, this time blocking her emotive probes. He couldn't quite read other people's minds, but he could construe the general outline of their musings. It had taken him years to hone his skills, but at long last he was gaining control over his mental equipment. Cathy was not quite as adept, but she was well ahead of him in sensing emotions.

Her reflection moved against the background of the twinkling lights, then retreated towards the bedroom door. He felt lucky she didn't seem to notice his own mirror image. Time was not as kind to him as it was to her. He felt heavier; he wasn't a man given to daily physical exercises.

Being naked always reminded them both of that first time at the Ritz-Xentung, when Dr. Catherine Mondellay had waylaid the young, handsome physician to her father's private suite. Yes, her father was that rich, only he wasn't there at the time. They'd been alone in the whole wide world. It was then that silk dress slid silently down her sinuous body for the very first time. Since that night they remained united by an unspoken pact, wedded by so much more than just some civil or ecclesiastic rites, or even pontifical announcements. Since that night they had remained united in body, emotions, in unspoken desires. And yes. Now they often even shared their thoughts.

Yet, what Peter recalled most about that very first night at the Ritz-Xentung was not of having sated his carnal desires, but the euphoric experience of two becoming one. As a student, later a young physician, he had experienced the pleasures of a number of young ladies, mostly nurses, but that was the first time, in years, that he felt like a virgin himself.

So much happened since Dr. Peter Thornton was forced to give up medicine, all thanks to the scurrilous gift—the enigmatic gift of healing—which had imposed itself, suddenly, and seemingly took residence in his hands. While initially beneficial to the recipients, Peter had found himself unable to withhold it from anyone seeking his help. The news of his talent, if such it were, had become so widely known that, all too soon, the excessive use of his gift had nearly killed him. It had sucked him dry of life juices, of the life force that apparently flowed through him toward the unfortunates in dire need of his ability. Also, he had found he had no competence to judge who should or shouldn't be the beneficiary of the power flowing through his hands. Finally, on one occasion, a man Peter had brought back from hovering on the edge of death, or nearly so, had lived only to take the life of another. Peter carried the guilt of that act to this day.

Since then, since those dark days at Chez Gaston in the lower part of the city, he'd withheld his powers; he used them, judiciously, only on very special occasions.

It had been Winston, the majordomo who did so much to look after Ruth's children, who had resuscitated Peter, literally, from the brink of death. Later, the physician who couldn't heal himself slowly recovered in Cathy's arms, and eventually lost himself in the dubious comfort of enforced anonymity. If it hadn't been for Ruth, his sister-in-law, and, later, for that strange coalition that developed between his old professor, Dr. John Brent, and Lena Walesa, the intrepid leader of Solidarity International, he would have ceased to exist. He might have vegetated somewhere, someplace, where people deprived of their personal will—shunned by the members of their own profession—abide; but it would not have been a life he would have cared for. With his expert medical knowledge, he would have terminated it himself.

Peter was no longer an 'ordinary' man. Over the arduous years since he became an outcast of the medical fraternity, he had worked hard to compensate himself for the loss of his favourite profession.

Since then he'd learned a lot, mostly thanks to Winston. The old—ageless, really—majordomo was always there, whenever most needed. He seemed to have the capacity to read Peter's mind. It was, at least in part, Winston's doing that Peter developed new interests. *Inter alia*, Peter had learned to read people's auras. Apparently everyone can do so. It takes time and effort, but the inherent ability lies dormant in each one of us. Peter hadn't known that at the time when he started to explore the esoteric aspect of his own nature.

But it hadn't been easy.

He'd spent endless hours, alone, in his room, in his sister-in-law's house, staring into the mirror, trying to discern any movement of light at the periphery of his face. Then his hands, his shoulders... Slowly, so very slowly, his eyes adjusted to the commands of his brain, his mind really, and he began to see hues beyond the usual range of light. Gradually his inner vision, for such it had to be called, came into its own. He could not only see auras, but decipher the meaning of different shades, even in people at a considerable distance.

He'd never forget the first time he saw a sphere of golden light moving uphill, towards Ruth's residence in Westmount. Winston had forgotten to consciously bring his natural luminosity under control. Of course, even its exquisite brightness remained invisible to people who resigned themselves to limit their sight to that set by mother nature.

Ah, yes, mother nature…

From the first proto-eyes that evolved over some 540 million years, the human eye was still limited to recording visible light in a tiny narrow spectrum. Framed by ultraviolet on one side and infrared on the other, man could see the violet, blue, green, yellow, and orange colours, contained between 0.000076 and 0.000038 wavelength. Beyond that, we remain blind to the brilliant mysteries of the universe. Theoretically, the X-rays, radio and cosmic rays, could be made visible, if only our brain had the capacity to interpret them. Our heads would have to be larger than a house. A large house. And it would be very, very hot inside it. Peter couldn't accept such limitations. Hence the study of the auras.

He often wondered if, on that day in Westmount, Winston had allowed him to see his aura on purpose, as a sort of reward for his hard work. Peter never saw Winston's aura again. Winston managed to conceal it even from his eyes. Peter wasn't sure why.

"It belongs to a different realm, Peter." Cathy overheard his musings at the subliminal level. When they were alone, her ability was something akin to telepathy. None of this made any 'scientific' sense. When still at the General Hospital, his colleagues, including some distinguished neurologists, had regarded reports of telepathy as 'false alarms'.

"Different realm?"

"All in good time," came the reply. This time the voice belonged to Winston. Or so Peter thought. The fact that Winston was nowhere near had nothing to do with this. Winston also didn't accept limitations.

Peter and Cathy hadn't discussed the matter since.

How would she know, Peter wondered, but this time he managed to hide this thought from her.

It had been years since Peter had walked the hospital corridors wearing a white coat. Not in his dreams, but wide awake. He smiled, remembering the stethoscope. It had become part of the uniform. He would not have been able to walk the wards without it. Nor could any physician, he supposed.

Well, now I can, he thought. I can go anywhere and not miss the touch, or the comfort, that the relatively simple device had given me—once—just hanging there.

Past. It's all in the past. Mustn't think of the past.

He looked at Cathy as she walked back towards the bedroom. Her figure was perfect. She was perfect. Beautiful, smart and, as if it mattered, rich. She... not he. He was virtually a nobody.

"Come, Peter. We have another five hours till breakfast."

He nodded. "I'll join you in a minute, darling. Go to bed."

His mind was still too active to be able to dismiss thoughts that forced themselves at his Frontal lobe. Yes, after all these years, he was still thinking like a physician. Frontal lobe, Parietal lobe, Temporal lobe, Occipital lobe... It's just a lot of lobes... What did the brain have to do with his mind? He suspected it was no more than a violin to a virtuoso. One couldn't play a concerto without it, but without him, without the musician, the violin was just a beautiful piece of wood and metal. And cat gut.

His thoughts returned to Cathy. She played a different instrument altogether. She was a virtuoso with atoms. With subatomic particles. She played with atoms and black holes.

Black holes that were no longer quite black.

That was where he and Cathy had finished their joint experiment about a month ago. Trapping a minuscule black hole in their thought-streams, cajoling it into a sustained existence. Into the space-time continuum. There was only one problem. Once the black hole became part of the material universe, it also became subject to its laws. To the law that included evolution. And evolution advanced at a rate somewhere between dead slow and dead slow. Some English scientist coined that phrase. Burke? James Burke? Or was he a broadcaster. Did it matter? Whoever coined the phrase, evolution advanced too slowly for Peter's liking.

For his emotional needs.

A new universe within a universe. Only it wasn't the same reality. Not nearly the same. Yet it was a reality which he and Cathy shared. Once... but they did share it. A month ago. Peter was determined to return to those elusive moments when he pictured a whole new world, growing, expanding; a world that wasn't there before—not seconds ago. What were the laws that ruled it? He wanted to ask Cathy but, somehow, the subject was not easy to approach. It sounded too much like a dream. A conscious dream, yet, even so, no less real.

He tiptoed quietly back to bed and slipped under the blanket. He felt exhausted. Not physically, but his mind would not give him rest. The years of relaxation exercises he'd practiced in the past seemed of no use.

As he closed his eyes, Cathy's arm came out of the darkness and draped itself, possessively, over his chest. This was by far the most relaxing thing he could hope for. Soon he'd leave this world and dive deeply into an alternate reality. Into a world where dreams, surely, are as real as Cathy's arm resting across his chest. Only he couldn't find the door.

Cathy served breakfast in the bay-window nook facing east. A small alcove, just big enough for the two of them. Orange juice, eggs, toast with Philadelphia cheese and coffee. For weeks now, they studiously avoided the subject of alternate universes. It was too absorbing, too demanding of their minds and emotions. They compromised.

"Are you still playing with your strings?" Peter asked innocently.

"Only on the piano," she replied with a straight face. Actually, she played the piano rather well.

Peter was referring to Cathy's work. As a theoretical physicist, spending part of her time at the CERN laboratories in Switzerland, she was wrapped up in weak and strong, electromagnetic and gravitational forces. She was also up to her neck in strings and superstrings, symmetries and supersymmetries, and other exotic characteristics of the M theory. To Peter it all sounded more like science fiction. Cathy had even spoken of ten or eleven dimensions, all curled up in some Calabi-Yau spheroids, or spaces, which were, to him, as complex as they were incomprehensible.

"Perhaps they are, Peter, but we must keep trying," she read or sensed his thoughts again.

"Why?"

"That's rather a silly question, isn't it?"

"Not if you accept that there are other realities," he countered.

"And how would that affect us, here? Here and now?"

"The other realities are here and now."

She played with the remnants of her fried eggs, then looked up from her plate.

"You really believe that?" She avoided his eyes.

For a moment Peter was very busy spreading cream cheese on his toast. Then he let go the knife and leaned back. His eyes searched Cathy's.

"I sometimes think that all of this here-and-now business is a lot of baloney. I find it hard to accept that primitive humanoids, on a primitive planet, circling a very average sun set on the periphery of the second outer arm of a minor galaxy, would be endowed with the power to comprehend the universe. We don't even know how large it is. And each time you guys recalculate it, it gets bigger. We also don't know, regardless of your strings, how small are our component parts. Planck's constant? Planck mass? Ten billion billion times the mass of a proton? Sounds huge—it's minuscule. These are just words."

"How long is a piece of string?" she smiled. When Peter didn't answer, she said, "It's about a Planck's length." Then she saw his expression. "About 10^{-33} of a centimeter. It's a sort of a joke in my, ah, circles."

Peter blinked, then downed his coffee.

"There are trillions of electrochemical reactions taking place in my body," he resumed. "Even as I speak to you and... well, as an ex-physician, I haven't the faintest idea how to replicate such a self-propelling biological robot as I am..."

"Easy, darling. Live and let live..."

"If you define life, for me. And that's another thing. If we are to believe the religions, before we have a chance to discover who or what we really are, we die. And then? *La morte è nulla!"*

He finished his minor soliloquy with an agonized cry emulating Iago's cry in the monologue in his favorite opera, Otello.

"Iago was furious, psychotic and filled with hate. You are none of these."

"I'm sorry. I guess, I'm just tired."

"It's the dreams, isn't it, darling."

"I suppose so. Though why would my long-gone profession keep coming back to hunt me, I have no idea. I wonder if Winston is somewhere behind it."

"If he is, you'll have to find out for yourself. He won't tell you. You know how he works."

"Yes. He makes you work for it. Each step you take you must earn. All he really does is create opportunities."

"By pushing you until you give up and decide to solve the problem."

"You really know him well, darling."

"I had to learn, to retain my sanity."

Cathy also went through the trials imposed, seemingly, by Winston. She was torn between the micro and the macro universes. As a theoretical physicist, she was mostly preoccupied with the very, very small. Since quantum mechanics had wrenched her away from the Einsteinian macro-universe, she sailed smoothly, until the later work reduced the Big Bang theory to the first fragments of a second, when the universe was, or seemed to have been, a tiny black hole. Not only had all matter shrunk to a pinpoint, but so did space. According to latest theories, before the big bang there was neither space nor matter nor time. Everything had shrunk into nothingness.

In a way, so had God.

At this point she became a cosmologist. Theoretical one, of course.

"You know, darling, no matter how much we might deny it, we are all searching for meaning. The meaning of life, of reality, but mostly we are all seekers of truth. We all want to know who we are and, perhaps even more, we want to know why we are here."

So did Cathy, only she pursued her curiosity with the passion she'd inherited from her father. Dr. Mondellay was one of the foremost physicists of the previous generation. Cathy was determined to be his worthy successor. She was.

Breakfast was over. Peter finished his second toast, one more than he ate usually. They were both lingering over black coffee, not wanting to get up and join the world, with which they both felt little affinity. They tried their best to leave the exigencies of everyday life behind them. Later that day, towards the evening, they would host a number of their friends in their nest suspended in the sky. The forty-ninth floor gave them regal command over the city. A lot more than they held over their lives.

"I'll clean up, and then, you are invited, Sir, for a walk on the mountain. Looks like a beautiful day."

Practically from the day they'd met, the Saturday morning stroll up and down the mountain was a rite that they both loved. Provided they were both in town. Cathy encouraged Peter to go up on his own, in her absence, but somehow it wasn't the same when she wasn't there. She made the grass greener, she imbued the autumn leaves with richer golds and reds, she even added a different fragrance to the air... when she was there.

"Look, Peter, they are ready to weave their own nest..." She pointed to a pair of robins going about their business. He would never have noticed, on his own.

"I bet he'll never catch her..." she said, a moment later, pointing up to a furry cloud, its jaws wide open, in hot pursuit of a feathery beast of some sort. She always saw shapes in the clouds. Perhaps she could have been a great sculptor. In complete contrast to her disciplined physicist's mind, outside her lab she compensated by filling her world with allegorical creatures. They seemed as real to her as her invisible atoms and quarks. Perhaps more so. At least she could see them. Often, almost touch them. And, usually, when she indulged her imagination, Peter was there. And he was real. Very real.

The table was cleared, dishes stacked in the washing machine. Cathy was putting on her walking shoes. Peter followed her to the bedroom to get his sweater. It was already getting chilly, this time of the year.

They spent the next two hours with their feet firmly planted on earth. It was beautiful, and once the sun came out from its cottony garments, Peter had to remove his sweater. They didn't talk much. Just walked, arm in arm, their eyes staring at the kaleidoscope of autumn around them. Much has been said and written about the Canadian fall. It was all true.

They came back refreshed. They still had time to sit back with a good book and rest their feet. Time enough to get ready for their guests in an hour or two.

It was about then that Peter stopped in his tracks. He knew the answer. Well, he knew the road he must travel to find the answer. He'd read about it some time ago, but he had dismissed it as hearsay. As another pipe-dream of pseudo philosophers—people too lazy to take the scientific route, who instead dabbled in black magic of metaphysical mumbo-jumbo. Except this is what he'd once thought about auras, not to mention of healing without the aid of medicine.

"The magic of today is the science of tomorrow…"

He had no idea whose statement it was, originally, but it was Winston's voice that delivered this snippet of encouragement to him right now. Some years ago he would have spun on his heels, expecting to see Winston towering behind him. Today he knew better. Winston was only seen when he chose to be seen. Sometimes Peter wondered if Winston didn't exist just in his own imagination.

There was hollow laughter echoing in his head.

"Well, you can't blame me, can you," the voice said. Peter was quite alone in the room. As alone as anyone who knows Winston, personally, can be—Winston Smith, the enigmatic majordomo at Ruth Thornton's house, in the elite Upper Westmount, with the sideline of looking after her children.

Cathy came in with a book. She walked past him, planting a breathy kiss on his lips. She did those little tokens often. They endeared her to Peter more than would great odes of love. She sat down by the window.

"Cathy?"

She waited patiently.

"It seems…" he began, his voice still tentative, "it seems that we are here for one purpose only—to learn. I'm sorry to disappoint you, my dear Cathy, but we are here to learn not about things, be they the cosmos or the heart of the atom, or even your beloved strings and M theory, but to learn about us. About you and me. About the consciousness that abides within us."

She looked up from the settee. There was something in his voice that made her open her eyes wide.

"If someone, or something, can program my dream to repeat itself, then, by all that's holy, so can I!"

She smiled with unadulterated pleasure. Peter was at his most attractive in moments of great decisions. Judging by his expression, this one heralded the beginning of a great adventure.

***

2

Reunion at the Aerie

Over the years, Peter had visited Dr. and Mrs. John Brent, his old professor, a number of times. He'd also dined, on a number of occasions, at Cathy's parents' house, at the top of Westmount. And, of course, ever since his brother died in that accident in China, he'd spent a good part of his years in Ruth's residence. It all added up to a debt of gratitude which, at long last, he could attempt to discharge. At least in part. All thanks to Cathy and her organizing ability.

This was the official house-warming party for people whom Peter and Cathy held closest to their heart. Even Winston was persuaded to come—though at first he refused to sit down in the presence of such distinguished members of the Montreal elite. Finally, Cathy made sure that he'd stay put by sitting on the arm of Winston's armchair, and threatening to slide onto his lap if he so much as blinked. To play safe, she also instructed Ruth's children, Moira and Jonathan, who refused to stay at home alone, to make sure that Winston remained in his Grand Puba Chair, and didn't dare to move to serve others. Not that the children belonged in such a group of elders, but, with Ruth's time being at a premium, she refused to go anywhere without them, if she could possibly take them with her.

His sister-in-law, probably the most beautiful woman Peter had ever seen, graced the opposite corner of the vast living room. Her dark complexion complemented the jet-black hair, with not a strand of gray, offsetting the dark-green long taffeta dress, which neither clung nor was loose, yet it made her look both inaccessible and desirable. A paradox that Peter, in his younger days, would have greatly admired. Together, the colours offset the lustrous blood-red rubies Peter had given her, once, in a moment of abounding gratitude.

She drew her legs under the chair, as if to make room for John Robb's lower limbs. Seemingly sitting up straight, he stretched himself on her left, trying hard not to let his arms and legs get in anyone's way. Better known as JR, he was as lanky as he was tall, but it was his legs that seemed to dangle from his spindly body for an indeterminate distance. When Solidarity International Canada grew to double its numbers south of the border, Ruth appointed JR to run the Canadian branch single-handedly. She oversaw the whole of North America, and was there to assist if needed. And, of course, there was Lena Walesa, at the Vatican, for emergencies.

Since the last 'war' that threatened peace in Europe, Lena had concentrated on overall coordination of Solidarity International, with little time for local problems. Each European nation had its own representative at the Vatican. In recent months the activities of AI, the artificial intelligence, generated by the USA calmed down, but the influence of Far-Eastern blocs, particularly the nanotechnology developed in India and China, began to infringe on Solidarity's interests. It was a dark and somber world they lived in. Struggle for power was nearing its peak.

But not tonight.

On Ruth's right stood a tall, gray-haired man in a navy uniform, who seemed ready to pose for a sculpture. For some reason he preferred to remain standing. A perfectly cut, immaculate, white uniform displayed his figure to best advantage. He was precisely the sort of man who should accompany Ruth on official, and even social, functions such as this. His name was Commander Francis Drake, probably dating back to his famous predecessor, the Vice Admiral of the same name, if some half-millennium into the past.

The remaining guests were disposed in the space between the two trios. They were made up of Peter's old professor, Dr. John Brent, with his wife, Lucy, hanging on to his arm, and Cathy's parents, making up a foursome that was already lost in some absorbing discussion. Peter smiled, suspecting that Dr. Mondellay was, for the umpteenth time, explaining to the Brents the intricacies of cold fusion, while Dr. Brent never tired of praising the now-lost medical talents of his old protégé, Peter himself.

Peter noticed that time was kind to the old professor. He seemed frozen in time from the day he'd introduced Dr. Peter Thornton to the illustrious group, when Peter had become the youngest inductee into the society of the Fellowship of the Royal College of Surgeons and Physicians.

Another time—another life, thought Peter.

The party was rolling under its own steam. With the exception of Commander Drake, all guests knew each other and were glad to share the latest gossip.

Peter mixed, stopping momentarily with each group, then leaned on the bar counter and surreptitiously regarded his sister-in-law over the rim of his glass. In the days before she became the Numero Uno of Solidarity for the whole of America, he owed her a great deal. Ruth, having lost her husband, seemed glad for the company he'd provided, though, at the time, he was working fourteen-hour days—first studying, then working as a resident at the General Hospital. Since that time, his sister-in-law appeared to have taken the enormous responsibilities of her new job in her stride. She wore her crown lightly, treating even the most junior of her assistants with equal decorum. Her staff loved her. She was a lady *par excellence*, in the truest sense of the word.

Peter attempted to read Ruth's thoughts. Just for fun, but also to find out something about her escort. He didn't learn much. Ruth was busy being a perfect lady, allowing JR to admire her rubies. Smiling disarmingly, she seemed deep in discussion with him. Peter hoped it wasn't business. Surely, she needed a rest. Actually, Ruth was also an accomplished actress. She managed to conceal, perhaps under a layer of fresh make-up, the last three days of intensive negotiations with the American trade unions, which must have left her exhausted.

Peter transferred his attention to Commander Drake, and... hit a blank wall. He'd heard about him; most of Montreal's higher echelons of society had, but, until today, for some reason Peter had managed to miss an actual introduction. During the last two or three months, Commander Drake had been in attendance at virtually all Solidarity International social functions, at Ruth's side. Social functions were always, at least partly, political in nature. Often, also under the umbrella of the Solidarity, Peter had been invited. He chose to stay away. He found exchanging sweet little nothings with the ladies and gentlemen of the political realm particularly boring. And now, at last, the statuesque *arbiter elegantiarum* was gracing his living room. From a distance, he looked even better.

All too soon, Peter found him an enigma.

There were three things wrong with Drake. One, he was definitely too perfect. Two, he looked a little too much like his late brother, Andrew. In fact he was Andrew less his brother's perennial scowl, and an equally permanent lopsided grin. And three... well three was from a very different category. Commander Francis Drake had no detectable aura.

Peter turned to make sure the drinks were being served well by the two men Cathy had borrowed for the night from Ritz-Xentung, who also 'imported' everyone's favourite dishes. With Peter and Cathy leaving the next day, the two men would later also take care of the cleanup. By the time he looked at the Commander again, Ruth was no longer at Drake's side.

"So what do you think, brother dear?" Ruth's voice came from behind him.

"Where did you find him?"

"In the wardrobe in my bedroom," Ruth said with a straight face.

"Care to elaborate?"

"There was Andrew's old skiing hat, you know, the old furry one. In it, not surprisingly, they found one of Andrew's hairs…"

"…and the rest is history," Peter added.

Sometime ago Ruth had started treating her brother-in-law as something between a genius and an eccentric. She wasn't sure which of the two she was now facing.

"You guessed?" she asked softly.

"No aura," Peter replied, even more quietly. Actually, everyone and everything has an aura, but for inanimate objects it is virtually imperceptible. Drake fitted this category.

Ruth remembered. It had been the absence of aura that had enabled Peter to recognize the spies in the Canadian Houses of Parliament. To recognize them and have them arrested.

"Why don't clones have auras? Aren't they biologically identical to us?" She thought her question was perfectly reasonable.

"You may or may not believe me, sister, but I have absolutely no idea."

After a moment's silence, Ruth went on. "The Solidarity insisted that I have a bodyguard for all social functions. Not just for being there, so to speak, but getting to and from. I had a choice. They made it clear that the, ah… man would have to be endowed with very special abilities. I had a choice to pick someone who would at least look vaguely familiar, or a total stranger. I mean in appearance."

"And you don't find the similarity to Andrew disturbing?"

"No more so than looking at his three-dimensional portrait. After all, that's what he, Francis, more or less, is." She tried to sound confident, but there was a slight hesitation in her voice.

"You are quite right. I would have done exactly the same," Peter said.

There was no point withdrawing reassurance from Ruth, even if he didn't really like the idea. On the other hand, he could see her point of view. If Francis had to have access to her home in Westmount, then having a 'total' stranger could have been even more unnerving.

"And he's programmed to be really nice to the children." She smiled, almost as if she felt guilty.

That must have clinched the deal. Perhaps there was some sort of genetic memory imprinted on Mo and Jo, which would make it easier for them to accept Francis, whatever his function. On the other hand, there was always Winston. He would never allow any harm to come to the children. Not Winston…

Since Peter had joined the Solidarity Movement, though not really as a full member, at least part of his salary came from the SI coffers. Since that fateful time, there had been an undercover war going on that most people were quite unaware of. The war was waged no longer for the heart and soul of man, but, at a deeper level, for economic dominance of the world. On the other hand, perhaps all wars have that covert reason. Until SI swelled its ranks on two continents—Europe and Canada—USA had dominated the world economically and, to a lesser extent, in other areas such as exporting its "culture", consisting mostly of English-speaking TV and movie products, for the masses. The Americans had learned early that if you cater to the lowest taste, the lowest common denominator, you also cater to the vast majority of people and thus make the most profit. This philosophy also kept their own masses quiet—if you discount the visceral roar of crowds punctuated by percussion-dominated noise accompanying the half-naked cheerleaders at the Super Bowls, various playoffs, and the World Series, where the "world" was confined strictly to the borders of the USA.

This began to change after China and India made great advances in nanotechnology, which enabled them to increase the efficacy of the human brain to a degree unheard of in the past. This, in turn, resulted in tremendous explosions in the fields of creativity, productivity and in any province in which originality allowed for growth and the resultant profit.

The USA countered with equally great strides in the development of AI. This included not only application of robots, androids, and later clones to carry out most tasks related to the maintenance of the standard of living, but also in the never-ending ambitions of the USA to act as the policeman of the world. This latter ambition led to a short-lasting but vicious 'war' which consisted, mostly, of the USA's attempting to substitute their own androids for the members of the governments of various European countries. Unofficially this was to counter the unification of the European economies under the Solidarity International umbrella, which, *inter alia*, controlled the incomes of the moguls of industries, banking, and other organizations, in which the top brass had been inordinately rewarded at the expense of the masses they employed and controlled.

Unfortunately for the USA, their indubitable success in replacing a considerable percentage of their labor force with AI units resulted in those displaced joining the SI movement. The Americans were becoming desperate and exasperated. With SI offering relative equality of income, genetic manipulation that prolonged life on the one side, and the Far-Eastern Blocs supplying the necessary acumen to enjoy life more fully, the Americans were squeezed. No one knew what the USA might do next, but everyone was living in the shadow of dire expectations.

"So you think I've done the right thing?" Ruth asked, gazing at her exemplary bodyguard.

Peter shook his head. He needed to clear his brain from thoughts fulminating in his head. He then followed Ruth's eyes towards Francis Drake.

"Of course, dear. Better a devil you know than a devil you don't..." That didn't come out right. Francis was no devil, and the model on whom he was based was a man of great charm and integrity. Even if he was my brother, Peter mused with a slight smirk. "I'm sorry, that didn't come out right," he repeated aloud.

"I know what you meant, Peter. There is a certain familiarity about Francis which I find reassuring," Ruth was unabashed.

So that was that. We were now hosting clones and androids, and if it hadn't been for Peter's unique talents, no one would have been any the wiser. Except for Ruth, and she, apparently, didn't mind.

Peter thoughts drifted back to the decadence that had been taking over the United States for some time. Canada had little more to be proud of. They had the Solidarity. But decadence was here, too. In the archives at the HQ, quite accidentally, he had found a disc marked 'modern music'. It was recorded as far back as the first decade of the present century, at one of the lectures at the University of McGill. The instruments consisted of tin cups, rattles, tambourine, bongos, maracas and drums. Must never forget the drums... Isn't this how it had all stared in the darkest Africa some 3,000,000 years ago? Minus the tin cups, of course. Ah, yes. There were also cowbells.

Peter shrugged.

The Hindus are right. We live in the age of Kali. We are continuously regressing. Exit Mozart, Beethoven, Chopin and Verdi and a thousand other talents, enter the bongos and cowbells. That, according to the experts, was progress.

He kept his thoughts to himself.

As for the rest of us, thanks to great advances in technology, we are also slowly conditioned to do less with more. Soon we will be surrounded with gadgets, artificial body parts, AI, and nanotechnological gizmos, and we shall do nothing at all. Just sit there, like vegetables, waiting to be fed by robots.

He wondered how many of his friends would have agreed with him, had he made his opinions known.

Nevertheless, dinner was a great success. They all agreed to make this a regular get-together, rotating between the two Thorntons, the Mondellay, and the Brent residences. JR offered to do his bit, but they all agreed that until he'd trap a willing young lady in his web, he was welcome to participate in the four domiciles as the tallest and the lankiest member of the group.

"Let's face it," Dr. Brent assured, "with those legs not many ladies have a chance of escaping very far..." There was an array of nods, "...and with those arms," he continued, encouraged, "you are bound to weave a web soon enough, and then we shall get even with you."

They all left in good humor, wishing Peter and Cathy Godspeed the next day.

When the Ritz-Xentung black-tie men finished the clean-up and left, leaving the kitchen spotless, Cathy picked up a book while Peter clicked on his computer. He had to find out if there was anything he could do to learn to control his dreams. He was amazed at the sheer volume of information. It ranged from scientific articles written by established names in the psychological and psychiatric professions, all the way to inspired dreamers who went on, at length, about controlled hallucinations and spiritual experiences. The latter had been interspersed with advice on judicious use of drugs, mostly hallucinogenic, which were supposed to stimulate more vivid dreams in 'normal' people. Peter hardly knew where to start, although he was quite sure he had no intention of stimulating himself to make his dreams more real than they already were. It was the unnerving reality they exuded that he wanted to diminish.

He also found that, although the western scientific community had done little work in this area, Tibetan monks had explored conscious dreaming for a long time.

And then a particular item attracted his attention.

The article began by stating that the human brain is made up of one hundred billion nerve cells, or neurons, and each one of these connects through one to ten thousand synapses with other neurons. He already knew from his medical studies that we have more nerve cells than there are stars in the Milky Way, whereas the number of possible permutations and combinations of brain states exceeds the number of elementary particles in the known universe. Having said that, the author hastened to add that the brain is little more than a means through which the mind finds its expression. Furthermore, according to the writer, the mind is but a means through which consciousness manifests itself.

For an ex-physician this was a little hard to swallow. On the other hand, so was his inherent ability to heal people with the touch of his hands. Or to observe their auras, for that matter. Peter sat back and began to read.

That same night, after he made sure that Cathy was asleep, he began his first exercise. He had been told that control of dream states could be learned, but that it required persistent, regular practice of... one hour each night. He had no idea how he would manage to stay awake that long. On the other hand, this was not the first time he would face the unknown with determination, which, so far, had invariably led to fruitful results. Later he'd learned that he could split the hour into two half-hour exercise sessions.

He lay back and began imaging various objects. He began with an apple, then a simple equilateral triangle. After a while he was ready to give up. What he was supposed to have been attempting was to stimulate the metabolism of some memory zones where the images were stored. His mind kept wandering until he concentrated on Cathy's face. Although a much more complex image, almost at once all other images dispersed, making the exercise quite effortless.

Even as his mind settled on his chosen image, he began losing awareness of his own body. At the same time, he reminded himself to breathe deeply and easily. Apparently controlled breathing can aid hallucinations. On the other hand, the last thing he wanted was to hallucinate...

He was very new at this game.

At four a.m., his electronic watch beeped once. From his early days in the medical profession, he had conditioned himself at his night duties to become fully awake at a single beep. Now, this ability came in useful. He repeated the exercise he had performed late last evening. Finally, on waking in the morning, he tried to put down in his notebook anything he could recall about his dreams. Here he failed again. He didn't remember a single dream. On the other hand, he also did not remember the nightmares he'd experienced on previous occasions. Beggars can't be choosers, he mused. He was used to having to work for a long time to get any results. It would take a lot to sway him from a chosen task.

The following night, he tried again. This time he jotted notes on one of his dreams. He knew that the REM rhythms, during which dreams occur, take place up to five times every night. He had no idea which dream he'd recorded. But, once again, the nightmare was missing and Cathy's face was firmly embedded in his consciousness. He had never realized just how beautiful she was until he'd spent time examining her beauty stored in his subconscious. Even if his pursuit of conscious dreams came to naught, this alone would have made it worthwhile.

The following morning, the world looked brighter.

The evening of that day, he and Cathy flew together to Rome. Later she would take the quick shuttle to CERN and return to the Vatican. Peter was still acting as liaison between Ruth and the headquarters in the Vatican. Since SI took over the maintenance of all the artworks previously under the patronage of the Roman Catholic Church, Solidarity had managed to restore a vast number of churches and the attendant works of art, which the Church could no longer afford to maintain. A great deal had changed since the late Vincenzo Magnani, known as the Last Pope, had left the Vatican and all its appurtenances in Lena's hands. As for the Church, Vincenzo returned it to the people.

"The Spiritual Church. The fraternity of souls that share the same beliefs. As it always should have been," he'd said during his resignation.

Later, some said that they had seen him in various parts of the world, where he was particularly needed as Papa. As the Holy Father—the Shepherd of souls. Perhaps they, too, were dreaming.

By that time, Peter felt at home even at the Aeroporto Leonardo da Vinci di Fiumicino. The day was just breaking, the sun glittering on the array of planes parked by the main building. The heli-cab, which was to take them to Città del Vaticano, was already waiting. Since the Solidarity took over, the Vatican never slept. Soon the helicopter deposited them, gently, at the tiny heliport. A man, dressed in the traditional, red, blue and yellow pantaloons of the Vatican Swiss Guard, took them to their quarters. It seemed that Lena took her duties as the curator of the Vatican treasures very seriously. Perhaps, too much so. The absurd uniforms were hardly a treasure. Still, people liked to hold on to fragments of tradition.

He and Cathy didn't get much sleep. It was still midnight in Montreal, and they were both in need of a nap. Also, Peter was determined to do at least some of his exercises. No sooner had they gotten to their room than Cathy collapsed on their bed. Double beds had been unknown in the Vatican before Lena took over. *Vive la différence*, Peter mused, as he lay down beside her.

They met with Lena in the SI main Headquarters. They hardly suspected that Lena would be at her desk since before they'd landed. She was that rare human who seemed quite happy sleeping between four and five hours per night, and look none the worse for it. As always, she presented them with her usual, alluring, expansive, Mother Earth image. She looked nothing short of glorious.

The women fell into each other's arms.

"Darling!"

"Darling!"

The platitudes were there only to help hide the genuine affection the women had for each other from the moment they'd met. Affection fuelled by admiration. Both women were well aware of each other's achievements.

"I'm so sorry I'm all tied up today," Lena said. "But you must have dinner with me..." She glanced at her diary. "Tonight!" There was a sigh of relief in her voice.

This was not a planned meeting. Peter and Cathy knew in advance that Lena had a busy day, but they both needed a day off. They flew over a day early, just to be together.

"Are you sure?"

Cathy knew what it was like to be busy.

"I insist. I can easily change my appointment to another day. There. That's settled then?"

It was a statement with a questioning tone for form's sake. Here Lena made all the decisions.

"At seven?" Lena added, smiling.

This was dismissal. Neither arrogant nor impolite. Just open and honest as friends should be to each other. She expected no less from other people. Even as Cathy and Peter were leaving, a man pushing a cart with a stack of papers was entering through another door. It appeared that in the Vatican, electronic age notwithstanding, paper still ruled.

So they had the afternoon to themselves.

Peter asked Cathy if she'd like to revisit his old memories. Arm in arm, they walked to the Basilica of St. Peter. He wanted to touch base with Vincenzo. The old Vincenzo. They entered the Basilica by the door leading to Scala Regia, as he'd done on that day, still lingering in his memory. He took Cathy past the Bernini masterpiece, the central altar, and led her to the end of the nave, to the steps leading to Cathedra Petri. Monuments of Paul III and Urban VIII continued to stand guard on either side of St. Peter's throne. Once again Peter read the ominous words, now merely reminiscent of history.

O Pastor Ecclesiae tu omnes Christi pascis agnos et oves.

He glanced at Cathy. "Pastor of the Church, you feed all Christ's lambs and sheep..." he translated.

She smiled wistfully. "It seems the diet didn't taste well to the sheep... they drifted to other pastures..." Cathy wasn't a Catholic, but felt sorry for the old pastor. It seemed that he deserved better.

Peter felt the need to be here, the place where, except for the archives, he'd last met Vincenzo—the Pontiff whose life he restored by sharing his own soul. Not the animal soul, not *nephesh*, erroneously translated in the Bible as such, but that part of himself which forever remains indivisible from the Single Source. The Soul with a capital S. The immortal part of himself. Perhaps omnipresent? It had been at that moment at the Vatican, when he first met the aging pope that he'd also discovered himself.

"You met him here the last time, didn't you..." Cathy whispered. He'd told her about that time. He could hardly share it with anyone else. It seemed like years ago—also, as if it were yesterday.

"It seems, darling, that only here am I sure of my own immortality. Everywhere else, I live with a shadow of doubt."

She let him dwell on his memories.

"I know this sounds childish, but I expect to hear his voice behind me. At any time…"

I am with you and without you. I am also everywhere and nowhere…

He heard the words, but only in his head. The Basilica was empty. He and Cathy were alone. This was not the day for miracles.

Outside the sun was warmer than at this time of the year in Montreal. Carefree, they strolled the Vatican Gardens. In Montreal they were both so busy that, apart from Sunday and sometimes Saturday mornings, they seldom had time to while it away. Not even in surroundings of such beauty—beauty and other-worldly serenity. It seemed that the corridors of power, once ecclesiastic and now in the hands of Solidarity International, had no access here. If power be the opposite of love, then this garden was replete with love. Here love and beauty abided in close harmony.

"I met him later that day, or it could have the following afternoon? I asked him if I was doing right by agreeing to work for Lena…"

Cathy, till then preoccupied with the view, looked up at Peter's face.

"And…?"

"Well, he gave me a peculiar answer. He said that I must always ask myself where it is that I am going. He said that once you know that, the rest becomes easy."

Cathy remained silent. Perhaps she, too, had doubts but didn't feel the need to share them. Or, at least, not right then.

"The dreadful thing is that a few years ago I knew, or I thought I knew, my direction fairly well…" Peter mused, his voice hesitant.

"…and now?"

"And now I feel as lost as a newborn babe."

They strolled, slowly, amid a profusion of flowers, huge, seemingly ancient trees, and sprightly fountains. In spite of its twenty-three acres of manicured lawns, pools and winding paths, this was the last place on earth one could get lost. Or even feel lost… yet, Peter managed just that. Lost like a newborn babe.

"It will come, darling. It will come. The important thing is that you're not standing still."

"Aren't I? Just what have I accomplished in my life?"

"You made me happy. Does that not count for anything?"

He stopped and took her in his arms. Right there where, since the latter part of the 13th century, Pope Nicolas III and his successors since had stood in quiet meditation. Right now he meditated upon Cathy—her wisdom, her proximity.

"Without you I would be even more lost," he whispered.

He was about to speak more when he distinctly heard a phrase echoing in his head. A phrase he hadn't thought about for a long time:

The wind bloweth where it listeth, and thou hearest the sound thereof, but canst not tell whence it cometh and whither it goeth: so is every one that is born of the Spirit.

Spirit? Peter hadn't thought of spirit since his seminary days. What is spirit, anyway? Perhaps, it's just an idea.

Amazingly, Cathy picked up on his thoughts.

"I think what they mean, Peter, is that the spirit is the source of all ideas."

More and more often he forgot to be amazed at Cathy's talents. Or was that simply love speaking through her?

And then they just sat down on the lawn and let time run its own course. After all, this was the first day-off either of

them had since way back when. For that day they had no
duties, no obligations, no schedules to keep. Except for
dinner with Lena.

Peter intended to show Cathy all other places he'd visited
before, particularly the library with its endless shelves of
priceless manuscripts. That was also the last place he'd seen
Vincenzo. People had said that he hadn't seen him. That
Vincenzo had died, some time ago. But they were wrong.
People like Vincenzo don't die. They might be in a different
reality, but they don't die. Ever.

A day of no commitments...

Instead, they just sat there. There was magic in these
gardens. Peter's depression lifted, awareness of beauty
around him took its place. They walked some other
meandering paths, dipped their fingers in the shallow ponds,
played hide-and-seek amid the box hedges of the Italian
Garden. Then they laughed at the sun playing filigree dance
in the prismatic mists of the fountains. Like two young lovers
on a honeymoon.

They forgot to have lunch and got back to their room just
in time to change for dinner. One never knew who might be
present. They were in luck. She was alone. The moment they
arrived in Lena's private chambers, two uniformed guards
brought in *hors d'oeuvres*. Then, on a table illuminated only
by four candles, plates seemed to come and disappear as if by
magic, silently, with the untrammeled grace of men who were
there to serve their favourite leader. It seemed that Lena was
not only admired and obeyed without question, but loved by
all who knew her.

They chatted till midnight. Not a word about business.
For the first time since they met her, Lena seemed in need of
rest, too.

"It's growing at an astounding rate," she said, gazing at
the last flickering glimmer of the candles set in pure crystal
candelabra. She was referring to the swelling ranks of the

Solidarity International. "I hardly have time to visit the Gardens…"

She knew about the enchantment of the gardens. Perhaps she also knew about the wonderful day Peter and Cathy had spent together—but… couldn't share it. Could it be that she was lonely?

That night, Peter again practiced his lucid dreams exercises. They weren't getting any easier. Ruth's face was overlapping with Francis and Lena's. Finally he fell asleep. He dreamt he was in that blasted sanitized corridor again. Only this time there were no doors. He'd sprinted the entire length yet saw no one through the gaping openings. Not a single patient. Not even a nurse. Yet, he was sure he'd been in a hospital. His hands were grasping his stethoscope, lest it fall off his neck. He woke up sweating. At least he didn't wake Cathy by smashing the headboard.

***

3

The Hub of Power

At 7:00 a.m. Cathy left for CERN. At 8:00 a.m. Lena walked briskly into the conference room. Everyone rose to their feet. There were seven men and three women, not counting Lena. She presided. Peter sat on her right, Dr. Chan on her left. The meeting was to be recorded with instant playback.

With the exception of Lena, and possibly Peter, the faces were morose. There was no need for Peter to hone his thought-reading skills. Franz Kafka once wrote that a book must be the axe for the frozen sea inside us. Well, now the atmosphere was so thick one could cut it with an axe. It was Lena's job to wield the axe. She had to stir the currents to snap not just Solidarity but the world from impending doom. The buck stopped here, at the Vatican, at her door.

And it all looked so very promising.

Solidarity had done more good to eliminate greed than any organization, any movement, in the history of man. Including Christianity, which started in poverty and ended up amassing so many worldly, material treasures that it collapsed under its own weight. Solidarity, by sharing the richness of human endeavor while concentrating on the development of genetics, eliminated most diseases, extended human life span, and added to leisure-time, which its members could enjoy thanks to the treasures it protected.

Alas, too much so. Now, thanks to Solidarity, human life span was extended beyond what was reasonable.

"Always the middle path, taught the great avatars," Peter murmured, when he saw the agenda for the meeting.

Well, Solidarity forgot. It was too good for too many good people. Longevity increased so much that 70% of its members spent half their life being unemployed. The retirement age could be increased, but then the younger generation would not be able to find jobs. A vicious circle. The economy was beginning to sag under the billion elderly hanging onto its coattails.

The Sino-Indian bloc had its own problems. About one generation ago the Chinese and the Indian governments, pushed by the extreme, socio-democratic influences, had been forced to open the nanotechnological benefits to the general population. Literally, to the masses. It had been hoped that the rise in general intelligence would stimulate people to take their fate into their own hands, and thus increase the general welfare of the two nations.

Not so.

The extensive use of nanotechnology increased the average human acumen to such an extent that there was virtually no one willing to perform the mundane tasks necessary to maintain even the most basic standard of living. The poorest of the poor would sit, mired in dust, on unpaved roads, playing three-dimensional chess.

The sublime or the ridiculous?

Perhaps both. Too late they realized the error of their newly found boon. Yet, by now, the genie refused to jump back into the bottle. Literally. In fact, the nanotechnological injections given directly into the bloodstream of countless millions of 'patients' had been absorbed by the genome, threatening to produce a nation, or two nations, of some 3,000,000,000 semi-autistic solons.

Without the willingness of the younger generation to work physically, and lacking the benefits of the USA technological achievements, their economic model was nearing collapse.

Like Solidarity, they had reached the point of no return.

And then there was the old US of A. Here the scientists concentrated on artificial intelligence. Whatever would reduce the human effort, whatever could eliminate human sweat and brawn, had been deemed to be good for the economy. Such attention to robots, cloning, or any other labor-saving devices, also served to create masses of unemployed, who demanded their share of the national product. Alas, such was held firmly by the greedy owners of the conglomerates, which had developed the various AI devices. To their further chagrin, Solidarity, without the slightest effort on its part, was making inroads into the American way of life. It threatened the stability of the rich.

The rich didn't like it one bit.

That much was known.

"Peter?"

Why always me, Peter thought. *Why me?*

"We shall not cease from exploration, and the end of all our exploring will be…" Peter began the T.S. Eliot quotation, and Lena finished it for him.

"…to arrive where we started and know the place for the first time."

They looked at each other. There was no smile of understanding. Just an enigma to be solved. You could hear a pin drop. No one dared to speak when Lena spoke. Yet Lena also stopped speaking. The silence stretched.

"Well…?" This time her eyes swept all people at the table. No one stirred. "It seems that we may have to *start at the beginning,*" she said at last, stressing the lasts four words.

Peter wished he'd already mastered the control of his dreams, and that any moment now he would change its course, and/or wake up. He sometimes imagined the world being destroyed by atomic warfare, or by an asteroid smashing into one of the continents, creating another ice age. But not this. He never imagined that the survival of the human race would be threatened by human ingenuity.

For some reason, an idea kept nagging him, somewhere at the back of his mind. It was like a tiny bee, tickling, but not actually alighting on his neck. It had something to do with his past. A long, long time ago. Also with knowing the place for the first time. The place. What was that place?

It was about then that Peter, for the want of something better to do, attempted to read Lena's mind. He'd never dared to do so before. On the other hand, he didn't have to. She'd never given an impression that she held any secrets before him. Was that what was nagging him?

No. That was not his motivation.

He wanted to find out what thoughts in Lena's mind did not reach her own conscious awareness. He wanted to dig deep, to look for and find the real Lena—what motivated her, what really made her tick.

He closed his eyes to eliminate all distractions. Time slowed down, then virtually stopped. He seemed to hover somewhere in no-man's land where the barrier defining us and them didn't exist.

He saw Lena as a little girl. Joyful yet serious, with unquenched curiosity. The image jumped to Gdansk. He didn't actually see it, but sensed that he was in the original Solidarity International stronghold. It was built after WWII on Ostrow Island, between the Martwa Vistula and the Kaszubski Canal. Directly opposite the Nadbrzeże Stoczniowe where her famous grandfather, Lech, gave birth to the Solidarity movement.

Dr. Gerhard Werner was about to leave.

"Eet eez zee third door on zee right," he said.

Peter was bending over Lena's inert body…

"Who are you?" Again a child's voice reached him from *a grown woman stretched on the bed before him.*

That's her secret, Peter thought. It was her innocence. She really was a child inside. Children like to play. Lena likes to play hard. To her, the whole of Solidarity International is a wonderful game. A game that, lately, seemed to have gone wrong.

He felt a light tap on his arm.

"You're all right now," he says, smiling encouragement.

Lena had been in a coma Dr. Werner and his team couldn't cope with.

"You're all right now," he repeated.

"Peter," Lena tapped his arm again.

"Sorry... I..."

"You look very pale. Are you feeling all right?"

"I'm sorry. I'm all right now. Really."

She studied his face, then smiled. "Well, my friends, it seems that we are back to square one. It should prove most interesting. By 8:00 a.m., tomorrow, I want proposals on my desk with suggestions on how to remedy the situation. Not just our, Solidarity's, problems, but the rest of the world. Do you think you can do that?"

The illustrious circle of the best heads in SI, gathered from the whole of Europe, gasped. Some eyes rolled, others collapsed against the back of their chairs. One or two faces went pale. Peter smiled.

She was right, of course. She didn't expect detailed proposals for redeeming the world woes, but she wanted ideas. No matter how crazy. It would be a great game, tossing them around. If she gave them too much time, they would eliminate their ideas themselves, unsure if they made any sense. Work would start later. In implementation. But you had to start with ideas.

She was a very smart woman, this Lena Walesa. Very smart woman, indeed.

As the meeting disbanded, Peter recalled another of T. S. Eliot's sayings. The poet, the dramatist, and a very wise man said that: "Only those who will risk going too far can possibly find out how far one can go." There was no danger of Lena stopping short. Children judged their strength by their aspirations. Not the other way round. Find aspirations and the strength will come.

Peter, as did all the other attendees of the meeting, spent the day racking his brains. Reviewing the history of Solidarity, making theoretical projections of variants that might affect Solidarity's future developments. Three times Peter escaped into the Gardens, three times he returned to his room, only to take quick, invigorating showers, and start his mental acrobatics again. By late evening he seemed to start again, from square one.

For the second night in a row he hadn't slept well. The moment he got into bed, he switched off the light and tried to dismiss all thought of Solidarity in order to practice his exercises. At first Cathy's image came fairly clearly, but soon it began to spin, rotate about its own central axis. He tried to follow the spin and began feeling his own body rotating, within a tunnel, as if on a spit. It was not an unpleasant feeling, though he got nervous when he felt himself slipping out of his body through an opening forming about the top of his head.

He thought that he was dreaming. He tried to hold on to the movement but got scared. He bit his teeth, hard, and sat up with a start. It was a very peculiar fantasy. Something like a phase that hovered between a dream and conscious reality. Was that the beginning of what he was searching for?

He tried to return to it but without success. Even Cathy's face eluded him. Then endless ranks of Solidarity members, waving banners spotted with vivid red blotches of blood, stretched out all the way to the horizon.

Consciousness is a fickle lady, was his last thought, before he collapsed into a dreamless slumber.

When Peter arrived in the conference room at eight sharp, the same people he had seen yesterday were already sitting, stiffly, in their places. Their facial expression did not bode well for what was to come. The next moment Lena walked in. She looked fresh as a proverbial daisy, obviously in a cheerful mood. Peter wondered if she actually had some good news, or if she was just looking forward to a new, possibly exciting game.

She stood behind her own chair, measuring the little congregation with her eyes. Peter reached out for her thoughts. They were clear, precise: *There is a poverty of ideas in politics,* she was thinking. A poverty of ideas. Peter withdrew his mental prongs.

She gestured to all present to sit down and leaned back in her chair. Then, without further ado, she turned to Dr. Chan.

"We shall start with you, Dr. Chan, and then continue around the table. I have your written notes, but I would like you all to describe your ideas in your own, simple words. Begin, Dr. Chan."

Dr. Chan, already a diminutive man, though really well known in his own field of genetics, seemed to shrink even further. His mouth opened, one or twice, and finally blurted out his proposal.

"I suggest introducing genetic imprint that would reduce the longevity of the cell reproductive system. If we tamper, just slightly..." he looked around nervously, "the telomeres, the repetitive DNA at the end of the chromosome..."

"Thank you, Doctor. Next, please?"

Peter, being on the end of the list of presenters, had time to study Lena's reactions. She seemed to be saying, "Why don't we just kill them all, it will solve all our problems." This sounded absurd, though perhaps she was referring only to those present. As for Dr. Chan, he was a genius at manipulating enzymes, but hardly at generating ideas outside his specialized field.

A woman about Lena's age, but looking haggard, stood up.

"You can remain sitting, Joan, if you like."

"Ah, yes, thank you, Ma'am. Well, I was thinking that we must, I mean should, find a way to stir interest in our members... perhaps other people, too, by organizing worldwide musical competition. Classical music only," she added quickly. We could do it on an ascending curve, the winners being awarded concert tours. I know we already have some of that, but what if we increase the frequency three or four or even fivefold..."

"What an interesting idea, Joan. Thank you very much."

Actually, in her mind, Lena was already selecting people from her staff who could take the idea further. Peter could almost see her wheels spinning in overtime.

"Next?"

A lady wearing just a little too much makeup raised her hand. "I believe that's me. I propose that we pick our favorite period in history and try to re-create it. But for all, not just the elite."

There was a chuckle running around the table.

"I propose when I was the duke of Padua."

"I'd rather be Marie Antoinette."

"And what is wrong with the Queen of Sheba?"

"Thank you, Mary. It's an alluring idea," Lena spoke, trying to stifle a giggle. Mary was very good at looking after the cultural heritage of the past years, but less so at practical solutions dealing with today's problems. Peter almost said: "Let them eat cake." Lena turned to the next person.

"Yes, John?"

"Create Olympic games for the centenarians? It would stimulate their ennui..." his voice trailed off.

He was the Solidarity's leading theoretical mathematician. He could see patterns within patterns. Although he did have a point that close to half of the SI membership was getting bored stiff.

"…or octogenarians…?"

"Thanks, John. You may have a point there. Next?"

The ideas flowed freely. "Colonize the moon?" To that day no one was sure if there was enough water. Anyway, the USA was working on that. "Colonize the oceans, underwater?" "Not that much air there, either," Peter murmured.

Peter sat only half-listening. Did anyone try praying for a solution? To whatever gods they believe in? There was little doubt that the human race was in trouble. For the first time in history, in various parts of the world, suicides exceeded homicides by a wide margin. This malaise was bound to spread. Bad things usually do. Like flus or other pandemics. It seemed, to him, that the Hindus were right. We were living in the age of Kali, and the human race was on the decline. Not in numbers, but in personal growth. We were changing our environment, not ourselves.

Next came the man responsible for our survival.

You might say that Dr. Philip Johnston (they were all Ph. D.'s here) was the SI caterer, though he also had a background in genetics. It was his job to make sure that the members of SI were well fed. These days supply and demand could not be left in the hands of the various governments, who were jealously concerned solely with their own citizens.

"Well," he began clearing his throat as though readying himself for a command performance, "it might take twenty or twenty-five years before we reap full benefits of my proposal."

He looked around to make sure he had everyone's attention. Strangely enough, not just Lena's… It looked as if he were competing for her job.

"What I propose is also tinkering with our genes, but not those affecting our longevity." Again his eyes scanned all present. "I propose that we limit the number of children our members have."

"Haven't the Chinese done that some time ago?" Lena asked quietly.

"Ah, indeed." Dr. Johnston was beginning to sound pompous. "However..." he let that hung in the air, "what can you offer a man who has everything?"

"A rhetorical question?" This was Peter. He was getting tired of the self-inflating doctor.

"The point is that if we first reduce, genetically, our members' capability to have more than, say, one child, we could then dangle, in front of his or her, ah, nose, the possibility of having more!"

No one spoke. The proposal was depriving humanity of their god's or nature's given right, but it had possibilities.

"Two or three, at the most," Dr. Johnston added when no one spoke. "In the way of reward for, ah, services rendered?"

This would, definitely, over time, reduce the demands on his own department. Being the fridge of the world couldn't have been easy.

Finally Lena spoke.

"And what about the non-members? Would they continue to breed like rabbits and, also in time, overrun us completely?"

"One would have to find a way of administering the dosage of, ah... hormonal inhibitors, ah... surreptitiously." The doctor spoke very quietly.

The population of the world was close to ten billion. The benefits to SI, specifically, and to the rest of the world, in general, would be undeniable. The pollution would be considerably reduced. Whatever the morality of the proposal, one could not dismiss it out of hand. Ever assuming it was possible to achieve through genetic manipulation, and to deliver the dose through, as the doctor called it, surreptitious means.

Lena looked pensive.

By now Peter could read Lena's mind like an open book. It came to him as a shock though, moments later, he took it as a matter of course: She was praying. To whom or what, he could not discern. He'd never suspected that Lena might still hold religious leanings. He assumed that one who is at the very top has no one else to turn to. Just God? An elusive, intangible, impalpable but reliable Power. Provided one added: "Let it be thy will." Otherwise, one tended to be disappointed too often. But she was praying that someone might mention prayer. The Throne of Peter was becoming too heavy for her. Even in all her innocence.

She was well aware that there were three main groups vying for international domination. Solidarity International united all people, mostly in Europe and Canada, that carried the gene of democracy in their veins. Real democracy, not the sort perverted by the young and ever fiscally hungry, ever disgruntled offspring of the original American GOP. But this accounted only for less than 25% of the population of the world. She felt responsible for the survival of her members, of her ideal, in a world bent on controlling others.

Competition was such that, for security reasons, mass cloning was already going on in all governments. Ruth's Francis was an example of this. Next would be clones of Lena and Ruth themselves. Displayed, like forlorn Mona Lisas, in the hope that no one would recognize the overly perfect illusions. Would that be enough to protect them? Even rats go crazy when contained in a confined space. And humans, right then, outnumbered rats on a relatively small planet that seemed to have been shrinking day by day. After all, only 29.2% of the earth surface was land. Colonizing the underwater potential was not such an outlandish idea.

No pun intended, Peter sniggered at this own thoughts.

Also, while China and India seemed more concerned with the development of the human brain, as though, ultimately, this would solve all their problems, USA's extreme right factions were becoming progressively more radical. Democrats were going underground. Literally.

Peter was getting tired just scanning Lena's thoughts. He had to be perfectly relaxed and had to concentrate at the same time—almost a contradiction in terms. Lena had an awful lot on her plate. For a moment Peter wondered if her Vatican predecessors, those old, tired men sitting on Peter's Throne, had felt the same pressures. He was glad that he avoided getting entangled in politics. Observing the workings of power was enough. He'd hate to be wielding it.

Everyone rose. The meeting was over.

"You didn't share your ideas with us, Peter," Lena was chiding him, yet did so with a broad smile. "This is not your cup of tea, is it? But I will want your views on the proposals generated by others. Can I count on you?"

He nodded. Suddenly he felt strangely depleted. It was only ten o'clock. He wondered if scanning human minds for any length of time could be draining him of his life juices? Am I abusing some sort of universal laws? he mused, not really wanting an answer.

He'd already submitted his own proposals in writing, from Montreal, on similar though not quite the exact same subject matter. He was here to discuss them. For some reason Lena did not mention them. Perhaps his notes had generated Lena's request for today's meeting. She would call him in her own good time. Perhaps she forgot; but that wouldn't have been like Lena. Or perhaps she read them and found them self-explanatory.

For now, they were all dismissed.

He had six more hours before Cathy was scheduled to return from CERN. He decided to go back to his room and practice his lucid dreaming. Lucid? Few things were lucid in his life, lately. Still, there were direct and indirect methods of achieving control over one's dreams. Or so they said on the Internet. He was determined to practice both.

He lay back as before, but this time he tried to observe whatever would present itself behind his closed eyelids. So

far, he hadn't had any success with this exercise. He lay
down, closed his eyes, and attempted to locate recognizable
images. He was supposed to do so in a relaxed state and
observe whatever presented itself, rather than trying to hold
on to any particular vision or object.

For a while nothing happened.

He got up and drew the curtains. He needed darkness.
The light he was attempting to observe did not come from
outside. It was supposed to come from within.

Soon the semi-darkness relaxed him. He cleared his mind
of the meeting, of problems that were facing the world. It
took him a few minutes. And then… and then fleeting images
of Vatican Gardens began to shimmer, elusively, behind his
eyelids. He didn't force them, didn't grab onto them. He
simply allowed them to float like clouds reflected in the still
waters of a pond. Then… he smelled the flowers. Roses?
From his right, the breeze carried the remnants of spray of the
fountain onto his face. How refreshing, he thought. It's
almost like being here… Then he heard Cathy's voice.

"Come, sit with me."

It was definitely Cathy's voice. Wasn't she in
Switzerland? She was only due back this evening. I must be
dreaming, he mused. A lucid dream at last? And the next
moment he became overpowered by the aroma. The richness
of the smell of roses mixed with that of Cathy's hair. He
loved what he'd seen, what he'd touched, but it would be the
fragrance of that day that he'd remember forever.

"Of course, you are, darling. That's what it's all about.
Just dreaming."

"You mean I am dreaming right now?"

"Aren't you?

"But it's so, so… real…"

"Of course it is. This is the true reality." She sounded
surprised.

He practically jumped out of his bed. The telephone jarred him from the Vatican Gardens with the brutality that only the here-and-now can offer. He reached out to the bedside table and picked up the receiver.

"Darling? I picked up an earlier flight. I'll be there in two hours at the most." Cathy sounded delighted. It seemed that Cathy could do more in a day than most people could in a week.

Peter assumed he was no longer dreaming.

"Give me the flight number and I'll pick you up in a heli."

"No need. The SI keep the heli-cab running to and from the da Vinci all the time. See you soon, darling."

And she hung up.

Peter leaned back and tried to analyze his dream. He saw images of the Gardens; they stabilized; he smelled the flowers, felt the spray of the fountain and heard Cathy's voice. All these things were very real to him. But... but he still had no control over them. Or had he? Was he not seeing and feeling and hearing exactly what he wanted? Was this what conscious dreaming was all about? Living your dreams?

Somehow he was sure that he'd hardly scratched the surface. Barely. But he'd made a start.

Cathy arrived breathless.

"I have lots to tell you. Lots! It's all about black holes that are smaller than an atom. Really. It's fascinating!"

Not to everyone, Peter thought, but he listened patiently. Cathy needed to unload her fresh update, if only to relax herself after an arduous day. After all, she had been up at six, left for the da Vinci at seven, and been running around CERN the rest of the time. Gradually she was calming down.

Only then did Peter take her to the, yes, to the Vatican *official* bar. There was only one, and access to it was restricted most of the time. He and Cathy were special guests. They sat down at the table overlooking the Gardens and sipped *spritzers* of the wine/soda variety. You could mix wine and lemonade, for a sweet *Sussgesspritzter*, the barman explained, or soda *Sauergespritzter*, which they opted for. It was refreshing, with no danger of getting drunk.

Their thoughts drifted to the previous afternoon.

"It was probably the nicest day we had together in a long time..." Cathy mused, her eyes misty.

"I've been there today," Peter said softly. He still wasn't sure how to treat his 'dream'.

"On your own?"

"No. You were there."

Cathy recognized Peter's voice. It was different when he talked, what Cathy referred to as, Winston things. She didn't know how else to call them. Winston had initiated her interest in the esoteric in such a way that it didn't really collide with her physics. As for Peter, after his experience with the healing gift, he was prepared to believe anything Winston told him. Well, almost.

"It's all one," the majordomo always said. "There are no physics and metaphysics. There are only physics and the not yet understood physics."

For at least a whole century, theoretical physics were and continued to fulminate at such an incredible rate that Winston's explanation was acceptable to her.

"So you've been busy?" Cathy was a little uncertain of her ground. Was Peter joking? "You dozed off..." it wasn't a question. "But there is more, isn't there..."

"Trust me. You were there. With me. You spoke to me," he sighed deeply. "You looked gorgeous."

It's good that I look good in his dreams, she thought. She took another sip of the spritzer. The bubbles kept rising to the surface, and, as she raised her glass, she felt a tinge of mist on her lips and cheeks as they burst. Peter watched her over the rim of his own glass.

"That, too," he said. "I also felt the mist of the fountain just before you called me."

"I give up. I want to know everything. Every detail. And don't make anything up to impress me."

Peter smiled. He knew that sooner or later it would come to that. He told her everything from the moment he reached their bedroom, up to the moment when she telephoned him.

"And let me tell you, that telephone was one of the most unpleasant noises I have heard in recent history."

For a little while they sat in silence. Their eyes wandering over the winding paths, their thoughts twisting around Peter's story.

"So you think it's beginning to work?"

For some reason Cathy was avoiding his eyes—as if she were afraid of his answer. A positive answer. While she admired and absolutely accepted Peter's ventures into what can only be described as alternate reality, she seemed jealous that she could not share them with him. At least, not all the time.

And there was more. For reasons she couldn't explain, she was afraid to lose him. She almost did when he had immersed himself into his power of healing. If it hadn't been for Winston, they would not be sitting here together. Peter had a tendency not to accept half-measures in anything. He was an all-or-nothing sort of man. And, all too often, the 'all' took him a long way from whatever others accepted as the norm.

Once again, as lucidly as possible, he told her the main points of his experience. When he finished, he gulped down the rest of his spritzer and gestured to the waiter for another. Cathy shook her head at having her own replenished.

"I can't imagine what would have happened if you hadn't called," he mused wistfully.

"It couldn't have been worse than your corridor installments," she murmured darkly.

"Worse? Worse! What I experienced in the Garden was wonderful. It was… it was…"

"Like the Garden of Eden?"

"Why did you say that?"

"Well, wasn't it?"

"In a way, I suppose. Only the apple tree was missing."

"That's why," she whispered. "You just accepted all the gifts without questioning…"

"I think you are making too much of this. After all, it must have been, I mean it *was*, just a dream." Then he looked down into the winding paths below them. "A very, very, very real dream," he mused, not quite believing it himself.

Peter left his second drink unfinished to take another walk in the Garden. They walked arm in arm, without talking. Minutes later, Peter's cellular intoned the first notes of *Chanson de Solveig*. He and Cathy had the same wake-up calls from *Peer Gynt*. They never got tired of hearing it.

"Thornton?" he practically barked.

"This is Julia, Madam Walesa's secretary. Madam was wondering if you could drop in for a few minutes."

Peter admired Julia's perfect pronunciation of Lena's name. It was spelled Walesa, but, in Poland, they pronounced it Vawensa. Frankly, for him, it sounded just as good in English, but he promised himself to make an extra special effort to be correct.

"Do you think I can bring Cathy with me?"

"I really couldn't say, Sir. But I suspect that Dr. Mondellay would be always welcome."

Peter clicked the cellular shut. On the way to Lena's office, he gave Cathy a quick review of his morning meeting. He trusted her to keep it confidential. Some ideas made Cathy raise her eyebrows.

"Did she pick any?" she asked when he finished.

Peter only smiled.

Lena was sitting on a straight-backed chair, apparently deep in thought. They weren't announced; Lena's door always stood open. Actually, not just Julia but two other people, both men, were staring at their computer screens in the anteroom. Peter was sure that, if need be, they would provide excellent protection. They did exhibit that 'perfect' appearance he'd learned to recognize as *too* perfect. He didn't attempt to scan their auras.

Cathy and Peter were halfway to her desk before Lena looked up. She smiled, pointed to two chairs in front of her desk, and remained silent. This was at odds with her usual abundant affability. Peter and Cathy took the chairs and waited. Lena studied both Peter and Cathy with acute concentration. At last she spoke.

"What would you do?"

She addressed both of them. She must have surmised that by now Peter would have briefed Cathy on the morning's meeting.

"I think, a century ago, the Chinese were right. They had no choice."

"But isn't it inhuman?" Lena's voice was hardly above a whisper.

"We live in an imperfect world. We must choose the lesser evil," Peter said.

Lena looked at Cathy, who nodded her affirmation.

"That's what I thought. But... well, it's so very non-Solidarity type of a decision. We..."

"You have done as much as you possibly could." This was Cathy speaking.

Lena smiled.

"I love you both. I wish there were more people like you two around."

Lena's voice sounded very sincere. To her, Peter and Cathy were first and foremost friends. Regardless of the business at hand. By then, for the most part, she was surrounded by yes-men. And yes-women. Adored by countless millions, what she needed was friends she could trust.

They still had two hours before a heli-cab would take them back to the da Vinci Airport. As they stepped into their room, the moment Peter glanced at their bed, he remembered the question he'd asked himself just after he felt himself slipping, head first, out of his body. In that phase, the no-man's-land hovering between dream and reality, he'd asked himself if this was the beginning of what he was searching for.

And now he had it. He was searching for the place he had to see, again, yet for the first time. In biblical days, the place, any place, tents, houses, villages, towns, they all symbolized states of consciousness. This was where he had to start again. From scratch. He had to retrace his steps to the initial state of his being. He had to rebuild his consciousness.

***

4

More Black Holes

On the way back to Montreal, Cathy and Peter didn't talk much. Mentally, and to a lesser degree emotionally, they both felt tired. They were also preoccupied with their thoughts. Cathy was trying to arrange what she'd learned to be able to share her news with her colleagues at the university. Peter—well, Peter's mind—was always delving into secrets which nature, for whatever reason, decided to throw at her chosen pinnacle of creation. In contrast to their previous visits, there now was a nervous tension in the Vatican that seemed contagious. At least the steady drone of the jet had a calming effect on them. For a while Peter watched the clouds suspended below them, then closed his eyes, and minutes later he was floating on the clouds himself. He wanted to tell Cathy how wonderful it was, when she appeared at his elbow, smiling her agreement. This was so much better than a Black Label he usually took at 35,000 feet above the Atlantic.

"Why do we need planes?" she asked, stretching luxuriously.

Regrettably, her physical body also stretched a little too much, knocking Peter out of his reverie. When Peter glanced at her, she looked asleep.

Back at the aerie, just to make sure all was well, Cathy immediately called her parents, while Peter made an appointment to see Ruth. Not as his sister-in-law, but as the North-American boss of SI. He'd long given up reporting by telephone. It was much too easy to tap in and take advantage of the information. Ruth asked him to see her early the following day.

"I intend to be in the office all day, tomorrow. Unless it's urgent, of course, you can just drop in, Peter."

"I think it'll keep," he replied and hung up. The moment he did so, he was sorry he hadn't inquired about Mo and Jo, and Winston. Am I getting old, he mused, or just self-centered?

Peter's frustrations were growing. He was now in his middle-40s and, at least in his own opinion, so far he'd accomplished nothing. Nothing he could be proud of. His healing abilities, alternate worlds, even the black holes, seemed to originate in different realities and thus did not contribute to his sense of achievement. Also, those past experiences did not affect his everyday life. Not here, on this tiny, confused, still so very primitive planet.

"Just think, darling, we have been fooling ourselves," he said, slumping in his armchair. "Imagine," he chided himself, "middle-forties and already having a favourite armchair."

"Young-forties," she corrected.

Cathy put down her glass and handed him a light Scotch. Actually, it was mostly water. "Nothing improves the taste of water as much as Scotch," he once told her. He also said, at the time, that it was the only statement he remembered originating from his father. He was very young when both his parents died.

There was little Cathy could do about his inner struggles. On a number of occasions she reminded him how very highly he was regarded in Solidarity by Lena Walesa herself, by JR, and just about anyone she'd ever met.

"And Mo and Jo simply adore you," she added, reading his thoughts from the expression on his face.

She then sat down and took a sip of dry Sherry. Her thoughts meandered between Peter and the work she did at CERN. Lately, to be closer to Peter, she worked mostly at the

McGill University labs, in Montreal, but an occasional hop to Switzerland re-energized her mental juices. Actually, the electronic communications, these days, were so advanced that she could be sitting on the moon and do the same research. The world was in the palm of her computer, so to speak. Her occasional trips to CERN sated her emotional needs as much as scientific.

Her latest passion was the event horizon of black holes— the theoretical boundary, the one-way surface of a black hole, beyond which there was no turning back. Once crossed, there was no escaping from the powerful gravitational grip that lay in the mysterious 'within'. And not even the top brains in theoretical physics knew what might lie within its black heart. It could be the elusive heaven. Or hell. Or, ultimately, another universe.

It was a broad field of research which overlapped with the entropy embodied within the black mystery. It was a field as unknown as Peter's seemingly esoteric area of research. Like Peter's, hers was a realm of its own. Furthermore, since Heisenberg postulated the uncertainty principle of quantum mechanics, nothing in Cathy's research was as dogmatic, as clean-cut, as it once had been.

"Today, physics and metaphysics seem to share similar unknowns," she told Peter. Perhaps Winston was right. He usually was.

Regrettably, Peter was getting more moody lately. It began when he realized that the tiny universe that he and Cathy had created only a few months ago could not be defined as real. Either that, or the potential universe belonged to a reality that only they could share. A private little realm, so private that it no longer seemed real. And now, more and more often, a mist, like an ocean of dense, dark matter, shrouded his thoughts from her; it had replaced his previous excitement, his previous spark of discovery. She tried to meet him halfway.

"By sustaining the ephemeral life of a transient black hole, we had created a world, a future earth, on which—in the fullness of time—we would be seen as Elohim, as creators. Even as ancient Hebrews had done…"

Even as she talked, his eyes drifted to a reality in which he chose, lately, to hide from her. After a while she continued, "We would be seen as Elohim, unto whose image and likeness our progeny would rise and evolve."

Cathy didn't really tell him anything he didn't already know. She merely wanted to raise some interest in something they could both share. For her, the mini-universes were easier to accept. After all, they were no less visible than the submicroscopic world into which she delved for most of her wakeful hours. She never really saw any of the objects she studied. Yet the quarks, gluons, gravitons, strings and superstrings, even photons, were as real to her as the light coming in through the window. Their intangibility didn't disturb her in the least—just as Peter could see the auras, all but invisible to other people's eyes.

Cathy understood his quandary. As euphoric as their shared experience had been, as far as she could gather, what they'd 'created' *was,* or had been, another universe. A real, *bona fide* universe. To his amazement, and equally to his partial dismay, she told him about the multiverse theory. The concept proposed that each and every black hole that emerged from the near-big bang environment exhibited theoretical conditions that had been very suggestive of—in fact, as far as they could tell, identical to—those suspected at the instant of the big bang itself. Such an environment had now been partially re-created within the CERN cyclotron. Cathy and her colleagues were peeking fifteen billion years into the past.

She remembered the joy they shared on that day when she'd told Peter about the first black hole blinking in and out of existence on the cyclotron computer screen. At the time, the life of that incipient universe lasted for a minute fraction of a second. But the potential was there.

"Just think, darling," she'd said, "each time a star dies, in a nova or supernova, it begins a process of collapse from which, ultimately, a new universe might be born... Like an oak from a paltry acorn!"

At the time Peter was elated. The demise of his own creative aspirations had not yet reached him.

"Each new," she'd continued, "each with unknown laws, over which we have absolutely no influence."

"Worlds without end!" he'd whispered, his voice in awe of what might be. "Worlds without end..." He remembered the phrase from the scriptures he'd once read.

For Cathy, science was akin to religion; for Peter it gravitated towards science fiction. There was little religion left in his life.

Now and then, especially after a boring day in the office, he, too, recalled that day. "And yet..." he mused, as he watched the ice cubes tinkling against his crystal glass, "and yet there is a Kingdom someone had spoken about. Like in the Gardens of the Vatican..."

"We shall always have the Gardens..." he whispered, then smiled, remembering *Casablanca*.

Cathy was till ambivalent about religions. She thought that the priests were wiser than scientists. At least they refused to rely exclusively on their mental powers. They leaned heavily on faith. Unfortunately, of late, they had little idea what to believe in.

Again she sensed Peter peeking into her thought-stream. He didn't mean to, but they were so close that it happened unintentionally. She didn't mind. They had no secrets from each other.

"In one respect," she resumed speaking out loud, though her voice had a dreamy quality to it, "they are identical to us, scientists. The priests, I mean. Neither of us have any idea, whatsoever, what had taken place before the big bang, or inside a black hole, not even whether there was but one black hole preceding our universe. What of the universe from which it emerged?"

"You mean they came…"

"Not they, Peter. The matter was supplied in our own material reality. But what of the rules and regulations? What of the laws of nature? The laws of science? The Universal Laws? What of the guidelines along which the new universe was to develop? What of the ideas…"

What of the Kingdom, Peter thought, but she heard him loud and clear.

That afternoon Cathy went to McGill. It was a pleasant day for a walk, and she decided to drop in at her lab and share the latest news from CERN with her colleagues.

Peter did what he hadn't done in many years. He wrote the words *Kingdom of Heaven* on his search engine. There were well over 22,000,000 entries. Obviously, if he wanted to find something useful, he was barking up the wrong tree. In fact, he felt, he would be better off to sit, cross-legged, under a Bodhi Tree himself, and await enlightenment.

"It worked before, it might work again," he murmured, half-seriously. "It might prove faster."

He was quite fed up with attempting to find enlightenment in computers, books, religions, or psychiatric mumbo-jumbo. As far as he could gather, they all touched the periphery of the unknown, the outer rim of the mystery of life, yet, with few exceptions, they never seemed to immerse themselves sufficiently to be able to come up with something useful. It may have been sufficient to create a religion or two, perhaps two too many, but not to free man from the religious bias.

Heaven and hell. The ultimate carrot—the ultimate stick. His mouth twisted in a derisive sneer. Peter was not a happy man. He leaned back in his chair.

Goethe, Dante, Mann, Milton, Verdi, Boîto, Gounod, Liszt... he mused, they, and countless others, explored the euphoria of paradise and the ultimate depravity of hell. To the mystics, philosophers, artists, composers and poets, such concepts were expressions of states of consciousness. To the religious, they stood for the ultimate, if inexplicable, virtually unattainable happiness, or the eternal suffering with no hope of reprieve.

"What depraved god would impose such anguish on his beloved children?" He laughed at the gullibility of the sheep. Then he stopped. Not so long ago, he'd been one of them.

No matter—perhaps, it is only a stick. Never mind that such an idea was foreign to the ancient Jews or Greeks. No matter... The Christian churches found hell a very convenient stick.

Shtick, he laughed outright. *Convenient Shtick!*

And then? he asked the hollowness in his own soul. *E poi?* His laughter was reminiscent of Iago's after his prophetic cry: *"La morte è il Nulla! È vechia fola il Ciel!"*

He closed his eyes. Paradise, he mused, was far harder to explain as a prospective carrot.

Most people found it much easier to imagine being permanently miserable than permanently happy. And the churches, before the Last Pope disbanded their folly, had been at a loss to explain how sitting on a cloud with a harp under your arm was supposed to compensate us for the loss of goodies, which we had been encouraged to part from.

Yet, if it hadn't been for Lena, for Solidarity, it all would have been for naught.

He got up and poured himself a glass of water with just a dash of Scotch. It helped him to think without getting too depressed. Before he sat down again, he picked up a copy of the Bible he hadn't looked at for some years. For a while he just sat there looking at the book that had once dictated every move, every decision, in his young life. Somewhere, among the thousands of heavily leafed pages, there was the original reason why he'd left the seminary. Then he had it. It was plain to see in John 10:34. Only the Church didn't like it. The Church had decided that Jesus had to become the *only* Son of God. And, as such, inserted the exclusion into the official Creed.

He remembered...

The Gnostics, the Cerinthians, the Arianists, and many others rebelled against this. But that had no longer been a problem. The stick was now all-powerful. The opposition had been simply anathematized or exiled. Lots and lots of them. The little guys and the priests. Like poor Arius. There had been others. *En masse.* The Church now had the tools to build an empire. It may have taken a little longer for the faithful to accept that St. Peter was to be His successor, but... well, we're only human.

The carrot and the stick were now ready!

Perhaps this was why I'd left the seminary, he wondered. And it could have been so easy.

Or... perhaps not.

Peter finished his drink and closed his eyes. He was going to find his own heaven. He was already pretty good at finding hell. Only his was not a permanent condition. And it was definitely self-created. Usually Cathy took care of substituting a shred of paradise in its place. With her mind or her body. Or just with her presence.

The next moment Peter was dozing in the armchair. His consciousness vacillated between wakeful and dreamy reality. He tried, as before, to visualize Cathy's face. No luck. Floaters seemed busy bouncing and sliding behind his closed eyelids, but refused to solidify into anything concrete.

He tried another exercise.

He imagined that he was bending his arm at the elbow. Then he tried to clench and unclench his fist. Only both exercises were supposed to be performed without using any muscles. What he was really attempting to do was to move his phantom arm. Only his arm wasn't phantom.

The phantom limbs were a well-known neurological phenomenon, but this was not what he'd been searching for. Nor did he hope to achieve a lucid dream. He wanted to be fully conscious when dreaming, rather as an artist is when in the act of creation. As Mozart must have been when dictating his oratorio, from his bed, when in an otherwise state of deep physical ailment. No. What he wanted was full command of his consciousness, not limited by the constraints of physical laws of the dualistic universe. Phantom or otherwise.

He became too agitated to continue with his exercises.

He was not getting anywhere fast. The most he succeeded, to date, had been that singular walk in the Vatican Gardens. It couldn't have been more real. It had all the ingredients of physical reality. Visual, movement, smell, feeling and sound, they were all there. It was as real as anything could be.

Ah, the smell of those roses...

He wondered if he would ever be able to re-create the experience. One thing was becoming clear. It seemed that Cathy was an integral component of his search—not that he knew, exactly, what he was searching for. Of one thing he was certain. What he perceived with his physical senses could not have been, could not be, all there is. There was too much evidence to the contrary.

His own experiences attested to that. As for Cathy? Well... she fitted into this in some strange way he couldn't quite understand. He was sure that she was an indispensable part of whatever it was that he was seeking. He recalled their last discussion on the subject. He had been reading Cathy's book on the Hindu philosophy. Since he'd donated all his books on medicine to the McGill Library, Cathy's books on theoretical physics *and* philosophy *and* ancient myths took over most of the wall space. She had very broad interests.

"I suppose you are my Devi," he'd said, looking at her silhouette outlined against the window. With the mountain behind her, she seemed to be emerging from the crowns of the trees—indeed like a goddess.

"Thank you, kind Sir," she replied. "Isn't that Sanskrit word for goddess?"

"Devi? In Hinduism, it is synonymous with Shakti, the female aspect of the divine, as conceptualized by the Shakta."

"Is that good?"

She sounded coy, but her eyes indicated interest. She'd spent months trying to stir Peter's interest in her books. Peter was much more of a doer than a reader. If he read about something new, he would have to prove to himself if it was true. If not, he tended to dismiss it. As for herself, frankly, she was interested in whatever Peter was doing.

"You are my counterpart. Although I possess consciousness and discrimination, without you I am impotent and void," he said. He also did his best to look crestfallen.

"I could have told you that long ago," she murmured.

"I dare say you could..." he heard her thoughts even as her words. She was as much part of him as he was of her. This time he chose to ignore her gibe.

"You may well be, quintessentially, the core form of every Hindu Goddess, but if you are the female manifestation of the supreme lord, that would make you also Prakriti, and me Purusha."

This exchange had taken place a few weeks ago. Now, reading this book also took him back to the last discussion he had had with Winston. Actually, discussions with Winston usually meant that Winston talked, and he listened.

"In Sanskrit," Winston had said, "puru, as in Purusha, stands for the cosmic man, or the self that pervades the whole universe. Cosmic man exists beyond time. He is both, the beginning and the final goal of creation. It corresponds to Adam Kadmon in the Kabbalah. In simpler words, it is that part of the individual which is immortal."

"They may be simpler words to you…" Peter cut himself short. He still tended to forget that all his thoughts were accessible to Winston. All his thoughts.

Cosmic Man fascinated Peter from the day he heard about the concept—so long ago… His mind drifted again to the old days, still in the Seminary, when he'd first come in contact with the Kabbalah. He suspected that the reason it kept coming up in recent days was Winston's ability to insinuate himself into his thoughts, into Cathy's thoughts, and even the children's mindset. There was something distinctly cosmic about Winston.

He was more relaxed now. Soon after he closed his eyes, two heads shimmered under his eyelids, moved up and down, and sideways, then solidified into familiar faces. They belonged to Moira and Jonathan. Both smiling, both carefree.

"Come, Uncle Peter, come play with us," they called in perfect unison.

The next moment the vision was gone.

Why can't I play like little children, he mused. Why do I take life so seriously?

He decided to go and visit Ruth's house. She would be at work, in her office, but he sensed the children's presence at home. If not, it would make for a nice walk. With Cathy working, he had about three hours, and it was only a twenty-minute fast walk to Westmount. It had been months since he was there. As he quickened his pace, he heard a familiar, sonorous voice at the back of his head.

"About time…"

I must be stupid, he thought. I don't even know if Winston's in.

Before he reached Ruth's house, two jumping yo-yos hopped down the street to meet him. At the housewarming at his condo, Peter hardly had a chance to exchange a dozen words with them. He knew and loved this incorrigible pair, virtually, from the day they were born. Mo, or Moira, was growing into a budding beauty, in direct line of her adopted mother's charm. Jo seemed to follow in his new father's footsteps. Boisterous, a mop of disheveled hair atop a head that never seemed to keep still. Only the penetrating eyes gave away that there was much more to the lad that hid behind first appearances. Even at his age.

"How did you know I was coming?" Peter tried to catch them both as they pirouetted around him.

"We called you, Uncle. Don't you remember?"

"You called..." And then he recalled the two faces hovering, then solidifying, behind his closed eyelids. "I most certainly do," he lied, hoping that neither of them could, nor would, read his thoughts. With Winston around, you could never tell. He was a formidable teacher.

The children took both his hands and led him to the front door. It opened as though by magic, no doubt practiced by the ancient majordomo.

"Welcome home," he said, stepping to one side. Winston once told Peter that home was wherever his feet were at the time.

"Hi, Winston, so nice to see you."

Peter had to look up to see Winston's grave face. There was seldom any expression on it, yet Peter knew, from first-hand experience, that the big man cared more for him and Ruth and the children than any man he'd ever met. Winston was a protector, a mentor, and, most of all, a friend you could trust. With everything. Might as well, as there was no hiding anything from him.

Nothing had changed in the house. The living room— Peter had learned last month—had all the windowpanes replaced with bulletproof glass. The same was true on Ruth's and children's bedrooms upstairs. The rest remained ordinary, though it was only a question of time before SI security would insist on upgrading the remaining windows. It was a strange world we lived in. Never was there such peace in the world as today. There were no military actions, no so-called armed conflicts, no threats that could be taken to the International Court. Yet you couldn't feel safe in your own home. Not if you were "somebody".

Instead of games, the four sat down and talked. They discussed children's schoolwork, the sports in which they participated, their favourite poems, the summer camp they'd attended. It was like in the old days, the days before Peter left soon after he'd been blessed with the spurious gift.

Was it spurious? Or had it been his inability to make full use of it? He dismissed the nagging thoughts and concentrated on the children.

Winston sat close to the door, regarding the three of them as a father would his favourite children. Had Cathy been here, she would have been included in that paternal gaze. It was obvious that Winston regarded them all as his life's greatest successes. Peter would give his right arm to be able to read Winston's thoughts at that moment. But the old majordomo was in full command when it came to allowing anyone to invade his mind. It was a field in which, by any definition known to man, he was a master.

After bringing each other up to date, the children couldn't avoid a race at the main stair. It was a tradition practiced whenever their mother was not in. She'd never actually said so, but implied that she thought it dangerous.

Winston positioned himself at the foot of the stair with a stopwatch, while Peter stood aside as the sole spectator. It was Mo's turn to go first. She stood on the bottom step, in a get-set-ready position. On a sign from Winston she sprinted to the top, straddled the balustrade and slid down in a flurry of hair flying around. Winston timed her to one-hundredth of a second. Peter had never met anyone who had Winston's reflexes.

Next came Jo. He assumed the position at the foot of the stair and waited. On a given sign, he repeated Mo's performance. There was neither laughter nor giggling during the race. It was a very serious matter. For years.

Jo won this time. By three one-hundredth of a second. They were always close.

"I'll get you next time," Mo murmured through clenched teeth.

"No, you won't," he affirmed.

"I will, too," she wouldn't give up.

Actually, the results were equally balanced. Jo was faster at running up the stairs, Mo at slipping on the rail and sliding down.

"I declare you both winners. I couldn't do it in twice the time," Peter said in as grave a voice as he could muster.

He hoped they believed him. Very likely, it was the truth.

Peter glanced at his watch. Cathy would be home in about fifteen minutes. He hugged the children and sprinted for the door.

"I'll race you, Uncle, to the street!" Jo shouted belatedly.

"I'll race you too," Mo echoed.

But he was gone.

"He's not bad at running," Winston said gravely as all three watched Peter breaking all unwritten records.

Peter loved the children, he also loved Winston, but Cathy was part of him. He simply couldn't let part of him wait for the rest of him to arrive. Not on his day off.

He collapsed in his armchair, wiped the sweat of his face with his sleeve, and opened a book he picked up from the table when the door opened.

"Hello, darling," he managed to suppress his halting breath. "Been waiting for you!" Ostentatiously he looked pointedly at his watch.

Cathy put away her briefcase in her office, glanced at the mirror, and leisurely made her way into the living room.

"Been busy?" she asked innocently.

"Reading," he replied. "There's so much to learn," he assured her pointing to the book opened on his lap.

She smiled, leaned over his reclining figure and planted an affectionate kiss on his lips.

"I'm so glad, darling. So very glad."

He looked up, questions in his eyes. She was always affectionate but this was suspicious.

"So what Mongolian delicacy are we having for supper tonight?" she asked.

He peeked, just peeked, into her thoughts. Then he looked at his lap. Apparently he'd spent the afternoon busily studying the secrets of Manjourian Cuisine. Upside down.

***

5
Lecture

Peter returned from the SI Vatican Headquarters depressed. His visit to see the children lightened his spirits somewhat, but the lassitude lingered. He didn't quite know why until he realized that the whole discussion with Lena, in fact the purpose of the meeting in the Vatican, had been to organize Solidarity resources in such a manner as to gain greater control over competing factions. There was an underlying current of struggle for power; something that—at least at the subliminal level—Peter disliked intensely. Lately, factions or blocs, whatever one chose to call them, repeatedly flexed their muscles. There was the Sino-Indian coalition, the European bloc and Canada, mostly subject to SI influences, and the USA. There was also Russia, but, over the years, it continued to become more fragmented and did not as yet find a way to unite their efforts. The same was true of the African and South American countries, although Brazil was becoming firmly established as the local power. Yet, for now, neither Russia nor South America threatened the hegemony imposed by the three most powerful bodies.

Peter realized, belatedly, that there was something intrinsically wrong about the competitive premise if power was the only objective.

He was still struggling with the idea when a gentle knock on the door brought him back to reality. He practically sighed with relief.

You don't usually invite Winston to visit you. He's been the majordomo at Ruth's house for more than a decade, and, over this time, he became not only a dear member of the family but respected for his views on just about any subject under the sun. For all that, he had never been asked for nor had he volunteered any advice concerning Ruth's work, her dealings with the Solidarity, politics, or any activities even marginally involved in the acquisition of power. It wasn't that he avoided the subjects; it was just that no one seemed interested in them when in Winston's company. When he was present, subjects seemed to come to the surface that wouldn't otherwise, regardless of people's personal interests. Power, in Winston's presence, was a no-no.

On this occasion, Peter opened his front door and Winston was there. For reasons Peter couldn't explain, he knew that Winston was coming in person. He strongly suspected that it had something to do with his morning report to Ruth, on the issues discussed at the Vatican session, which, when all was said and done, dealt with the acquisition and the maintenance of control over people. Whichever way you turned it, it came down to the question of power.

"Power is the opposite of love," Winston once told Peter.

And now, day after Peter's return from the Vatican, for no apparent reason, Winston stood at his door. They shook hands, touched shoulders as was customary between friends; though in this case, Peter's shoulder barely reached Winston's chest.

Peter offered Winston a customary drink, which he, also in his customary fashion, declined. Winston was very self-sufficient. Also, he shunned small talk, the usual remarks about the weather, state of health or other tidbits, which 'normal' people seemed to find obligatory when first meeting, or visiting someone's house.

Almost immediately he made the purpose of his visit clear.

"I'm glad you enjoyed your trip to the Vatican. I note that you also reported to Madam Ruth on your discussion. There are things that, I believe, had not been discussed."

Winston seldom if ever explained how he came to certain information that could be only partially inferred from what Ruth may have said at home. As for Peter reporting to Ruth this morning, regardless of what he'd told her, Winston could not possibly have known. Or at least, he couldn't unless he had access to spy-mikes in her office. And JR made sure that Ruth's office was scanned, swept and electronically cleaned, regularly, for any evidence of such.

Winston was an enigma.

Peter waited for what was to come. He sat down in his favourite armchair. Winston stood by the window, looking at the Mount Royal. Even though the big man was facing away, Peter sensed gentle probing. Nothing definite, just as though some thoughts, recent memories, crossed Peter's mind for no apparent reason. After a little while Winston turned and faced his host. Peter felt distinctly uncomfortable, feeling more than knowing that he was now being scrutinized in depth. Winston was studying his aura. Finally, the majordomo lowered his bulk into the chair facing Peter. He began without any further preambles. Peter knew better than to question or interrupt when Winston decided to share his thoughts with him.

"I know of few people who are not acquainted with the phrase: 'Power corrupts, absolute power corrupts absolutely'," he said, his eyes locked with Peter's.

Peter nodded.

"More often than not, we cite this expression without analyzing its deeper meaning. Why does power corrupt? Were all our kings and princes, our presidents and ministers, popes and bishops, mullahs and preachers, judges and advocates and other men and women wielding power... corrupt? If so, how does this corruption manifest itself?"

Peter relaxed, though he realized that he'd never analyzed the intricacies of power as such. Winston seemed to be reading his mind.

"In physics, power is the energy made capable of doing work. In mechanics, it is that which tends to produce motion.

In engineering, power is the energy of all kinds taking different forms such as mechanical or electrical. In mathematics, it is a sort of inverse of a root. In optics, it is the degree of magnification. It is also the ability to act, to react, to conduct oneself in an autonomous manner. I do not believe that any of the above tend to corrupt."

Peter smiled. This was a preamble, after all. It was also more like Cathy talking. He wondered if his old friend had picked her brain. Winston continued.

"We associate power with birthright, prerogative, privilege, right, management, ascendancy, dominance, dominion, sovereignty, influence, prestige, force, strength... we are beginning to tread on dangerous ground. Power is also synonymous with authority, command, control, domination, jurisdiction, mastery, might, strings, sway, supremacy, superiority... leading directly to corruption of one who practices such on one's neighbour. But only *leading* to corruption."

Peter raised an eyebrow. "You stressed the word *leading*?" Winston seemed unaware of the interruption.

"After all, there are many who wish to be led, who feel the need to be controlled or at least restrained, who wish to live under the jurisdiction of a powerful authority. And one may also wish to exercise mastery over one's own weaknesses."

Peter nodded, as though saying, "I see."

"We are still not walking on very dangerous ground. Not yet."

Winston sighed, seeing Peter's facial expression, then smiled at Peter's thoughts.

"Although there is a distinct suction heard as we steer our boots laden with self-righteousness through the quagmire?" Peter offered aloud.

"Not exactly the way I would put it, but you have the idea of what I'm driving at."

For a while they sat in silence.

Peter realized that the corruptive influence of power was not in how we applied it towards others, but what it did to us. To our psyche. It riled the waters, it distorted our vision, polluted our souls? Why... he wondered.

"Surely I exercise power; physical strength, will power, power of decision, overcoming fear." Peter talked quietly, as though thinking aloud. "It is also within my power to forgive, to atone, to help—when requested. We've also heard that love is the greatest power of all..."

"That last is an oxymoron." Winston's bass interrupted him with vehemence. "Power is the opposite of love. Even as Absolute Power is the opposite of Unconditional Love."

"Power is the opposite of love," Peter repeated. "I've heard that before..."

Power is at its most powerful when it is not exercised at all. When it metamorphoses into love. Winston's lips hadn't moved, but Peter heard him distinctly in his head.

Did this make any sense?

Power when it's no longer power, it becomes love.

The next moment Peter found that he was alone. He looked around, smiled, and resigned himself to the fact that he'd never understand Winston. Had he really been here? Had he, having planted the seed, left unobtrusively, silently, the way he usually moved in Ruth's house? Like a ghost slipping in and out of the rosewood paneling. Like Cathy's black holes, Winston seemed subject to different laws.

Peter had learned, long ago, that there was no point trying to understand Winston's ways. In the past, Peter had ample evidence of that. He saw Winston's comings and goings, as if the old man had his being beyond the confines of time or space. In other respects, he was almost absurdly 'normal', whatever that word was intended to imply. Yet Winston came and went, in and out of our reality, never admitting that he did anything unusual, anything that could not be accomplished by anyone who chose to make the effort. Effort to what? Learn? Peter had learned to see and interpret auras. Could everyone do it? According to Winston, that answer was a resounding yes.

"Most of us use but a minuscule fraction of our capabilities," Winston told him the last time Peter asked how Winston managed to walk through walls.

"And the answer is…?" Peter had pressed.

"There are no walls," Winston had replied. "They exist only in your mind."

On that occasion Peter couldn't get any more out of him.

Peter's mind drifted back to the seed of the solution that Winston had left behind.

When Cathy called from the lab, Peter mentioned the last part of the conversation he'd had with Winston. She said that, essentially, Winston was right.

"If you could counter the negative charge of the electrons, there would be no problem. You could walk right through them."

That didn't help him either. He decided that, at least for now, he'd leave the heretofore impenetrable walls alone. Later, when she returned from the lab, Peter resumed the discussion on the subject of power. He told Cathy about Ruth, and about his report that stressed the need of control and power. He also told her about Winston's enigmatic visit.

"I really think he was here, this time, only he left, unobtrusively, when he'd made his point."

"That would be in his style," she nodded. Cathy was also wise to Winston's ways. "Put the kettle on. I'll be home soon," she said and cut the connection.

They sat back, sharing a pot of green tea. Her parents had given Cathy a most beautiful set of the finest china Peter had ever seen. It was hand-painted, and virtually translucent.

"So what did Winston say?"

"Not much, but enough to make me think." Peter wavered. "Mostly that power corrupts…"

"I could have told you that…" she smiled sweetly.

"There are consequences. It seems that the corruptive influence of power applies only to the kind, the noble, the saintly. The others are already corrupt. They have nothing to lose, so to speak. But the goodly, those who firmly desire to do so much for so many—they are in danger."

"You are thinking of Ruth and Lena…" Cathy mused aloud. Peter nodded.

"No matter what the effort, what sacrifice, power corrupts. Those who are willing, and sometimes able, to sacrifice their very lives to do good unto others… they are often the victims of power. And not just power wielded by others."

Cathy sipped her tea in silence. She thought Peter was pushing the envelope too far. Then she looked up from her cup. "There is one ethical axiom that can save us from the wiles of power," she put down her cup and looked Peter in the eyes. "The end does *not* justify the means. Ever."

Peter looked at her with admiration.

It seemed sad that no matter how noble the intention, how wonderful our hopes, how altruistic, how prodigious the apparent benefits… the end does *not* justify the means. And those who wield power are in a position to sacrifice more means than those who do not. This brought him back to Ruth and Lena. His doubts began to swell.

He mused aloud.

"Power first proposes, then imposes, finally forces us to obey. 'For our own good', of course. It takes away our freedom of choice, offers to do our thinking for us, lowers our resistance until we succumb to it. Power corrupts our minds, our ability to be individuals, to respect individuality."

Cathy was also lost in thought. As she looked up, there was a mixture of sadness and admiration in her eyes.

"But mostly," she said, "it corrupts the one exercising such power over others. Corruption is another word for compromise. Both jeopardize ethics. The greater the compromise, the greater the corruption."

Peter nodded. "It is as Winston had said: power is the opposite of love. You can always compromise on power, never on love. You can give the citizen some freedom; you cannot give them only a little love. Love is indivisible."

The next thing Cathy said was interrupted by something very unpleasant yet akin to laughter. It sounded like a chuckle wrapped in a derisive sneer.

"Have you heard, darling? Compromise is said to be the soul of politics."

Peter didn't laugh at all. He was thinking of Lena; but, most of all, he was thinking of Ruth. He wondered if all this was brought about solely by the explosive rise in world population. He wondered what Winston would say. Could he help? Or was it already too late…

Winston had been introduced to the Andrew Thornton household after his prospective benefactor was already dead. Andrew, apparently on his deathbed, fashioned a whimsical letter addressed to his wife, that the man carrying it, bearing the name Winston Smith, should be hired as majordomo. There were no explanations, though it became evident, over the years, that in the months immediately preceding Andrew's untimely death the men had become quite close. Not that Winston talked about it. It just came out in the course of otherwise quite normal conversations.

Winston was also a jewel with the children.

He commanded their respect and obedience, without ever raising his voice, let alone his hand. He never competed with what might have been perceived as Andrew's authority. In fact, he instilled in Mo and Jo love for their father. For the father they never had a chance to know. He told them, and them alone, stories which made their father more real than a man could be, should he have lived at home, but spent long hours at the office. Perhaps that was what most endeared him to Ruth and, to only a slightly lesser degree, to Peter.

Winston really was a jewel.

Peter glanced at his watch. It was time to go to bed. The TV programs were devoid of anything of interest, let alone value. They catered to the lowest common denominator, or possibly a bit lower, in an effort to drag the viewer to the dismal level of the teenage producers. The TV programmers were making millions, unless they were members of the Solidarity. Then their income could only reach five times the average. Those were the SI rules.

With their biological clocks upset by the recent trip to Europe, Peter and Cathy decided to stop reading and get an early night. Peter still had his dream control exercises to do, and Cathy felt a little more tired than usual.

"Shall we go?"

Yet Peter still lingered. "You know, darling, it seems to me that power, like religion, tends to set us apart. Love, on the other hand, love and faith bring people together." He was still trying to dissect the Vatican meeting.

He also wondered if there was any way to turn people's minds from one dyad of concepts to the other. From power and religion, to love and faith. And then, sadly, he realized that this was precisely what the great avatars had attempted to do. For centuries. Even millennia. Was man destined to tread the water mill forever?

The Wheel of Awagawan, he thought; not for the first time. The Wheel of Awagawan.

How sad.

It had been good to have Winston practically at one's elbow all these years. Living at his sister-in-law's house was a blessing which he'd never fully appreciated. He used it for years as digs, while studying for his medical fellowship, only to lose it all in a single week.

Sic transit gloria mundi, he thought. But there was no more sadness in his musings, just a lingering trace of disappointment.

It had come much later that Peter and Cathy began to suspect that Winston was behind his apparent 'misfortunes'. That it was he who had, by some mysterious means, imbued Peter's hands with the power of healing. It was also Winston who had opened his eyes to realities that reached beyond Peter's wildest dreams. Yes, Winston must have been behind all that and more.

On occasion, Peter had witnessed Mo and Jo being exposed to the same realities. The funny thing was that neither Peter, nor Cathy, nor the children, nor even Winston himself had ever named that realm in which Winston seemed completely at home. We all lived in the earthly reality, with occasional departures, through dreams or visions, to a realm that seemed insubstantial. With Winston, it seemed the other way around. He shared our reality for our sake only, while he remained distant from our everyday trials and tribulations. As distant as one can imagine. Winston lived in a reality of his own, graciously descending to our paltry level for our sakes only. To put it simply, Winston was not really of this world. Nor was the reality he lived in.

This might also explain why Mo and Jo had relatively few friends of their own age. By some means or other, Winston managed to fill the void which most children craved to satisfy. There was the school, of course, and the summer camps; but, for the most part, both youngsters seemed incredibly self-sufficient. More so than Peter had ever been.

And today, though least expected, Winston had dropped in. Perhaps if Peter were more advanced on his spiritual climb, he might have noticed that there was a very clear correlation between Winston's visits and Peter's personal troubles. For now, Peter couldn't see it. In time, he would.

Peter's lucid dreaming exercises were not bearing much fruit. An avalanche of contributors on the Internet insisted that consistency in exercises was of the greatest importance. Peter was anything but consistent. He worked hard and expected results. Since the 'gift' had destroyed his career, with the exception of his studies of aura, most of his work had given him little sense of achievement.

After Peter had reported to Ruth, he was told to wait for orders. Not that Ruth would ever use such words.

"Thank you so much, Peter. We shall study your report and take appropriate action. I hope you will help us when we reach some conclusions." Throughout all this, Ruth favoured him with her irresistible smile.

Peter hated waiting.

On the other hand, he wasn't a normal employee. If it hadn't been for his old professor and Lena, he wouldn't have been an employee at all. He was needed to solve problems that others deemed unsolvable, or to coordinate the efforts of experts originating in different fields of interest. He had to make sense of them and translate them into a language that ordinary mortals could understand.

Often, that included himself.

His commissions came in waves that had nothing to do with everyday operations of Solidarity. When they came, he might have to give up sleeping for a few days. Even risk his life. The rest of the time he was given free rein to use his time and develop his own interests that might advance his usefulness in general terms.

Lately, with little work, Peter was becoming more elusive. He decided to spend more time with the children. After all, he was their only uncle. He owed it to his brother. And to Ruth.

Cathy switched off her bedside lamp. He leaned over and kissed her gently. She hardly reacted. Must have been really tired. He lay still for a while.

"Sometimes I think that I am on the track of finding my true self. And, for some reason, he, she or it is playing hide-and-seek with me," he whispered, not knowing if she was asleep already.

"I quite like what I found already," she murmured back.

"So do I," Peter assured, running his hand over Cathy's body.

"That's not what I meant, and you know it," Cathy said, but she turned her head to hide her smile of pleasure. It's nice to be loved just for what one is. Or even in spite of it, she mused.

"I love you for both, though I'm hard put to find the latter," he murmured, and switched of his own light.

Exercises came next.

That night Peter decided to start at the beginning, and then continue with the same exercise for a week. The exercise was relatively simple. There were direct and indirect techniques. Although the indirect ones were favoured by most instruction manuals, the instructors recommended that they be performed only on waking up. This was not enough for Peter.

He would continue to develop his dreams' recall, by writing down whatever he remembered immediately on waking up; but he needed techniques he could practice more often, and have more control over. Hence, he decided on the direct methods.

He closed his eyes, relaxing his body from his toes upward to the top of his head. Then, just to relax his mind, he imagined himself basking in the penumbra of subtropical palms. Lately this part was becoming harder. His mind was filled with accumulated frustrations that were hard to eliminate, as they remained undefined. It was like disliking shadows without knowing the source of the light. Nevertheless, the smooth, tall Royal palms, curving away, just a little, from the trade winds, helped. He even felt the gentle Caribbean easterly washing over his body.

He had to achieve a free-floating state of mind. Lapses in consciousness, memory gaps, even falling in and out of sleep was his aim. The rule was, however, not to fall into deep sleep.

In a few minutes, he felt he was ready.

He performed the same exercises as he did on waking; but, as a direct version, he could sustain them for a longer time. The phantom movement, visualization behind the eyelids, listening to the sounds generated in his head, all had their place in direct techniques. The exercises were so relaxing that, at least with part of his awareness, he had to pay attention not to fall into deep sleep.

Actually, by then, control of his dreams was only a small part of Peter's new hobby. Apparently the so-called lucid dreams were also but a means to an end. Ultimately, it was supposed to lead to out-of-body experiences, or OBEs, such as he'd already enjoyed a number of times, though without having any control over them. These techniques were purported to include manifesting items, supposedly, from thin air, and overcoming most, if not all, restrictions imposed on us all by the adamant laws of nature.

He hoped that, with time and effort, he would master the techniques which, heretofore, appeared to have been the domain only of great spiritual masters, mystics, or saints of various religions. Of great visionaries.

Peter smiled dreamily when he recalled Winston's words concerning visions.

"All visions are subjective, Peter. Subjective religious visions are called revelations. Subjective non-religious visions—unless held by famous people—are often referred to as hallucinations."

Peter had heard a psychiatrist giving a lecture at the MGH, when the speaker, a lady of some considerable repute in her field, defined an out-of-body experience as a symptom of schizophrenia. Father Pio, Sai Baba, not to mention Jesus Christ, would have been pleased to hear that.

Peter still had no idea what sainthood had to do with any of this. Perhaps charlatans who possessed these techniques didn't advertise them. Nor did Father Pio of Pietrelcina. He is said to have been in two places at the same time. Two places thousands of kilometers apart. Not bad for a humble Capuchin priest coming from a small farming town in southern Italy.

There have been others.

The out-of-body projection, or regarding reality from outside one's physical body, has been known about for millennia. Also known as astral projection, or the projection of the astral body, it has been practiced, in the West, by Neoplatonists, Theosophists, Rosicrucians and, more recently, by members of a new religious movement called Eckankar. In Egypt the astral body was known as the *ka,* or subtle body, attached to the physical body by a psychic silver cord. The Taoists in China spoke of alchemical practices involving the creation of an energy body. In India such practices have been described in Yoga Vashishta-Maharamayana of Valimiki. During the last few weeks, Peter had found that literature on the subject abounded worldwide.

Peter also found that many artists, in a variety of disciplines, were well versed with the secrets of astral projection. He decided, there and then, not to be left out.

On the other hand, he mused, it all could have been orchestrated by Winston. Not the others, of course, but his own involvement.

The breeze on his face was getting stronger. He opened his eyes. He was alone on a sandy beach, stretching on a *chaise longue* under a solitary palm tree, which was bending quite substantially away from the rising wind. The sea was still balmy, but the horizon promised a change of weather. Even as he watched, the swell began to move up the beach. This was followed by a ripple that broke the lustrous surface of the water. A storm was coming. Judging by the clouds on the horizon, a big storm. Perhaps a hurricane?

He reached out as far as he could see. He was amazed at the power of his vision. He could actually see the individual waves forming into breakers on the line where the water met the sky. He reached out farther, and, to his disbelief, he could hear the breakers smashing into mountains of foam. He felt that, should he want to, he would be able to taste the salt in the spray...

He looked on in awe. The ocean was ready to display signs of horrendous power.

He stirred uncomfortably.

"What is it, darling?"

He heard Cathy's voice over the growing whistle of the wind. It was growing exponentially.

"What?"

"You were flapping your arms..."

She switched on the lamp on her bedside table.

"I'm sorry," he muttered, and then sat up. "Do you know anyone in Florida?"

"Dad is leaving tomorrow morning to spend a month with the Boltons. He said this time of the year the hurricanes are over and the tourists haven't arrived yet."

"Call him and tell him to delay his departure by a day or two."

"But he must already have plane tickets!"

"Call him," Peter repeated. "Call him now. Find an excuse."

The time was 11:46 p.m.. Cathy's father was bound to be asleep by now. She picked up the receiver.

"Dad! I'm dreadfully sorry to call you so late. But I simply must see you tomorrow. I need your opinion…"

"Of course, darling. It's a good thing that this time of the year one doesn't have to book planes ahead of time. Call me tomorrow."

"Thanks, Dad. Thank you so much. Goodnight!"

She looked at Peter, her eyes none too friendly.

"OK, out with it."

"There's going to be a bloody awful hurricane over Florida tomorrow," he said. "Or a tsunami," he added pensively.

"Oh…"

"Goodnight, darling," he added. He really didn't feel like explaining. He was already in hot water.

"But don't they forecast such things well ahead of time?" Cathy asked, still propped up on one elbow.

Not in my dreams, thought Peter. At this time he had no idea what or when was likely to happen. Perhaps in the alternate reality time moved at a different pace.

"I want you to tell me, by breakfast time, what it is that I am supposed to consult my father about," she said, and switched off the bedside lamp.

Peter didn't sleep well that night. He hardly slept at all. He hoped that he might use the semi-dormant state to do his exercises, but he got nowhere very fast. The precondition to success was a state of relaxation, and he was far, far from it.

First thing in the morning, Peter clicked on the TV and tuned to the weather channel. Adverts. Whenever he wanted some news, he hit the ads. He had a good mind to throw the TV out of his 49th story window. Only the windows didn't open; not at this elevation. It would have been too dangerous, they told him. He wondered why on the 29th floor it would not be.

"Feel free to jump, Dr. Thornton, it's only 29 floors!"

That's right. The super still addressed him as doctor. Pete wondered how he knew. Only, of course, he would never have said that. No matter, he waited for the ads to be over. Would jumping from the 29th floor be good for your health? On the other hand, throwing someone... like those ads artists...

Idiots.

Peter was angry. At that particular moment, at the whole world. If his dream was a dream, and not some sort of astral projection, then Cathy wouldn't speak to him for a week. Nor should she. After all, she put up with a lot from him. He was of little use to anyone, let alone to Cathy. And now, apparently, to her parents.

Next the local forecast... announced the disembodied announcer.

I don't want the local news, you blithering...

They were not to know. He waited patiently. He learned all about the prospective weather in Montreal, the Laurentians, Eastern Townships... Also Quebec City, the Gaspe Peninsula...

Next, the general weather forecast.

Promises, promises. Next came the ads, *then* would come the general weather forecast. By now ponderous clouds were gathering inside Peter's head. Then a ray of sunshine: Cathy came out of the bathroom. She looked as though she'd forgotten about last night.

Don't you wish... he muttered under his breath.

"Hello, darling, a good night?"

New York is expecting a morning ground frost...

"Not bad, you?"

A belated weather system is forming...

Peter looked at the TV.

There is a depression forming southeast of Cuba. Within three hours it is expected to develop into a tropical storm. Gusts are already approaching 40 miles per hour. At present the depression is moving towards northwest. It is expected to grow in intensity.

Someone handed the weatherman a piece of paper.

...this just in. The winds are reported to be just over...

Peter changed channels.

—NEWS BREAK—
The winds of the tropical storm are reported to have now increased to seventy knots. That's, ah... over eighty miles per hour. That is a hurricane category one. It might increase to category three before it reaches the coast of Florida... Winds not less than one hundred and twenty knots... that's, ah... that's almost a hundred-forty miles per hour, are expected to hit the eastern coast of southern Florida late tonight or early tomorrow morning... A surge of eighteen feet...
The reporter was doing the conversion in his head.
This is unheard-of this time of the year, the reporter concluded weakly, his face showing a mixture of surprise and disbelief. *By now, a tropical depression, which might rise to a storm, would always dissipate before it reached land. Today it grew. No one expected such weather this late in the season. No one.*
...a tsunami...?
That last the baffled weatherman whispered as though talking to himself.

Even fifty years ago, this would have been impossible. The weather patterns had been changing for decades. The changes in variables were occurring three to four times faster than in the past. This cut into the early warning system.

Even so, there was guilt painted all over the reporter's face. They should have spotted this build-up earlier. The meteorologists must have left their posts too quickly.

No one expected it…

Peter's face grew grim. It didn't make sense. He shared the reporter's disbelief. Such winds should have been noted well ahead of time. They must have relaxed their vigilance—it was well past the hurricane season—although weather, of late, was becoming quite unpredictable. They were also wrong in their calculations. 120 knots amounted to more than 220 kilometers per hour. That's a category *four* hurricane. So is an eighteen-foot surge. Peter's father was a sailor—Peter remembered those things.

Cathy's invariably radiant face turned ashen. Peter clicked off the sound. They'd both heard enough.

"Y-y-you saved his life…" she muttered haltingly, something between horror and admiration showing in her eyes. She forgot that her father's flight would probably have been cancelled.

"I only did…"

"You saved his life," she repeated. "You saved my father's life…"

She run up to Peter and threw her arms around his neck. After a nightmarish night, he took a deep breath. It was over. At last. On the other hand, somewhere at the back of his head he felt—no, he knew—that it was just the beginning.

*** *

6
N.A.S.I. Headquarters

To a casual visitor, the offices of the North American Solidarity International Headquarters looked like any other office building in this part of the world. There were the usual security measures, the uniformed guards, the metal detectors, and a variety of electronic pattern recognition spotters that were less visible.

None of these concerned any of the employees. They had their own subcutaneous implants that confirmed their identity and opened the doors for them—as though by magic.

Others had to undergo the rigors of scrutiny that was growing in complexity year by year. In addition to the usual detectors, there were retina scanners, X-ray gateways, sniffing dogs and even electronic devices that could actually set off an alarm on detecting certain chemicals. SI security teams tried hard to make all these measures as unobtrusive as possible, yet deemed them necessary for the safety of their own people and their guests.

All these were essentially at the main entrance to the building. A second set of security measures were arranged on the roof, where a private heliport commanded even greater security, and many VIPs, presumably for their own safety, tended to take this mode of travel. The service entrances were, of course, also equipped with an array of stringent precautions.

The SI Headquarters was better guarded than the Houses of Parliament or the Bank of Canada. Apparently, in those locations few people were deemed worthy of the efforts of suicide bombers or funds worthy of a robber's attention.

Peter was the only employee who had unhindered access to the Headquarters without having to undergo the implant emplacement. As a compromise, he agreed to carry, dangling on his neck and under his shirt, a similar device that could be scanned by the detectors. Being removable, he had to have it updated on a monthly basis, and/or when returning from abroad. Lately, due to the proliferation of clones, there was talk that portable devices might not suffice. After all, if a doppelganger could take the place of a real person, then, surely, devices could also be stolen and/or reproduced.

Ruth Thornton's office occupied the whole of the top floor. Her private kingdom was accessible from below by a special bank of elevators and protected from above by a small army of agents, as well as by a special layer of material built into the roof. The substance, originally invented by Florida State University, was said to be 250 times stronger than steel, while being 10 times lighter. It was an engineering marvel, which precluded any attempts of bombing the Headquarters from above.

"We are an impregnable bastion of democracy," Ruth quipped, to add weight to her argument. On the 43rd floor, she did not consider windows, all fitted with three layers of bulletproof glass, to present any danger.

"For now," JR murmured.

John Robb was not only running Solidarity Canada, but remained its chief of security. This included the maintenance of the state-of-the-art technology in all aspects of the Headquarters. JR took it all in stride in a way that would make a Praying Mantis proud.

Ruth liked her office. Although all four walls consisted of extensive, virtually continuous computer screens, she could, at any time, switch from the masses of data to a veritable array of landscapes stored in the voluminous "Read-only-memory".

"Just a few gigabytes," she assured Peter. "At least I think so," she added, with a dose of disbelief at her own words.

It had been JR who'd installed this alternative projection system, in gratitude for Ruth's having appointed him to be in charge of SI Canada. Peter recalled when, on one occasion, he entered Ruth's office for an appointment a minute or two early, and found himself overlooking the Sugar Loaf Mountain from the top of the Corcovado. Right behind him the Cristo Redemptor towered over him, silhouetted against the cloudless sky. With a touch of a button Ruth erased the vision. At the time, Peter had wondered how long she'd felt the need to restore her batteries after the last tempestuous meeting she'd had, earlier that morning, with the American consul. Nevertheless, seconds later, then as now, she was all smiles, her eyes still reflecting Rio's sunshine. She managed to look demure even when sitting behind her simple desk, with but a mass of buttons built into the surface, all within reach of both her hands. Her desk, four soft-backed armchairs, and her own control armchair were the only furniture in the room. A single carnation in a slim crystal vase graced her desk. The rest of the world was hidden inside the seemingly blank walls.

The meeting had been called to discuss the latest directives that had arrived from Rome. Peter found it amusing that the word from the Vatican was still considered gospel. Not that Lena Walesa was infallible; but she did have at her disposal the best brains of Europe, Canada, and sizable portions of the ROW. For the uninitiated, ROW stood for the 'rest of the world'.

As in her private office, the conference table was empty of files, papers, or even portable computers. The transparent glass top seemed to float over the carpet which, together with the acoustic ceiling, muted all but the most extraneous sounds. Ruth enjoyed silence. She also didn't encourage her staff to fiddle through their files when they should be paying attention to what was being said at the meeting.

"If you can't hold it in your hand, then carry it in your head," she'd said, at the very first meeting Peter had attended some years ago.

Ruth also found files and electronics cluttering the table distracting. After the first few times, people came to the meetings fully prepared.

"Please remain seated," she said, as she flowed into the room.

In her late forties, she still moved with the grace of a woman half her age. Then again, with the progress Solidarity had made in genetic manipulation, most women did. Or, perhaps it took five decades to develop just such grace. Peter admired his sister-in-law for many of her attributes. He never understood how his late brother, Andrew, could leave her for months on end, to supervise construction jobs in diverse parts of the world.

Peter sat back and decided to amuse himself with studying the auras of his colleagues. There was little to choose from. They all displayed talents commensurate with the jobs and positions they each held. Perhaps the two were interconnected?

He moved on to Ruth. She, well, she was definitely different.

Obviously, he'd seen Ruth's aura many times before. From the day he'd learned to detect and read them, hers was a clear blue. On occasion it tended just a bit towards purple, mostly when she was worried, or towards turquoise when…

Ruth pressed a button, and a wall screen came to life. Lena appeared to be sitting in her own office, busy signing documents. Within seconds she looked up.

"Thank you, Ruth—and welcome all. You've all been briefed. I need your comments."

JR fidgeted. One never knew if he had something to say, or if he couldn't find sufficient space for his legs.

"Yes, JR?" This was Ruth.

"Unless we are given statistical benefits for immediate cloning, I would not consider it a priority. To date, with one exception, SI has managed to stay away from the American indulgence for VIP doppelgangers. And anyway, how would we implement such a subterfuge?" JR was always practical.

The one exception JR referred to was Ruth's personal guard, Francis Drake. Even now, Drake was biting his nails in Ruth's private office. Or did whatever clones do to fill their time.

"The object, JR, is to confuse the enemy, not ourselves. If they don't know which is real, the benefits are obvious," Lena said without a hint of preaching.

"Then why not make two or three..." he murmured.

"Don't murmur, JR. Your observations are always valuable," Lena chided gently. "As for your question, it may come to that..." she left the sentence hanging.

JR's aura turned a little fuzzy. It wasn't normally quite as clear as Ruth's, but the blue was still quite outstanding. No one, not even Peter, could aspire to the golden hue that denoted the highest degree of spiritual development. Winston was the only one, though looking at his you'd never have guessed it. It seemed that Winston could manipulate his colours at will.

The rest of the people exhibited a range of pinks, oranges and reds, with occasional brownish overtones, which didn't bode well for their character. No matter. They may have been good at the job they had been selected to do. And that was the least of Ruth's problems. At least they all had auras. They were all human.

"I would suggest that we all make a list of personnel we believe should take advantage of the latest cloning technology. We can make all the preparations, and leave the final decision pending," Ruth said, looking pointedly at the wall screen. In an overpopulated world she was keen to keep the new biological units to a minimum.

"Excellent. If we are ready, the implementation is said to take only a few days."

There was a joint intake of air.

"A fully grown human being in a few days?"

"Surely, it must take longer…"

"Are you sure…?"

Lena smiled at the last query. "Yes, Joan, I am usually sure when I make a statement." Lena knew all present by their first names. They addressed her as Madam, or Ma'am. She had long given up trying to persuade them all to call her Lena. There was something distinctly regal about Lena.

Joan tried hard to slide under the transparent tabletop. Obviously, to no avail. "I didn't mean…" she began and thought better of it. "Yes, Ma'am," she said and sat up straight.

This is like kindergarten, Peter mused. Lena Walesa, the kindly teacher, and a bunch of children trying hard to please her. He also wondered if Lena was telling them all she knew. Lena seemed to be studying the faces of all present. To his amazement, Peter realized that, although she was not present, he could detect her thoughts. Not exactly read them, but be very aware of them. Lena, he felt, had a very orderly mind. And more than anything, she knew exactly what answer she wanted to hear, before she asked her question.

As for the people around the table, Ruth and JR stood out by a mile—the only two who did not fit into the kindergarten analogy. It was quite amazing what nonsense churned inside most people's heads. They didn't even think what might *be* right or wrong, only what might be perceived as such. Thank heaven we have Ruth on our side, he mused. Once again, he felt proud of his sister-in-law. She took on the job of North-American leadership without batting an eyelid. When, way back when, he had questioned the modality of her qualifications, she was surprised. "Someone has to do the job," she'd said. "If we look for the most competent person, years will pass, and we'll not find her. Or him."

"I heard last night that the White House personnel with number five and four clearance has been cloned, or will be," Ruth glanced at her watch, "by the time this meeting is over."

So we, too, had our spies. Peter wondered how she had managed to insinuate her people into the highest strata of the US Executive Branch. At least, he assumed they were 'real' people—not some brand-new version of androids. Solidarity had many sympathizers, even south of the border. Either way, Ruth would have her way. Ruth or Lena. In terms of philosophy and political orientation, the two seemed inseparable.

"I suppose you must fight fire with fire," he said to Ruth as much as to anyone present, or Lena, for that matter. He knew that Ruth was counting on his support.

Ruth nodded her thanks.

"JR, will you make up the necessary list?" This wasn't a question.

"Yes, Ma'am," JR replied, nodding his agreement. Ruth's last tidbit had convinced him. "We'd better be ready."

"Peter, would you like to give us an overview?" Ruth smiled sweetly at her brother-in-law.

The list consisted of organizing DNA samples of all present at the table. There were other details, in which he was already well versed. What Ruth wanted was a little scientific background, to set people's moral reservations at ease. Peter, once a physician, was more qualified in those matters than any of them.

"People think of clones as 'fully blown people'. Not so. Not like Dolly, the original sheep cloned from a somatic cell, using the process of nuclear transfer, made at the beginning of this century in Scotland. That was, pretty much, a real sheep." Peter spoke softly, remembering his discussions with other physicians some years ago. "Nevertheless, in less than seven years, she had to be euthanized. It turned out that her telomeres were short, accelerating the aging process. The problem of telomeres, the region of repetitive DNA at the end of a chromosome that protects the chromosome from destruction, could never be solved. Hence, in later years, composites, which used to be called androids, are now referred to as clones. It really meant copies. They were like three-dimensional photographs that resembled the original in every detail. At best, they could be considered half-human. The psychiatrists also tell us that the clones are not endowed with the accepted sense of self."

Nor with any aura, Peter thought, but kept that to himself.

"Thank you, Peter, I think we can be less preoccupied with ethical concerns we may have had," Ruth looked at the wall screen.

Lena heard what she wanted to hear. Even as Ruth looked on, Lena's face began to darken and then dissolve until, as with the Cheshire cat, only her smile lingered behind.

The meeting was over.

Peter never took time to wonder why animals, even trees, had well-defined auras yet robots or androids do not. The most advanced computers could, in minutes, perform 'mental' tasks, which would take humans years to solve. Without the use of nanotechnology, man would be outmatched by even average computing machines. Yet, humans had something that did not even begin to manifest itself in any form of artificial intelligence. Unless you define intelligence as the ability to survive. But even there, so far, humans ruled supreme. We were, of course, most adept at killing. Better than any other life form on earth. Was that what made us so superior? Our ability to destroy?

Could a machine turn against a human? Or was man necessary to pull the trigger? There were laws of robotics in science fiction. What about real life? Could a machine be intelligent enough to want to survive?

When Peter returned home, Cathy was already there. A splendid lunch was waiting for him. His favourite. Smoked salmon with finely chopped, marinated onions, mixed with capers. It was the only occasion when Peter touched alcohol other than a dash of Scotch in his water. Well, a glass of wine, with dinner. And, well, an occasional beer with JR. But with the Atlantic salmon Peter took a dash of vodka—often two or three. Preferably *Jarzębiak,* a Polish brandy, elaborated on the fruit of the rowan tree. It offered brandy's bouquet and the smoothness of vodka.

Cathy was all smiles.

"I gather dad has forgiven you?"

"He sends his love and thanks," she said.

Methinks, Peter mused, I'm in the genius category—for now. Wonder how long it will last...

He raised a tiny thimble of the dark golden vodka and threw it down his throat. He thought Poles knew how to have fun.

"Dad called his friends in Florida. They are watching the weather forecasts. The wind, offshore, is swirling around category two. They are hoping..."

It did not matter. Cathy wasn't mad. She was grateful. And he wasn't hallucinating or showing early symptoms of schizophrenia. Maybe there was something to this astral projection. Only, at least for now, he had absolutely no control over it.

Cathy was watching him closely. She always did that when he was pensive.

"After we've eaten, I want you to tell me all about it." She looked him in the eye. "Will you?"

"Only if you promise that you will not regard me as completely bonkers."

She smiled her assent. "Just this time," she promised. "Just this time, my love."

The salmon was superb, the Jarzębiak perfectly chilled, and the fresh, crispy baguette completed the feast. For a while they talked about neutral things. Thanks to Solidarity, Peter was kept abreast of political activities throughout the world. They discussed items of general interest.

Then, black coffee in hand, they moved to the armchairs.

"So how did dad take it? Was it hard to convince him?"

"I didn't tell him, not to start with, that you got the information from a hallucination, ah... sorry, from a dream. He is a scientist; he would have found it hard to swallow. But he's also broadminded. Once he'd checked the weather news, I told him the truth. He had to believe me because before midnight, last night, no one suspected there would be yet another hurricane this season. Often one can see one forming all the way off the shores of Africa, only no one was looking. At least not down south. Also, it never advanced with such alacrity. The info had to come from somewhere, so it might as well have been you."

"Not the most flattering recommendation," Peter murmured.

"And just how would you have reacted a year ago, even six months ago, if you'd been given such news?"

"I stand corrected. Frankly, I hardly believe any of it myself. Even now."

Cathy started laughing. "You are worse than he is! You don't believe anything you don't check out yourself."

"I wouldn't be surprised," he conceded resignedly.

"So... tell me..."

Peter spent the next fifteen minutes telling Cathy about his latest experiments with the dream/OBE/astral projection/soul travel research he had been doing, these last few days. Then he described his vision, if such it was, on some forgotten beach.

"I have no idea where it was, but I knew that there must be a reason for my vision, my... for what I saw. Until proven to the contrary, I always believe there's a reason for everything. Only it was not just a *vision*. It was, well, it was an experience. I could see it, feel it, hear it... I tell you, darling, it was real. Very, very real. All my senses had been sharpened as never before..."

She listened without interrupting. After a while, she got up and topped up their demitasses. She decided not to go to the lab today. After all, she was mistress of her own time.

Though he didn't immediately admit it, Peter was as impressed with his dream as was Cathy. The strange thing was that, when he began this new line of research, he never intended to develop prophetic vision. All he really wanted was to get rid of his nightmares, which took him back to his medical past. He also couldn't figure out why such nightmares would occur in his present *modus vivendi*. He wasn't exactly saving human lives, but he did perform a function for the SI that, according to both Ruth and Lena, was indispensable.

"So what now?" Cathy asked, placing a fresh cup at his elbow.

"What indeed? At least, for now, the nightmares are gone. Forever? Few things are for ever."

Cathy nodded. She was well aware how fast science was hurtling into the unknown future. "You will continue with...?"

"Of course!" he swung his arms in desperation. "What else can I do?"

"Darling, you are doing a great deal."

She did her best to settle him down. Peter had higher expectations of himself than of anyone she'd ever met. He practiced the exact opposite of the adage, 'do as I say'. His motto was, "Do as I do, regardless of what I say."

"Well, there is one other thing. It's sort of playing a strange tune at the back of my mind. I can't be sure, yet, but there may be a way to actually gain control over this dream business."

He told her about the variety of exercises he was doing, and many more he hadn't tried yet. The Internet was fully loaded with masses of information, many laying claims to different yet impressive results. Cathy looked spellbound by his story.

"How come I've never heard about those things? I mean, one was brought up to associate such things with mystical inspiration, or, more often than not, with charlatans."

Peter smiled.

"You and me, together. Yet there are people there, on the net, with medical backgrounds, scientists, as well as a bunch of people with various religious orientations," he conceded. "I have to sort them all out, pick out the best, and see where it will take me."

"I suspect you'll want to learn flying, next? A trip to the moon on gossamer wings…"

"Only if you fly with me."

"I promise…"

The *Peer Gynt* suite jingled on his cell phone.

"Sir?" It was one of Ruth's secretaries. "Madam would like to see you at your convenience."

"Today?"

"Yes, Sir. As soon as possible."

"At my convenience as soon as… Never mind. Tell Mrs. Thornton I'll be there in half an hour."

"The office?" Cathy posed a rhetorical question.

"Sister dear, my dear. Her secretary sounded nervous."

"That means Ruth is nervous. You'd better go."

Peter made sure his ID dangled on his neck and left immediately. It was a ten-minute taxi ride. Peter was let in without the usual runaround to which most guests, not endowed with the subcutaneous implant, were usually subjected. He was, however, escorted by two uniformed guards to Ruth's office. While Peter's face was well known at the HQ, JR issued new instructions regarding possible clones. He'd noticed that, in the elevator, he'd been scanned to within an inch of his life by a sort of state-of-the-art MRI/CT scan combination.

"Go right in, Sir."

A secretary waved him into Ruth's office. He never got used to its size nor to the virtually continuous wall screens, with masses of data relating the facts and figures of Solidarity activities around North America and, in part, the rest of the world. It was like a global window into SI comings and goings.

Ruth was facing away from him, speaking into a mike. She must have sensed his presence, because she spun her armchair and waved him into one in front of her desk. The armchairs were also the very latest state of the art. Within seconds of sitting down, they adjusted themselves to his personal contours, and began massaging his back, arms, thighs, or whatever came in contact with its surface. The days of stiff backs were over.

Ruth pushed away the mike and faced her brother-in-law. Peter thought that she and Lena could, jointly and severally, charm the pants off any man. He peeked into her mind. It wasn't hard. He had expected to be called in.

"So now you want me to be a glorified aura detector?" he asked.

Her thoughts were not fully formulated, but they implied that Peter was to scan the SI staff and visitors for the presence of clones.

"What else could do the job?" Ruth knew that he knew. Or guessed? She still wasn't sure about the thought-reading business. Except by Winston. Winston could do anything.

"What about the GDV effect?" Peter asked.

"Which is?"

"Gas Discharge Visualization. It's been used in Russia, Sweden… for years. Never mind. It's a camera for bio-electrography. It is being used in diagnostics in most, if not all, eastern medical applications. I'm… I'm considerably out of touch with medicine these days. Hardly surprising…" For some inexplicable reason he felt guilty.

There was no point explaining that Professor Korotcov had confirmed earlier research conducted by Mandel and Milhomens, which produced promising and surprisingly coherent information, about psychological and physiological conditions in patients, by examining the stimulated electro-phonic glow around a human finger. Peter had read about it a while ago, about the time when he began studying auras.

"Is that something to do with Kirlian effect?"

"Yes. It does not photograph an aura. What it does is to photograph the visible electro-photonic glow of an object in response to pulsed electrical field excitation. It was known to Nikola Tesla late in the nineteenth century. Then the Russian named Kirlian took it further."

And the rest is history, he almost added, remembering that if it hadn't been for his sudden interest in auras, he'd probably have remained ignorant about the latest research in this field.

"And you think it will detect auras, or lack of them, in non-human objects?"

"That's not quite accurate. Animals and even trees have auras. But it might be possible to detect the fact that the object, as you say, is not wholly human."

"I suppose that would do the trick," Ruth said, her face still more pensive than usual. "I'd really have to rely on you, Peter. This field is completely foreign to me."

"Understood."

"Until you prove it one way or another, I am putting you in charge of any action that might be required to make sure that the SI is free of clones or androids."

"You want a bell to ring when Francis walks by?"

"Don't be flippant, brother dear. This is a very serious matter. If I understand Lena, it could be a question of life and death."

He nodded. "I suppose it's up to me to research the, ah, Kirlian effect?"

Ruth nodded.

"Can I borrow JR?" he added hopefully.

"That's up to JR… if he has time."

Ruth was not in a giving mood. No matter. Peter was sure that JR would love to have his gases stimulated. With or without a cool beer.

"See ya!" Peter smiled and left.

The problem was that Peter had no idea if the GDV technique would work on auras. It's not as though he could discuss the matter with anyone he knew. With the possible exception of Winston. Winston was always an exception.

Peter was both right and wrong. Since he'd scored his unprecedented success of spotting androids posturing as people in the Houses of Parliament, in Ottawa, JR had been dabbling with GDV on his own. He had no ambitions to upstage Peter, or to develop abilities of reading auras himself, but JR was a tinkerer. So far, however, he couldn't have come up with anything worthwhile or he would have told Ruth, who, in turn, would have informed Peter. Thus, as far as Peter was concern, he was on his own.

***

Part Two

LIMBO

Much Ado About Nothing
"sundry times publicly acted"

William Shakespeare

7
Much Ado About Nothing

Originally, **Solidarity International** had been created with very noble aims. All the original postulates the Solidarity had set out to achieve have already been achieved. The salary scales were contained within a maximum of 5x average incomes. Medical services were provided to all its members for free. All employees had a stake in the company they worked for. Retirees had living pensions. It was amazing how much can be saved by cutting out millions from the coffers of greedy medical specialists, pharmaceutical conglomerates and, even more so, from lawyers' fees, and the absurd compensations awarded by publicly appointed judges who have been, for years, completely out of touch with reality.

Things were rolling under their own steam.

For now, Peter performed the duties of a glorified detector machine that happened to be biologically based. He once said that we are all mobile robots nature designed to feed the army of germs living within us. However, if he and JR succeeded in their electro-photonic endeavour, Peter would lose even that distinction. His usefulness would be limited to feeding his germs. Billions of them. Trillions?

It seemed that the Bard was right. Solidarity International was becoming intensely preoccupied with much ado about nothing. This was probably the underlying factor contributing to Peter's emotional condition. He was approaching the mood he'd sunk to when he'd learned about his newly acquired gift of healing. Years of study, work, self-denial, all dismissed by the whim of powers which he didn't even recognize as real.

Boredom breeds discontent. If it hadn't been for his self-imposed discipline of practicing his dream control exercises, he would have collapsed in a heap of self-pity.

Nevertheless, the discontent that he had managed to suppress by keeping busy with broad-based research for the SI, now that it was all done, was coming back to him. The original disbelief, then dejection, and now, slowly gnawing at his gut... revolt. These emotional states first invaded his consciousness on the day he'd embraced the dying lad, in the Montreal General Hospital. The whispers had already been spreading, on the tongues of young, impressionable nurses, of his enigmatic touch. For a while, he'd managed to contain them. He almost returned to his status of a first-rate physician, and then... wasn't it Lucille? Lucille Ouellette? The boy's mother...

"Just touch 'im," she'd begged. No tears, no wailing, just a soft whisper, *Just touch 'im...* He still remembered her French Canadian accent.

"I'm a doctor, a physician. I don't touch people. I examine them and then prescribe medications," he'd wanted to scream at her. Only he hadn't. He hadn't even said it. Perhaps he should have.

The boy was dying.

Peter recalled leaning over and holding the lad to his chest. Just for a while. A short while...

To this day he wasn't sure why he'd done that.

And now he was ready to kill. Not that he would, but he felt disconsolate, frustrated, tired of constant self-denial. Yet kill he might. Winston said it wouldn't matter. We were immortal.

"There is only one kind of survival," Winston had said, "the survival of our memories. The only soul that one can lose contact with is *nephesh*, our subconscious. Nevertheless, this definition of soul is limited, or confined, to the accumulated experience stored in the subconscious from a single incarnation. Just this one life." Winston's hands embraced the sphere of the air around him. "Your true self is immortal, indestructible, and cannot be injured in any way."

There, we're immortal!

In his present mental condition, Peter interpreted Winston's statement as license to kill. Isn't this what nature does to preserve various species? Nature kills using our hands. He held up his hands in the air.

"The Lord giveth, the Lord taketh away," he muttered to himself. "These hands can do both. Heal and kill, with equal facility."

As an ex-physician he knew of a dozen ways he could kill with impunity. We are nature, integral parts of it. Kill or be killed. Kill others, so that you might live.

Not that he would. He could simply kill himself. Just once. To murder others, indiscriminately, he would partake in nature herself. Cooperate with her. Like Genghis Khan. Or Stalin. Or Hitler. Or even Twigg, muzzled by his VP Linker—the last of the great killers.

Aye, perhaps I could kill…

Not yet.

He came to the office every day, like a regular employee. As he used to, at the hospital. God, those were the days. He used to be busy then. Really busy. He enjoyed life to the full. There were no nightmares to visit him in his dreams. He lived his dreams. Yes, he lived to the full. He'd felt like Sherlock Holmes, diagnosing the truth from scant, often intangible facts.

There were more than eleven thousand employees at the SI Headquarters. He began by asking various people if there was anything he could do for them. To assist them in any way. Any way? He caught them off guard—they were all busy with their assigned tasks. They all—yes, all of them—took his offer of help as a joke.

On the other hand, his roving the various departments was a relatively unobtrusive way to meet people and scan their auras. Some were so dull as to be hardly visible from any distance. Any distance at all. He had to get close. After all, wasn't that his new, engaging job? Once he had a broad range of interests. Even outside medicine. Now?

They all knew that he was the boss's brother-in-law. Wasn't he the man who did things in the Houses of Parliament, not so long ago? Something to do with spies? He flew to the Vatican on a moment's notice. He knew Miss Walesa personally—they were on first-name terms. Imagine that? On first-name terms with Miss Walesa! They say he used to be a physician…

Peter was a legend before his time.

"He's just checking up on us," he heard their thoughts, following him down the corridor.

A corridor just like at the hospital, only the colours were not as bland, and the smell was not saturated with antiseptic cleansers. And the light fixtures were of a much better quality. The sick didn't need good light fixtures. All they wanted was to get out, as soon as possible, and go home.

Or feet first, Peter mused grimly.

Days turned into weeks, weeks into months. By January, walking to the office was no longer fun. Not in the Canadian winter. There wasn't a single clone gracing the SI Headquarters. Neither clone, nor android, nor a robot other than with SI insignia. Those were needed to distribute items too heavy for people to carry. They didn't even look like people—well, not much. Only when they retracted the wheels and put on a human face. Sort of human, just to blend in better. Before that, people had been scared of them. Now, they all had pet names.

"Get Giorgino to give you a hand…"

"Let Picolla do it for you…"

"Why don't you call Roberto…"

Yes, one could call them and they came. Quickly. Willingly. Obediently. Not at all like people.

For some reason all the robots had been given Italian or quasi-Italian names. No one knew why. Perhaps, to tell them apart from real people? Or maybe there were not many Italians working at Headquarters, and those who were, had had their names long Anglicized.

He was careful not to touch people. He would become useless as a spy. The last thing he needed was a horde of people lining up to benefit from his gift. He wasn't even sure he still had it. Also, somehow, people seemed to have forgotten his reputed abilities. It's hard to remember things you don't really believe in.

Whatever happened to the days when he dove, head first, into genetics? In spite of his medical background, he'd learned more in a month than he had in years of medical studies. And then robotics… Americans had made colossal strides in the development and implementation of Artificial Intelligence: their androids looked more human than the humans. Or, as they used to joke at the seminary, they might have been *plus catholique que le pape.* Who knew, perhaps the clones had been programmed to be Catholics. They certainly were not intended to think for themselves.

He shrugged at his own vindictive thoughts.

And then there was his dive, headlong, into the completely unknown field of nanotechnology? He'd found it amazing what the Chinese and Indian scientists had done at the micro-scale. They could inject nanoparticles into the bloodstream that countermanded the programs nature instilled herself. As a physician, Peter wouldn't have been able to deal with such patients. Neither physically nor mentally. By the end of the second decade of this century, Nanoneurology had become an established science. By the middle of the century, it had displaced the old style neurology with all the old speculative suppositions. The plagues of the past, the cancers, Parkinson's and the whole gamut of cardiovascular diseases, had been practically eliminated. At least for those who could afford treatment, or… were members of the Solidarity.

Peter had to decide if the beneficiaries of nanotechnology were still wholly human. At least, as compared to androids and/or clones. The problem was that they still had visible auras, but the hues they emanated, especially those who underwent neurosurgical manipulation, were completely different. Perhaps it was time to redefine humanity. In the past, these would have been ethical problems that various religions would have dissected in a million ways to find an acceptable answer. But this was the Age of Aquarius. Everyone tended, or had been intended, to water their own ethical garden. If you didn't break the law that protected the individuality and/or the property of another, you were your own ethical boss. You also carried your own ethical responsibilities.

Those were the challenging days. The rules had been set and were running relatively smoothly. The rest was mostly much ado about nothing. Even family life had changed diametrically. Children who benefited from various treatments often surpassed their parents' abilities before reaching adulthood. Alas, not their sense of responsibility. Emotionally, they remained children.

It wasn't always easy.

Each day, returning from the office, Peter threw himself into his new hobby. At least, that's what he called it. After all, he did it only for himself, to sate his own interests. With the exception of that one case of the hurricane, he saw no way that others could benefit from his research, even if he became successful. Yet he had to pursue it, if only to remain sane.

His one consolation was that Cathy was showing signs of interest in OBE. Or, at least, in lucid dreaming.

"It would be most incredible fun to be able to control one's dreams. Imagine..." And there followed a series of dream-like fragments that fulminated in her fertile imagination.

"There would be nothing we couldn't do... Oh, Peter, just think, if we could dream the same dream... together."

When it came to her romantic life, Cathy was always practical. She already was a spinner of dreams. She just needed more control over them.

"Will you help me?"

Frankly, he had been waiting for this moment. He hadn't told her that on three occasions he'd actually seen her in his dreams. He was sure that his attention and desire had induced Cathy's presence into his chimerical excursions. Regrettably, to date, although, as his notebook at his bedside would attest, the recall of his dreams had improved enormously, he couldn't be sure that he actually wielded any real control over the dreams as such. It had been months now. He had snippets he regarded as partial successes. On a few occasions he woke up thinking that he was still dreaming; once he found himself in the middle of his living room in the middle of the night, without any recall of how he had gotten there. If sleepwalking was part of the experience, then he had no use for it. Somnambulism did not excite him at all. If anything, he regarded it as dangerous.

"I'm not exactly an expert, darling." He was pleased, but definitely abashed.

"You know more than I do?"

"In theory. I'm good at theory. It's practice that gives me problems."

Peter knew what the problem was. He was too tense. Much too tense. He was also frustrated, had low self-esteem, and generally lived in a badly camouflaged state of dissatisfaction. Any one of these would block access to his subconscious. He was rapidly losing the art of relaxation.

"If you help me with theory…"

She left that hanging. Perhaps she could, he mused. Perhaps, with her superb ability to find good in virtually anything, she could help him. Then he sighed. There I go, thinking of myself, again, he chided himself.

The next day Cathy left for CERN. It wouldn't be for long, but it came at the wrong time. Wrong for him. Peter felt like learning to fly from his 49th story window. Thank God they don't open, he mused.

There is a reason for everything, he heard at the back of his head. It was Winston's voice.

Cathy was away till Friday. Three days of bachelorhood was the last thing Peter wanted, but it gave him a chance to spend most of the night practicing indirect techniques of out-of-body projection.

On her return, as usual, she was up to her neck in black holes, and a number of other enigmatic and invisible whatnots that didn't make the slightest sense to Peter. He was now convinced that theoretical physics in no way differed from science fiction, with a strong bias towards fiction, and a good admix of fantasy.

She was also engulfed in her event horizons.

"But, Peter, a massless black hole no longer has an event horizon. It…"

Apparently the space got sucked in together with that once gargantuan mass and…

"There goes the Cheshire Cat, again," Peter offered.

"If only. It seems that there is nothing left. Not even the smile."

It was in moments such as those that Peter was glad he opted for real things. Things like auras, astral bodies, perhaps Tao spirits, and suchlike. Things he could actually see, feel, touch, often hear and—most of all—enjoy. For Peter, physics became completely intangible.

By Saturday, after a brisk walk on hard, crisp snow, Cathy came back to the subject of the control of dreams. Apparently she'd read up on the stuff on her flight to and from Europe. She was much better versed in the Chinese version of astral projection than Peter. In fact, when Peter was younger, in the seminary, such flights of fancy had been seriously discouraged. Later, studying and practicing medicine, you couldn't raise the subject without becoming a laughing-stock. If you couldn't touch it, smell it, or see it, even with the aid of electron microscopes, it wasn't real.

"They say there are, in fact, two bodies. The body that leaves yours, when you sleep, is the *yin shen.* Or, at least, it is similar to the 'dream' body." Her fingers placed the word dream in inverted comas.

Peter wasn't particularly interested in Tao, or its meditative practices, but he loved looking at Cathy when she talked. She invariably seemed totally involved in the subject she was discussing.

"There is also the *yang shen,*" she added. "It can also leave your body of flesh and blood, yet it is still material body and form and can be seen with human eyes. It seems to be both—physical and spiritual—with independent existence."

"Is this supposed to make it clearer?" Peter was more confused than ever.

"Well, it is a projection of the real spirit..."

"...and thus it can do anything it jolly well wants?" He was only half-serious.

"I thought you were serious about this," Cathy snapped. She'd really put a lot of effort into the research on the plane.

"Sorry. I really am, only you seem to have too many bodies in Tao. I rather assumed that we have only one body, which can slip in and out of its physical shell, or manifest through it."

"I am not telling you what I think, only what is accepted in the Taoist perspective." She still sounded a little hurt.

"And I appreciate it very much," he said, and drew her towards him. Sitting on a love seat facing the Mount Royal as it was being sowed gently with clean, white, tremulous snowflakes, he found it difficult to get really angry.

"You are a one-track mind," she whispered, but did not resist. Lately Peter was so preoccupied with his nocturnal exercises that she missed his physical contact.

"Whatever body you wish to project at me, I'll take it," he said, his voice getting raspy. "How about…"

"I thought you'd never ask…"

Half an hour later, they were still discussing projections of various parts of their bodies. Then, they got serious.

"So astral projection was really practiced by the ancient Chinese…" Peter mused.

"Actually, the more advanced monks did not regard the projection of *yin shen* as the ultimate goal of Tao, although it was usually the result of many years of meditation. On the other hand, they also held that ordinary people could experience the projection of *yin shen* quite spontaneously."

"So there is still hope for us?"

"Well… it helps if you are near death…"

"No, thank you, I'd rather…"

"Or… you are not going to like this," she warned.

"Further away from death? Try me."

"Or, if you are a borderline schizophrenic."

"That describes me to the letter."

"I love you, too. Although I find you more schizo than frenetic. Normal people bore me. You, darling, never have."

Peter was ready to return to the discussion of projections of her physical body. On the settee, facing the mountain. Or on the carpet. Or anywhere.

That night, they lay side by side, their fingers interlocked. Peter was dreaming, very lucidly, of just such a time when they would attempt to leave their bodies, if that's the right word, and join forces "on the other side" of reality. He realized that he didn't even have a language to express his desires, his aims; nor even his exact purpose. It was as if he desperately wanted to go down the road, not knowing at all where the road was leading.

Before attempting to relax, he had to push away distracting thoughts.

Perhaps I am a borderline schizophrenic, he mused. I'm certainly indifferent to most usual exigencies. I have been told that I tend to withdraw into my shell, particularly when among people of dubious intelligence. When healing people with my hands, I have had a sensation of omnipotence, though, at the same time, I had absolutely no control over it, but rather a sense of persecution. With all these, Lena and Ruth, not to mention Cathy, regarded my intelligence to remain unimpaired. All classic terms for schizoid behaviour. There is nothing borderline about me.

Is there?

Only, the patient is not supposed to be fully aware if it. So far, I seem to be, he murmured, a crooked grin twisting his mouth.

"Darling, you are not relaxing," Cathy whispered.

He squeezed her hand in acknowledgment. "I know, I'm sorry," he muttered.

Slowly, very slowly, her very presence pushed away his turbulent thoughts. Whatever happened, he wanted this to be a trip together. Wherever it took them.

Gradually his awareness of the bed, of his body, even of touching Cathy's hand, began to dissolve in an ocean of calm. Dense fog filled his vision, then patches of darker and lighter mists floated effortlessly behind his closed eyelids.

He wanted to call out to Cathy, to bring her closer to him. He was convinced that she was there, close by, probably calling him… he reached out with both hands, groping in the swirling haze. He grasped at the wisps, at ghosts swirling in the omnipresent fog, which his eyes could not pierce. *Where am I?* he asked.

Where am I? he called out, as loudly as he dared. He didn't know if one is allowed to speak loudly in such places as this. Was Cathy here? He hoped not. When he wanted to travel together, it wasn't to such a place. He sensed that there was nothing as far as his mind could reach. A swirling mass of nothingness. He was suspended, alone in the middle of a reality that was not real. He was suspended in a whirlpool of unfulfilled desires. A non-place.

He was suspended in limbo.

He woke up sweating. In the light of the digital clock, Peter discerned Cathy sleeping peacefully. As he looked closer, he could barely see a gentle smile on her relaxed face. I wonder where she went, he mused.

Why didn't I go with her?

Why didn't she take me with her? Only then did he realize that this whole exercise was his idea. When you're playing with fire, you get burned, he thought.

Or… or you get lost in fog, a voice whispered in his head.

Which are my thoughts? Those I formulate or those that seem to formulate on their own in my head. Perhaps I am a schizophrenic. I hear voices. On the other hand, I did hear those ephemeral whispers from the day I've met Winston. Does he have something to do with this?

My inner world is empty.

That's it. My inner world is empty. Ready to be created, like that black hole Cathy and I sustained, momentarily, before it could wink out of existence. Only this was different. The fog was gray. The light in it was diffused, unformed, like ideas that were not yet manifested.

Cathy was still sleeping.

Peter lay back, afraid to close his eyes. He stared into the darkness. Gradually, his eyes adjusted. He could see the ceiling, then its surface stretching on all sides towards the horizon. It was beginning to turn blue. He felt the warmth of the sun caressing his body.

"It's gorgeous, darling, isn't it?"

"Yes, sweetheart. It is gorgeous wherever you are."

He felt the sea lapping the collapsible legs of their beach-chairs. Soon they would have to move farther up the gently sloping sand.

"Not a cloud on the horizon," Cathy whispered. "Not a care in the world…"

He smiled his gratitude. For some reason he assumed that his being there was her doing. Somehow, in the middle of Canadian winter, she'd managed to transport him to the balmy tropics.

"It wasn't me," she whispered. "We both wanted it, deep down. In your subconscious…"

And then fog began to drift in from the sea. He wished he didn't try to rationalize what had happened. The moment he did, it began to dissolve. To dissolve into the precinct of Limbo. Once again.

"Or the antechamber of hell," he thought grimly.

"Peter, Peter! Wake up!" Cathy was tugging at his shoulder. "Wake up, darling…"

He forced his eyes to open.

"What happened?" His voice was raspy.

"You all right?" There was real concern on her face. "You sounded as though you were seeing the devil himself."

"Ah, yes. The antechamber of hell." He wiped the sweat from his forehead. He was beginning to understand. "It's not what you want, it's what is at the back of your mind. In your subconscious."

"What are you talking about?"

"About soul travel."

"What happened, Peter? You look awful."

Cathy had occasion to see Peter in very diverse moods, but this was one of his weaker moments.

"That's roughly how I feel, thanks, darling."

"I'm serious. You really look as if you'd seen a ghost…"

"You were right the first time. Not a ghost but the devil himself. Actually, he wasn't home, but his domain…"

He shivered convulsively, trying to shake off the lingering vision. Cathy remained silent, waiting for him to continue.

"You know, darling, there is the good and the bad, or the holy and the evil. But none of them are as bad as the stuff in-between."

"Whatever happened to the middle path?" she was still bending over the bed, studying his face. Then she sat down and stroked his hair as she had, once, in the old rustic cabin in the Laurentians, when she was bringing him back to life. It seemed that was in another lifetime.

"It's not that. It's something to do with an image I recall from John's Revelation…" he closed his eyes. For a moment he was sitting in a straight-backed pew; an elderly priest was delivering a homily.

I wish you were either cold or hot… because you are lukewarm, and neither cold nor hot, I am about to spit you out of my mouth.

Peter blinked repeatedly. Then he looked up at Cathy.

"It's something to do with this. With not caring, deeply. It's to do with emotions. I think," his eyes drifted again to some unknown regions, "I think this whole other realm is motivated by emotions. Not will power, not mind, but emotions."

"Why do you think so, Peter?" Cathy felt drawn into his dilemma.

"Because I went there, I drifted there, without a definite emotional need. I found myself in Limbo. A place, a reality, where you feel nothing, where you are null and void. Like fog that is drifting yet has nowhere to go."

"Could that be why he, two thousand years ago, stressed so much the need for love?"

Cathy had been brought up in the Confucian/Taoist tradition. Strictly speaking she wasn't a Christian—not by baptism—but they both knew whom she was talking about.

"It seems to me that whatever we can find *there* is, or can be, so powerful that entering its domain without love in your heart might have very, very dire consequences."

"And what exactly is this *there*?"

"If I knew, I'd probably also know how to get there, without getting lost on the way. But, you know, what really scares me is just how very real it is."

Whatever it is. The Limbo, the hurricane forming on the horizon far too distant to be seen with human eyes, or even the smell of roses in the Vatican Gardens. Whatever and wherever *there* was, it was magic.

By then, Peter had recovered his usual hue. He'd be all right. Cathy got up to make breakfast. Nothing like black coffee to wash those cobwebs away. She had but one regret. She was desperately sorry she couldn't help him; that she couldn't share Peter's experiences with him. For her, they were still just theories. And then she remembered: so were 90% of her theoretical physics.

Peter was still trying to work out the lesson he had just been given. It seemed to him that, apart from Cathy, he didn't really care about anything very much. He liked some people, certainly Ruth's children. There was also Ruth herself, his old professor John Brent and Lucy. He also held a special place in his heart for Lena, and definitely for JR... There were a few people he cared about, but... hardly loved. Hardly to the extent that he would jump in the fire for them. Or into a raging current.

"Actually I probably would,' he muttered, "but not in cold blood."

But... he wasn't sure. Not really. Not as sure as he was of his love for Cathy. Towards others he was neither cold nor hot. Lukewarm. Yes, lukewarm described him best. Apparently it wasn't good enough. He was motivated by loyalty, a sense of duty, often by curiosity, but seldom by just love.

He swiveled his chair towards the window. For a while he watched the snowflakes making their convoluting journeys down, apparently determined never to reach the ground. At this height, they seemed suspended in the air, some warm currents carrying them up as well as down, gently swirling, uncertain, or perhaps just uncaring what is to happen to them.

Lukewarm? A little like me, Peter sighed. Getting nowhere. If only I knew where I was going, it all would be so much easier. The only thing that shows any promise in my life is the unknown. On the other hand, not knowing stimulates one's ambitions only if there's purpose to it. Only if it urges one to action.

You're like the snowflakes. You are swept up and down, aimlessly, without rancor but also without love; indifferent, careless yet not carefree. You need help. Why do you always need help? We all do, only few of us admit it...

He didn't say any of this, but he heard all the words distinctly echoing in his head. And then a familiar phrase drifted, uninvited, across his churning mind.

The wind bloweth where it listeth, and thou hearest the sound thereof, but canst not tell whence it cometh and whither it goeth: so is every one that is born of the Spirit.

Like the flakes outside my window... Only I don't even hear the wind. But I have heard this sentence before. Long, long *ago.*

And then anger stirred with him.

Only I don't seem to be born at all.

I'm hardly alive.

***

8
A Trial Run

Up to that day, Peter's meandering paths through the various departments of SI Headquarter were routine. By definition, routine is boring. It was a way to pass his time, and to get paid for doing nothing much. To earn his keep. He refused to be a hanger-on to Cathy's parents' millions. The book Mrs. Mondellay had written about him, assigning him the royalties, no longer reaped abundant profit.

"I never imagined I was so interesting," he'd said, having been told that that *One Just Man*, as she'd titled the book, remained on the bestseller list for more than a year.

As for his present assignment at the SI, it wasn't really his fault—not in the strictest sense of the word—that he was the only one Ruth knew who could read auras; or, to put it differently, to tell a human from a non-human.

Nevertheless, his new commission began to reap results.

He first realized that there was something amiss when he noticed that, each time he approached the bank of elevators in the main lobby, one of the guards found it necessary to slip away. The guard must have seen him approaching through the glass entrance doors and was gone before Peter could get near him. After it happened for the fourth time, Peter refused to treat it as a coincidence. He knew the guard was missing, because he was not only an unusually handsome man, but also an inch taller than the average guard. Years as a physician had trained Peter's eyes for details; even as small at those he'd now spotted. But what really caught Peter's attention was the guard's uncanny resemblance to Francis Drake. Not in facial features, but in the general appearance— of being just a little too good to be true. A fraction too tall, the silhouette just a tinge too straight, the shoulders just a little too broad—generally suggesting a paragon of virtue. People are not like that. Not usually. Occasionally they slouch. They lean on one elbow. Their heads hang down. It looked as if someone had made very sure that the guard would get the job.

For a while it didn't strike Peter as peculiar, because the guards had been selected for their impressive postures, and encouraged to move around, just so as not to offer an easy target. They were supposed to mix, to rub shoulders with men and women, while the metal detectors in their uniforms' pockets recorded any abnormalities. They must have been doing their job well, as the Headquarters' security had never been compromised. At least, not from the main entrance lobby. There was that single breach, when Ruth was kidnapped, but that happened through the roof entrance, where the access from the heliport had not had sufficient precautions. And even then, Ruth had been partially responsible. She had trusted a man who once had already proven not to be reliable.

Peter approached the main entrance, then turned and made as though he had forgotten something. He walked back, mixed with a few people, then took up a position behind a six-foot cedar hedge. From that concealed location, with a collapsible monocular that he'd inherited from his father, he regarded the activities of the guards. After a few minutes, he approached the entrance again and, as usual, made for the bank of elevators. The taller guard, seconds ago towering at the main desk, was missing. Peter, while pleased with his subterfuge, was getting a bit annoyed. Not so much that the guard was apparently trying to outwit him, but that he did so in such a blatant way.

Last night, he'd asked Cathy if one could manufacture a black hole and have people you didn't like fall into it.

"Well, some years ago, Strominger and Vafa advocated designer black holes..." she began, then she caught herself. "Peter, you're not serious!"

He wasn't, though there had been times when he'd have liked to have had a black hole ready at this bidding. His life might have taken a different turn. On the other hand, since he'd lost his chance to be a physician, nothing else stirred comparable passion in him. Not really. First the seminary, then medicine. Then, auras notwithstanding, he felt empty.

Now, for the first time in years, he felt the thrill of a hunt. *The game's afoot, Mrs. Thornton,* he mused. He wondered if, before taking any action, he ought to report his findings to Ruth. After all, here, at the Headquarters, she was the boss. He chose a compromise. He knocked on JR's door.

John Robb was alone in his office. His secretary must have been out on some errant. Since becoming the unofficial SI expert on Artificial Intelligence, JR had grown in stature, as had his office. At least as big as Peter's, with room for two secretaries. Only both stations were empty. JR noticed Peter's inquiring look.

"Just out to get me some real coffee. Can't stand the stuff that comes out of this machine."

He gestured Peter to a chair.

"Both of them?" Usually, JR kept both secretaries busy.

"Ah, Marie didn't feel so well. I let her go home." JR was generous to a fault. He was also, basically, a loner.

Peter slipped into the chair in front of the large desk and told JR about his recent successes as a detective. Contrary to Ruth's office, JR's desk was cluttered with stacks of files, pieces of wires, a soldering iron, and a number of bits and pieces Peter didn't recognize. When he finished telling his story, JR rose to his full six-foot-eight and began pacing his office. Large as it was, he covered the distance, wall to wall, in four strides. Peter had never seen legs that long. Perhaps JR was an early android, before they perfected the system. On the other hand, any AI with such proportions would have been terminated long ago. That was the problem with us humans. We were all eminently imperfect. At least by the standards set by the classical Greek sculptures.

JR stopped pacing and disappeared. When Peter swiveled his chair, JR was towering directly behind him. JR just stood there, staring at Peter.

"Did you see more than one?" he asked.

"So you're assuming that I was right?"

"Peter, for as long as I've known you, you were always right. Did you see more than one, ah... suspect?"

"But I haven't gotten close enough to him to confirm the absence of an aura."

JR nodded and started pacing again.

JR, as security chief, was the only member of SI, other than Ruth and Lena, who knew about Peter's special abilities. Not just suspected but had been officially briefed about them. Outside this trio there had been whispers, lots of whispers, but nothing concrete. Peter insisted on that. He had no desire to be regarded, for the second time in his life, as a freak

"Why don't you sit down, JR. You keep disappearing from my field of vision."

Incidentally, what Peter meant was that he was observing, almost intuitively, JR's aura. It was a pulsating bright blue. The man was thinking. Hard. Only Peter could hardly tell him that. *Excuse me, JR, but your aura is pulsating...* It was not the sort of thing one could work into a conversation.

JR stopped, stared down at Peter, shrugged, then settled behind his desk.

"There's never enough room for my legs under this thing," he said, tapping the glass and metal desk, probably twice as large as Peter had in his office.

"Try pushing your chair back," Peter muttered. In addition to the clutter, there were three computer screens on JR's desk, but he did most of the work by twitting buttons built into both armrests of his armchair. He didn't have to sit as close as he did.

"Why thanks! I'd never thought of that!" JR was one of the brighter stars of SI. He really was an intellectual marvel. It was the simple things that stumped him. He found it easier to memorize a chess game than to tie his shoes. Well, almost.

"So?" Peter asked. "What do we do next?"

"We wait."

"Wait?" Peter didn't find this funny. There was hope here for a little action, and now... "Wait?" he repeated, disappointment in his voice.

"You never answered my question, and they always work in pairs," was JR's cryptic response.

"Just how would you know?"

"It's my job." JR looked surprised. Seeing questions in Peter's eyes, he added, "In the States—they're all from the States, you know—in the States they always produce them in pairs. The hard part is the design—you might as well use it more than once. Also, the first one does the work, the second is a backup. Mostly in case something happens to Number One."

"And you know that for sure?" Peter was a little annoyed that, in a matter of speaking, he'd failed in his job. He'd missed the backup. He'd have to go back to the grindstone.

"They are identical. Really, you cannot tell them apart. Not without taking them apart. Ha, ha! Funny that!"

Peter was in no mood for jokes.

"So what do I do next?" Theoretically, Peter was working for JR.

"You tell me how to locate Number One. I'll put a tracer on him, and he'll lead us to his Number Two."

"Won't they spot you when…"

"Not personally, Peter. My, you really are out of touch. I have an army of security guards, mostly in civvies."

"But… how did they get inside the building? Don't you still need an implant?"

"That's part of the problem. I suspect they were shipped in crates as some sort of office equipment, perhaps furniture, and had the means to get out of the crates on their own. But I'm just speculating."

"Of course…" I really am out of touch, Peter thought. "So, once inside, they have to remain, ah, inside."

"Unless they can find a way to be shipped out… but for now, the important thing is to locate the Number Two and nab them together."

Peter nodded. And take them apart, he mused. He couldn't quite picture taking Francis Drake apart, just to find out what made him tick. Still, Francis was not a spy. On the other hand, he was not really human, either. Life was becoming complicated.

Peter couldn't, and certainly shouldn't, share with Cathy the nature of his work. The more she knew, the more it might endanger her life. Judging by what had happened in Europe some time ago, the competition was playing for keeps.

On the other hand, Cathy had no such qualms about sharing her work with Peter, if only he could understand it. She'd mentioned the 'designer' black holes. Apparently the theorists were quite serious about them.

"When we say 'construct' a designer black hole, we mean theoretically. Not a real solid black hole, so to speak. To make one we would need pressures, or gravity, similar to those in the first microsecond after the big bang."

Peter pretended to be crestfallen.

"Are you sure I cannot help?" he asked, even more facetiously.

"All you need to know is," Ruth continued, ignoring his comments, "that pursuing the calculations of the entropy of a five-dimensional black hole, we progressed to ten, then eleven dimensions, all curled up on the theoretical..."

"You can curl up black holes?"

"No, Peter, the dimensions are curled up... never mind. What I am trying to say is that reaching out into other dimensions is no longer the province of black magic, but..."

"...but rather black holes," he finished for her.

"Well, in a way. There certainly is more even to this reality than meets the eye, or... or any other of our senses."

"It all seems to exist in our minds. It's a question of agreement. We agree that this or that is real—and, henceforth, it is."

"We now agree that, at least beyond the event horizon, there are not fewer than eleven dimensions..." she said, her voice as wondrous as his when he talked of the horizon beyond the scope of our physical eyes.

"What you are really trying to tell me is that I am not completely bananas."

She leaned over and planted a saucy kiss on his mouth.

"You are completely everything to me, except for bananas," she assured him gravely.

"Seriously, though," Peter recovered sufficiently to get back to their discussion, "it really does seem that creating reality is left to us. Didn't he say... *whatever you bind on earth will be bound in heaven?* And vice versa? Something like that. Nothing is real until we decide that it is. Until we bind it. Until we make it real. It seems that the creation of what's real and what isn't is left in our inept hands."

Cathy was thinking about her subatomic particles, which she could neither touch, nor feel, nor experience with any of her senses. She could only bind them to earth, to our reality, with theories. Like Einstein, she was trying to know the thoughts of god.

"Ah, Peter, if I could only bind them…" she whispered, lost in her own musings.

They went on like this all evening.

Peter needed even such rambling discussions to take him away from the monotony of his work at the Headquarters which, important as it was, did not tax his brain unduly. He realized that each day he returned home feeling more and more disgusted with himself. Even his latest discovery, which could be construed as at least a minor achievement, had been whisked away from him. Once the enemy became known, JR was much more competent in dealing with the problem. Peter's new hobby of conscious dreaming, or the practice of out-of-body projection, became his only escape. And now, after his latest experience, he began to have cold feet even in that area of research.

"What am I to do, Cathy? Whatever I attempt becomes polluted by my inadequacies."

Cathy wished she could help. She offered to assist him in all his astral research. Yet, it seemed, this area had to be mastered on one's own, before one could share it with others. And Peter wasn't ready.

"It will come, darling. It will come," she whispered, but she was worried about the man she loved dearly.

In the past, Peter had been escaping from the office to get home. Recently, the escape became a two-way street. If it hadn't been for Cathy, who alone acted like balm for his roiled nerves, he would have hidden in the darkest black hole he could find and waited to emerge on the other side, in some different, hopefully better, reality. For now, however, Cathy was not prepared to provide him with this way out.

That morning JR was waiting for him just outside the main entrance, curled up, if a man his size could curl up, behind the cedar hedge. He whistled softly, gesturing Peter to join him behind the fence, which, once before, had served Peter as an observation spot.

"I'd like you to show me which guy you suspect of being a clone," he said, without any preambles.

JR came equipped with a telescope of his own that looked like an old-fashioned instrument, favoured by the masters of ancient square-riggers.

"Land ahoy," Peter murmured, when JR handed him the archaic instrument.

"I got that from my uncle," JR said. "An old salt." When that didn't seem to impress Peter, he added, "He was a collector."

Archaic or not, the telescope did its job. Peter couldn't help liking JR's turn of phrase, nor his permanently good humour. He actually met JR's uncle once. A true raconteur of old naval stories.

"Twenty years in the Navy," Peter recalled JR's uncle's assurances. "Never drunk on duty—never sober on liberty."

It turned out the expression came from a portrait painted by Charles Cole. JR's uncle had a framed copy on the wall.

Peter could only describe his suspect's position. He obviously didn't know his name, as asking for it, during the guard's absence, would be bound to raise suspicions. JR would have to actually recognize him.

"What do you intend doing," he asked, handing the spyglass to JR and describing the guards' position. He couldn't say just the taller one, as at any time the guards turned, leaned over the desk or sat down.

"Third on the left," JR said after a while, handing the telescope back to Peter for confirmation.

"Got it in one."

"I'll remember him," a slight smile played about JR's lips. "Now here's the game plan. I'll go inside first. Presumably our suspect will stay where he is. It is obvious that he's onto you, and your devious ways, but they don't suspect anyone else capable of possible recognition. I'll make for the elevator, come back some minutes later and hide behind a column. When you come in, I'll follow him to wherever he's hiding. OK?"

He offered his watch to synchronize time. "Give me, ah, seven minutes precisely, and then make for the door."

"If you're a minute late, I'll freeze to death."

Until now, neither of the men seemed aware that the temperature was well below zero.

"Seven minutes from... now," JR said, and let his long stride take him towards the main entrance.

Peter pretended that he was not yet frozen still.

The seven minutes felt like an hour. As he hadn't expected JR to surprise him, he had carried only a light coat, which he used for fast walks to the office. He always walked. It was virtually his only concession to exercising his body. But standing still, so as not to attract attention, did nothing for his circulation. After two minutes he decided he would be less conspicuous if he paced up and down, look this way and that, as if waiting for someone. Three minutes later, he began to feel his toes again. During the last two minutes he glanced at his watch every few seconds. Then he squared his shoulders and made for the main entrance.

Even as he approached, he saw one of the uniformed guards leave the console and edge to his right. He hoped JR was in position to follow him. There was nothing, at least for now, that Peter could do.

He walked past the other remaining guards, both saluting him as he made for the elevator. He made straight for JR's office, intending to wait for him to hear the news.

After ten minutes, there was no sign of JR.

"Tell Mr. Robb I'll be in my office," Peter told the secretary and made for the door. Just outside he bumped into JR. If it hadn't been for his dangling height, he wouldn't have recognized him. JR wore a Vandyke beard, a French beret at a capricious angle, and carried a square portfolio under his arm.

"The SOB disappeared," he said without being asked. "I followed him the moment he moved, and he wasn't there any more. Or anywhere. Like a ghost."

JR pulled Peter back into his office.

"Ghost is exactly what he's lacking," Peter murmured.

"We'll have to do it all again. What makes me wonder is how does he know you're approaching on your way out?"

Peter looked up at JR's face hovering a foot about his own. He felt embarrassed and annoyed at himself for not having thought of that himself.

"There must be two of them. Or... at least two."

"I know. I told you, they always..."

"...work in pairs. The other one must keep a look out for the elevators and warn his counterpart. Sneaky devils."

Within minutes they had a game plan.

Peter would walk down the last three flights of stairs, come out at the mezzanine, and try to spot anyone suspicious who had a good view of the elevators. If the two guards were as easily recognizable, there would be no difficulty in recognizing him.

"You'd better wear a disguise," JR murmured, as he reached into the left drawers of his desk and produced three wigs, a variety of mustaches, and an equal number of beards. They ranged from mousy gray, to pale gray, to nondescript brown.

"Must be non-descriptive," JR admonished. "You always spot a blond, often one who's silvery gray or near black. It's the colours in-between that are hard to place."

JR made a lot of sense. Peter had the distinct impression that JR was enjoying this subterfuge a lot more than he cared to admit. He sounded like a big boy who was given a new toy; or at least sounded like a lad discussing a game of cowboys and Indians.

And... he, John Robb, was running Solidarity Canada.

Ah, those Crazy Canucks! It was the name of the group of Alpine skiers who rose to prominence in the World Cup during the later part of the last century. It still stuck to describe people taking unwarranted risks. Or... just being a little crazy. The skiers were Mo and Jo's idols.

Peter decided to try and get into the spirit of the game. Since he had stopped living at Ruth's, the absence of children removed him from a daily dose of fun and games. And now? Never mind that the android guards may have been programmed with deadly intentions. He might as well try and enjoy the chase while it lasted. Dutifully he selected a disguise best suiting his taste, and looked critically at his clothing.

"No one ever looks at those," JR assured him. "We are all relatively similarly dressed. Even women. When you spotted that android, you never looked at his uniform, did you?"

As Peter was trying out various disguises, JR looked on, his head cocked to one side. He was smiling.

"You know, Peter, we are not even sure that they are androids..."

Peter sat back. He's right, again, he thought. We aren't sure. For some reason he didn't enjoy this thought either. Had he been wasting his time? Again?

"Are you making a point?"

"We might as well enjoy it," JR said, his smile getting broader.

So that was his point. This time Peter's smile was also more sincere.

"What would I do without you, my friend?" Peter asked. He recalled that, not so long ago, it had been he who had convinced Ruth to promote JR to his present position. And now, even as he was trying on a series of mustaches, he noticed that JR's fingers were playing a steady tattoo on his twitters. JR was working.

A gentle knock was followed by a blond head appearing in the door. "Mr. Jones is here," she announced.

"Just a moment, dear. Peter, put those away, please." He then turned to the blond head. "Ask him to come in."

A short guy walked awkwardly into JR's office. Immediately he got to the point.

"It's a cupboard with spare elevator parts, Sir. You can hardly see it. The marble door is flush with the wall panels, and if you don't know where to look, you won't find it. But we don't have the key to it, Sir. Only the elevator people have access."

"Thank you, Jones. Good job," JR waved him away. "I thought as much," he added, after the man left his office.

"What was all that about?"

"While you were trying on the hairy stuff, I twitted the maintenance guys to find out where there might be a cupboard, in the immediate vicinity of the bank of elevators, in the main lobby, where one could get inside."

"You think he's hiding there?"

"Where else? I had two other men watching every other escape route, including the stairs."

"Two... so you were all prepared?"

"I'm in charge of security, Peter. As I told you, it's my job."

"I thought you were running SI Canada."

"That's running on its own. You know, a well-oiled machine? I'm more of a trouble-shooter. I'm more concerned with where is the other guy. Unless we can locate them both, they'll communicate their apprehension to their, ah, masters."

"Apprehension? You mean arrest?"

"Right. Ideally, I'd like to reprogram them to send back phony information."

"You can do that?"

"We can try."

Peter was becoming acutely glad that he was not running SI Canada, or any other SI branch. Politics was a dirty business. You have to think like your enemy.

"So what's next?"

"Tomorrow morning I'll have men posted in the main lobby. Around ten, walk down the last three flights to the mezzanine, and try to spot the other guy. Here, put this in your lapel. I'll hear your every thought."

"You what!?"

"Just kidding. It's a mike sensitive to your particular voice. When you tell us where the other guy is, we'll move in on both of them."

"Tomorrow at ten?"

"Today people will be going home, soon. Tomorrow earlier, there's also too much traffic in the lobby. Tomorrow at ten."

"Roger."

"Who's Roger?"

"Never mind. They used to say that in the Air Force. See you tomorrow."

Peter gathered his chosen 'hairy-stuff' and bid JR farewell. For some reason he resented it that JR was enjoying himself quite so much. He wished he was. He really tried. I have to see the kids more often, he promised himself. It wasn't the first time he'd made that promise to himself.

"And I wonder what's happening with Winston," he said that aloud.

Then he turned to make sure there was no one behind him. The last thing he wanted was to be accused of talking to himself.

Cathy was full of beans. She'd visited her parents. She was surprised to find Mo and Jo playing Scrabble with her father. They made the game a little more exciting by allowing not just English but also French words. All three spoke French fluently, as all good Quebecers should. Most did. As well as English and Mandarin. Actually English was mostly for business and international affairs. French took care of cultural events. Mandarin was a High Society's *je ne sais quoi*.

For some reasons, on social occasions people liked to great each other in Mandarin. Perhaps it was as close as they could get to a 5000-year-old culture. They used Standard Mandarin, of course. Even Mandarin had many dialects. Or perhaps they just felt like Mandarins, like plutocrats of some old imperial court. Ladies favoured designs derived from old Manchurian dresses, while the Mandarin collar was in for men. It had long ago displaced the tie, which Peter always deemed as one of the more idiotic inventions.

"At last one cannot strangle oneself on a moment's notice, although, with some people I know…"

Peter loved seeing Cathy in cheongsam, a body-clinging, one-piece dress. Cathy had the facility of making it fall down on the carpet with the touch of her fingers. He'd never forget that first night in Ritz-Xentung.

After doing a great number of lucid dream exercises on his own, Peter asked Cathy if she'd like to attempt, once again, an out-of-body experience together. Since a good few days had passed since that unfortunate night when Peter practically gave up the ghost, she agreed. This time Cathy took hold of Peter's hand and held on tight. Then she intertwined her elbow with his, as though making sure he'd not escape her.

Try as they might, they kept falling asleep, until one or the other would unwittingly wake the other by tugging at his or her elbow. A few times Peter felt he was losing touch with reality. Then Cathy would confess to the same feeling. They just couldn't synchronize their efforts. By one a.m. they gave up and, without further ado, made love. After that, their travel took them straight to heaven. Wherever heaven was. As far as they were concerned, they were already there.

"Wherever we travel together, I definitely want to take your body with me."

"And what about me?" she sounded disappointed.

Peter furrowed his brow, pondering her request. Then, nodding gravely, he said, "Oh, all right, you can come, too."

***

9
Ennui

There were just two things that kept Peter relatively sane: Cathy and his mystery hunt with JR. As for his attempts at OBE, they tended to keep him off balance, somewhere between shreds of hope and growing despondency. So far, his soul travel was limited to experiences that could as well have been assigned to the field of dreams and/or nightmares. He still commanded hardly any control over his chimerical states. Against his better judgment, he continued to try with persistence born out of desperation.

"If I don't do that, what am I to do?" he asked Cathy.

She had no answer. From the day she met the brilliant, spirited young physician, Peter continued to decline into a no-man's-land that hovered somewhere at the edges of alternate reality and utter boredom. He was more disheartened than he'd ever been in his life. Once again, his thoughts drifted to Winston. When still living in Westmount, he'd never realized what enormous influence the old majordomo had on his life. Ostensibly invisible, yet his presence filled every nook and cranny of Ruth's house. Winston was part of the woodwork. He seemed to permeate the air you breathed.

"I wonder what's up with Winston," he murmured.

Cathy smiled sadly. She missed Winston, too.

"Perhaps we should invite him over?" she offered.

"How do you invite a butler?" Peter asked. "'Would you like to drop in for a drink?' Winston doesn't drink. 'For a chat?' Winston doesn't indulge in small talk. 'To give us a lecture?' On what subject? I don't even know what to ask him…"

Cathy admitted that Peter was right. You didn't ask Winston 'things'. When you did, you might wait for months to get an answer. No. Winston filled the void in your mind—when needed. He had to be there. To be around. Often she thought that he was. Peter also used to feel his presence. But not lately. Something had gone amiss.

At least, thanks to JR, Peter had moments of subdued excitement. Yet, even there, JR seemed to derive more pleasure out of their righteous shenanigans than Peter ever could. Just a few years ago, Peter had amused himself in detecting the nature of a disease from a complex and elaborate array of symptoms. His work saved lives. Now? Now he was assisting in nabbing a guard, a possible android, with JR doing most of the thinking.

"At least, it gives you something exciting to do," Cathy did her best to cheer him up.

"Exciting?" He smiled sadly. "I don't even know if I'm on the right track."

He was. If he hadn't been quite so depressed, so bored, he'd have realized that no one but he could have ever spotted the inconsistencies in the guard's appearance, stance, or even behaviour. It took a scientifically trained mind to detect those 'symptoms'. That and his special talents: a sort of sixth sense.

Peter left for the office at the usual time. On entering the building, he noticed the usual absence of the presumed android. Presumed—because he could never get close enough to assure that the guard did not exhibit even a minuscule aura. Some people, some very primitive minds, hardly displayed any aura at all. It was as if they were still half-dead. Zombies. Only no one knew that. Not until one started talking with them. Then they seemed hardly awake. Those people were hardly capable of formulating a grammatical sentence.

Peter met one such man, panhandling close to the SI building. That very morning, in spite of biting cold, the man was at his usual post. The strange thing was that panhandling, though not illegal, was hardly necessary. The SI fed anyone who was hungry. They also gave a roof over the heads of all comers, human and animal alike. Could it be that those half-awake men, or women, didn't know that? Peter nodded to him, wondering at his blank stare.

"How are you?" Peter asked, determined to tell him about the SI benefits.

"Eeh? Who me?" The man also mumbled something incomprehensible.

"Well, yes." Peter smiled encouragement.

"Why, you know, why, er, do you ask?"

"I thought you might need help?" Peter framed it into a question.

"What, you know, what makes you, you know, ah, think that?"

Peter walked on. The man didn't need help. His diminutive aura attested to that. A tree exhibited more life-force. Perhaps it was his karma? The man was determined to remain a nomad, to stay exactly where he was. A bitter smile twisted Peter's mouth. He, too, was a nomad once. Perhaps... in another lifetime?

On reaching his office, Peter got down to business. He had a private washroom, in which he donned the disguise he had borrowed from JR. By the time he finished, he looked like a second-string actor auditioning for the role of a disguised Sherlock Holmes. No matter. Unless the android, the suspected android, was an expert on aspiring thespians, or could read individual auras, Peter would not be recognized. As a finishing touch he inserted a quarter inch pad into his left shoe, which gave him a slight limp. Finally he put on the maintenance staff overalls, which evidently JR had left for him in the washroom, and clipped on the concealed mike.

He was ready.

At five to ten Peter walked down the corridor to the bank of elevators. Joan, his secretary, didn't even bat an eye. This wasn't the first time Peter dressed up in peculiar clothing. She pretended she didn't notice.

Peter took the freight elevator down to the fifth floor, got out, and took the stairs through the remaining floors, down to the mezzanine. He was the only one who got out of the elevator, and the only one using the staircase.

From his chosen position, he could just see the reception desk. The handsome brute of a guard was on duty. So far, so good, he told himself. He assumed that the clone's doppelganger would position himself in such a way as to observe the passenger elevators. If they had been warned, as Peter suspected, of his ability to spot androids, then they would now keep an eye on the elevator hall.

"In case you'd come down, unexpectedly, and upset the apple cart," as JR had put it picturesquely.

Peter scrutinized each column, each nook—not that there were many—and saw no one that resembled anything but human. Even at this distance their auras, though faint, were clearly visible. It was also clear that the original culprit had no aura at all. Not even a vaguest sheen.

Peter whispered into his lapel. "Number One confirmed. Definitely android."

Well, that was that. As for the other android, there was no sign of him. He reported his disappointment to JR.

The next moment four men approached the desk from different directions. One of them spoke to the android, and together they walked to the bank of elevators. Obviously, the 'man' would be interrogated.

"You can go back to your office now," Peter recognized JR's voice. His friend sounded very pleased with himself.

Before leaving, Peter scanned the whole Entrance Hall once again. Then he stopped. A glitter attracted his attention. Then he saw two more. He looked closer. For no reason Peter could imagine, tiny mirrors had been placed in various locations. Unless… unless they were the spare eyes of the android. Unless the guard could cover the whole entrance hall, *and* the bank of elevators, without leaving his post. The mirrors were tiny but might well suffice for the android's enhanced optics.

Peter changed back in his office to resemble his old self. Joan smiled broadly.

"A good hunt, Sir?"

Peter smiled back. He did not feel free to discuss it. Not yet. Ten minutes later, JR stormed into his office.

"You'll never believe it. Those things cost a million dollars a throw. A million dollars!"

"And…"

"By the time we asked the first question, the neuro-network of the SOB turned to mashed potatoes. They have a self-destruct system."

"So we'll never know who sent him?"

"Oh, we know who sent him. Only Washington is interested in our activities. They think we are a threat to their work force."

"So all's not lost?" Peter said hopefully.

"All *is* lost. I was going to feed the Yankees false information, remember?"

Peter remembered. He also remembered something else.

"So where is the doppelganger?"

"Search me," JR kept pacing Peter's office. He always did that when he was nervous, or when he was thinking. He'd once told Peter that it stimulated the blood flow to his brain.

"I think I can answer that," Peter said smugly. It wasn't often that he could beat JR at his own game.

JR stopped dead in his track, his whole body leaning forward as if he were facing a strong wind.

"Well? Are you going to keep me in suspense?"

"The other guy is in the elevator maintenance locker, where you thought the Number One would be hiding."

JR straightened his body without falling over. He regarded Peter with surprise and disbelief. "Go on," he said at last.

"Well, it took only one android, at least at a time, to scan the whole lobby. With their AI optics, it wouldn't be a problem." He told JR about the mirrors. "So if there is a Number Two, and you say there is, he must be in the cupboard."

JR lowered himself into the chair in front of Peter's desk.

"Why... the son of a screaming banshee..."

"Not accurate but descriptive," Peter murmured. Strictly speaking, physiologically that android had never been born.

"What?"

"So how can you get hold of him without mashing his brain?"

For a while JR looked dead to the world. His eyes were closed, his body slumped like a heap of disjointed limbs, all thrown, haphazardly, over the armchair. Peter had no idea if JR was OK. Then he remembered his lanky friend doing an impersonation of a stick insect before. It was when Peter needed his help after Ruth had been kidnapped. Here, he did it again.

As suddenly as JR had collapsed, he sprang to his feet with amazing agility and reached the door in three strides, waving his excuses.

So much for explanations, thought Peter.

On the way home, Peter saved a cat from a group of hooligans. Four youngsters were chasing the poor beast and throwing snowballs at him. Or her? Peter managed to affect the hooligans adversely. Quite suddenly, all four seemed to have become very tired. They all sat down on the snow and panted. Peter was quite unaware that his power of healing was a two-way street, let alone at a distance. He'd never tried to hurt anyone. Certainly not intentionally. Even now. He merely thought that the boys should feel the way the cat felt.

After a momentary sense of achievement, by the time Peter got home, he was as bored as ever. Or as he had been before the android escapade. He was getting better at hating himself. And the worst thing of all was that he wasn't quite sure why.

He felt like disappearing. He felt like taking JR's disguises, changing his appearance, and going off, somewhere, to help people. Or even stray cats. Like in the old days. Just before he died. Almost died. Died to his previous life. Would have—if it hadn't been for Winston. And later Cathy.

Dear Cathy. Then she and I could go back to that cottage in the Laurentians.

Just the two of us. Just like in the old days.

Once again an ocean of doubts accosted him.

What is it all for? Why are we here? What's the point of it all?

Cathy wasn't home yet. He slumped into his armchair.

Why can't I populate my garden with petals of beauty, with thoughts of god? Am I forever attached to my worthless body? Worthless...

...trillions upon trillions of cells, each perfectly formed, working in perfect harmony. Systems, circulatory, endocrine, immune, digestive, nervous, respiratory... dozens of them, all superbly coordinated... Veins like rivers irrigating endless fields spanning from toes, up through my legs... Others commencing at my fingertips only to swell into tsunami when they reach my torso... Pushing and pulling, flowing and ebbing, restoring, purifying, feeding... until they reach the very center, the seat of my passion, the heart of the matter,

the heart of my material body, the miracle of engineering such as never was...

Till now?

There the streams bounce back, once more, again and again, endlessly, tirelessly, seemingly forever... Eventually to rise to the apex of this wondrous creation, to the seat of all thought, to spring in this mortal, physical world and imbue it with a new, original particle of immortality. Forever meandering, searching for the meaning of it all.

"Peter?"

Forever searching for the meaning of it all...

"Peter?" This time Cathy spoke louder.

Dreams boring, useless, uninspired: a desert, from station to station, a never-ending desert, a moonscape...

"The dead feeding the dead," he said out loud.

"Yes, darling, let them. You just take it easy. Just take it easy..." She sounded worried.

She took Peter's arms and guided him to the bedroom. There, she took off his shoes, lifted his legs and covered him with a blanket. She knew what had happened. The last time Peter used his special powers, the same thing occurred. Their use seemed to suck life out of him. Like at Chez Gaston, only he was strong then. At least, to start with.

Peter didn't stir till early morning. It must have been a dreamless night. By breakfast time he was all right. He just looked a little guilty.

On his way to the office, fresh air helped to clear his head of any aftermath of yesterday's internal soliloquy. Such moments of introspection came upon him, suddenly, at times he least expected. After all, he and JR scored a minor victory over the opposition, whoever they were. At least, so it seemed. As for his helping the stray cat, well, it was also a minor matter. Even if Peter had collapsed, physically, it would have been just for an hour or two. The rest, the vast majority of his problems, remained dormant in his head. In his mind. He felt he had to take the next step, only he still had no idea where the road was leading him.

As he entered the lobby, the doppelganger of the guy with mashed-potato brains was at his post as if nothing had happened. He had been either reconstructed by JR's team, or they managed to do something with, or to, Number Two, without melting his neurons. The 'man' looked identical. It must have been Number One, after all. Could two clones look that much alike? But if it had mashed its own brains, then it would have to be Number Two. Perhaps the two androids didn't have time to compare notes? Only how come the Number Two didn't make for the cupboard on Peter's approach?

Peter heard a chuckle right behind him. With all his size, JR could move not only with great agility, but almost silently. A little like Winston.

"The androids have so many nano-metallic components in their brains that magnets can freeze their synapses. Now, at least, this beauty will broadcast our news. Ha, ha!" JR grinned like a boy that got away with a great prank. He looked like a very happy camper.

So, the game was over. Exit excitement, return to ennui.

The following night, Peter didn't sleep at all. At least, he didn't think he was sleeping. He seemed to slip in and out of consciousness, as though waking and dreaming, both at the same time. He seemed as aware of being in his bedroom, with Cathy by his side, as he was of floating, then settling down in some nondescript locations, momentarily, as though he were searching for some place, somewhere familiar, yet long forgotten. It wasn't an unpleasant experience, as he was also aware of a peculiar sense of freedom, of not being hampered by his recent dark images of listlessness, of lassitude born of ennui.

After a seemingly timeless while, he found himself sitting apart, on a stone bench. Below him stretched a series of semicircular rows of seats, such as in an amphitheater, reminiscent of structures Romans had built all across the Middle East. He was vaguely aware of the Romans' predilection for open-air theaters.

Only then did he sense the echo of yesterdays. The auditorium was full, yet, down there, close to the proscenium, a pair of heads looked familiar. Even from behind, Moira and Jonathan's curls were unmistakable. He'd seen this image before. Long, long ago. Simultaneously he seemed aware that time, as he knew it, didn't really matter. That it wasn't real.

The stage was empty, yet the attention of all those gathered seemed directed at its center. Then Peter heard the unmistakable voice.

"You must let go. You cannot cling to one and the other. If you hold on to one, the other will destroy you. If you let go, it will save you."

Peter had no idea what the words meant, but the voice belonged to Winston. After he heard the words, the air vibrating at center-stage cleared, and Peter saw the old majordomo standing, motionless, his white gown moving slightly as he seemed to envelop all present in a silent embrace. Moments later, Peter saw, again, the shadows on his bedroom ceiling beginning to stir with chimerical filigree of the first rays of dawn.

At long last, he fell asleep. Hardly two hours later he got up, fresh, rested, as if he had had a perfect night of sleep, uninterrupted by any peculiar images.

He showered, shaved and dressed, and throughout all this felt light-headed. In fact, for the first time in months, he felt happy. If asked, he would not be able to account for his change of mood.

"You know, Cathy? We are complex, enigmatic beings," he said. Even the quick morning kiss seemed filled with joy.

"Of course, dear."

Cathy was pouring the coffee.

"I've spent months trying to dream in full consciousness, trying to lose awareness of my body, yet..."

This time she looked up. Only now did she notice. Peter did look different. He looked excited, baffled, but... whatever it was, he no longer looked frustrated.

"Yes, go on," she encouraged.

"Yet last night I decided to give it a rest. After months of seemingly unsuccessful exercises, I just relaxed; at least, I thought I did. What I mean is that I relaxed mentally. Deep down. I, well, I told myself, let there be what may. I was through with fighting, trying, forcing myself into some mental states I knew nothing about. In a way, for the first time in perhaps years, I accepted my fate, not even knowing what it might bring. That's when it happened. Although I can't be sure. Time is so fickle when you're semiconscious."

He looked down at his coffee suffused with a wisp of rising steam.

"Did something happen?"

"If you mean, did I dream something? Well, I can't be sure. I seem to have just lain there, next to you, watching the ceiling..."

"...and?"

He described to her the Roman amphitheater, the people all dressed in what looked like Roman togas. The two familiar heads...

"I never saw their faces, but I knew those heads belonged to Mo and Jo. For some reason they were unmistakable. Everyone looked as though they were listening intently. Only I could neither hear, nor see anyone on the stage. Not for quite a while."

He put down his coffee cup and stared Cathy in the eyes. She either imagined or thought that she knew what was coming.

"And then you saw Winston," she murmured.

"And then I saw... how did you know?"

There was a prolonged silence. Then, very carefully, she replaced her own cup. "Because I was there," she said, hardly above a whisper.

For some reason, Peter had mixed feelings. He wanted to surprise Cathy, to share with her a seemingly momentous achievement in his chimerical endeavours and, well, she beat him to it.

I should be overjoyed. Isn't this what I'd been hoping for? For the two of us to travel together? Have I been traveling? Was any of this real? Or am I really a borderline schizophrenic? Or is she just saying this to humour me?

He could no longer look Cathy in the eyes. He was ashamed of his thoughts, his tacit accusations, his jealousy. The inner world was not just his to explore.

"Winston was repeating the warning from the Gospel of Thomas," she said, looking at the sun reflected in the snow-capped tops of conifers.

Slowly he looked up.

"I was reading it last night, after you went to sleep. His lecture was based on a saying attributed to Jesus." She got up and picked up a thin book lying on the low coffee table. She opened it on a marker. *"If you bring forth what is within you, what you have will save you. If you do not have that within you, what you do not have within you will kill you,"* she read aloud.

Peter was less sure of himself. He cleared his throat, drank some coffee, and murmured, "That's not exactly what I heard."

Cathy looked up, trying to catch his eye. This was important. Did everyone hear only that which they were meant to hear?

"He said that we must let go. That we cannot cling to one and the other. He said, *'If you hold on to one, the other will destroy you. If you let go, it will save you.'* Or something like that. Now, after what you just said, I can no longer be sure."

"The two quotations are not that far apart," Cathy said reassuringly. "I rather suspect that we all hear whatever is most important to us. Perhaps I must bring forth—and you, darling, must let go."

Let go of what? He reverted to his rebelling mood. Have I not given up enough? What else do I have to lose?

He was hoping to hear Winston's voice at the back of his head. But there was only silence, filled with a continuous humming noise. He gazed at Cathy, hoping for help. But Cathy was just looking out at Mount Royal. She seemed far, far away.

What else am I supposed to give up, he mused?

***

10

The Green Monster

For the next three days, Peter felt exhausted, with an undercurrent of anger. The euphoria he felt after that fateful night had evaporated into thin air. He felt as though he'd been upstaged, as if his nocturnal exploits had been relegated to ordinary events, accessible to hundreds of people. After all, wasn't the amphitheater full of quasi-Roman citizenry?

Don't kid yourself, Peter. There's nothing special about you, about your abilities.

And even there, he didn't even sit in the amphitheater. He was outside, exiled, like a man who might contaminate others with his presence. He felt like a parasite. Sponging knowledge that didn't belong to him. Well, if I can't join them in the auditorium, then good riddance. There are other ways to skin a cat.

On the way to the office, he decided that if you can't beat them, then you might as well join them. If I can't have spiritual power, then mundane goodies will have to do. His financial resources were sufficient, but compared to others, especially from his past, he was still a poor cousin. Furthermore, there was no reason for him to be bored.

It was all my own fault, for peeking over the shoulders of others, where I was not wanted.

The semicircular amphitheater shimmered before his eyes. Then it dissolved in powdery flakes hovering in front of his face.

Is this the winter of my discontent? Richard was not alone...

The flakes seemed bent on landing on his face. He screwed up his eyes half-shut to protect them. He could get to his office blindfolded. He didn't care if he trod on somebody's toes. He'd been careful all too long. Let them look out for themselves. Different people have different needs to satisfy.

And then, that lopsided grin, which twisted his handsome features of late, appeared again.

"I," he affirmed in his mind, his lips forming the actual words as though speaking out loud, "as of now—I shall look after *numero uno.*"

In that moment, Peter decided to achieve total financial independence. Then, and only then, would he decide what to do. In the meantime, he'd remain with Solidarity, but only for Ruth's sake. As a consultant. But, he thought, he'd trust no one's but his own judgment.

There was an instant payoff. For the next while, he did not recall having any dreams of any kind. He felt free.

He set about achieving his aim as he would prepare for a complex diagnosis. He extracted the relevant programs from the Internet, scanned them rapidly, then read in greater detail those that seemed of greater value. In just about all his endeavours, Peter was always guided by precise methodology. Even in his study of dreams, he employed the same orderly manner. Dreams, however, for now, went on the back-burner.

He decided to live his dreams. He knew he could.

If it hadn't been for his orderly mind, he wouldn't have become a Fellow of the Royal College of Surgeons and Physicians by the time he turned twenty-seven. He could hardly be blamed for having lost the privileges in the same calendar year. That was beyond his influence. What he did now, was not. In this realm he, and he alone, was the boss.

Peter already had a smattering of experience on the Stock Exchange. He knew that, in order to make real money, he'd have to do it on the American market. All people, from all over the world, who rejected the Solidarity postulates of relative equality of people, used the American Stock Exchanges to outwit one another. The Dow Jones, the NASDAQ and the S&P 500 would henceforth be his playing field. There were still many people for whom the Green-Eyed Monster of premeditated greed was the guiding light.

"Did you ever play the market?" Peter asked JR, who'd just put his head through the door of his office.

"She's out, again," he said, in the way of apology.

Peter had sent his secretary to get some discs for him from the SI basement archives. In the office they seldom used paper. Hardly anyone did, anymore. Except for Cathy. She loved the feel of a book in her hands. As for ebooks, usually one would import them directly onto one's computer, but some more specialized versions remained on discs. Anyway, Peter wanted to take them home, and one was not allowed to 'export' data electronically from Headquarters. Not without official permission, and Peter had no desire to advertise his new interest far and wide.

JR was still suspended in mid-stride, waiting for permission to come in. Peter waved him in.

"Well?" he asked again.

"The Dow Jones? The NASDAQ? American Exchange, Toronto, London, Beijing, Singap…?"

"Yes."

"No."

"Thanks for being so tightlipped about it," Peter grinned. "We are alone. I know this is not strictly in accordance with SI policies."

"Then, yes."

"Then, sit down."

JR transported his body to the chair opposite Peter's desk. He didn't sit down but, as usual, he collapsed into it.

"Fire away," he said, flickers of fun already playing in his eyes. Knowing Peter, he was suspecting a new caper was in the works.

"I can't tell you too much, yet," Peter winked, "but I want to know if one can bankrupt the exchange."

A long, low whistle came out of JR's pursed lips. He regarded Peter from under his eyelashes, trying to determine if Peter was serious. For years JR had known his friend to be one of the most selfless people he'd ever met. Peter's motivation could not have been greed. There had to be other reasons, probably from the Vatican.

All along, Peter was reading JR's thoughts. He couldn't help grinning to himself.

"Theoretically," Peter explained belatedly.

"Of course," JR seemed mollified. He almost added a wink of his own. "Well," JR said after a long pause, "there's hacking."

"Don't they have the best barriers in the world?"

"Probably. It could be that the Nanotechs were not sufficiently interested to break through them. Yet. After all, the whole world is using the Dow to do business. It's an exchange of a lot more than money, as such."

"So you think the barriers are no match for the best of nanotechnology?

"Barriers have, well… barriers. Limits. Nanotechnology is open-ended."

Ideas were formulating in Peter's mind. At least for now, he'd stay away from the Canadian, not to mention the USA markets. There were many others in the world. With the exception of Beijing, not as big, but big enough. All he really wanted was to channel some of the billions they made to his own accounts. Such were still to be opened, under an assumed name, of course.

For more than a century in the States, and even longer in a number of other countries of the world, the economic growth was controlled by an ever-shrinking minority. Known as Plutonomy, the system created the means through which the minority held the overwhelming majority of the wealth. It was in direct opposition to the aims of Solidarity International. A formidable opposition.

Peter felt the thrill of danger. Not an unpleasant sensation. It made his blood cruise faster. He was just beginning to get elated. And, after all, it was just a game. He didn't really need money. He just wanted to know that he could have it if he wanted to. How much easier, he thought, was it to be thrilled this side of the great divide—in the physical reality. How much faster...

Yes, definitely a game, he grinned to his own thoughts.

JR left soon after their little discussion. He'd only dropped in to tell Peter that the Number Two was 'alive' and well, and regularly reporting, to an unknown address in Baltimore, on things that JR found most innocuous, in a very complex way. Occasionally JR added a juicy bit of info, making sure that it was completely out of date. He wondered how long it would take the enemy to suspect that something was fishy.

"The longer it takes, the longer they won't bother to send replacements. It's our best insurance," he added.

They agreed to meet tomorrow, with JR supplying Peter some ideas regarding Peter's investment portfolio. JR thought it would be great fun. Peter did not try to dissuade him. For the first time in a long time, he was beginning to enjoy himself.

Peter's idea, though announced spontaneously to JR to cover his tracks, was not as crazy as it sounded. At the beginning of this, the 20th, century, the Americans had a president who, with a small, handpicked clique, in a mere eight years, managed to destroy the USA economy and bankrupt dozens of banks, investment houses, mortgage companies, and other financial institutions. His successor, though seemingly bright and charming, seemed to imagine that money grew on trees. Peter imagined that he might be equally as successful in drawing the forbidden fruit from the same silviculture. Not to ruin anyone, as the corrupt president did, but to push aside the rich, the very rich, if they stood in his way of making a billion or two. Of course, Peter had no desire to bankrupt the USA, let alone the world's economy. Nor, for that matter, to ruin some perfectly functioning banks or financial institutions. All he wanted was to get his share, at the expense of people who, once again, were getting filthy rich at the expense of other people.

It sounded fair and square. After all, the USA had recovered, as had the rest of the world, and the dismal, if some well-meaning, presidents were soon forgotten. Of course, the resultant system had been engineered so that only the middle-income people paid the exorbitant income tax, to pay off the accumulated debt.

"After all," Peter told Cathy, "it was as the Bible said, the rich grew richer, and the poor lost what little they had."

"What?" Her reaction was that of horror.

"Well, sort of." Peter scratched his head. It had been a while since he'd read the Bible. "I think it was, 'For he that hath, to him shall be given: and he that hath not, from him shall be taken even that which he hath.'"

"Darling?" She managed to make it sound like an insult. "This statement is symbolic. It refers to spiritual riches…"

"Oh, yeah? Tell that to southern fundamentalists!"

They went on like this for a little while. Till the very end, Cathy wasn't sure if Peter was serious. Frankly, the longer they talked, the less sure was Peter himself.

Looking back at history, in just a few short decades, the Americans managed to pay off the trillions of dollars of debt, which their inept forefathers had accumulated. However, since then, the ugly head of the Green-Eyed Monster was stirring again.

It appears that we all learn from the past. Not how to avoid calamities, but how to recover from them.

Peter had but one regret. Since he and Cathy tied the knot, he'd never done anything behind her back. They shared everything, often including their thoughts. Now, Peter had to make sure that Cathy, even accidentally, wouldn't discover that he was doing something surreptitiously. He wanted billions for the sheer fun of making them, but he wanted Cathy more. Still, he smiled grimly, *qui ne risque rien, n'a rien*. So far he was very good at getting *rien*. Well, no more. When he next met with JR, the lanky leader of SI Canada offered his own spin on the French adage.

"Who doesn't take a risk, doesn't go to jail," he grinned.

Not without a reason. For close to twenty years after the last financial calamity, the United States Department of Justice was still offering free room and board to dozens of lesser crooks in the financial field. The bigger risk-takers were already in jail. Most of them died there. Yet, the prospect of incarceration never seemed to deter others from attempting to outwit the law. Perhaps the law itself was crooked.

Nevertheless, according to JR, there was only one way to score big in a short time. Peter would have to open hundreds of fictitious accounts. All over the world. Since the last market collapse, the new rules demanded that debts, nowadays defined as leverage, had to be paid in full within a mere 24 hours. What it actually meant was that one had access to a limited credit for a whole day. As the world turns once every 24 hours, the period could be extended indefinitely by playing one leveraged amount against the other.

"The trick is to stop before they get onto you," JR winked. "Greed, as you know, my friend, doesn't pay."

JR fitted perfectly into the Solidarity framework. As head of SI Canada, he was being paid 5 times the average SI income. It was already more than he could spend, without having to give up some of his pleasures, such as solving insoluble problems.

As for his scheme, frankly, it was all a bit over Peter's head. JR, however, thought of it as an exciting game of chess, played against the world's best computers—the various banks', the Investment Houses' and the Financial Institutions' computers. It would all be electronic. Not a penny would change hands. It would be a glorified catch-me-if-you-can.

"A sort of catch-as-catch-can," JR indicated his favourite wrestling move, though Peter had no idea how anyone with his physical attributes could possible wrestle. On the other hand, JR was always an enigma.

"And you don't need any money for this, ah, this, ah...?" For once Peter was at a loss for words.

"No, Peter. What I propose is a sort of Ponzi scheme that is not a Ponzi."

"Ponzi?"

"The credit is given to Charles Ponzi," JR explained, "but in fact it originated in a Dickens novel of 1857 entitled *Little Dorrit*."

"How the devil do you know all this?" Peter was quite impressed.

JR began to studiously inspect his nails. "I'm in security, remember?" He appeared to use this phrase as a catch-all.

Peter nodded. That may have explained part of it, but... "Isn't that illegal?"

"Not if it's not really a Ponzi. A Ponzi scheme is a fraudulent investment in which you pay your investors from their own money, or from money supplied from subsequent investors, in amounts greater than the profit their money makes. Thus, ultimately it must fail. We wouldn't do that."

"And people didn't suspect anything?"

"Not for quite a while. It's based on the assumption that all people are greedy. They want something for nothing. Although you offer them returns that are much higher than can be reasonably expected, for as long as you're paying, they keep investing."

"From new investors' money... Why, that's dirty!"

"Nevertheless, some six decades ago, a man named Madoff separated countless people, and organizations, from their hard-earned money. He was said to have stolen some sixty-five billion. Not bad, even for a former chairman of NASDAQ."

Peter whistled softly. "Sixty-five billion dollars?"

"In good old US currency." JR smiled. "And in those days the US greenback was worth a lot more than it is today. But we wouldn't do that."

Unwittingly, Peter let out the air from his lungs with a long wheeze. Sixty-five billion... He also realized that if it hadn't been for inherent human greed, the scheme couldn't have worked. His father-in-law once told him, "If it looks too good to be true, it probably is." Ponzi schemes always were.

"So just how would we, ah, differ from your Ponzi operation?"

"Hardly mine, my friend. I have no need for money," JR corrected.

"Sorry, my scheme..."

JR nodded. He liked to have his facts straight. "Well, it's to do with derivatives."

"Which are?" Contrary to JR, until the idea struck him last night, Peter had never had any interest in money whatsoever.

"It's something that is derived from something else. For instance, the futures contracts. It is an agreement to exchange the underlying asset at some future date, for a pre-agreed price."

"You're way over my head, JR." Peter was again scratching his head. "Couldn't you put together for me some sort of computer program that would play such a game on its own?"

"Of course! It's the only way to do it. You open an account offering to deposit a sum of money, which you borrow at another bank, which lends you the money because you deposited some money with them which you borrowed... and so on. That's why you need all those accounts, all over the world. Simple!"

"And just where is the profit?"

"Well, there isn't any—not really. But what happens is the leverage angle. Each time you deposit some money, you increase the leverage amount you can borrow. The sum is growing exponentially. Ultimately you can borrow billions."

And then forget to return a small part of it? Like a billion or two? Or... keep going and be a multibillionaire on paper. Well, actually, on the computer screen.

"So I could be a multibillionaire without having a penny?"

"Well, I suppose so. As I was saying, it is only a game..."

There was something implicitly attractive about the Green Monster. Actually the name really belongs to envy, but envy is fueled by greed. If people didn't envy other people's money, their sense of greed would not be as fulfilling. Keeping up with the Joneses is based on that. Envy fueled by greed.

Peter had occasion to feel the lure of the Green-Eyed Monster. Not so much greed as envy. In the seminary, he envied the saints their piety, their self-effacement, their humility. Until recently, he had always believed in his own self-worth.

Originally, when later he took up medicine, he had been motivated by his willingness to help people. To eliminate suffering from their lives, to restore their health.

Originally.

Within but a few short years, his motivation changed to the driving ambition to know more than other students, then more than other interns, later to be the best resident doctor in the Montreal General Hospital. He believed that he'd succeeded. He knew he'd succeeded. He always did. Failure was not a consideration. His fellowship attested to that, even if his motivations may have been fuelled by erroneous ambitions. For some reason people never accused him of having an inflated ego. Perhaps he really was that good. He worked like a slave and he expected returns.

And now he was ready to be rich. He had no need for money. He had Cathy. She was the quintessence of his wealth. But he refused to be bored. He was ready to take risks. Even if only on paper. He didn't really envy other people's money. What he did envy, well, quite a lot, was other people's ability to achieve total independence from the foibles of this world. He still felt that he was a pawn, thrown this way and that by the currents of life, over which he had no influence. That, he was determined, was about to end.

All the way home, Peter was wracking his brains how to approach the subject of his new escapade, without actually telling Cathy what it was about. She always supported all his schemes, even as supposedly deviant as attempting to heal people with the touch of his hands. Not the run-of-the-mill type of endeavour, he mused. But this was different. While he was fully committed to the venture, there was a shade of uncertainty at the back of his mind. To get her involved, he had to tackle the subject from the point of view of pure science, or religion. He had no idea how to bring science into greed or envy. It had to be the other.

That evening, after dinner, he added a little Merlot to Cathy's wineglass and settled in his armchair, waiting for her to join him. He thought it too risky to mention greed, as such. Anyway, the two were sisters.

"What would you say is the nature of envy?" he murmured, looking over the edge of his own glass. The rich red of the wine shimmered in stark contrast to the emeralds of her eyes.

"What a strange question," she countered.

"They say that in hell the cauldrons of simmering oil filled with those who committed the sin of envy need no guards to push them back with their red-hot tridents. The other fryees pull the aspiring escapees back into the oil themselves."

"I thought you didn't believe in hell."

Cathy regarded Peter, trying to guess what he was really driving at.

"Well, most of us associate envy with financial standing, power, or a prestigious position…"

Cathy sat up. Peter saw that she was hooked.

"Envy is not limited to egos suffering from obscurity," she affirmed. There was challenge in her tone of voice. She reached out to add more wine to her own glass, then changed her mind. Peter waited, sipping on his own.

"Thomas Alva Edison held over thirteen-hundred patents," she pointed out. "Yet his accomplishments evidently led to such an inflated ego that he fell under the spell of envy. At one time, he preferred to destroy the reputation of Nikola Tesla, by spreading garrulous nonsense about the dangers of his competitor's invention."

Cathy glanced at Peter before continuing. He seemed happy just listening.

"Tesla invented the A/C. That's alternating current, not air conditioning," she added with a smile. "Anyway, Edison laid some nonsensical claims regarding the efficacy of his own discovery," again, she looked pointedly at Peter, "the direct current—though he was already well aware of its limitations. In time Tesla was well and truly vindicated, but not before Edison drove him to near-bankruptcy by his envy."

Trust Cathy to use science to illustrate her point. She

was now completely drawn in. When she talked 'science', her eyes lit up. She was on a mission.

"Tesla, in his turn," she said, "condemned Einstein's early achievements out of hand, without ever giving them the benefit of the doubt, let alone a serious study."

"The scientist's ego is as fragile a structure as an unstable atom," Peter put in, rather proud of his simile.

"Not to be left behind, and blaming it on the principle of uncertainty, Albert Einstein virtually dismissed the theory of quantum mechanics by claiming that 'God does not play dice with the universe.' Coming from an acknowledged genius, a feeble argument at best. Wouldn't you say that Einstein might have been motivated, at least in part, by envy that among his peers quantum theory was sublimating his theories of relativity?"

Peter had absolutely no idea what Einstein did or didn't do to Cathy's quantum theory. He tried a defensive tactic.

"But, darling, scientists, great and small, do not hold monopoly on envy…"

For a moment Peter recalled his discussion with JR. Have I been motivated by greed or envy, he wondered.

Or was it just by boredom?

Cathy seemed quite agitated. Was she suspecting something? She could, usually, sense Peter's feelings, if not actually read his mind. This time she was drawing a blank. What was he up to, she mused.

She took the last sip of her wine and sat back. For a while she continued studying Peter, still trying to pierce his mental defenses. Peter suspected as much and concentrated on nonentities. She smiled, knowingly, and decided to change the subject. Or at least, to turn it on its side.

"If we must pass judgment," she resumed, when Peter remained silent, "then, surely, 'by their fruits we shall know them'. Edison gave us an incandescent lamp and many other life-enhancing gadgets. Einstein gave us a new vision of our universe and filled it with wonder beyond imagination. From Tesla we inherited the radio and alternating-current transmission."

Cathy smiled, still attempting to probe Peter's mind. She knew he was shielding something.

"I envy none of them—I am grateful to all," she concluded.

Envy is a green-eyed monster, Peter mused, but not as monstrous as the people who fall permanently under its spell. They are, truly, the lost souls.

The next morning, Peter left for the office early. Greed or envy notwithstanding, he wanted to see if JR had come up with anything. He wasn't disappointed. JR was already in Peter's office, a whimsical smile on his lips.

"You are serious about this?" he asked Peter, without any preambles.

"What have you got?"

JR reached into his jacket pocket and pulled out three discs. He weighed them in his hands, as though they were heavier than they actually were.

"This must be handled with care," he said. "With great care."

For just a moment Peter felt uncomfortable. Whatever he'd done in the past, he was either forced into it, compelled by circumstances, or else he was very sure of his ground. This was different. Also, the technology involved was well beyond his ability to understand. He wondered if he could learn enough, and quickly enough, not to put both his feet into something from which he might not be able to extricate himself. In the past he had Dr. Brent, Ruth, even Lena, staunchly at his side. That was a very powerful trio. In this little enterprise, for the first time, he was alone. If there was danger of being compromised, then he categorically refused to implicate his friend JR. He told him as much.

"Understood," he said, understanding little. He'd never think of protecting himself at Peter's expense.

JR inserted the first disk into Peter's computer slot. The screen lit up with a pattern that Peter found quite meaningless. JR pressed a few keys, and Hindu-Arabic numbers replaced the previous scribbles. They were dotted with ordinary letters, and interrupted, here and there, with some syllabograms Peter had never seen before.

"Just how do you make head and tail of this?"

"As I told you, nanotechnology is open-ended."

"And that means…"

JR looked up. "You didn't know?"

"Didn't know what?"

JR walked around Peter's desk and slumped into the armchair. He watched Peter with an intensity of perception Peter had never noticed before. Peter tried reading JR's thoughts and sensed nothing. Just a whirl of information much too fast for him to interpret. Then it dawned on him. JR was a Nanotech.

He looked up expectantly. "Just when did you…"

"…become a Nanotech? You cannot allow anyone to take advantage over you. Not if you're running even a small branch of SI." When Peter continued staring at JR, his lanky friend explained. "It had been decided that while Lena and Ruth must make do with God-given neurons, they must have, at their disposal, a few Nanotechs. I assumed you knew, and that was why you called me in on this scheme."

"I knew there was a cadre of Nanotechs in SI, I just didn't think you were one of them."

Peter remembered the discussions. In Mumbai, India, and a few other places, one could purchase a vast range of nanotechnological improvements. Mumbai had the best reputation. The implants were not limited to enhancing your intellect. They could improve your lung capacity, increase or decrease your blood pressure, even reduce your weight by manipulating the efficacy of your digestive system. JR, or SI, had only been interested in the ability to outthink the opposition. The rest was handled by their own genetics program.

"We had been selected by polygraphic techniques to assure that, as best as could be assured, none of us would use the advantages of nanotechnology for our own gains. Then we took individual trips to Mumbai for insertions. They wouldn't give any one of us the full range of their technology, but each one of us gained slightly different advantages, and together we can outmatch anything the Sino-Indian bloc can throw at us."

"Just when did it all happen?" Peter was a little annoyed at not having been informed.

"It's in the report on your computer. Triple X security clearance. You have that. You can look it up whenever you want to." By then JR was regarding Peter with a look of a gentle teacher admonishing a slightly backward child.

"Been a b-bit busy," Peter half-stammered.

He hadn't been busy at all. He felt embarrassed. Perhaps there was no need for him to have gotten quite so bored. It could have been the damn dreams. He had been losing touch with reality. He shook his head. "I'm sorry, I'll catch up on all that stuff pronto."

JR smiled. "Of course," he said. Then he pointed to the first disk still throwing numbers and letters on the screen. "On this one, you insert your name, your signature, and the number of banks you wish to partake in your venture. The name and signature do not necessarily have to be your own. I'd say some degree of confidentiality would be advisable. In fact, for the record, this operation is based in Johannesburg, with branches in Guanzhau, that's China, New Delhi, India, and, of course, Calgary."

Peter looked up. "Why of course?"

"Because anyone who finds Calgary on the set of references will not suspect big business being involved. For half a century now, since oil went out of business, Calgary became known for a great variety of small enterprises. There are millions of them. Virtually impossible to trace."

So that was what being a Nanotech meant... You just about knew everything about everything. And then some, Peter mused, but kept his observations to himself. He could not resist, however, letting out a near-silent whistle.

Actually, Peter was wrong. Nanotechnology improved the recall; the capacity of the brain remained the same. You just learned to use it better.

"And the other disks?"

"Once you establish the network, you begin the operations. You decide on the leverage you want and proceed. I'd suggest you keep the leverage well below the legal limit of fifty percent. Banks are allowed much more, but that might attract undue attention. You could, if you want to, increase it to fifty, once your network is established. The whole thing is, of course, set on automatic. It will continue to grow exponentially until you stop it."

"How?"

"I suggest you call me."

"And the third disk?" Peter's head was getting woozy.

"That's there only if you want to make withdrawals of actual money. I mean by converting it back from derivatives to cash, commodities, or say, real estate. I rather think that is not your intention..." he let that drift away.

After all, JR had not been officially informed as to the real purpose of the exercise. He knew, however, that Peter often acted on explicit instructions of both Ruth and Lena. That was enough for him. After all, he also knew that Peter had been instrumental in getting him his present position in SI.

Peter's cell-phone jingled. JR got up and made for the door. "Call me if you need me," he threw over his shoulder," and he was gone as fast as he'd come in.

There was a giggle in Peter's anteroom and then silence. Joan, Peter's secretary, always liked JR. Most people did.

The man had an uncanny talent for saying the right thing to every person. It was almost as though he were reading their minds.

"Thornton?" Peter spoke into the mouthpiece.

"Can you join me in my office?" This was Ruth.

"On my way," he rose even as he spoke.

Ruth was the kindest, nicest, most generous person he knew in Canada. Perhaps the world. But she was also the most efficient boss of SI North America. You don't keep your boss waiting. Not even if she's your sister-in-law.

***

11
The Third Crash

Ruth's **pretty, young** and pert-looking receptionist was new. She literally jumped to her feet, knocked on the inner door, and opened it for Peter to go in. On this floor, Peter was a minor celebrity.

"Hi, sister?"

Ruth pointed to a chair. "Will call you back, John."

"Robb?" For a dreadful moment Peter was afraid that JR had told Ruth about his harebrained idea.

She ignored his question. Her face was friendly. "Peter, we have a problem."

He relaxed visibly. He was about to say, "I thought as much", but thought better of it. This was business. He nodded.

"How can I help?"

"I have no idea, Peter. But I have to touch base with someone before I bother Lena with every little detail."

Ruth leaned back in her oversized chair, which looked like the control center of an intergalactic spaceship. Not only did it display twitting buttons on both her armrests, but also there were other projections, probably earphones, which came and receded over her head, and other paraphernalia for which Peter didn't even have names.

"This was before your time," she began, seemingly unaware that she was only a few years older than Peter. "The first economic crash had taken place in October 1929. Rich people went to bed fat and contented, only to wake up poor, often penniless."

"Still fat?" Peter couldn't resist a snide remark. Once again, Ruth ignored him. She knew her brother-in-law.

"Eighty years later, in 2009, history repeated itself. This time, once again, the American taxpayer stretched out his helping hand to save the institutions that robbed him," she continued.

And now, Peter thought, the rich and ugly were ready for picking, but hopefully, without the taxpayers' participation. He felt lucky that JR had enlightened him on the subject just minutes ago.

"A crash engineered by an incompetent president and some Ponzi schemes?" he offered.

Ruth looked up, sat more straight and smiled.

"You seem to be well versed on the subject, brother dear?"

"One reads," Peter lied with a straight face.

His ego continued to place growing demands on him. But Peter did know that the Solidarity's success in Canada was partially precipitated by a leading technological firm, which invalidated their employees' pensions while paying millions in bonuses to their executives, whose ineptitude forced the firm into bankruptcy.

Nevertheless, Ruth's sudden elation was short-lived. She slumped back into her spaceship. "Our people tell us that we're in danger of history repeating itself," she said slowly, studying Peter's face.

He held his breath. Had JR's research into his scheme, their scheme, reached her ears already after all? He felt waves of hot and cold rushing up and down his spine.

"Your sources?" he decided to play for keeps.

"Washington," Ruth said. "Our people picked up a trail of what can only be described as a Ponzi scheme on a global scale." She looked at Peter, smouldering fires stirring in her dark eyes. "This could affect our members," she said. "While we guarantee a living retirement wage, we encourage independent thinking. What we do not encourage is rampant greed."

So we are back to the Green-Eyed Monster, Peter thought. Only someone, somewhere, had beaten him to it.

"And just where do I come in?"

"Think about it. I'm called a meeting tomorrow at ten to do some brainstorming. You will be there." She pressed a button on her chair.

The door opened and a smiling face bowed slightly.

"Mr. Thornton is leaving now. Give him access to all the latest data we got from Washington."

Ruth's ears were already covered by earphones. Her face showed concentration. The girl smiled lightly as Peter followed her out of Ruth's office. Ruth was growing in Peter's eyes. That's some sis-in-law I've got, he mused. And a second later he realized, I'd better watch my step. He had no wish to lose his present income.

There were things he had to do. First, he had to protect Cathy's inheritance. He had no idea how extensive her father's holdings were, but he had to make sure that he wouldn't expose them to unnecessary risks.

Then, there were the SI holdings. Not nearly as large as those of some American corporations, but they were there to assure the SI retirement pensions. He'd have to get JR involved in that. Perhaps JR could also give a hand with Dr. Mondellay's portfolio. Peter soon realized that the protection of SI's pensions was, most probably, what Ruth had in mind. He might be able to play two hands in the same game of poker. He smiled, feeling a thrill of expectation.

About then a thought struck him that, at tomorrow's meeting, JR might put two and two together—and make five. He might well assume with his Nanotech brain that Peter already knew about the Washington scheme, and that Peter had approached him ahead of time. This could be both good and bad. Good—if he retained JR's commitment to his own cause, and bad if JR blurted that he and JR had already discussed it. Peter imagined that, so far, only he had been apprised of the US Ponzi situation. He picked up the cell-phone.

"JR? It's me. About the stuff we discussed. We're meeting with Ruth tomorrow. I wouldn't discuss it at the meeting. It might be misunderstood by some. Let's see how it works first, and then…"

"I got you, Peter. Mum's the word." JR was full of quaint expressions.

"Thanks. By the way, how can I protect the SI holdings from my own…"

"It's built into disk number two. Also, no SI holdings are in derivatives. Lena was very strict about that. You're on safe ground."

As simple as that…

Peter was amazed that Lena was conversant with the foibles of the market. On the other hand, one of her functions was to preserve the cultural heritage accumulated by the Catholic Church, and that, as JR would probably say, took a very pretty penny. She was some woman…

That left only Dr. Mondellay. And possibly Dr. Brent. It was at moments like this that Peter was glad he did not have many friends. There's something to be said for being a loner. Even if it does drive you crazy, on occasion. He was sure that Ruth, with her almost holier-than-thou morals, would not dabble in derivatives herself, either. It was too much like gambling. He picked up the telephone and asked for Dr. Brent.

There was a flurry of fast, heavy breathing when the secretary recognized Peter's voice.

"Why, Dr. Thornton, how nice to hear your voice. You never come to see us…" She really was aflutter like a schoolgirl on her first date.

"I promise I will, ah…" he was wracking his brain to remember her name. All he remembered was that she was middle-aged and very nice.

"I'll tell Dr. Brent that you called, Sir. Does he have your number?"

Peter gave her his cell number, said a few nice things and snapped his cell shut. She was nice but she was lonely. She tended to go on.

Peter was ready to go to lunch when Dr. Brent returned his call.

"Hello, my boy. I hear good things about you. Lena tells me that you are keeping your eye on the security of the SI Headquarters."

Peter forgot that Dr. Brent and Lena had sponsored his present position at SI, together. For some reason they must have continued to keep in touch.

"Sorry to bother you, John," it had taken Peter years to learn to address his old chief of medicine by his first name, "but I just heard that the financial world is in for another hayride, thanks to our American friends. I am told that investments in derivatives might be in danger of collapsing."

"Derivatives? Derivatives of what?"

"Well, what I mean is that if you have lots of money invested in…"

"Peter, when do you imagine I have time to play with investments? What little money I have I give to Lucy, and as far as I know, if there's any left over, she buys Canada Savings Bonds."

"I'm so glad to hear it, John. How's Lucy?"

"She's just fine. She mentions you now and then. You should drop in and say hello."

"Will do. Please give her my very warmest regards."

"Do it yourself, young man. Ha, ha. She'll enjoy it more coming from you."

"Of course. I mean, I will." They met not so long ago at his condo party, but Lucy was a social animal while John was much too busy to indulge in such frivolities.

They both hung up simultaneously. Dr. Brent sounded a little rushed. To run the Hospital at his age must have been taxing. Peter had forgotten how hard they all worked at the General.

That left Dr. Mondellay, Cathy's father, but Peter decided to check on him through Cathy. So far so good. He clicked on his computer and inserted the first disk. With a strange feeling of being naughty, he pressed the Enter button. An hour later he selected the banks he wanted to deal with. Actually, to deal through. JR offered a long list with some peripheral comments. The computer would open accounts. The investor's domicile would be in India. Why? India is a big place. He was hoping to get lost among nearly two billion people. There were countless trillions of electronic transactions taking place daily on the subcontinent alone. Perhaps per hour? For the first time in his life, he, Dr. Peter Thornton, was joining the rat race.

Finally, his *sub rosa* work being done, he remembered his even more secret function at SI Headquarters. With little enthusiasm, nodding with a knowing smile to his secretary, he left his office. She knew, of course, about his function. She, Ruth and JR knew about it, unless the last two decided to enlighten anyone else.

Peter spent the rest of the day touring different departments, making up reasons for dropping in on people on the spur of the moment. He was becoming quite adept at lying. He was telling himself that it's all in good cause, but it left considerable distaste in his mouth. On the other hand, he was hardly likely to spot an android by announcing his presence and asking people if he could examine their auras. Lying came with the territory. He hardly expected that what might be considered a spiritually oriented ability might lead him to become an expert at prevarication. By now, he could cross swords with any politician.

So far, with the exception of the main lobby, his snooping had come to naught. While boring, it also proved what a good job JR was doing with his security team. The floors, as JR would put it, were clean. Frankly, the only function Peter's meandering route served was to make him acquainted with practically every employee at Headquarters. He'd become known as never before. Hardly his dream-come-true.

For once, Cathy was already waiting for him at home. She came early, and spent an hour or two doing what women do around the house when alone. Men usually pour themselves a drink and drop into a comfortable armchair, pick up the Financial Times, or click on a News program on TV. Women seem to putter around, seemingly doing nothing much, yet, by the time they finish, the house is converted into a home. In some practically invisible way, they add to the place a feel of warmth, coziness and an inimitable sense of being lived in. And if they are very smart, they also leave behind their unique presence.

Peter loved it when Cathy got home first.

Once settled down, he mentioned the dangers that were swooping upon us, poor folks, from down south.

"It's unofficial, I wouldn't mention it to anybody, but I'm concerned about your dad. He ought to think about his investments." Peter tried to sound as offhand as he could.

"Dad's investments? I don't believe dad ever invested a penny in his life. All his income comes from royalties paid by people, the world over, for his cold-fusion invention. Remember?"

Until the last day or two, Peter was completely divorced from anything remotely connected with making money. Or, at least, from making money for money's sake. He was rewarded for his work, but he lost interest in increasing his 'take-home' on the day when he had been forced to give up his fellowship in the Royal College. Before that day, and since, money had always been a byproduct of his work. Never a motivation for doing it. Apparently Dr. Mondellay was moulded from the same clay. And that was in addition to Dr. Bartholomew Mondellay's putting the first Chinese man on Mars. Cathy's father was no ordinary man.

Now that Peter was ready to activate the disk number 2, he began having cold feet. What if he hurt innocent people on the way? What if schools, widows, orphanages… what if the wrong people pay for his bit of fun?

Later that evening he realized that he hadn't thought of Winston for some time. What would Winston have done? *Don't be stupid, Peter, Winston would never do such a thing. It's not his, ah, cup of tea.* Yeah… but…

No matter how he twisted his logic, Winston would never have become involved in this sort of charade. For whatever reason. And then, out of the blue, he recalled a thing Winston had once said.

"You cannot lose, Peter, what is yours in your consciousness. What is part of your true self. And further, you can never keep, for long, what is not yours."

Was this an absolution for his forthcoming prank? He did not intend to keep his millions, perhaps billions. He only wanted to see what it feels like to own the world. Or a small slice of it. Like those magnates of the past. And… some still living today. Would it make him feel superior? Invincible? Almighty? Would he experience a sense of Power? Power with a capital P? Or would being even a theoretical member of Plutocracy fill him with distaste or even disgust?

Peter was still mulling over the possibilities when he and Cathy retired. He forsook his OBE exercises and fell, exhausted, on the pillows. He had never suspected that *sub rosa* activities, not conducted out of a sense of duty only, well, only out of a misplaced, artificially induced sense of greed, would take a lot out of you. He recalled a saying that it is harder to earn a crooked dollar than an honest one.

Just before dozing off, he smiled at the thought that, only recently, *sub rosa* activities had become synonymous with covert activities. In his younger days, five-petalled roses had been carved over the confessionals, promising that the exchanges that would take place would forever remain secret. Hence, Latin for "under the rose". So much had transpired since those days, and yet...

And yet the memories lingered on.

It did not turn out to be a pleasant night. For a week now he'd lost his ability to recall any of his dreams. His notebook, at his bedside table, lay open, the pencil sharpened, his recall missing. He hardly expected that night to be any different. Yet three times he got out of bed, paced his living room, stared into the night, into the lights shimmering on the slopes of Mount Royal. Each time he'd been awakened by a nightmare: a vision so garish that he began to suspect that someone had slipped him some delayed action drugs. He knew of hallucinogens that acted in strange ways.

Exhausted, he returned to his bed, trying to stay awake for as long as he could. His eyes, having adjusted to the darkness, could just discern Cathy's features, superbly relaxed in angelic repose. What a clean conscience she must have, he mused.

Cathy, my dear Cathy...

He lay on his back trying to retain the image of her face behind his eyelids. He had no success. Yet again, he opened his eyes to stay awake.

Within minutes the ceiling darkened, then turned into churning clouds of dark, acrid smoke. He felt flames all around him. He was suspended in a gooey substance, like thick liquid honey or even thicker oil. It certainly smelled more like the latter. Its temperature was rising, until its engulfing warmth turned to painful caress. He felt drawn into it, deeper and deeper, until the viscid, sticky concoction began closing over his head. He could hardly breathe. It sucked him in with indomitable force, such as he'd never experienced before. Inexplicably, he sensed that vaporous miasma wasn't real, yet could do nothing to extricate himself from its embrace.

When he finally came awake, at dawn, his bed was wet with perspiration. If Cathy hadn't been by his side, he would have walked out, never to sleep on this bed again. He rose slowly, tiptoed towards and stood by the window. From there, he addressed a silent soliloquy to Cathy's sleeping body.

There is one very positive outcome of my nocturnal tortures. I did not hear voices. I did not imagine that government has planted devices in my brain, to spy on my thoughts and monitor my actions. Nor did I think that aliens have taken over my body. What is even more important, throughout the dismal experience, I was aware that it was not reality. That, no matter how tactile, no matter how many of my senses had been involved, it was still just a vision.

Thus I am not a schizophrenic, after all.

He looked away and made his way to the bathroom. He needed a long, relaxing shower.

I may be going in the wrong direction, but at least I am going. I'm no longer standing still. I am alive.

And as he felt the drops of hot water caressing his body, he mused, this time aloud, "I wonder what Winston would say."

By 9 a.m., JR was waiting for him at the front desk. The android, which magically emerged from the elevator maintenance cupboard, seemed less tall by JR's side. JR towered over everybody. The android, which stood in for his fried-brained colleague, greeted Peter with a stiff, but perfect smile. JR grinned his best boyish grin.

"I don't believe you've met..." he murmured, then drew Peter aside. "Wanted to touch base before the meeting with the boss," he said, walking towards the bank of elevators.

Peter followed obediently.

On Peter's floor, JR pulled him to the side of the corridor. "When do you intend to try out the, ah, system?"

"Why do you ask?"

"Because, if the SI attempt a similar venture to counteract the Yankees, we might cross paths and, well, act against each other's interests."

Yankees was not the historic New York baseball team. It was the only way JR referred to the USA Washingtonians. Actually, most of the time, anyone south of the border was a Yankee. Also, Peter noticed that JR no longer thought that Peter was acting on behalf of the SI. For a brief moment he felt lost, but recovered quickly.

"SI will obviously take priority in such a case. Will the disks need adjustment?"

"Wait till after the meeting. I won't know till we hear details from Mrs. Thornton."

Peter nodded.

"Of course." This was serious. In any other circumstances, JR would have said 'the boss'.

They arrived at Peter's door.

"You want to come in?"

"No, thanks, I have some work to do before the meeting." And his spindly legs took him back to the elevator in a smooth, gliding motion.

The man was a workhorse.

Precisely at ten, four men and three women walked into the conference room. Ruth was already there. In a few words she repeated the news she'd shared with Peter yesterday. Then she sat back and waited.

No one volunteered.

"Well?" Ruth ran her eyes over the little gathering.

Actually, all present had been briefed, in advance, what the meeting was going to be about. Then, even as JR opened his mouth, they all spoke at once.

"Are you sure?"

"Are your sources reliable?"

"I thought there were laws…"

"Surely, not again…"

JR raised his hand, reaching halfway to the ceiling. "I believe," he said, "what Mrs. Thornton expects from us is not an expression of disbelief, but suggestions what action, if any, we should take to counteract the news we have been presented with."

Ruth smiled her appreciation. She didn't like meetings. Like Lena, she believed that a camel is a horse designed by a committee. However, the SI constitution demanded a modicum of democracy.

Silence returned to the room. She met JR's eyes. He nodded. There was some sort of understanding those two had developed since JR took over SI Canada.

"Very well. I expect written proposals on my desk by ten a.m. tomorrow morning."

She got up and walked out of the room. Except for JR and Peter, the rest of the delegates looked like children who were told that they'd have to stay after school. They gathered their little gray files, and filed out of the conference room. JR and Peter stayed behind. After a few moments, Ruth came back.

"Peter and I have been working on a scheme that might do the trick," JR said, winking at Peter. Then, leaving out certain details, he described, in broad terms, what could be done to Ponzi the Ponzis.

"We cannot do this as SI, but Peter offered to risk his good name and reputation and run the countermeasures under his own banner, so to speak."

Peter could have hugged JR. He was not only the smartest, but by far the nicest friend he'd ever had. Actually, all his friends were an exemplary lot. Belatedly he was beginning to realize that he was a very lucky man.

"Thank you, Peter," Ruth said. There was admiration and gratitude in her voice. Peter was beginning to feel very embarrassed.

That afternoon, JR made a few programming adjustments and, within an hour, this time together, he and JR put disk number two into operation.

No matter under whose flag, Peter still found the idea of being a multibillionaire exciting. Perhaps some of the euphoria was missing, now that there was no profound secrecy surrounding the 'game', but still, billions are billions are billions. There was a nice ring to it.

He and JR sat, next to each other, watching the large computer screen in JR's office. The one in Peter's was too small. The numbers whirled at an absurd velocity. Only the totals on the right hand side of the screen were legible; the others moved, changed and adjusted too quickly for the human eye to follow. By the end of the day, Peter had made his first hundred million dollars.

"It's a slow start," JR murmured.

"It's only on paper, right?" Peter said. He did not share JR's concept of speed.

"Not even. They are little more than electrons floating around the world at the speed of light."

Peter took a deep breath. He never thought being a multimillionaire would be so innocuous. He hardly felt a thing.

They both left the office at six. JR was whistling softly. It was evident that he was enjoying himself immensely. Peter didn't quite share his friend's sentiments. In fact, within an hour of getting home, he was beginning to feel the weight of the money. After all, the whole earth consists of tiny, elusive, invisible atoms, each having even tinier electrons whirling around their nuclei. There are a great many of them. And, as of that day, great many seemed to swirl around him.

At ten o'clock that same evening, *Peer Gynt* jingled on his cell phone. It was JR. He was chuckling.

"Well done, my friend," was his opening salvo. "Two private Yankee banks which are specializing in derivatives are searching for credit. I believe we've done it." He chuckled again. "At this rate, we will have engineered the Third Crash by… by Thursday noon."

This was Tuesday, but Peter didn't care.

The next day things were relatively quiet. Peter did his usual tours, smiled at people, tried to be nice and friendly. He couldn't help but wonder what he, a multimillionaire, was doing wandering the corridors, knocking on people's doors under some pretext or other. Every hour or two he shrugged, shook his head, and continued.

I don't care, he kept telling himself.

I don't care!

Actually he did, but he couldn't divorce himself from the idea that all those sums on the screen were just that. Sums, tiny numbers, scribbled on a computer screen. Suddenly the idea didn't sound all that good. Frankly, he was also getting scared. He wasn't quite sure why, but a sense of unease began somewhere at the back of his neck, and crept up, stubbornly, to his forehead. He kept frowning. He'd ventured into a field he knew absolutely nothing about. Neither about computers nor about business.

He tried hard not to think about it. After all, it was set on automatic.

Then, on Wednesday night, it hit him. It was something JR had said, must have been the day, no, two days ago. It hit him like a bolt of lightning from a clear midnight sky. "It is set on automatic. It will grow exponentially until you stop it."

Until you stop it.

Peter had forgotten. By then, trillions of dollars worth absolutely nothing were spinning at the velocity of light around the globe. Banks, attempting to meet the promissory notes, were collapsing like flies swatted by an elephant's tail. Next came the building societies, which relied on those banks for credit. Finally, the greediest of the greedy, the investment houses, which banked on no one understanding the intricacies of derivatives or the insidious iniquity of Ponzi schemes, began to drown in their own greedy quagmire.

As quietly as he could, Peter slipped from under the blanket. Cathy hadn't stirred. He picked up his clothing, crept out of the bedroom and closed the door. Minutes later he was running all the way to Headquarters. As his lungs fought for air, puffs of steam formed in the freezing air. His feet crunched on fresh snow. He ran, slipping, catching his balance and running again. He ran to the elevators, almost knocking down the night watchman. He ran down the corridor to his office.

"Damn!"

He'd forgotten the key. He kicked at the lock with all the force he could muster. It snapped, with a dry, metallic sound. Alarm bells filled the night silence. He dove for the computer, its hum telling its own story. The next moment he was covered in cold sweat. As he pressed the shut-off key, the computer continued to hum. He tapped the slot to extract the disks. The disks were not there. Both were missing.

The computer continued to hum.

***

12
Panic

Peter **swore, slammed his fist** on his desk, then collapsed, exhausted, into his armchair. "Damn the alarms," he swore again. *Damn my stupid schemes. Damn JR. No. That's unfair. It was all my idea, or at least I put it in his head, I can't blame anyone but myself.* Thoughts, desperate thoughts, were whirling through his mind.

The next moment two men, stunners drawn, barged into his office.

"Stand up and keep your arms away from your body!" one said. His voice was familiar.

Peter shrugged. He got up, keeping his hands up. The guard gasped.

"Mr. Thornton?" he mumbled, visibly at a loss for words.

"Yes, ah, George?" Peter was squinting at the guard's lapel. He wasn't sure of his name. The man often saluted him on his inspection tours.

"Yes, Sir. Sorry, Sir. We thought..."

"It is I who am sorry, George. Emergency. Forgot my key. You can fix the door in the morning."

"Yes, Sir." George, still looking as if he'd been hit by his own stunner, saluted stiffly and backed out of the office. Peter sank back into his armchair, momentarily, closing his eyes.

I've engineered the third economic crash. People have written records of their holdings, they should be all right. Banks, like governments, don't produce anything. No comestibles, no goods of practical use to humanity. Banks have only electronic possessions. Imaginary. Theoretical. These may have been erased. Superseded. By trillions upon trillions of transactions. Growing exponentially at the speed of light.

Peter's mind was spinning in circles without rhyme or reason. His first rational thought was to call his secretary and ask her if anyone had had access to his computer in his absence. It was close to one a.m. Even if she told him, there would be little he could do with the information.

"It wouldn't help," he muttered to himself.

He had no idea if the program could run, forever, without the disks. He was not exactly computer savvy. All he knew was that the computer was still humming. Softly, as though trying to be quiet during the night. Peter knew how to use it as well as anyone. He knew how to find information on the Internet. As for its internal functioning, he was as green as the man next door. As anyone who didn't specialize in computer programming.

He wondered if he should call Ruth. For some reason he couldn't force himself to call JR. He had no idea why.

He woke up stiff, for a moment wondering where Cathy was. He must have dozed off from sheer nervous exhaustion. The next instant he became aware of his office. It all began coming back. He glanced at his watch. It was 5:30 a.m. He rubbed his eyes. Only then did it all come back to him in vivid, painful detail. He looked at his computer. It was off and it was humming. Something was very wrong. *Did some people conspire against me?* A sense of panic was returning to him. What the devil was going on?

It was too early to call Cathy. He almost jumped out of his skin when his cellular sang. Cathy was on.

"Peter? Where on earth are you?"

"Sorry, darling, emergency. I'm at the office."

"Are you all right?"

"Yes, of course, darling. I'll call you as soon as I can. Must go." He clicked the cellular shut. He was hoping his voice had been calm and reassuring.

He was getting very good at lying. They say that the first lie is the hardest. Soon it gets easier. By now, he felt, he could lie as glibly as a used-car dealer. Only he didn't enjoy it. Perhaps... not yet?

It was coming on 6:00 a.m. He wondered if there was any point in calling JR. John would be in the office in two/three hours. *Might as well wait. Not make a fool of myself, again. What else could go wrong?*

He almost relaxed.

Then he thought of the speed of light. The universal constant. You can't be married to a physicist and not know such things. Three hundred thousand kilometers per second, he mused darkly. 299,792,458 meters per second—Cathy always insisted on accuracy. *How come I remember such things?* About one hundred and eighty-six thousand miles per second. Too much. Much too fast. About 7.5 times around the earth per second. That's a lot of transactions. His mind was a whirl of numbers.

PER SECOND!!!

He jumped to his feet, only to collapse again.

Whatever might have happened, it probably already had. I forgot to terminate the program. I just forgot. It's no good to panic now. Everyone else will. Once they wake up... Dark thoughts crowded his brain.

I wish I remembered how to pray...

He felt totally spent. Exhausted, as he would be after a week of continuous duty at the General. Or like that day in the yard, behind Chez Gaston's. As he closed his eyes he could see the neon sign. *Gaston Brown, Proprieteur.* Another time, another life. *A brisk walk around the backyard. So cold. So very cold.*

Winston? Winston? Are you there?

A gentle tap on his shoulder woke him up. He'd dozed off again. He still felt worn out. JR's smiling face was looking down at him.

"Good stuff, hey?" JR could be very Canadian when he wanted to.

JR was looking at Peter's computer. Next to it, a small, portable TV was competing for his attention. "I think we did it," he said. He looked very pleased with himself.

"I couldn't switch it off," Peter confessed lamely.

"Well, now. Thank heavens for little mercies," JR murmured, punching a few keys on Peter's keyboard. "I know. I fixed it so you couldn't." He was still grinning. "I thought it would be OK as long as you didn't pull the cord out."

For a moment Peter wondered if his friend had gone mad. Stark raving mad. Trillions upon trillions of transactions must have raced around the world; by now quadrillions and then some. JR must have gone mad.

"P-pull the c-cord out...?" He'd never thought of it.

"I've set it to reversal," JR murmured, as if saying the obvious. Then he looked down at Peter. "You can close your mouth now. Your little peccadilloes are all erased. Or will be within minutes."

"My... erased...?"

"You are no longer a multibillionaire, my friend. Actually you are, only nobody knows it. You can write any check you like, for any amount. Only, well, no one can pay it. Well, almost no one. Not south of the border. It's a bit complicated." JR was grinning wider and wider. It seemed that he was right in his element.

Peter wasn't sure if he should laugh or cry. All erased? His first reaction was on the lines of "how dare you?" His second, "thank God!" For a while, he had no other reactions. He must have looked flabbergasted.

"You all right, Peter?" JR sounded worried.

"I, ahh, I... ah..." Peter cleared his throat. "Of course I'm all right. At least, I think I am. Aren't I? Should I be? JR, what the devil is going on?"

"I'll tell you what. Go home, get some sleep, then get some Heineken. Or Holsten Premium. Kronenbourg?" Peter was staring at him. "You know, imported beer? Oh, never mind. I'll bring my own. I'll drop in and tell you all about it, all right?"

"And you'll start another little Ponzi..."

"...we don't use that word openly." He pointed to the door, which he'd left half-open. "It's illegal," he added in a whisper. And then the roar of his laughter filled Peter's office, the anteroom, and probably the corridor all the way to the elevators. Peter had heard JR laugh before, mostly chuckles, but he never imagined that such an emaciated body could emit such uproarious bellowing.

Peter wasn't quite sure, but he thought he'd noticed just a touch of hysteria in this gleeful outburst. Gradually, JR settled down.

"Have a good rest, while I report to Mrs. Thornton," he said, still catching his breath. "Hope she'll like what she'll hear. "

And with these ominous words, JR disappeared in three measured strides towards the corridor.

Peter took JR's advice. He was in no shape to do anything constructive, anyway. JR looked relaxed, as in relaxed after a serious binge, but still, that was enough for Peter to take the load off his feet. Cathy would be out and he might get some real sleep, uninterrupted by thoughts that were as dark as many a nightmare. Ironically, he wondered what his next dream would be like. He didn't have to wait long.

He took a taxi home. On entering his condo he threw his coat on a chair. Somewhere along the way, between the entrance door to his apartment and the bedroom, he dropped off his Mao-styled tunic and shed his shoes. He collapsed on the bed in one smooth motion.

He completely forgot to call Cathy. For the next five hours, he was dead to the world. The naps in the office did not seem to offer him any rest at all.

If he dreamt anything, he had no recollection of it. On awaking, he felt more rested than he'd felt in a week. Probably it was the release of tension. He didn't care. He was looking forward to seeing his lanky friend.

Then he heard movement in the sitting room. Cathy was back. Just as he sat up, she peeked into the bedroom. She was holding a pair of shoes.

"Where would you like these?" she asked.

"Sorry, love, I was a bit..."

"I think I shall put them away with your coat, hat, gloves, scarf..."

"Really, darling. I'm sorry."

She smiled. He wasn't usually so untidy. In fact, never *that* untidy. Not even when he was a student, living in Ruth's house.

"I think you'd better tell me about it," Cathy started, looking at him expectantly.

"Well, I dropped the coat on the chair, I think, then..."

"Peter!" That was stern.

"JR will be here soon. He'll explain." When Cathy continued to look blank, he added. "He'll bring his own beer. Imported," he added, after a pause.

Frankly, he would not have been able to explain what happened even if someone paid him the billions he'd made, and apparently lost, in quick succession.

Cathy shrugged. "Breakfast?" she asked. It was late afternoon.

"I'd love it."

She rolled her eyes and left the bedroom. Peter dragged himself off the bed and staggered to the bathroom. Perhaps he wasn't as rested as he thought. He felt stiff, or groggy, as if he'd danced all night. Not that he ever did, except that time in Ritz-Xentung, and that was with Cathy. God, she looked great that night. A lascivious smile widened his lips. Did she ever... he mused, enamoured with the image hovering in his genitalia.

"Still does," he added to himself, shaking the remaining cobwebs from his head.

Some minutes later he was enjoying a belated breakfast, with Cathy sipping green tea. She let him eat in silence, though curiosity was chewing at her nerves. It was the first time ever that her husband left her for the night without a word. After a while, she turned on the TV.

> "...seventeen banks have closed their doors to the public. The New York Stock Exchange stopped trading just after the opening bell. Ah... make that twenty-seven, no, forty-seven banks..."

Cathy looked at Peter, who swallowed hard. The speaker continued.

> "The President of the United States will address the nation momentarily. In the meantime, we repeat again. The experts state that this is the worst crash since the first decade of this century, when a total of eleven trillion dollars melted from the United States economy. The US Treasury did not answer our calls. So far, no one offered any explanation for the alleged fiscal collapse. It seems as incomprehensible as it was some sixty years ago."

Without a single comment, Cathy turned down the volume and stared at Peter. He began to feel more and more uncomfortable. At last he couldn't take her steady glare any longer.

"What?" he shrugged. "I didn't do that?" Unfortunately it sounded like a question.

"And you had nothing to do with it, right?"

With a piece of fresh baguette, Peter wiped the rest of the fried eggs from his plate and turned his eyes to the mountain. Yet another coat of snow was just beginning to refresh the Mount Royal with virginal chastity. He felt much better now.

"No doubt, the universe will continue to unfold itself as it should," he murmured.

"Don't be flippant, darling. Aren't you playing with fire?"

Cathy was definitely suspecting something. Then Peter remembered asking her about her father's investments. She was a very smart lady.

"JR will be here, soon," he murmured, glancing at his watch.

Cathy turned up the sound on the TV. The screen was showing crowds of people demanding to be allowed into their banks. Some were waving their fists, two or three began throwing rocks.

"Where do they find rocks in the middle of New York?" she asked incongruously.

In the background one could just discern the sound of a police siren. The riots were imminent. Peter looked away. What have I done… he mused. *What on earth have I done?*

The scene shifted to Chicago. Things were quieter there, but there, too, groups of people were gathering at banks' doors. The camera shifted to four different locations. Apparently only some banks had remained closed, and people must have wanted to withdraw their holdings from those that were still open. After the panic in New York, Chicago was still relatively peaceful.

"For how long?" Cathy asked, reading his thoughts.

Peter was afraid to think, lest she continued to read them. *What would come next? Mob rebellions? Bloodshed? Mass murder? Did money hold people together? Like common faith? It wasn't evil. Its abuse was. Isn't all abuse evil?*

"Peter!" Cathy was staring at him. "You're turning pale..."

"Sorry. It's my imagination. Let's turn off the TV."

She did. For a while they sat in silence. They both put their attention on the thick snowflakes floating outside their panoramic window. After the scenes on TV, there was an unearthly peace in their carefree movement. Some were caught in the updraft, and flew upwards, defying gravity. Like puffs of cotton, alive yet indifferent, they seemed to have their being outside the confines of time.

For Cathy and Peter time also seemed to have slowed down. For a brief moment, Cathy wondered how much cash she had at home for groceries and suchlike. Then she relaxed. North of the border there was peace and quiet. They sat there, in an uneasy silence, till *Peer Gynt* announced that JR was downstairs in the lobby.

"Come right up," Peter said, taking a deep breath. At last, he thought. At last.

JR arrived, carrying a small crate of Lowenbrau.

"Carried it all the way from Munich." he grinned. He looked and sounded lighthearted. "Germany. What's that? Germany... you mean the beer. It's been around since 1383. That's longer than I've..."

"...been an Nanotech. Your head is full of..."

"...completely useless stuff!"

"JR, is that really you?" Cathy recognized his voice in the hall, but he had never sounded so boisterous. She was waiting for him with a large stein in hand. "This one's from Germany, too," she announced, handing it over.

Peter gave one bottle of Lowenbrau to JR and carried the rest of the carton to the kitchen. He put it in the fridge and returned with two glasses and a bottle of Merlot. He'd noticed that Cathy had already prepared two platters of *belles gueules*, presumably while he was still asleep, though she couldn't have known that JR was coming. On the other hand, you never knew with Cathy.

"This is from Argentina," Peter announced. "Just to be different."

They settled in three armchairs facing the Mount Royal.

"My, you have a view... Cheers."

JR looked and sounded happy. All three raised their glasses, JR emptying a quarter of his in a single swig. Peter and Cathy continued to stare at him expectantly. JR seemed to think that he'd dropped in for a chat. At last Peter couldn't wait any longer.

"So how did Ruth take it?"

"How do you expect. We did exactly what she wanted!" No wonder JR looked so full of beans. "The Ponzis have panned out." He took another swig. "As far as we can see, every single one of them."

"I hate to butt in, but could you let me in on your rambling?" Cathy's tone said that enough was enough.

JR glanced at Peter and cleared his throat. "It's a little bit confidential, Cathy..."

"It's a long flight down through that window," she countered.

"It's all right, JR. She can read my thoughts."

JR nodded. In an incredibly concise and clear manner, he explained to Cathy the history of Ponzi charlatans, and then how it applied to today.

"It's hard to believe it's possible, but with the wonders of technology we played the Ponzis for patsies. We managed to outwit them at their own game."

Wonders of technology and a single Nanotech brain, albeit a very special one. Peter was also incredibly grateful that JR carefully omitted mentioning his own participation in the whole affair.

"And it was your beloved husband who actually initiated the whole idea. Brilliant, I tell you. Quite brilliant!"

Peter groaned. A moment later the full weight of JR's words reached him. JR managed to turn his frantic attempt at usurping money into a brilliant scheme which, according to JR, would ultimately, somehow, save billions in SI interests. Perhaps, if you eradicate a pandemic, everyone gets to be more healthy? Peter slumped even deeper into his armchair, although, at that precise moment, he felt about a million tons lighter.

"Ch-ch-cheers," he raised his glass.

By then Cathy was gazing at him with admiring eyes. "Cheers!" he repeated, raising his glass towards JR. Whatever have I done to deserve this, he wondered?

It transpired that, immediately preceding his *coup d'état* of the Ponzi empire, JR had converted what little holdings SI held, outside commodities, into bonds and/or financial instruments, which were outside the influence of the ineffectual derivatives. Ruth was amazed at his abilities in the field, which, to date, had been outside the confines of his specific department. There's a big difference between security and securities, she knew. She also knew, instantly, that Nanotechs held an amazing edge over mere mortals. Fortunately, power carries responsibilities, and JR was among the very few to whom Ruth could entrust such loyalty. Nanotechs could be as dangerous as they could be useful, as the Americans had learned the hard way. Some years ago, a small group of Nanotechs of the Sino-Indian bloc almost crippled one of the main AI research stations. It had been then that the Americans decided to double their efforts to develop artificial intelligence still further, to maintain their own tenuous advantage in the economic balance among the fully developed nations.

The world was becoming a very complex place.

The ridiculous thing was that power, as such, power to affect millions, seemed to rest in the hands of individuals.

Not governments but individuals. By the same token, although the governments of the world had finally ratified nuclear nonproliferation treaties, a single man or woman could construct and detonate an atomic device. The same was true of Ponzi schemes and other artificial constructs that could, and often did, affect millions if not billions of people.

JR was going through his third Lowenbrau, and the delicious *belles gueules* were rapidly disappearing from both platters. All three were finally relaxed, though Peter still had to redefine his place in the new scheme of things.

Washing down the last *pièce de résistance* with the last gulp of beer, JR climbed out of the deep armchair and stretched his considerable height.

"Well," he said, "that's about all you need to know for now. I hope, gracious lady, you, too, are reasonably satisfied with my explanation of what kept your dear husband in office most of the night. It wasn't as simple as I made it sound, but the conclusions and results are correct."

"Won't you stay for dinner?"

"What, and lose my divine shape? I've been masticating your delicious *amuse-bouches* all evening and, at least for now, I couldn't swallow another bite. Also, I have to follow up on a thing or two in the office."

It was nearly seven o'clock and JR was going back to the office.

"No peace for the guilty," he threw over his shoulders and made for the door. Neither Cathy nor Peter could keep up with him. He was in the elevator lobby before they reached their own front door.

Cathy and Peter didn't eat supper, either. Peter was still digesting his breakfast, and Cathy seemed well satisfied with the *hors d'oeuvres*. The wine also made her sleepy, particularly as she had also missed some sleep last night, worrying about Peter.

As for Peter, well, he began thanking his lucky stars. JR not only did not present him as a greedy SOB that fell under the spell of the almighty dollar, but managed to paint him a portrait of a knight on a white steed, charging to save SI from a fate worse than death. This reality, he mused, is just too unpredictable. Tonight, he promised himself, I'm going back to my study of dreams.

But he didn't. All he dreamt about was of being a little fish swimming in murky, unpleasant water. He didn't like it one bit.

The moment Peter got up, he clicked on the TV. He wished he hadn't. If yesterday the riots, and rumors of riots, had been in the air, today they hit the United States with full force. He'd never suspected that, apparently, the whole nation was up to their greedy necks in the insidious Ponzi schemes operated by even more dishonest brokers.

There were also reports of murders, when irate investors were told that their financial idols, invariably multi-billionaires, forfeited on their obligations. In different states, mostly in Florida, seven palatial residences had been set on fire. People, men and women, who seemed to have lost even the slightest modicum of civilized behaviour, had attacked members of the household escaping the blazing infernos. Some of the attackers emptied their guns, others wielded garden implements, spades, forks, or whatever they thought would create maximum damage. These were scenes that could have been taken out of the worst Hollywood horror movies, or nightmares, such as Peter never imagined could be born in a human mind.

Finally, the cameras moved to show another mob that had already formed in front of the White House. In the general uproar Peter could not hear their demands, but the cameras showed a forest of placards, evidently produced haphazardly, demanding compensation, retribution and, in a nutshell, the heads of the perpetrators of this collapse.

Peter doubted if even one of them realized that a Ponzi scheme couldn't succeed without the active and repetitive participation of willing, avaricious investors. Greed breeds greed even as violence breeds violence.

The evidence for that last axiom became soon evident. The camera shifted to a group of helicopters, which began spraying the festering, weaving mob with something that caused people to cover their eyes and their heads with their clothing. Then, individual people, now semi-blinded, began to charge this way and that, like fish trapped in the nets of proficient fishermen.

Canada fared a lot better. It wasn't that Canadians didn't invest, but for as long as Peter could remember, Canadians had been, and still were, interested in commodities. While they were lucky that their territory yielded so many natural resources, Dr. Bartholomew Mondellay's invention continued to open the frozen, incredibly rich-in-minerals sub-arctic territories, which added to Canada's already well-balanced coffers. SI was very well aware of this fact, as were the relatively few working members of society who were not already members of Solidarity International. For now, on the Canadian doorstep, all was well.

"Was it worth it, Peter?"

Cathy had been standing by Peter's shoulder for some time now. She, too, was stunned by the extent of the reaction. The Ponzi schemes must have been huge, and fuelled by the same AI technology which had enabled JR to stop them.

"If JR hadn't stopped them now, then, within months, a year or two at most, they would have collapsed under their own weight. The damage would have been considerably greater."

"How can we be sure?"

"Cathy, I'm not a financial expert. Far from it. But in 2008 one man skinned seemingly ordinary people, as well as some supposedly charitable organizations, out of sixty-five billion dollars. That was just one man! Now imagine forty or fifty such schemes working in different parts of the country using today's technology."

Peter looked up at Cathy, who still seemed unconvinced.

"I put it to you, darling, that if JR hadn't cut off their greedy fingers yesterday, the riots would have been far, far greater. They also would have resulted in mass murder, as against, tragic as they are, individual people."

The helicopters, having dropped their load, presumably tear gas, retreated over the Ellipse, towards the Washington Monument. An inset map in the top left corner of the TV screen was following their progress. The helicopters—there must have been at least a dozen of them—veered southwest over the Jefferson Bridge towards the Pentagon.

"It looks, almost, as if they were prepared for such a contingency..." Peter mused aloud.

"You mean the White House was in on the—what is it—a Ponzi scheme?"

"Yes, darling. It seems it is a yes to both your questions."

"B-b-but how could they? Those are their own people?" Peter had never heard Cathy stammer before.

"It's to do with power, darling. Money is power and power corrupts. The more money you have, the greater your power."

"But what for? What on earth do they hope to accomplish with it?"

"Both money and power are like an aphrodisiac. Also like a narcotic. It has its own rewards."

"But that's sick. It's psychotic..."

"We are all a little psychotic. It's only the degree that matters. The degree by which we veer from the norm."

"But norm is dull!" she practically spat out the words.

"Exactly. Normal means average and average means dull. But you can't tell that to the people, to the masses. Most of them would hate to stir away from what is accepted, what is considered normal."

"And the alternative?"

"You are looking at the consequences of a few dozen men veering away from the norm. At other people's expense…"

"So power really does corrupt?"

It wasn't a question. It was a confirmation of an axiom, which Cathy found so very hard to accept. For her, God was all-powerful. It seemed like a contradiction in terms.

***

Part Three

POWER

Power is the opposite of love.

Stanislaw Kapuscinski
Collection of Essays, Essay on *Power*,
Beyond Religion Volume I

13
World Without Money

For generations, money has been used as a symbol of value. After the last fiscal crash in 2008, the US Treasury printed a few trillion dollars just to fill the gap created by human greed and stupidity. Peter wondered if, on this occasion, they'd still dare to lumber people with debt, which had taken their fathers and grandfathers nearly two generations to pay back.

And mothers and grandmothers—women had to work to help men balance the national books.

Peter suspected they'd still print billions, if not trillions, surreptitiously, without bragging about it. Why? Well, old habits die hard. *You cannot put new wine into old sacks...* Peter smiled at the distant memory. Lately, more and more often he had flashes of his early days at the seminary. Not the ritual and the dogmas, but the basis from which it had all started.

Nevertheless, he also suspected that nobody would attach any real value to the once almighty dollar. Organizations and industries, which were members of SI Canada, paid all its members relatively equal amounts of money, though currency never actually changed hands. Credit, however, was extended in Canadian currency. In Europe, where they still used money for some transactions, the Euro was still holding its head, if barely, above water. Renminbi? Rupee? The ruble? Brazilian real?

Would anybody care?

Not unless they had to.

A quart of wheat for a day's wages, and three quarts of barley for a day's wages, and do not damage the oil and the wine.

Peter smiled again. The Black Horse of the Apocalypse was about to rule supreme. Barter. Like in the old days. Very, very old days. Tit for tat. Service for service. It's fair, isn't it?

There was a catch. The Black Horse had the power to bring famine—to kill with hunger. That *was* its power. Ultimately its job was to restore balance. Ultimately...

Peter remembered. The Revelation of John always fascinated him. This may not be the end of days, he mused, but it will certainly be the end of an era.

Washington would hate it, but it would have to try to follow the example of the people. The barter system precluded taxation. It left the Treasury coffers empty. They'd have to tighten every belt in the nation. Slowly stability would return.

"God is money!"

"Not any more!" Echoed those who had lost faith.

In God? Perhaps. But mostly in the value of money.

Dead, too, were the slogans of yesterday. Gold was still valued at $5000 an ounce, only you couldn't eat it. Neither could you sleep in it; nor did it provide a roof over your head, keep out the cold—and this was winter. Nor could you ride it to work. Oh, you still had to work, only you'd be rewarded in kind. You still needed some money, if you could get it. For travel. For going abroad. Some people still liked it. They kept the faith. But if you had an ounce or two of gold, what would you accept in return?

The value system had to be reexamined.

A new beginning?

Ruth, John Robb, Peter and three other senior members of SI Canada, plus one representing SI USA, were sitting on one side of the gently curved table. They were facing a giant wall screen on the other side. Soon it would show an equal number of men and women who'd face them from across the Atlantic. From the Vatican. To a casual onlooker, once the screen was activated, it would seem that all fourteen people were sitting at the same table.

It was an emergency meeting convened by Lena Walesa on a moment's notice. No one would come prepared. No one could be certain why the Chief called the meeting. All were busy trying to outguess each other. It wasn't too difficult. The monetary system had collapsed. Nobody trusted the once mighty dollar. The other currencies still carried some authority, but people were withdrawing their holdings throughout the world.

"Capitalism is dead. God save Capitalism?" JR intoned into Peter's ear. Lately the two were inseparable. They were invariably sitting next to each other.

"Perhaps, in a different form? Solidarity used it." Peter replied. "Do you really care?" It was a rhetorical question.

"Used it. Not abused it," came a whispered reply.

Yet, after this brief exchange, JR remained the only person at the table who seemed totally at ease. John Robb, it had been whispered, the architect of the change in the fiscal profile of the world. No one could know for sure, but there were whispers. JR and Peter Thornton. Peter wondered if he really was guilty of feeding JR the idea. If so, would he be devoured by Lena, or praised? Would he tell her the truth?

Unlikely. As far as Peter could gather, in fact was deeply convinced, for JR the whole affair was little more than a game. Peter had never met a man—or woman, for that matter—less interested in money than JR. His definition of luxury was a pint or two of imported beer.

A quart of wheat for a day's wages...

For some reason, the Revelations of John kept nagging Peter with the persistence of a thirsty mosquito. What a time to remember the Bible, he mused. He tried smiling. It would do to look less than grim today. Everyone else did.

Ruth had called the meeting for 10:00 a.m., Montreal time, 4:00 p.m. in the Vatican. She said that it might be good if we met a half-hour earlier, to bounce some ideas. Also, she'd said, at 9:30 a.m., the President of the USA was going to address the nation. Not us. His nation.

"We might as well listen to him together. Might have some reactions," she said in an audio message all present found on their computers on arrival in the office. Peter wondered how Ruth slept last night. Of course, she had met with JR already.

The time was 9:25 and all but Ruth were waiting in their assigned seats. At 9:29 Ruth walked in and nodded to her personal secretary. A smaller screen, left of the table, came to life. All turned to stare at the White House Oval Office. It was empty. Seconds later the 48th President of the United States, John Herbert Walker, walked in and sat stiffly behind his desk. He looked drawn, yet seemingly sure of himself. If anything, his face hinted at studied indifference. He glanced over his shoulder as though he were being watched. Then, also seemingly on purpose, he squinted into the camera. There was something vaguely insincere about his behaviour.

"My Fellow Americans. As you might already know, yesterday, at midnight, our FBI agents, acting on the authority of the Vice President of the United States, arrested twenty-two CEOs, together with their senior staff, of major American brokerage houses. You can rest assured that they will answer for the fiscal conditions which we are all facing today, ah… to the full extent of the law."

The President's voice sounded raspy. Even as he spoke, he began looking, then sounding, haggard. It was a fascinating performance. Towards the end he looked like a man grasping at straws. With a hand that seemed to be shaking, he took a sip of water.

"Nevertheless, their crimes, if proven, must not be used as an excuse for mob rule. We are a nation where we hold individual freedoms in highest regard. However, under the present circumstances, as of ten o'clock this morning, I have no choice but to suspend them. I hereby declare Martial Law. I have given orders that any person wielding or even carrying any firearms outside their own property will be shot on sight. The Martial Law will be lifted the moment I'm advised that the rule of law has been restored."

Tough words from a tough-looking man. Yet, there was something staged about it. The President rushed the last few words as if anxious to get away from the camera. He succeeded. The TV screen went black on his last word. No comments from the stations; no comments from the White House staff; no questions being asked or answered.

After nearly 300 years, the Second Amendment to the Constitution of the United States, adopted on December 15, 1791, had been suspended. At least for now, the American love affair with firearms was over.

Many would celebrate. Others would use it to shoot themselves. In protest, of course.

There was a quiet sound of air escaping from the lungs of all present, followed almost immediately by a corresponding intake, as the main wall screen came to life. After a quick phantasmagoria of effects, which assured that the signals would be scrambled and reconstituted at the speed of light in both, the Vatican and Montreal, Lena appeared on the screen. Seeing her smiling face, everyone visibly relaxed.

"Welcome to the New World," she announced. In spite of her smile, she sounded serious.

There was a murmur of response. Peter realized that JR was not the only person to whom money was of absolutely no importance. Lena was the other.

"Just as I'm sure you were, we, too, have been privileged to hear the announcement by the President of the United States. I think we can recognize it as a marked evolutionary leap for the American citizenry. If only his suspension of the Second Amendment could be ratified on a long-term basis, we would all benefit greatly from this otherwise as yet undefined state of affairs."

She didn't even mention the collapse of the US dollar. Perhaps it did not have such a great effect in Europe.

Ruth glanced around the table, then fixed her eyes on Lena as though Lena were right there, present in the room. "We were hoping to hear your impressions of the fiscal imbalance that has swept through the United States," she said, still staring at Lena.

"A very interesting development. I believe it leaves Solidarity on a much stronger footing on the North American continent."

That it did. Peter wondered how anyone could be quite so dispassionate about money as Lena sounded. He knew that she cared deeply about just about every member of her organization. It was very much *her* organization. Yet, there she was, as cool, as pragmatic, as only the leader of a movement that had swept the world could be. Peter realized that he could live to be a hundred and fifty, and never become quite so detached. Compared to Lena, he was a bundle of nerves and emotions.

Ruth sat back. "You mean that Solidarity need not take any steps to protect itself from the possible outflow?"

Lena smiled. "You of all people, Ruth, know that Solidarity is not concerned with the making, only with the distribution of wealth. It seems to me that, following the financial fiasco that has overrun the United States, the distribution is likely to become more, and not less, equitable."

JR was smiling from ear to ear. Apparently he was the only one on the Canadian side of the table who was thinking along precisely the same lines.

"B-but all the people who have lost..." an elderly gentleman, Dr. Mendel, in charge of medical insurance, mentioned feebly. Lena made some people nervous.

"...will learn to do with less. Wealth is not defined by the number of dollars you own. It is a state of consciousness. I know millionaires who feel poor. I know paupers who are rich beyond our wildest dreams."

Peter sat back. Behind his closed eyelids he saw the image of the Last Pope. Vincenzo's face beamed back at him. History produced many art collectors. The ancient Pharaohs, the Rajas of India, the Borgias, who besides art had developed expertise in theft, rape, bribery, incest and murder, as had many of their rich, regal, and not so aristocratic contemporaries. Later, numerous Sheikhs and Emirs kept up the good work, and were eventually followed by a number of billionaires. They all had riches beyond rhyme or reason. Yet none could equal the artistic heritage of the Holy Roman Catholic Church. It wasn't that popes, with the possible exception of Julius II, claimed exclusive ownership of their heritage. But they certainly treated it as their own, private domain, over which they wielded absolute power. Anyone who disagreed with them was executed or condemned, often in this world and in the next.

And then came the Last Pope—the man who had given away more than any man in the history of the world. Who had given away everything he had, or held sway over, and had become rich, as Lena had said, beyond anyone's wildest dreams.

Vincenzo, my friend...

Silence continued to stretch. Peter expected such words from Winston, but Lena?

"So Solidarity need take no steps to counteract the present conditions..." an ancient-looking man spoke haltingly, as though still trying to understand what had happened. He was looking after the Church's heritage in North America. A challenge not many could meet. He alone needed money to do justice to the artworks under his tutelage.

"We have a duty to protect our members as best we can, and..." Ruth knew Francis Morton, Ph.D., the man who spoke, as a man who cared deeply about the job with which he had been entrusted, "...and the heritage, but never at the expense of our members. We have the duty to uphold our constitution, not to make anyone rich."

"Remember our motto," Lena said softly, hardly above a whisper. "It is not how good you are. It is how hard you work to be as good as you can be."

Peter relaxed even more. This was not a brain-storming session to overcome financial difficulties. This was a briefing conference to make sure that no member of Solidarity International would get, in any way, involved in what happened south of the border. Peter glanced at JR. By then, his friend was busy examining his nails. He seemed miles away, as though his interests lay elsewhere. They did. He was working out, in his head, the number of new members SI would gain as a result of the upheavals.

Peter felt that he'd never really analyzed the real motivations behind the Solidarity movement. It may have begun in the Stocznia Gdańska, in Poland, where, in 1970, Lech Walesa mobilized the Polish workers to stand up for their rights against the Soviet oppressors, but this was a very different organization. These people were no longer against things; they were *for* a superior mode of living. Paradoxically, had he known that his granddaughter would sit on the throne of the Vatican, Lech Walesa would have turned in his grave. Lech was a devout Roman Catholic at a time when the Church was instrumental in keeping up the Polish spirit. Now? The old Vatican was no more. Nor was the Soviet Union. Nor was the Church—at least, not in its previous form.

This was a very different world.

So I am safe, Peter thought, and immediately was ashamed of thinking, again, of his own interests. He remembered Winston's words, "If there is one evil worse than power, it is the self. The ego." Peter never forgot those words. He also never managed to overcome the warning inherent in them.

For the next ten minutes Ruth and Lena exchanged some administrative matters, which were of relatively little interest to those present. There were no more instructions to give, not as such, but rather a consolidation and reiteration of policies which motivated the Solidarity's principles.

"We are not after power," Lena repeated. "We refuse to tell people what to do. We offer our way of life to all that wish to participate in it. That is all. That must remain all."

The screen went blank.

Peter was reasonably satisfied. But if Solidarity was such an upstanding organization, why did Ruth approve of the scheme that JR concocted at his instigation? Perhaps the temptations were becoming too great even for the stalwart members of the Solidarity? Even for people who for years had been living in what might be called financial abstinence?

Were members of Solidarity becoming the new righteous? Were they the new Order of Knights in shining armour that lived according to the dictates of the New Age?

Am I the odd man out?

That evening, at home, Peter decided to tell Cathy about the meeting. He had been working for Solidarity for a few years, but he'd never joined the movement. He'd never become a full member. An associate, they called him. He just shared in all the privileges but had no moral obligation to conform to the constitution. As a matter of fact, he'd never read it. The reason he objected to full membership was that he refused to have an electronic beeper inserted subcutaneously under his hairline. "What if I went bald?" he'd asked them at the time.

It may have been his medical background or, what is more likely, his latent memories of the last three verses of chapter 13 in the Revelation of John.

> *He causes all, the small and the great, the rich and the poor, and the free and the slave, to be given marks on their right hands, or on their foreheads; and that no one would be able to buy or to sell, unless he has that mark, the name of the beast or the number of his name. Here is wisdom. He who has understanding, let him calculate the number of the beast, for it is the number of a man. His number is six hundred sixty-six.*

To the best of Peter's knowledge, the identification tag inserted subcutaneously near members' foreheads had nothing to do with the number 666. Nor were the members limited in their shopping; but it did control their unobstructed access to the Solidarity building and/or installations. This included bank accounts, their line of credit, and Medicare. He felt his freedom would be impaired. Cathy was completely free from any superstitions. She thought such an insert was no more than a convenience.

"You know, darling, this Solidarity bunch, well, there's a lot more to them than meets the eye," Peter mused aloud.

She began watching him over the top of the book she was trying to read. She didn't comment.

"And that Lena woman, well, she's really something…"

Cathy put her book down. She knew her reading was over for the evening. Lately Peter was either lost in thoughts, or in need of sharing them.

"It seems, almost, as if the good of the Vatican has rubbed off on Lena, leaving all the negative aspects buried with the old... the old..."

"Regime?" Cathy smiled sweetly. He kept forgetting that Cathy was not really a Christian.

"What a strange word to use."

Although Peter was, as he called it, completely "cured" of the religion of his youth, there were still hang-ups that lingered in the dark corners of his mind.

"I know what you mean. Lena brought with her a new-world feeling, a freshness, that truly inspires people to discover within themselves their very best."

"What a wonderful way of putting it..." he murmured.

For the first time in a week, Peter dreamt that he was dreaming. He saw Cathy's face reflected in the window. They were both looking at a beautiful garden. They felt that soon, very soon, they'd both be walking there. Side by side. As it should be. The garden was even more beautiful than the one in the Vatican. And this is how he knew he was dreaming: he could actually smell the roses—through the glass. And he realized that it may not have been a dream after all. It may have been Cathy's hair he smelled, not the roses. Or... perhaps both?

Peter switched on the small bedroom TV. He wanted to see the news. Lena may have been above it all, but Peter's feet were still planted firmly on the ground. Peter half listened, half read the strip at the bottom of the screen which added more news for the discriminating customers.

As so often lately, his mind was wandering.

Newton was right, he thought. Every object in a state of uniform motion tends to remain in that state of motion unless an external force is applied to it. He remembered that from school. Now, however, an external force had been applied to the US financial system. It was no longer in uniform motion. In fact, it could be said that, for the last two days, it had remained static. Until recently, the market, controlled by a small group of people, continued to unfold, without interruption, and would have continued to unfold until...? Until what? An inevitable collapse? Or until an external force supplied by JR affected its course. There was absolutely no doubt in Peter's mind that the market would have collapsed soon, in a few months at most, regardless of JR's intervention. Only, the later it collapsed, the greater would be the damage the collapse would have caused. He thought of each electronic message orbiting the earth at the rate of some 27,000 every single hour.

But, he reasoned, there is also Newton's Third Law of Motion. It states that for every action there is an equal and opposite reaction. This was more difficult to discern.

The Third Law could be interpreted in a number of ways. First, money represented power. By definition, as Winston once told him, power precludes love. Power separates the rich from the poor, the greedy from the generous, the takers from the givers. In this respect, the Power of Washington could be said to lie in direct contrast to the aims of Solidarity. The two philosophies were unfolding the world in diametrically opposite directions. Solidarity was the antithesis of power. The SI leaders were rewarded in the same way as all members who offered all their efforts for the betterment of their community. This could not be said for the Washington Clique. This included the Executive, the Lawmakers and even the Judicial arm of the Triumvirate of Power. Wall Street with all its tentacles was but the consequence of the underlying philosophy. The Triumvirate, like the Holy Trinity of the past, imposed its power on all citizens, though on some much more so than on others.

Soon it became abundantly evident that one cannot wield power unless there is someone on whom it can be wielded. The beast needs slaves to feed on.

Cathy was watching the TV over his shoulder.

But there is more... he sensed her immersed in his thought stream.

For thousands of years, people wanted to be governed. They elected priests, kings, presidents, also governors, senator, mayors, even sheriffs or policemen, to tell them what to do, how to behave. And then—and now, in a profoundly intangible way, we all became immersed in the Age of Aquarius. Each man, each woman, each soul wanted, or had to learn, to tend to their own garden.

That's what Winston had said.

"Originally power was wielded by gods. By Elohim. Don't forget, Peter, Elohim is plural. The deities of the Old Testament were strict, unforgiving, vengeful. Two thousand years later a man said that 'I and my father are one'."

"And now, dear Cathy?" All along she was following his train of thoughts. "And now it seems that, at long last, we have to learn to cater for ourselves. If we'd wasted the last four thousand years, the ages of ram and fish, if we came to this age unprepared... our thoughts scattered, our neighbours set apart, we will not cope. We shall vacate our bodies and wait till the age of Kali runs its course, and Brahma falls asleep, once again, to dream of another reality."

"Peter, look," she pointed to the small screen.

The impressive figure of the President, John Herbert Walker, flanked by two senior vice presidents, stood before a battery of microphones. Since the population of the USA reached five hundred million, four VPs were being elected—two executive and two senior assistants to the president.

For a minute or two, there was silence. The four VPs stood like mummies—immobile, frozen in time. They didn't even blink. Almost immediately, Peter realized that all four were androids. Who knows, perhaps so was the president, although he did blink once or twice. Perhaps he was a later model? Then the president's eyes centered on the lens of the camera. He spoke with a well-modulated voice, like one trained in the art of elocution.

> "Fellow Americans. It has been brought to our notice that a new pandemic of unknown origin is spreading in various parts of the country. The Martial Law Committee headed by Senator John McBeegh has decided that, starting tomorrow, the Department of Health will initiate a mass vaccination program of all citizens of the United States of America. Due to the virility of the virus, the program is compulsory. It applies to all citizens of all ages. Those who decline will be excluded from access to the food distribution centers, which are opening in all parts of the country. We shall keep you advised of all developments."

"And thus control your coming and your going," Peter said, a twisted smile on his lips.

"So it has begun?"

"*...and the rich and the poor, and the free and the slave, will be given marks on their foreheads,*" Peter quoted from memory, adapting the prophecy to the present time. "*And no one would be able to buy or to sell...* or gain access to the food-banks."

"I bet the vaccine has 666 stamped on its label in invisible ink." Cathy completed his thought.

"Yes, darling, it has begun. Famine is next."

***

14
Jonathan and Moira

Winston Smith joined the Thornton family on that fateful day when he presented himself at Ruth's door, bearing a letter from Andrew. It took place soon after Ruth's husband died in an accident at the construction site on the Yang Tse river. Winston Smith remained with Ruth, Jonathan and Moira ever since. He went through the stages of a butler, a cook, a general factotum, then majordomo, and finally a cherished member of the family. Throughout that time, he managed to maintain a certain distance of respect, rather than servility. He never abused his position in the household, though it would be hard to imagine how he could. He was loved equally by Ruth and Peter, and absolutely adored by the children. For many years Peter benefited from his elusive presence. In a peculiar, incomprehensible way, Winston managed to be all things to all people; to supply everyone's needs, from fulfilling domestic chores to acting as the most valuable adviser to all of them. Even now, Peter, though living apart, when he came across a true dilemma, first turned his thoughts to Winston.

"What would Winston have done?"

This question, though often *à contre coeur*, almost invariably provided the answer. Winston was just as inimitable at a distance as he was face to face. Perhaps indomitable would be a better word.

On many occasions Winston made his presence known in no uncertain ways. Peter could not only hear his words clearly annunciated, seemingly at the back of his head, but he could see the majordomo's considerable bulk standing before him, to wit, in flesh and blood, only to dissolve into the air minutes, or seconds, later. Originally Peter assumed that his imagination was playing tricks on him; that he suffered from overwork, exhaustion, even peripheral bouts of schizophrenia. Over time, however, he'd given up such facile explanations.

Cathy shared Peter's sentiments.

"Winston is Winston," she said, her jade eyes filling with wonder. "You don't question his comings and goings. You appreciate his presence. In person, or hovering within your head."

That was roughly how Peter felt about him; only in his case, there was just a smidgen of jealousy that he, Peter, couldn't match any of Winston's accomplishments. Not even his cooking. At any rate, this was Sunday afternoon, and Winston had said he'd drop in today. To the best of Peter's recollection, this was the first time, ever, that Winston actually announced himself. Usually... he only announced others: guests or visitors.

Peter's thoughts were interrupted by the door chime.

The tall man bowed as though being admitted to the Holy of Holies. As he straightened up, his hands were still held together.

"*Namaste*," he said.

"*Namaste*," Winston repeated, facing Cathy.

Peter and Cathy both returned the *anjali mudra*, the Hindu salutation, which meant many things to many people. Usually it meant simply: "I bow to you." At a deeper level, it said: "I bow reverentially to you." In Winston's case the meaning went still deeper. It really said, "I salute the immortal perfection that resides within you." That, and not less. His posture and his tone attested to that. Winston didn't believe in imaginary gods. His divinities were real, tangible, yet omnipresent.

After early unfortunate events in Winston's career in Canada, he'd sailed to India, where he'd spent a considerable time at the feet of a number of teachers. Swamis, they called them. Like *Namaste*, the title has many meanings in Sanskrit, but as regarding Winston, it meant 'spiritual teacher.' When telling Peter about it, Winston had smiled. "It's a little misleading," he'd said. "He never spoke about spirits." It was a rare, Winston-type joke.

On his return home to Canada, Winston brought a number of customs with him, rare, exotic customs, which enriched his own as well as Peter's life. Like the *Namaste* greeting. What could be more beautiful, Peter thought, than to salute the 'real' you?

"The children missed you," were Winston's next words. "They asked me to speak for both of them, and ask if either of them had offended you in any way."

Peter wished he could disappear into the ethers, as Winston often did. He felt guilty, ungrateful, selfish.

"I have no excuse," he mumbled.

"Wonderful," Winston answered and clapped his hands.

The front door opened and two smiling faces danced into the living room. Mo ran to Cathy, Jo to Peter. A moment later, as though on command, they changed directions, with Mo jumping up to reach and hang on Peter's neck.

"I missed you, Uncle. I really did," she said.

Jonathan seconded the motion. There was no bitterness, no accusation of any sort. Just a shadow of sorrow that now was dispelled by the present reunion.

"Mommy's in the office," Jo explained. "Uncle Winston told us that you wanted to see us."

"And then she's going to a function," Mo added. She would not be left behind in providing Uncle Peter with information. She did not elucidate what function her mother intended to attend.

Peter gave Winston a grateful glance. It was just like him to think of others. How could Winston know? On the other hand, how does he know everything else? Peter suspected that Winston had access to everyone's mind. He certainly did to his. And Cathy's. And the children's, of course. Sometimes Peter found it difficult to separate his own thoughts from those that he suspected had been generated by Winston. It was as though the two of them became of one mind. It never lasted, but he treasured those moments of inexplicable union. Some time ago, Peter had had the same impression when he met the Last Pope.

Peter really wished he could see the children more often. Ruth and Andrew had adopted both when Ruth learned that their parents had died in an accident. Only a few years later, the children had lost a father for the second time. It was soon after that tragedy that Peter had moved in with them. Peter never imagined that he could take Andrew's place; but, at the time, he was a hard-working resident at the Montreal General Hospital, and one could do worse than having him as a male role model. Later Winston appeared on the scene, but at the time theirs was a very different relationship. While Peter was quite willing to 'horse around' on the thick carpet, or pretend to play cricket in the backyard, or chase squirrels on Mount Royal, Winston was a combination of a grandfather and a figure of authority such as few children ever encountered. It was a very strange household.

In those days, Peter used to address Winston by his surname. Smith this, Smith that. He thought it proper form to address a butler in this fashion. Winston never batted an eyelid. He acted as a good and proper butler should. He even served Peter his Friday night Dry Martinis. Later, after Winston had single-handedly saved his life, Peter couldn't believe how smug he must have sounded. Most of all, Winston was not even his butler, only Ruth's. Yet...

He caught Winston's smile.

He remembered, belatedly, that Winston was privy to all his thoughts, even the most intimate ones. Effortlessly, without any probing whatever. Not by surreptitious peeking, only, well... by becoming one with his mind, even though he didn't quite understand what Winston had meant by that.

There is no essential difference between self and other.

Peter heard Winston's words as clearly as if they'd been spoken aloud. Then Winston's smile lightened his face. *In fact, it seems that self is an illusion.*

Serves you right for asking stupid question in your own head, Peter scolded himself.

There are no stupid questions... he heard Winston's voice, again, coming from within himself. Peter knew the rest of the adage: ...there are only stupid answers.

He suddenly noticed that both children had been watching and listening to this exchange. When it was over, Moira smiled. Jonathan murmured, "There, I told you so!"

"No, you didn't," came a prompt reply.

"Yes, I..."

They noticed Winston gazing at them and thought better than to pursue their constant competition. At the same time, Peter realized that there was an even closer communion between Winston and the children than between the majordomo and himself. Perhaps the children had no hang-ups about accepting pearls of wisdom from a butler.

When will I learn, he mused.

Cathy served tea and cold drinks for the children. There was also a tray of chocolate biscuits, which she remembered Mo and Jo loved.

"How are you progressing with your exercises?" Winston asked.

Peter knew intuitively that his friend was asking about his dream and out-of-body attempts. He also knew that Winston was more aware of his progress than he was himself.

"I know, my friend. The beginnings are always hard. Remember the auras?" Winston murmured.

Peter remembered the endless hours he'd spent in front of a mirror trying to discern even a most illusive outline of colour outside the contours of his head. Now, he glanced around. Cathy displayed a wonderful blue with tiny sparks of gold. Both children's, though small, were almost as pure as

Winston's gold that Peter had seen once in Westmount, though the children's auras did fluctuate rather a lot, touching all colours of the rainbow. As for Winston, he kept his directed inward. Should he relax his control, the room would have been filled with sunshine.

Peter nodded. "Harder than I imagined," he answered.

"You mustn't try so hard, my friend," Winston spoke aloud, though very softly. "Did you know, if you stimulate your right parietal cortex with an electrode, you'll have an out-of-body experience?"

How did he know about the parietal cortex, Peter mused.

"It's in your head," Winston answered. "You would feel that you were floating near the ceiling, watching your own body down below."

"Are you saying that it's all… it's all a physiological, or just a neurological, hallucination?"

"No, Peter. I am saying that if all you want is an OBE, then there are easier ways to achieve it."

Peter would have to digest this statement later. At the moment, he noticed that sometimes when Winston spokes, Mo and Jo seemed to freeze in their tracks, their attention riveted to every word the majordomo was saying. This time, however, they continued to play Scrabble with Cathy, as if the three of them were alone.

There was only one possible answer. Both children were already adepts at soul travel. But what of Cathy? Surely, she was just beginning, just as he was. Surely… not my Cathy…

Peter felt as though she'd sold him out. He felt betrayed, as if treachery were taking place under his own roof.

Cathy didn't look up from her game. Perhaps she was involved deeper with the children than he was. What if it was just a game? It wasn't the game that mattered, it was the children.

Why am I thinking all the time of myself?

For the umpteenth time this week, Peter felt deeply ashamed of himself. It was at this moment that he felt

Winston's presence. Not his physical presence, but that inimitable feeling that all is right, all is as it should be. The peace that, in his experience, only Winston could offer and sustain.

"What am I to do?"

"Heaven, Peter, is for the adventurous. For the brave," Winston's voice whispered in his head.

Peter had nothing he could say. He felt lost. In spite of Cathy and Winston and the children, he felt deeply alone. Also, Winston had never used the word heaven before. What did he mean by that? Peter was sure he did not intend to convey the image of the conventional, religious type of heaven to which, if we were nice, we were supposed to tiptoe after death. Whatever that was.

What am I to do, he asked silently, feeling a lot younger than either Mo or Jo.

"Do you remember Chez Gaston?"

Winston looked deeply into his eyes, and seconds later Peter saw a drab, dark room, upstairs, in which he'd spent months healing others and destroying himself. It was as real, as tangible, as though he were there right now. He nodded, feeling weakness in all his bones.

"Why do you think you had run yourself down to such a degree?"

Peter recalled becoming weaker and weaker, until finally he'd collapsed in total exhaustion.

"It was like trying to have an OBE by stimulating your brain with electrodes." Even in his head he felt Winston's compassionate smile. "It wasn't you, Peter, who did the healing. Not the physical, transient you. Why did you assume the consequences upon yourself?"

Peter shrugged uncomfortably. He was just beginning to see the distant light. Everything at the seminary pointed to what would happen after he died. Eternal life... only, you had to die first. Peter never understood this overwhelming predilection of people, who supposedly believed in eternal life, yet remained committed and preoccupied with death and dying. Perhaps this is why he took up medicine. He wanted to serve the living. Alas, power greater than his buried that dream.

Sometimes he mused that his own drive to find the intangible, like the auras, or his quest for an out-of-body experience, was nothing more than a committed attempt to escape death. Did he do it out of fear? He closed his eyes, in an attempt to concentrate.

Winston's face shimmered in front of his own.

"Well, Peter, is it out of fear?"

"No. It is not. If I really did have a motivation other than fear, then it must have been curiosity. I suppose, what I really wanted to find was my own true nature."

"You refused to accept that your biological body is all there is?"

"I suppose so."

"Well? Is it?"

It was a strange question to pose to a physician. Actually, an ex-physician, he reminded himself. And for some reason, for the very first time, the answer that formed in his mind pleased him.

"Uncle Peter, it's your turn. Aunt Cathy has beaten both of us. Now you try." Jo was standing before him, hands akimbo, his chin thrust out, refusing to take no for an answer.

"Aunt Cathy beats everybody. That's not fair," he whimpered. He did his best to look miserable, which precipitated a burst of laughter from both children.

The game was already set up. The problem Peter faced was how to lose the game without Mo and Jo's reading his mind, or his facial expression, that he was doing it on purpose. It wouldn't do if his guests lost two games in a row.

He needn't have worried.

By the time Cathy, with the welcome assistance from Winston, whipped up a small dinner, Peter lost fair and square, without even trying. He didn't have to cheat at all.

"And next time, don't even think about it," Mo threw over her shoulder. Peter pretended not to understand what she was talking about. Mo appeared to have dismissed the idea of Peter's intended cheating and concentrated on food.

While Peter lived in Westmount, he and the children had, obviously, seen each other daily. It had been difficult to see the process of growing up advancing at the usual pace. Then, when Francis Drake moved in, and Ruth told him that the 'Commander' had been programmed to be 'very nice with children', Peter thought, or imagined, that he'd been replaced by a later model. Apparently not so. Children learned as much from other people's mistakes as from their own. Androids don't make mistakes. In addition, they had been growing up with Winston watching their every move. And that was a very different cup of tea altogether.

Now, after hardly a few months of living apart, Peter couldn't shake the idea that both Mo and Jo had surpassed him on the road of self-discovery. They may have left him a long way behind.

Lately, Peter was not at his best, but the next morning he did spot two more androids, very unorthodox ones, pretending to be busy on the roof heliport of Headquarters. He called in JR, and when he told him about it, JR looked surprised.

"I changed all security guards on the roof yesterday. That's impossible," he looked both surprised and disgusted. "We rotate them to make sure they stay sharp and don't go to sleep on the job. Once they get used to a place... Anyway, did you notice their badges?"

"No, JR. I always try to keep my distance, if possible. If I get too close, they have been known to run under cover, remember?"

"Of course. Sorry. You just make me nervous. First Rome and now this."

"Rome?"

"You know, the Vatican. They had a break-in, some files are missing. They didn't find any fingerprints or..."

"Android don't have to have any," Peter said.

"We have no idea if they were androids, Peter. You are becoming obsessed. Well, maybe not," he corrected himself. "Not with the guys on the roof. What worries me is that we all thought the Vatican defenses were impregnable."

Only now did JR fold his legs and slide down on the armchair. "I've got to take it a bit more easy," he confessed to himself. Actually, for the first time he looked haggard.

"There is something else, isn't there," Peter half read his thoughts, and half guessed from his facial expression.

JR looked at Peter as though weighing if he should confide in him. Then he shrugged. "You'll find out sooner or later. Francis has been neutralized."

"Francis Drake? The Commander? Ruth's bodyguard?"

JR nodded. "We still don't know how they did it. Last night he went out on some pretext and never came back. Smith called me about midnight. My men found him at the bottom of the street, near Sherbrooke. He'd been run down by a heavy truck."

"I thought androids, or enhanced clones, have fantastic reflexes..."

"That's why I'm worried. I think the Yankees are playing tit for tat. Only less elegantly."

For a while they sat in silence. Peter was sorry. Francis Drake really did remind him of his brother Andrew. Peter knew that Drake was a semi-artificial creation, but, well, it was as Ruth said. It was like looking at a three-dimensional portrait of his late brother.

"Did I tell you the twosome seemed unorthodox?"

"In what way?"

"Well, you couldn't really put your finger on it, but they seemed, well, imperfect."

"So if it hadn't been for the absence of what you call aura, they would have gone unnoticed?"

"Probably."

Peter decided to be kind. JR seemed to have forgotten that the guard at the front desk, though 'eminently' perfect, also remained unrecognized until Peter had pointed him out. "They were—unrecognized, I mean. I checked the files. They've been around for some months. Maybe longer. Moles, I presume."

"You mean recruited or implanted long before they might be needed..."

"That's how I see it," Peter remembered his experiments at the Houses of Parliament, in Ottawa. Those agents had also been around for a while, without any destructive instructions. "Just sort of waiting for a better day."

"Better for whom?" JR said through his teeth. He didn't find it amusing.

JR had to determine what might have been the possible, let alone probable, purpose for the androids stationed on the roof. He was all too aware of Ruth's kidnapping, some time ago, which turned out to be little more than a show of strength. Not very wise, as it precipitated very stringent security measures. Apparently, not stringent enough.

Obviously, JR was thinking of our friends from below the 50th parallel. The Sino-Indian bloc was still preoccupied in gaining control, and extending their influence, into Russia and Africa. At least for now, South America appeared to remain reasonably neutral. Nevertheless, SI must have been stepping on someone's toes. Or else, not for the first time and notwithstanding the economic problems, the USA could have been just flexing their muscles.

"Thanks, Peter. I'll make sure the two guys are being watched."

Before leaving, they made arrangements for Peter to point out the two culprits from a distance, so that JR could take appropriate measures. At this stage, the exercise seemed innocuous. Little more than house-cleaning. It seemed that way. Neither thought the matter was overly pressing. After all, the two androids were only two of about a dozen security agents occupying the heliport landing pad and the ancillary buildings on the roof. There was little they could do but report to their master on the comings and goings of visitors, and Solidarity International always prided itself of having few secrets.

"We are an open organization. What little privacy we indulge in is only to protect the interests of our members," Lena liked to repeat.

It was the interests of the members that worried JR. He was responsible for their physical safety, and he made no secret about it.

Slightly enervated, Peter decided to double his efforts on his inspection rounds, in case the Yankees, as JR continued to call them, tried some other tricks. What Peter found deeply annoying was that, even during his days at the Montreal General, he had counted the Americans among his best friends. Their medical research was aboveboard. They were highly intelligent, often brilliant, invariably generous in both the material sense, such as granting scholarships, and sharing their knowledge. He couldn't help but like and admire them. Later, he found it difficult to accept that such wonderful people could be lumbered with such an inexplicably morally bankrupt ruling class.

"They say that all people have the governments they deserve. I don't believe this is true of the Americans," he had told Cathy only the other day.

"They are trusting, which makes them too credulous. They've all been hoodwinked," she had agreed.

It seemed like the only explanation; that, and their dismal participation in their elections. They must have been already disenchanted with their politicians.

To this day Ruth continued to receive, at her home address, sporadic invitations for Peter to attend various medical symposia. Peter never officially resigned from his Fellowship. It was kept for him, in abeyance, as if he might, one day, lose his healing ability. What a strange world this is, he mused, that healing power disqualifies me from being a physician. And then he remembered the handful of men blessed, or cursed, with unusual healing powers, most of them destroyed by the medical establishment. Arigo, Groening, Cayce, more recently Cabez and Kordos and many others all the way back to biblical times.

Peter followed JR to his office and borrowed the disguise he'd worn during the Main Lobby caper. The demise of Francis Drake—clone or not—did egg him on to increase his efforts. He couldn't accept that a clone, with highly enhanced reflexes, would not have been able to avoid a track running into him, without very knowledgeable and determined efforts on the part of the driver. Had the driver also been an android?

Peter donned his disguise and returned to the roof. There he positioned himself at the reading desk, where pamphlets praising Montreal's sites of interest were strewn to tempt important visitors who were waiting for helicopters, or to be picked up by a welcoming committee. The waiting room offered a panoramic view of the arrival area.

He didn't have to wait long. Not more than twenty meters away, Peter noticed two men carrying some sort of equipment towards the landing platform. They were accompanied with two more men, who exhibited a conspicuous absence of an aura.

Peter directed his telescopic lens at the quartet, ran about twenty high-speed snapshots, and put the camera back in his pocket.

Next Peter tapped on his electronic notebook, then again on the computerized schedule. "10:00 a.m., replacing landing lights to be completed before dusk," it said. But why would security guards perform the functions of maintenance men? He tapped JR's security bulletin and twitted the question.

> Until further notice, maintenance work at points of access and/or egress (there was a lengthy list that included the Until further notice, maintenance work at points of access and/or egress (there was a lengthy list that included the main lobby, the roof, garages, service door and others) will be carried out with enhanced security procedures.

He supposed that meant the security guards would have to get their fingers a little dirty. He scratched himself under the false beard and discreetly left the waiting room. The ID plate hanging on his neck, under his shirt, opened the door for him. Without it, he could have been arrested by the two androids. Wouldn't that be funny?

He didn't laugh.

Minutes later, JR was examining the photos. He shook his head in disbelief.

"I spoke to these guys yesterday. They sure looked normal to me. What is more, they've been around for years…"

He sank back in his armchair. His face lost its ruddy colour. "Good God, Peter. They've found a way to insert substitutes for the regular employees."

"They are very smart people," Peter murmured. He remembered better days, when this would have been a compliment.

***

15
Ruth Thornton

In 1945, **Sir Winston Churchill,** historian, writer, and artist, also at the time the Prime Minister of the United Kingdom, was deeply convinced that the British Empire still matched the USA as an economic power. Alas, even a man of his indisputable stature had been wrong. There is an adamant mistress that controls the world. Her name is Fate. She would make us utterly helpless if it weren't for one fact. She invariably acts in a predictable way.

The rule is quite simple.

A man is born as a tiny, helpless baby. Slowly, ever so slowly, he eats, absorbs, matures. He grows, learns, expands his vision, his area of influence. His wealth. Sometimes, he or she becomes powerful. And then, one day, by accident or design, he or she dies. Suddenly. Often, with hardly a whimper. A hundred years of life extinguished in seconds.

The rules of economics are similar.

An empire that had its birth at the end of the 15th century, after expanding for some 450 years, died almost overnight, with hardly a whimper. That is the secret that Fate assigned to us. It takes years, centuries, to grow a successful economy. It takes as long to build an empire—the collapse, however, is almost instantaneous. No matter what efforts had been made by Winston Churchill, Anthony Eden or even Margaret Thatcher, the fate had already been written in the sand. *The Moving Finger writes, and having writ, moves on.*

Omar Khayyam was right, even in 1859 he knew. The British Empire was over.

The United States of America were no different. For years they towered over the rest of the world. Not just militarily, but economically. The mighty dollar was the preferred reserve currency the world over. And then, almost suddenly, in 2030 China's GDP overtook that of the US. Eleven years later, the same became true of India. By 2053 the GDP of the USA had been surpassed by Brazil.

The USA became one of many.

For a number of years, the US presidents doubled over to save the financial empire. Alas, the president proposes, the Congress disposes. And already for years, Congress had been in the pockets of an army of pollsters who advanced the causes of Plutocracy. The USA fiscal policies became untenable. They thrived on debt, like leeches attached to the rest of the world. And then came the second wave of Ponzis.

The final collapse was unavoidable. Overnight, the USA went bankrupt. But... but they had to blame someone. They had to find a scapegoat. The most convenient culprit lay next door. Solidarity International.

They did it! It was Them!
They destroyed the economy!
Socialists!!
Communists!!!

Not the overwhelming national debt, nor living on credit to maintain one's undeserved standard of living, not the small minority living in obscene abundance at the expense of the majority, but Solidarity International.

The accusations were many. They needed a scapegoat. Few remembered who the communists were, but SI was relatively well known even in the States.

The first article appeared in the New York Times on December 1, 2071. The title displayed a single word.

T H E M

The word was plastered across the whole width of the front page. The citizenry had long indulged in science fiction—light on science, so as not to offend their sensibilities or overstrain their intellect—which seemed to sate the need of the common man for adventure at someone else's expense. THEM became the rallying cry. US and THEM. Many, for the first time in months, read their paper. The message was simple.

If it weren't for Solidarity International, none of our present woes would have happened.

THEY were responsible. It was **THEM**. That was enough. THEY will pay.

The other dailies picked up the tune, and on the next day Solidarity International became the two most-hated words in the English language.

On the third night of December, in the middle of a snowstorm, Ruth Thornton's bodies were thrown, in a heap, in front of the Houses of Parliament, in Ottawa. Not just her body, but hers and a dozen others, androids, identical to her in appearance. They lay in a pyre. The copies were no longer of any use. They became redundant, like the original. JR noted that the Americans must have been preparing for this for some time. Why else produce such a number of Ruth's doppelgangers? No one claimed responsibility. No one admitted to the guilt. Someone had to pay. Ruth was selected from the available choices. She was at the top of SI North America. The buck stopped at her feet.

THEY PAID, said the next headline. Followed with an early Merry Christmas.

Ruth's body was brought back to Montreal the same day. Also the same day, her ashes were scattered in the tiny park on the top of Westmount. That was were Andrew's ashes fed the trees that seemed to grow in great profusion. Peter held Jonathan and Moira's hands. Behind him Cathy, Winston, JR, Dr. and Mrs. Brent stood quietly. It was a spur-of-the-moment funeral. No one said anything. They all had their own, private memories. They all loved her. Some part of them died with her.

The wake took place in the Thornton Westmount residence. Pete and Cathy stayed overnight. Later Mo and Jo would move in with them. Or they would move to the house. It did not really matter, as long as they were together.

On Friday, the week following Ruth's funeral, two official-looking gentlemen knocked on the door of the Westmount residence, where Winston and both children continued to reside. The fact that the children had actually been staying with Peter and Cathy had apparently escaped their notice.

The two men stated that a certain lady, from across the street, who preferred to remain anonymous, had lodged a complaint at the local police station that two very young teenagers were staying alone with a strange-looking old man in the house. Apparently two other men, both looking as suspicious, were also seen meandering the grounds. The lady said that she was watching the house for some time, and was greatly concerned about the children's safety.

"Really, she'd said, two young teenagers, no parents and that strange-looking man, and those other men? I mean really, you know, I ask you, she'd said," said the policemen, reading from his notebook. "And now, Sir," concluded the plainclothes policemen, "we are asking you…"

Winston invited both plainclothes into the hall, then, with stoic persistence began to look into the first man's eyes. A moment later, he did the same with the second man. The two security guards who, Peter insisted, should remain on the premises after Ruth's death, seemed to ignore the whole affair. Winston had looked into their eyes before.

Moments later the two policemen bowed deeply, then saluted, then backed out of the house, turned around, and, still seemingly in a daze, proceeded on their way. The lady from across the street was never heard from again.

He was standing on a small platform, cantilevered over a sheer drop of thousands of feet. Straight ahead, on the other side of the chasm, his eyes followed an eagle that soared, seemingly borne by rising air, until it all but disappeared in the blue sky, from which hung scattered clouds, no bigger than the cotton fields below, from which they may well have originated. Even as Peter looked on, the green hill ahead swelled, darkened, then seemed to split as a single rocky outcrop which extended itself upwards, to create a forbidding aerie. The solitary eagle swooped down from behind the cloud and alit, effortlessly, folding its formidable wings.

"He often comes here at night," Peter heard. The voice sounded familiar.

"He?"

"Couldn't you tell? JR. He thinks of himself so unwieldy on earth that here he spends most of his time flying effortlessly. I never saw him flap his wings. Just rising and falling on air currents. He's very good at that."

Peter thought JR was very good at most things.

"That he is... that's why he's here, so often. Or maybe because of it." A smile followed these words.

Peter was quite spellbound. If this was a dream, then he didn't want it to end.

"Turn around, Peter," a different voice reached him from a distance that was impossible to define. It was a whisper in his ear; it was also a calling from afar, urging him, perhaps, to come closer.

He turned.

No more than ten feet away stood Andrew, his arm draped protectively over Ruth's shoulders. Only he wasn't the Andrew Peter had known and remembered. This man was much younger, perhaps in his late thirties. And Ruth? Ruth was everything Andrew had always said about her before she and Peter met. A beauty such as could, and momentarily did, take Peter's breath away. Yet, unmistakably, it was Ruth. His sister-in-law. The very same Ruth who, only two days ago, had asked him to drop in at her house to see the children more often.

"They do," she'd said. "They really do miss you, brother dear."

Now, she just smiled.

"Hello, Uncle Peter," Mo peeked from behind Ruth's skirt.

"Hello, Uncle Peter," Jo echoed, tugging at Andrew's arm. "Can we go and play now?" They both looked their real age, about 12 and 13 apiece.

"It's all right, Peter," a familiar voice resounded in his head. Then the air shimmered and Winston appeared out of nowhere. "Sorry," he said, "But I couldn't leave Cathy alone."

And out of the same shimmering air Cathy materialized, though, for a moment, she looked anything but material. She was holding on to Winston's hand. "Are we here yet?" she asked.

"Look around you," Winston's arm swept over the panorama. "Welcome to my little…"

"…Kingdom?" Cathy asked, still disbelieving the evidence of her eyes.

"Only in name," Winston corrected. "Actually it is ours. No one holds dominion here. We are all one."

Good old Winston, Peter mused. Always enigmatic. Even here. Winston's response was his usual benevolent smile.

The next moment Cathy was tugging at his elbow. ·

"Peter… Peter! You'll oversleep. Time to get up."

He opened one eye, then, with considerable dismay, the other. "I'll never forgive you for this," he whispered.

"I know. I was there." There was also a trace of sadness in her voice. "It won't go away."

"It just did." Peter was still grumpy.

"No, it didn't. We did. It is still there."

At this Peter sat up, his eyes wide, only now fully awake. "You were there!" he almost shouted.

Cathy looked at him like a mother admonishing a child. "Shhhh, you'll wake the children. Also, I just told you so, darling. We all were."

"Ruth was there," Peter said, hardly believing his own words. "Ruth and… and… Andrew?" Now he was convinced that he was dreaming. But how did Cathy know about this? Do we dream in unison?

"We do all things in unison, even when we are apart," she said softly.

"Now you talk like Winston."

She only smiled. "You'll be late for the office. I suspect, today will be a busy day." She left to prepare breakfast.

"Children? What…" Mo and Jo. They slept overnight. Winston remained alone in the house, in Westmount. The children thought spending the night with Uncle and Aunt would be nice.

Only now it all hit him.

Ruth's death, the pyre in Ottawa, the scattering of her ashes on the top of Westmount… it came back to him like a tsunami. He fell back on the pillows. How come she was there, he mused. *She was dead. I saw the breeze carrying her ashes. What is 'there'… or better still, where is it?*

"Peter," Cathy's voice reached him from the kitchen. She was ahead of his questions. "We are all there. It is here that we come just temporarily."

"Now I know you've been talking to Winston," he grumbled.

He felt that she and Winston conspired to confuse him. Even the children seemed guilty of that. Nevertheless, he jumped out of bed and took a quick shower, which brought him back to reality. Almost. For a while he still hovered in no-man's-land. And then he heard laughter.

"Uncle Peter is soooo funny!" Jonathan said, peeking out of the study where Cathy had prepared makeshift beds for them. For once Moira agreed with him. Perhaps, at long last, they were beginning to act their true age.

"Yes, he is," she affirmed, seemingly surprised at her own acquiescence. "He certainly is," she repeated, nodding gravely.

"Breakfast!"

They both charged to the table in their pajamas.

"Just this once," Cathy admonished.

There was a single grain of luck in all this. The schools were already closed for Christmas. Most of Mo and Jo's tutoring was done at home, but they attended some classes just to develop relationships with other children. It was Winston's advice. Cathy decided to take a few days off, to look after the children. Winston would be coming over later.

Some years ago, Ruth, with Winston in the background, had interviewed eleven prospective teachers before she selected three of them to give Mo and Jo their daily lessons. Those consisted of three subjects only. Math, languages (Latin, Ancient Greek and Sanskrit), and philosophy. After three years, the children had reached the university entry level in all three subjects. When not discerning mathematical patterns to develop algebraic thinking and logic skills, or discussing, in Latin, the influence of Ovid's, yes, Publius Ovidius Naso's *Metamorphoses* on Western Art and Literature, Winston encouraged the most juvenile behaviour Mo and Jo could think of.

"To balance things," he'd say when Ruth thought he was going too far. "We must make sure that they remain children for as long as possible. Once they grow up an ego is born..."

Peter, listening from aside, recalled feeling vaguely uncomfortable. He felt Winston's eyes on the back of his neck, as if he personified the offending ego. It felt as though Winston thought ego to be the greatest sin a man was capable of.

When Peter got to the office, they were all waiting for him in the Lecture Theater. Every head of department, deputy-head, every major consultant, group leaders, research staff, departmental security heads, even the heads of various maintenance groups. In some respects, SI was a very democratic organization. When Peter walked in, everyone stood up. It all happened in near-total silence. There was an atmosphere of sorrow in the darkened hall. They were remembering Ruth Thornton, their Chief. It seemed to Peter that they all loved her, each in his and her particular way. Ruth was the sort of person that generated good spirits. Also a sense of love. Of oneness.

He turned towards the stage. Behind an empty chair in the middle of the long table was a massive bouquet of red roses. It was an explosion of colour among the grayish uniforms most SI members wore. Peter climbed the three steps leading to the stage, mesmerized by the sheer size of the flower arrangement. Then he saw a small note. It said, "We all love you". It was signed Lena Walesa. For a moment Peter thought he smelled the Gardens of the Vatican.

There was a seat reserved for Peter on the stage. Normally he sat at Ruth's right hand. He took his usual seat, as he would upstairs, next to an empty chair. As though on command, everyone sat down.

Peter wasn't quite sure what was happening. He'd never attended a general meeting of SI. His participation was limited to local agendas. After all, he was only an associate member. This time a note had been left for him, in his office, to go to the theater.

JR stood up.

"Thank you all for coming. We are all aware of the tragic circumstances that brought us here today. We all loved Mrs. Thornton, and, I am sure, we shall continue to love her. However, life must go on. We are here to select her successor."

He stopped and looked over the dozen or so people at the main table, then the few hundred in the hall.

"May I have your nominations, please?"

For a moment there was silence. Ruth had been appointed by Lena. She was the first leader on the North American continent and, at the time, there was no one, as yet, to vote for her. The organization had been run from the Vatican. Now, Ruth had created a structure that functioned independently though in full cooperation and with approval of Lena Walesa.

John Robb, as the Chief of SI Canada, took interim charge. His intent was to have a secret ballot, but Ruth's murder happened so suddenly that they were all caught unprepared. To vote, one needed candidates, and there were none. JR was the obvious choice. After all, he was running SI Canada and, by all accounts, doing a great job. Of course, if he accepted, they would have to appoint someone else to take over his job. Which would be even harder. Essentially, by now, JR was the CEO, whereas Ruth was more in the nature of a nominal Chairman, or Chairperson, as some liked to call it. In all but name, JR was Ruth's right hand in practically all matters, a job that would not be easy to fill.

The oldest member at the table, Professor J.P. Jackson, Chief of Research in genetics, raised his hand.

"I propose Dr. Peter Thornton," he said in a clear firm voice.

Peter tried to shrink into his chair. He was wracking his brain whom to propose other than JR. He knew that JR was a superb, self-motivating Number Two. Number One needed an overall vision, not a superb compendium of specific expertises.

Two more hands went up.

"I'll second that," said Mrs. Carlton, the vice president of Operations. "Dr. Peter Thornton."

"Dr. Peter Thornton," two more hands went up.

Peter almost laughed. At least six years had passed since he had been referred to as Doctor, so many times, in a single day.

Half the auditorium was standing, the other half was fast rising to their feet. A murmur rose to a clamour of voices, from which one name emerged in constant repetition. The spontaneous hullabaloo changed to a chant.

"Peter Thornton... Peter Thornton... Peter Thornton..."

At least, no more doctor, Peter thought. What am I doing here? I'm not even a member. Not a full member.

JR raised his hands. Quiet returned. He turned to face Peter.

"Peter Thornton. You have been selected by acclamation. Do you accept the leadership of the North American Branch of Solidarity International?"

Peter had no idea what the responsibilities entailed. In desperation he dropped his head to gather his thoughts. This gesture was taken as a nod of acquiescence.

"Ladies and Gentlemen. I give you our new Chief, Doctor Peter Thornton."

No one had ever witnessed JR exhibit a wider smile.

A second pandemonium broke out. Everyone wanted to congratulate him. To shake his hand. To touch him. As the queue filed by the podium, Peter began to feel tired. By the time it was over, he felt exhausted. He sat back and tried to figure out what he had landed himself into. Then he realized that he had no strength to get up. He lingered on. After some ten minutes, JR escorted him to his old office. Time enough to move offices tomorrow. For now, Peter gained computer access to all Ruth's files. There were many Megabytes of them. Many. He began scanning them with progressively bleary eyes. It reminded him of the days he'd been cramming for medical exams. They say that history repeats itself, he mused, but there was no smile on his face. Only wonder.

He discovered that SI had a file on every single member. Nothing intimate, but all the information necessary to be able to assist them. In case of some accident, SI could provide instant response. The organization really cared for its members.

But most of the files dealt with overall policies, relations with public authorities, politicians, industries, manufacturers, people of influence. All areas which, until that moment, Peter had managed to studiously avoid.

Ruth... Ruth... what have you done to me?

Actually it wasn't Ruth. She was willing to continue with this arduous task. It was that old gentleman, who proposed Peter Thornton's name on the ballot. Ballot? It was a farce. There was no ballot. He was sentenced without being allowed to present his defense.

For a moment he closed his eyes.

This is for you, Ruth. And you, Andrew. Have fun.

The next day there were whispers in the corridors of SI Headquarters that a number of people who felt quite sick, but refused to miss the elections, left the hall feeling just fine. They found it a good omen.

When Peter returned home, Winston was already there. Cathy wanted to go shopping, but Winston arrived with enough food for the four of them to last a week. Cathy managed to persuade Winston to stay for dinner. Although Peter had reserved a guestroom for him in the condo, Winston declined to stay the night. He felt the house in Westmount should not be left unattended.

"Frankly, dear Cathy, Mrs. Thornton's house is the only home I've ever known. I like it there. Every square inch has memories."

Cathy understood that. Her job demanded a great deal of traveling, and she often longed for being able to spend somewhere long enough to start calling it home. Now, at last she had it, and it seemed that Winston shared her needs.

Later, the five of them would have to decide if the children were to stay with Peter and Cathy permanently, or if they all should move to Westmount. For now, the kids didn't seem to mind sharing a bedroom. There was no false, puritanical modesty between them. Later they'd make new arrangements.

When Peter got back from Headquarters, he was still reeling from the events of the day. After he'd left the office, JR called Cathy to tell her what happened.

"I'm sure it came as a considerable shock to him, Cathy, but I really couldn't imagine anyone else taking the reins. Please, forgive me."

Cathy was only a little less stunned than Peter.

"But why? He's so... so..."

"He is capable of anything he puts his heart to, Cathy. We both know that."

She couldn't deny that there were few things Peter couldn't do when he tried. She smiled weakly at the mouthpiece and hung up. She was still using the old-fashioned telephone. It continued to offer more privacy than any radio device. "Thanks for letting me know," she whispered to the dead receiver.

There was another surprise awaiting Peter. As he dropped his coat and overshoes in the hall, Winston, of his own accord, presented him with a drink. Peter had long given up his Friday Martinis, but today was special and, in a way, in spite of Ruth's death, it seemed like a time for celebration. It was reminiscent of the old English saying, "The King is dead, God save the King!" As Peter walked in, he was greeted by Winston holding out a silver tray with a very dry Vodka Martini. Like in the old days.

For a while no one mentioned Ruth, or the events of last night. Peter was convinced that it couldn't have been just his individual dream, or a hallucination. It was just *too* real. Anyway, Cathy confirmed that this morning. Did others have similar memories? Winston? The children?

When the main course was over, Winston broached the subject in his usual, impersonal way.

"Most people don't know this, but dreams are often latent memories of the time they've spent there."

There? He remembered. He knew. And the children?

The moment Winston started talking, Mo and Jo replaced their forks on their plates, and sat up even straighter than before. Their eyes seemed drawn by some magnetic force to the old majordomo. To their adopted Uncle.

So they also knew...

"You know, Peter, I met your brother about three months before he met with the accident. Of course, there is no such thing as an accident. But about that later. At the time, Andrew had been diagnosed with a local disease that attacked his liver. The resultant degeneration was already in an advanced stage. In China, then, it was deemed incurable, and here it was quite unknown. I offered to show him the meaning of immortality. He refused."

Peter looked at Cathy, then at the children, and finally he managed to calm himself down. It wouldn't do to interrupt Winston.

"Andrew said that he'd only accept my offer if I swore that I'd also take Ruth across the Great Divide." He looked sadly at the children. "Of course, I couldn't do that. No one is allowed to interfere with the free will of others."

"He refused an offer of immortality?" Cathy's voice was a mixture of incredulity and admiration.

"For the love of a woman..." Peter added, looking at Cathy. I can understand that, he thought. He wouldn't want to be immortal without Cathy at his side.

"No one can offer immortality. We are already immortal. What I offered was a deep awareness of it, which one usually gains from visiting the true realm. With a little practice, and a lot of faith, it can be done with someone's cooperation..."

"Is this how you took me there?" Peter was staring at Winston, as though daring him to deny it.

"My dear boy, I was not aware that it was such a hardship for you."

"And in the Vatican? And the sea shore? And..."

"Peter, I cannot do anything against your will anymore than anyone could be hypnotized against their will. It's a question of tacit agreement. When the consciousness is ready..."

But Peter wasn't listening. He pushed his chair back, walked around the table and embraced Winston, who didn't have a chance to get up. He put his arms around his giant chest and held on for dear life. Later Cathy told him that this was the only time, ever, that she saw Winston embarrassed.

After a little while Peter let go.

"Thank you, my friend," Peter murmured, and walked back to his own place.

It was beginning to dawn on Peter that everyone at this table seemed more advanced in matters of consciousness than he was. Was it consciousness? There had been moments when he was suspecting that up there, wherever 'there' was, was the real thing. That down here, on earth, in this valley of tears, all was imaginary. It was almost as though whatever we imagined, often on the spur of the moment, became our personal reality. Even considering a 150-year life-span, in terms of eternity, it was little more than a wink of an eye. On the other hand, eternity had no time. No beginning and no end. It just was. Or is.

"You are getting there, my friend," he heard Winston's voice, though Winston, in that particular moment, was talking to Jonathan.

Peter was beginning to find all this more and more confusing. And then Winston looked at him and Peter heard distinct words, this time aloud.

"It gets easier after a few million years..." and the huge majordomo winked, precipitating an explosion of laughter from Mo and Jo. Peter had known Winston for a number of years, but he had never, never seen Winston wink before.

This time he decided to get even. Quite openly, he probed Winston's and both children's minds. It didn't seem that they objected. They seemed quite open, accessible. At least now he knew why they were all laughing. After only a minute or two, he'd already forgotten that up there, there is no time. Not really. Unless... unless you chose to make it.

This last paradigm didn't make it any easier, either.

They spent the rest of the time reminiscing about Ruth. The old days, when Peter had just moved into her house, when she was still working at the United Nations, when Winston Smith was a forbidding as well as formidable majordomo.

For the first time, Peter wondered why he saw so little emotion between his late sister-in-law and the children. It was true that they had both been adopted, but the visible signs of affection usually displayed between mother and children were not there. Then he remembered. Ruth and the children must have spent most of their time on the other side of the Great Divide. Up there, in the reality he found so hard to espouse, people were not only affectionate, but, in a way, they intertwined, melted and fused into a single emotional entity. So much more than any human entity is capable of down here, in the dualistic reality, where we seem to celebrate what makes us different, rather than what makes us one.

Which was the true reality? he still wondered.

Then Peter recalled that break-in, in Westmount, when he dislodged an intruder from the upstairs window, breaking his leg, and healing it the next moment. Those were very different days. Yet, Peter missed them. He had virtually no responsibilities then. He was completely self-centered.

"Yes, my boy," Winston said, looking at Peter with paternal love, "you've come a long way." They were a long way off from the days when Peter addressed Winston as Smith, and Smith address Peter as Sir. It was almost a role reversal.

That's funny, Peter mused, and I thought I was just starting. But he didn't probe anyone's thoughts for confirmation. A little humility goes a long way.

There were smiles all around.

Later, as he lay down to sleep, it came to him that only now, after all these years, did he understand why Winston appeared that day at the Westmount residence front door, with a letter from Andrew. It had been to keep his promise to do his best to bring Ruth over, across the Great Divide. All else was just coincidental.

That night he dreamt that he was floating over vast, endless fields, stretching to a horizon where the earth and the sky seemed to merge into one. They were, by some miracle, filled with innumerable flowers. Red roses, each one of them. He was sure that finally he'd mastered access to Winston's Kingdom. And then he saw two men, in wide cowboy hats, galloping towards a farmstead. It turned out he was floating over Canadian prairies. It was a real dream. Only the roses were a gift from Lena.

"Ah, well," he mused, "perhaps heaven is omnipresent, after all?"

***

16

Strings

It was one of those murky, gray, discouraging evenings, when you felt you ought to be doing something but didn't really feel like doing anything at all. The ambience permeated the air, pushing all of them, even Mo and Jo, into the backs of their armchairs. Since Peter's appointment, they all spent most of their evenings together, at the condo, regardless of where they slept. Invariably, Peter was the last to arrive. They were still on temporary footing, unwilling to make a final decision. Winston had a room rented on a lower floor; the children seemed happy, at least for now, to camp in the study.

For once, Cathy had a captive audience. She spent the last half hour explaining the theory of strings and black holes. Talking of strings, she did her best to explain that the fundamental one-dimensional object was, or is, an essential ingredient in string theory. Then she talked about strings' coupling constant, or strings splitting and joining together into one. Then she held their attention when she talked of the vibrational patterns that strings assume. Finally she explained about the first, second, third and fourth superstring revolutions.

"So the fundamental building blocks of nature are not zero-dimensional particles, but minute one-dimensional threads we call strings."

No one contradicted her. Peter tried to look interested, Winston drew his shaggy brows together, and the children, very slowly, backed out of the room and disappeared into the study. *En passant*, she mentioned how the Schwarzschild solution permitted the existence of black holes, and concluded with an emotional treatise about the devastating rupture that spacetime suffers in the vicinity of a singularity...

She sounded like a walking encyclopedia of theoretical physics.

"Don't you find it just fascinating?" she asked, nearly breathless. "Just imagine..."

Peter thought it was time to change the subject.

"You continue to educate us, Cathy, in the *how* of things. Don't you ever ask the *why*?" He stressed the two adverbs.

"I leave that to the philosophers," she admitted freely.

"But, darling, if you don't know why, does it really matter how?"

"I always listen when you talk about your hobby horses," she countered, evidently not pleased with the direction the conversation was taking.

"You can only change things if you know the how, Peter," Winston joined in after a prolonged silence. "Cathy," he turned to her with both arms wide, as though trying to embrace everything she'd just said, "if you were god, how would you have done it?"

Cathy, ready to continue her spat with Peter, opened her mouth, then closed it again. She knew, instinctively, that Winston was asking her how she would design the universe. A tall order for a little girl, she thought.

"I never thought of it that way," she conceded.

"If you had, you would have both, the why and the how of things. They are really interconnected."

And having said that, Winston seemed to have gotten lost in his own thoughts. Perhaps he just began designing another Kingdom. You could never know with Winston.

As silence prevailed for a little while, Jo put in his head through the door, followed in quick succession by Mo. They already knew that Aunt Cathy was a little obsessed with strings. Also with black holes, but mostly strings. Actually, they'd both read up on string theory on the Internet, but didn't want to hurt Aunt Cathy's feelings.

"They're all vibrating, yet each individual strand is playing its own tune, combining into symphonies of celestial music," she resumed, quietly, doubting if anyone was listening.

Peter thought her eyes shone the way Mozart's must have when he composed the *Sanctus* chorus of his *Requiem*. She was in her own, private heaven.

"*Tuba Mirum*," Jo insisted.

"*Benedictus,*" Mo insisted.

Peter heard both contentions, though neither of the children opened his or her mouth. It didn't really matter. Mozart's eyes probably shone with equal fervour throughout the time during which he composed the *Requiem*. Nevertheless, Peter decided to guard his thoughts in this crowd. They had no reservations about treating his mind as their own. Winston took one look at the children and the probing stopped instantly. Was there anything these kids couldn't do? Seconds later both were on their way to play in the study.

"There are different strings, Cathy, that tie us together. The human genome consists of about 25,000 genes. Genes are the thread that connect us to more primitive animals." This was Winston talking, though he, too, quite unashamedly, was extracting the information from Peter's mind.

For a moment Cathy was lost. "B-but… yes, of course, only I thought, you both wanted to learn what makes me tick." The hurt feelings painted on her face would have been more convincing if her eyes weren't still smiling.

"We know what makes you tick, Cathy. And, if I may say so, you're ticking very nicely indeed," Peter said gravely.

"Ha, ha, my darling husband. Wait till you'll want to talk about your Solidarity," she countered.

"*My* Solidarity? Come on, darling, you must be kidd..."
He stopped. On this continent, it now *was* his Solidarity.

Peter still couldn't adjust himself to the position imposed on him. He went to the office earlier, came back home later, and he still left work undone. It seemed that everyone had questions for him, usually on subjects he knew nothing about. And, though he hated to admit it, it really was *his* Solidarity. His to command, his to preserve, his to improve, his to cherish and love... Ruth would have expected that from him.

"Brain is the means through which mind communicates with our body, and external environment," Winston cut in, trying to attract their attention. He intended to lead them into the subject of unity with nature, but gave up. His previous ability to command the audience had deserted him. He smiled in resignation. The mental juices of his audience were too scattered to be pulled together.

Cathy really was a little sad. It seemed to her that she was beginning to lose touch with Peter. Not just due to his new appointment. She could hardly recognize him. She kept herself busy with strings and the M theory. Peter's new job so preoccupied him that, at times, she was feeling lonely. She tried to compensate by trying to learn to be a mother to the two orphans, though they seemed to be quite exceptionally self-sufficient. In the morning they'd walk to Westmount with Winston, attend to their studies, and return to the condo early, in high spirits, hardly looking for motherly love.

That same night, she lay on her back, staring at the filigree shadows clouds rushing in front of the full moon cast on the tulle curtains. She never drew thick draperies when the full moon was out.

"It's much too beautiful to hide," she'd told Peter. "And, we only have it once a month, clouds permitting."

But even the fleeting shadows didn't comfort her soul.

...what is it that I am really seeking? Why can't I be satisfied with the beauty of a flower? With the curve of a tree

spreading her arms to give shade to lovers on a hot summer day? Why must my world recede in reverse direction to the progression of the stars? Even as they continue on their flight into the expanse of the unknown, so I, for some reason, search for the same meaning within the very heart of matter.

My thoughts dance, effortless in the microcosm of the same god that created the galaxies, the myriad upon myriad of stars, dust clouds, nebulas, furnaces of fires yet to be lit...?

And here am I, retreating in the opposite direction, searching for god among the electrons and protons, among the quarks and bosons, among the dancing, vibrating strings of energy...

They had to decide about the children's future. The house was a little farther away from the SI Headquarters. On the other hand, it was still within walking distance, and the children had a garden in which to do the things that children do outdoors. Also, Mo and Jo had developed a few friendships in Westmount, which would no longer be as available or convenient to maintain.

Peter was happy to have the children sleeping in the study. He had enough work in the office to want to bring it home. Winston didn't seem to mind taking the daily walks, to and from Westmount, and do the shopping on the way. Sometimes, children helped him to carry the groceries. As for Cathy, well, she and Peter didn't have children of their own, and for Cathy this was a new experience, which she seemed to enjoy more every day. Slowly her loneliness seemed to dissipate under their lively presence. The children took to her as if they were intended to be together from the beginning of their lives. Provided she didn't overdo the string theory. Also, she hadn't had a real holiday for as long as she could remember, and staying at home, pretending to be a mom, was more fun than she was prepared to admit.

"Are there strings in Uncle Winston's Kingdom?" Jo asked out of the blue.

With children around, there was always an abundance of questions. Questions she'd never think of formulating on her own.

The name *Winston's Kingdom* stuck to the place they visited together on those occasional nocturnal excursions. While Peter was still trying to analyze whether hallucinations, group or otherwise, were also manifestations of schizophrenia, both children treated them as something perfectly natural—not hallucinations, only trips. Of course, having lived under Winston's wing for some years, they had had plenty of time to become accustomed.

Three weeks after Peter was acclaimed the Chief of SI North America (actually his official title was the President of SI North American Operations), problems began in earnest. He no longer had time to wander the corridors of Headquarters, in expectation of spotting another android. Whether the 'opposition' knew it or not was a moot point. They were certainly smart enough to plant a number of moles, so presumably they had a well-developed network of spies.

For now, this was the least of Peter's problems. There were reasons to believe that the Americans had been grasping at straws for some time. With their fiscal institutions in dire straits, their main problem became the supply and the distribution of food. As Peter and JR suspected, the 'pandemic' was a phony excuse to implant nanotechnological identification systems, which the USA had bought from China for a few squadrons of AI fighter planes and six battalions of robotic, fully equipped soldiers. Of course, the word "bought" took on a different meaning, since the dollar had lost its intrinsic value. They bartered one for the other. It became the only way in which the US could indulge in international trade. On the other hand, they were by far the most advanced country in terms of artificial intelligence. As such, they had plenty to barter.

China had its own problems of controlling its population, and the robots would come in useful. With 55 different ethnic groups, many of them trying hard to protect and reintroduce their own language, not to mention to illegally swell their own ranks, some sort of 'morally' neutral army was a must. The word 'morally' was more than ambiguous, since the robots/android/clones could be, and had been, programmed to recognize only the original programmer as authority. Of course, they could be reprogrammed, but that required such mental abilities as JR's. No doubt the Chinese had their own JRs in abundance, and if not, India was right next door and ready to help. Most probably the only directive they would not be able to override would be the protection the Americans built into them, to protect themselves.

Nevertheless, none of the above was of any concern to Peter. What did concern him was that, as Chief of SI in North America, he had occasion to visit Ottawa. He was on his way to see the Prime Minister when he noticed at least a dozen androids, or other semi-artificial constructs, completely devoid of aura. The sheer number of them was thought-provoking, if not actually frightening.

He discussed the matter with JR. Peter could no longer do the snooping and identification himself. Sneaking up on people was not becoming to his new position. Yet, there was no one else capable of detecting the delinquent auras. They were completely at a loss.

In near desperation, Peter mentioned his new dilemma at dinner. Cathy showed concern; the children showed little interest. And then Winston looked up from his plate.

"It could be a nice little game," he mused, looking at no one in particular.

"Game? Winston, my friend. This is anything but a game." Peter was becoming exasperated.

"Life is a game, Peter. You're taking it too seriously."

When Peter opened his mouth to lecture Winston on the responsibilities of his office, Winston raised his arm. He must have guessed at the flood ready to pour from the great Chief of SI North America.

"Bear with me, my friend, I mean you no harm." For some reason, this had the desired effect.

"I presume you have an idea?" For a moment Peter imagined that Winston would volunteer to do the snooping. Winston smiled disarmingly, having read his mind.

"You'll need George, Little Freddie, Maxine, Joanna and, yes, and the Johnson twins. You'd arrange, through your contacts, of course, a visit of the little group of eight to visit the houses of Parliament, and such ancillary buildings as you see fit."

"You mentioned eight, I count to six…" And then the idea got to him. "You think it would work?"

"They would need some sort of stickers which would adhere to the culprits' clothing and be recognizable to the RCMP or whoever does the security arrangements at the governmental buildings."

"All right, you two, what have you cooked up?" Cathy was on the edge of her seat.

Caught up in the heat of the possibilities, quite rudely, Peter ignored her. "But wouldn't it be dangerous for the children?" he asked Winston instead.

"How would you react? Would you suspect that you're in any danger? Would you suspect anything at all? It depends on the sticker, I suppose, but I'm sure JR can come up with something sufficiently innocuous." Winston was perfectly relaxed. Of course, he always was.

"Peter!" Cathy had enough of the cat and mouse. "Now!" She really wanted an explanation.

The plan, like all best plans, was simple. If fact, one might say, it was childish. JR would provide reasonably 'invisible', as in transparent or of some nondescript colour, stickers, as in glue, or Velcro, or whatever would adhere to the usual clothing worn be the suspected androids. Then a group of children would be taken on a conducted tour of the government building, wandering all over the place, occasionally running into people, as children often do. The particular children running into people would be Mo and Jo. They were a little old for the game, but would still get away with it. Teenagers can behave quite irresponsibly. They would bump into suspects, while, well, sort of misbehaving. The supervisor, the person looking after the children, would scold them, and take them along with some words of apology to the person into whom they had bumped. Once the children were a good distance away, the RCMP guys and/or dolls clad in innocent plainclothes would move in and gently but persuasively cart the culprits away.

"But how would they identify…"

"The stickers could emit infrared, or ultraviolet, or supersonic, or magnetic rays which would be picked up by the RCMP," Peter concluded triumphantly.

"While the other children would act, unknowingly, as perfect decoys," Winston murmured. He sounded highly amused.

For a while Cathy remained perfectly still. Still and silent. Then she looked up, her eyes brimming with determination.

"I categorically refuse to have my children used for undercover work." She sounded as if she'd made up her mind.

Peter, Winston and both children looked at her with astonishment.

"But Auntie…" Jo was first.

"But Auntie…" Mo followed. "We are not little children…"

They must have already been looking forward to a trip to Ottawa, not to mention to be involved in such an exciting game. Thanks to living with Winston, they'd obviously both been very adept at reading auras for some time.

"B-b-but..." Peter followed.

Cathy got to her feet. "Unless..." she said, and there was threat in her voice, "unless I'm the children's supervisor!"

With that she actually stamped her foot on the soft carpet which failed to have the desired effect. Luckily, such was unnecessary.

Seconds later, Peter held Cathy in his arms, the children were trying hard to squeeze between their two bodies, and Winston started clearing the table.

For the first time in a little while, Peter felt happy and relaxed.

But not all was fun and games. For some time now, the Americans, in spite of their spying ventures, had been facing great food delivery problems. The truckers were asking for extra compensation, as were the suppliers of gas. Even now, not all trucks were electric, and proponents of cold fusion couldn't get the approval of Dr. Mondellay's invention through Congress. Too many connections would lose out on it. Thus distribution remained the main problem. For now, the military AI export provided for ample supplies being shipped in from Africa which, during the last ten years or so, had become the breadbasket of the world. The continent had always enjoyed vast areas of incredibly fertile land, propitious climate suitable for up to three harvests per year but, until a decade or two ago, local squabbles deprived them of profitable exploitation of their wealth. Now they had it. They took payment in terms of military, electronic, AI, and nanotechnological equipment and technology. Canada also provided them with genetic know-how, although, at least for now, the northern part of North America was foodwise self-sufficient.

In the meantime, the Americans were becoming desperate, and desperate people often resort to desperate measures. Apparently, their spying operations had been only the beginning.

Meanwhile, within three days JR produced a variety of stickers. Also, as the titular head of SI Canada, he contacted the top echelons of RCMP, who said that, in the light of previous services rendered by the SI, they would be delighted to participate in Winston's little charade. Needless to say, JR didn't tell them how the children would recognize the androids. "It's a new thing we are working on," he said, "Not free to talk about it yet." The operation became known by the code word *Charade*.

Peter, Cathy and JR also agreed that they'd conduct regular sightseeing visits to SI Headquarters in Montreal, with different groups of children to camouflage Mo and Jo's repetitive presence. Incidentally, each time the 'charades' were mentioned, Mo and Jo jumped for joy. There were moments when they acted half their age. The concept of any real or imagined danger was completely foreign to them. Nevertheless, they were perfectly aware that one could not, and would not, mention any of this outside home. In spite of their all too often very juvenile behaviour, they were very, very precocious children.

By early January of the following year, Moira and Jonathan had identified an incredible total of seventeen androids in the Houses of Parliament alone, with four more in the Supreme Court, and an astonishing twenty-two at—of all places—the RCMP National Headquarters. All androids had been dismantled and used for research.

Three weeks later, the SI Headquarters yielded a relatively small number of spies. After three visits, only four androids had been picked up.

"A negligible number by National Standards," JR quipped, proud of his own security measures.

"Or, perhaps, we're not quite as important as we thought," Peter murmured.

By mid-February, still in bitter cold, both Dakotas, Minnesota, and Wyoming registered food riots. The irony was that they had been the food producers, but the government decided to distribute more than what they considered their fair share to other states. Things were getting tough. Tempers flared, aggravated further by the fact that the enforcers were not human and refused to discuss the programming they'd received.

Paradoxically, the next wave of riots came from the very south. Florida's obese population demanded their ration of 'fat-building food' such as triple-cheeseburgers; as did the Texans, with the population of Alabama and Missouri not far behind. At least those people stayed warm while they destroyed the storehouses, which further diminished their prospective allotments.

Simultaneously, SI North America received a stunning 2.7 million applications for membership. Consequently, Peter Thornton expected a new wave of anti-Solidarity activities. He warned JR to take special measures to protect all senior members, including and particularly himself.

"Remember, my friend, you are the one person I simply couldn't do without," he assured JR gravely.

"Some people, you mean, are a little more indispensable than others?"

Peter wasn't smiling.

Next came the disappearances. Some years ago the Americans had tried to put pressure on various members of the European Union to lessen the influence of Solidarity in those countries. They concentrated on political personages, including ministers and various high-level civil servants. After a while, the matter had been resolved.

In Canada, which they now considered as dangerous as they did the Vatican in the past, they took a different tack. Leaving the politicians alone, other than spying on them, they concentrated their scurrilous efforts on the leaders of industry. Presumably they thought that if their neighbours had economic troubles, their own would seem less unpleasant. This was not a direct attack on Solidarity Canada, except that the members of Solidarity had been usefully employed by the industrial concerns. It was a more insidious tactic altogether. They wanted to foment dissatisfaction among the ranks, and stir them to turn against SI management.

A second wave of disappearances, as before in Europe, was followed by attempts to tamper with communications, phony, misleading ads on TV, railway tracks being switched, and other such pranks, which, though inconvenient, were hardly of a dangerously disruptive nature. After Ruth was murdered, there was no more blood spilled, but... this was a different kind of war, as if conducted by overgrown boys.

The sad part of it was that there were probably as many Americans against those actions as had been members of Solidarity. The average John Doe was, and remained, the most pleasant, generous and friendly individual that walked this earth. The vast majority of the citizens were completely unaware of their government's shenanigans.

For a while, Peter and JR remained at a loss how to respond. It seemed that unless they could find a way to fight fire with fire, little or nothing would be accomplished.

Peter began to fantasize what unpleasant things he could do to the 'Yankees'. He would not go so far as to kidnap people, nor would he resort to murder. He could not force himself to sink that low. But he might find a way to put out of commission thousands of robots—which responded adversely to specific magnetic fields. This would include also thousands of androids—which took over most duties at the United Nations. Likewise the mass transit systems, in fact most functions that had been automated, were, by now, in the USA, controlled by artificial intelligence. And anything that can be programmed can be jammed. It would not be permanent, but it would create havoc such as they'd never had to face before. Even more so than they'd already suffered by or from the Ponzi schemes, although JR's contribution to that was, quite frankly, doing the nation a big favour. In the meantime, Peter had to do something to discourage the CIA, or possibly the Pentagon, from continuing their underhanded games.

On the other hand, the new leader of SI North America hated to think what Winston would say about such actions. The only people who would really suffer would be well... the people. Those who did in fact murder and kidnap their neighbours would remain relatively unpunished. Peter never forgot that, but a year ago, the same people had kidnapped his sister-in-law. Yet he had refused to make the war personal. It would destroy him even as it was now destroying the Americans.

"You cannot end war with war," Winston had repeated on a number of occasions. "You can only end war with peace." It was an old adage, and it was true.

But how do you offer peace to people who do not even admit that they are fighting a war? As always, there was a solution. It came from the Vatican.

Lena in her early fifties looked as good as a 'normal' woman would at thirty-five. Seeing admiration in his eyes, her right-hand man whispered in Peter's ear: "It's amazing what a clean conscience does to you." He seemed as much in awe of her as Peter was.

On arrival, Lena embraced him as though he were a long-lost brother. "I never thanked you, Peter, for taking over Ruth's job. I also never told you how very much I miss her."

She did tell him, a number of times, just not in person.

Peter had flown to Rome early that morning and, as usual, took a helitaxi to the Vatican. He slept like a log on the SI executive jet, which had sleeping arrangements worthy of a five-star hotel. He was the top honcho now, and he was given top honours with the attendant comforts. His income rose to 5x the Solidarity average, but the perks were an extra.

The technology was becoming so very advanced, and moving forward at such a fast pace, that he didn't even trust the scrambler to protect the most intimate exchanges of ideas. And Solidarity Canada needed all the help it could get.

Lena led him to her private apartment. "We don't really need a committee for this," she said. "If between us we can't find a solution, then we should both look for a new job."

She may have been joking, but if so, her tone didn't convey any humour.

But they were not alone. Lena had forbidden all her senior staff to be alone, anywhere, at any time, for any reason. Yes, that included using the toilet facilities, although the guard was told to remain just outside the doors. Peter should have guessed that, as he was escorted every step from the moment he'd put his foot on the Aeroporto Leonardo da Vinci di Fiumicino's tarmac. For some reason he didn't find it strange. He thought it came with the territory, so to speak.

For a little while, Lena and Peter reminisced over the old times. Lena had many memories of Ruth, which Peter hadn't known about. As Lena talked, his opinion of his late sister-in-law, already high, grew exponentially. In turn, Peter told her more about Ruth, the mother; the way she always, in spite of all her overwhelming responsibilities, found time for her children.

"She must have gone short on sleep for weeks at a time, but the children never, never complained. Although," he added, "Winston may have had something to do with that."

Lena held up her hand.

"I think I've got it," she said, her face lighting up with unadulterated joy. There was nothing mechanical about Lena. It was just that she usually managed to hold her emotions in tight, very tight reins.

She got up and started pacing her living room. Some of the old splendour of the Vatican still lingered here. The somber eyes of past popes and cardinals followed her from the majestic portraits adorning the walls. They didn't seem to disturb her, but Peter tried hard to avoid meeting their cold stares.

"You know, Peter, why the Last Pope asked me to take over looking after the heritage? That's common knowledge. What is not so well known is that when he also dissolved the clergy, suddenly, there was all this income from countless churches where people continued to drop money for their maintenance. Old habits, I presume. Masses of museums, works of art, basilicas, cathedrals, continued to attract vast numbers of tourists, while, almost overnight, there were no more hundreds of thousands of clergy to support."

"And that makes such a difference?"

"Peter! At the time the Last Pope dissolved the priesthood as a job, as a profession to be supported by others, the church was maintaining, one way or another, well over 450,000 clergy. Some of the higher echelons were commanding quite high incomes. Since then, I've agreed to support many of them, particularly the old and infirm. The vast majority of them are, of course, retired. But at the beginning, even at a very small living wage of, say, thirty thousand US per annum, which was to include the maintenance of their often well oversized, and in great need of repair, living quarters, that adds up to thirteen point five billion dollars. Imagine, Peter, year after year, billions of dollars. Year, after year, after year. And believe me. Very few, indeed, commanded incomes as small as thirty thousand."

"I gather that you are not exactly short of money?"

She smiled sweetly, as only a person who has no need of money can.

"Solidarity is rich beyond our widest dreams. Since we treat the entire heritage as a tourist attraction, which the churches most certainly are, the maintenance is taking care of itself. And, in addition to the, say, fourteen billion-dollar saving, we have the Solidarity membership fees. That is why I said that I think I have a solution."

Lena touched her left ear. She nodded and said she'd be right over. Apparently, she always carried that discreet communication gadget with her. Evidently, she had previous commitments. She smiled and left the room. Moments later, her secretary conveyed to Peter her excuses. She would be all tied up till dinner.

"Had Miss Walesa known you were coming, Sir, a little earlier, she would have made preparations."

It was true. Peter had come on a moment's notice. He was desperate in Montreal. He still was. Lena's mention of a solution would have to keep till tonight.

He spent most of the day relaxing. It was his first day off since he'd been elected to his office. For a little while he just made himself comfortable, leaned back in his chair examining the splendid, slightly domed ceiling, painted with biblical scenes by past, unknown to him, masters. Then he nodded to the ever-present guard and went out to stroll, once again, the Vatican Gardens. It was already quite warm. The buds were bursting, offering promise of an early spring. He spread his mackintosh on the slightly moist lawn, stretched out, and started counting little clouds drifting from the West. Perhaps from Canada, he mused. Then he tried to analyze his motivation of coming here, to see Lena. Was it fear or the need for vengeance?

The next moment he was asleep.

***

17
Revenge

Peter opened his eyes feeling wonderfully refreshed. No, he hadn't dreamt of Winston's Kingdom, nor had he experienced any nightmares. He slept as only a man who was in great need of sleep would. With total abandon. It hadn't really been lack of sleep that brought him to the brink of exhaustion. The new pressures did it.

Never before had Peter Thornton been lumbered with the responsibility for not just a patient or two, or even a dozen, but for the wellbeing of millions of people. Since Dr. Mondellay's invention of portable cold-fusion generators provided the needed energy, the population of Canada had grown to about 64 million. SI's portion of it added up to more than 42 million, with another 17 million, or so, south of the border, where the SI ideals were still in their infancy. That added up to 59 million people who relied on Peter's guidance. Taxing for a man who all too often didn't know where he was going himself.

"Don't worry, Peter," Winston once assured him, "we are all here to learn."

"Maybe, but it sure makes you tired," was Peter's sardonic reply.

Yet, here and now, awaking in this magic garden, Peter actually felt carefree. Perhaps it was the nearness of Vincenzo in his mind that relaxed him. Vincenzo, the man who single-handedly changed the world.

Lying here, under the expanse of azure sky over the Vatican Gardens, he was hardly aware that his dominion was a mere drop in the Solidarity Ocean. Since early this century, in great part due to the immigrants, the population of Europe had more than doubled. Lena, with her Europe, parts of North Africa and fringes of the Middle East, catered to more than 2.3 billion members of all nationalities. And the total membership was growing at an average rate of about three million per month. Lately—faster.

Not a year, a month!

Peter glanced at his watch. He still had two hours. He decided to go to his room—the same one he'd stayed in with Cathy just a month or two ago—to clean up and change. Just as he emerged from the shower, dripping wet, his cell phone jingled.

"Miss Walesa will see you now, Sir," said a congenial female voice.

"If she did she might suffer a shock," he muttered.

"I'll tell her that, Sir."

Before Peter could withdraw his comment, the secretary hung up. Ah, well, he thought, it won't be the first time I've been caught with my pants down.

Ten minutes later he knocked on Lena's door. Two security guards, one on each side of the door, bowed respectfully. Peter wasn't used to such honours. He bowed back.

Lena was alone. He was surprised that she had dressed for dinner. Her generous contours did wonders to the tight-fitting black dress. She walked to the door, took his arm, and led him to a small sitting area, where two Martinis were already waiting in crystal containers filled with ice.

"Vodka, very dry," she said demurely. When he raised an eyebrow, she added, "Don't forget, Peter, the blood coursing in my veins. I've been brought up on Polish Vodka."

Of course—she did originate in Poland. Nevertheless, her comment was all the more amusing since Peter had never seen her drink anything other than wine, and that in great moderation.

"Don't worry, Peter, I'm not about to seduce you," she said, suspecting that she might be making him feel a little uncomfortable. "We have so few special occasions that I thought I'd celebrate your arrival in a proper manner. How's Cathy?"

"She asked to be remembered to you," Peter said truthfully, and raised his glass. The Martini was perfect. It reminded him of Winston's treats on Friday nights.

The next moment Lena the hostess dissolved into thin air, and Lena, the most powerful woman in the world, took the stage. She pointed to one of the armchairs, taking the other herself.

"I mentioned this morning that I thought I had a solution to the North American problem. The USA problem, to be more precise. You looked so run-down that I thought a day off for you was long overdue. I've spent the day in consultation with a number of people who claim expertise in fiscal matters. They confirmed my suspicions."

Peter sipped on his Martini, Lena's remained untouched, nestling on ice.

"The problems the US faced in 1929, and then in early 2008, remained unresolved. On both occasions they threw massive sums of money at the financial institutions, while ignoring the cause of the problem. It was like treating the symptoms while ignoring the cause of the disease."

She looked up to make sure she had Peter's attention. He nodded.

"It seems, and I am not referring to any moral judgment, that the problem was greed. The whole economy of the US was based not on cost plus overhead and profit, but on how much the market would bear. This remains true to this day. It is also in total denial of all that Solidarity stands for."

Peter was beginning to see a glimmer of light at the end of a very long tunnel. She, Lena Walesa, was not satisfied with the work she was doing. She was determined to change the way the world worked.

"As I mentioned this morning, we are rich. And we are rich because we don't pay ourselves what we could, only what we need to lead comfortable, elegant, decent lives. Not a single member of Solidarity has been coerced into joining our movement. Our growth is based exclusively and entirely on free will. Yet... it works. This leads me to believe that people are not intrinsically greedy. It is only a relatively small group that suffers from this malady. I've decided to purge America of this group of people."

"How?" Peter couldn't contain himself. Lena smiled.

"By removing the patsies. The system is based on robbing a very large group of people of relatively small amounts of money. Again, the skimming of money is based on the 'how much can the system bear'. If four hundred million people pay seven-hundred-fifty dollars a year for cable TV, the total adds up to three trillion dollars each year. The supply network is already in place, and the maintenance costs are minimal. This allows the media moguls, the oligarchy, to pay themselves absurd salaries. The same principles are involved in all the voluntary and non-voluntary federal and state taxation systems, as well as in all aspects of entertainment, such as professional sports, the movie industry, and other commercially based, mass-produced and mass-distributed products. So far, thanks to JR and, I understand, a young man who prefers to remain anonymous, we have removed only the financial organizations from the equation. The rest are still all there, and, relatively speaking, still thriving. Well, says Solidarity International, enough is enough."

"Cheers to New America," she said raising her glass. This time she did take a minute sip of her Martini.

For a brief moment Peter felt uncomfortable about the mention of his purported anonymity. Then he shrugged, squared his shoulders and asked, "You do have a plan, of course?" It sounded halfway between a question and a statement. Lena continued smiling.

"We are going to take our revenge for all the harm they've done us."

Peter's eyes narrowed. This didn't sound like Lena at all.

"We are going to help them," she concluded triumphantly.

"H-h-help them? But h-how?"

"The announcement will be on the airwaves tomorrow morning. It will be broadcast from our satellites." She glanced at Peter, as his eyes grew round. "Don't worry, Peter. We are not going into the satellite launching business. What I mean is that, for services rendered, once a month we are given free time to broadcast our announcements worldwide."

This time Lena downed the rest of her Martini and pointed to the dining table. "Shall we?"

The business part of the meeting was over.

The *scallopini alla bolognese* was superb. Cathy never served *prosciutto*, and she reserved cheese for after meals. In Lena's private kitchen, Peter soon discovered, there was no 'after meal'. Dinner was a one-plate serving, with fruit and coffee or tea to follow.

"Just love Italian food," Lena confessed, which probably accounted for her Mother Earth figure. If it hadn't been for her 18-hour-a-day workload, she'd have to forego the cheese.

For coffee they moved back to the sitting area.

"I propose to offer our American friends credit based on our Constitution. However, I also intend to inject some funds into their fiscal system on condition that all employees, including the upper echelons, board of directors *and* the lawyers they employ conform to our rules." She stressed the *and* with a knowing wink. "I'm referring to our maximum of five times average income rule. Only the income will be based on Solidarity average, not whatever they would like to concoct."

"I thought that was already available to them."

"To individual people who've heard about us and applied for membership of their own free will. We are still not as well known as you imagine, Peter. We try to keep a relatively low profile."

"And you think they'll take it?"

"If not, new organizations will rise, in direct competition with the existing, mostly defunct ones. I'm not going to do the job for them. Solidarity, as you know, is based on voluntarism. Those who accept our conditions will benefit. Those who don't..." she spread her arms. She gazed expectantly at Peter, presumably waiting for some sort of reaction.

"I thought you'd want to destroy them," he murmured.

"The thought had crossed my mind," she admitted. "In a way, my proposal will. With luck, and over time, it will destroy an economic system based on greed. As for actual destruction, well... I thought of Vincenzo. I couldn't do it to him."

So he also left his mark on her, Peter mused. What an extraordinary man he was.

"You see, Peter, none of this is mine. Not even ours. We are just the custodians of what people, through the ages, have offered to enrich the heritage of the human race. There is no room for hatred, here. Nor for vengeance."

"You cannot end war with war," Peter repeated Winston's words.

He wondered where Winston got the adage. The majordomo never seemed to read; yet he was more knowledgeable than were most people Peter ever met.

"Abraham Lincoln said that America will never be destroyed from the outside. 'If we falter,' he said, 'and lose our freedoms, it will be because we destroyed ourselves'," he said softly.

Lena smiled. "The president was a very wise man. We do not propose to encroach on their freedom. *Au contraire.* We want to give them yet another option."

Said the spider to the fly, thought Peter, but he kept his thoughts to himself. The US was pushing the envelope of half a billion people. Not a bad coup, if Lena could swing it.

Next came the floods. While famine was punishment enough, the floods made the delivery of food even harder. Lena's announcement received no official response from Washington, but, during the first week, there were close to half a million inquiries regarding the offer of credit.

You can't build Rome in a day, but this was as promising as anything Lena had hoped for. Within the next three weeks, 27 new banks, or old-restructured banks, opened their doors. There wasn't a single inquiry from any investment institutions. The financial oligarchy crawled under the rocks and stayed there. They might have been afraid for their lives. Also, salaries limited to five times the Solidarity average just weren't in their cards. It would be like asking a hockey or a baseball player to perform for the same salary as a professor of a major university or a neurosurgeon at the Montreal General Hospital. There was still great skepticism regarding the stability of the US dollar, but, over time, people would recover from what became known as the Ponzi Fiasco.

Heads had turned when SI North America bought ten American helicopters to deliver food to the Solidarity members in stranded areas on a 24/7 basis. Although the media made great efforts to diminish the service as "just another propaganda ploy", the people who were fed didn't agree. Finally a local daily in Wyoming printed a front-page headline, which became a rallying cry from coast to coast:

YOU CAN'T EAT PROPAGANDA
BUT SOLIDARITY SURE TASTES GOOD

The number of applications to become members of Solidarity grew from 1.7 to 3.9 million during the first two months. It seemed that even as the floods receded, Solidarity flooded the United States with ever-greater acts of generosity. Lena called it the Vincenzo Revenge.

For a while, the onslaught of androids invading the Canadian institutions abated. There were sporadic outbursts in various parts of the country, but they looked as if they were individual attacks, more in the nature of industrial espionage, than having a political motivation. In fact, Washington kept amazingly quiet. They could not tax people who, officially, had virtually no income. And those who did, well, their incomes fell below, or almost below, the taxable minimum. Any measure that would increase taxes imposed on lesser income was not an option. The riots would be more wide-spread than even they could imagine. If Washington was desperate, then they didn't show it. Perhaps they were hibernating, waiting for what spring might bring.

Peter found it hard to believe that a mere three months ago he was determined to avenge Ruth's death. He'd visited some American concerns in Montreal, including the consulate, in an attempt to read various functionaries' minds, in a feeble attempt to find Ruth's murderers. He's done a lot of maturing—these last few months. He'd assumed responsibilities, which he, by now, treated very seriously. He'd learned to work with people, an art he'd never developed before. To his surprise, he discovered that most people had dreams, most were trying hard to do their best. Lately, when he practiced his OBE exercises, it was no longer to escape the reality that he disliked, but to extend it, to grow, and ultimately to be able to help others do the same.

He had a single conversation with Winston on this subject. "OBE," the Majordomo had said, "is not a stepping out of your physical body. It is the stepping out of the constraints you impose on yourself, by freeing yourself from that which sets you apart. It is the stepping out of your ego."

Peter defied the odds. Instead of being corrupted by power, he used it to empower others. He was becoming a very different person.

"Did I tell you, darling, that I love you?" It was a question Cathy was asking more often. "Because I really, really, really do…" She was developing a habit of staring at Peter with starry eyes.

The rapid swelling of the Solidarity ranks reminded Peter of the meeting he had had in the Vatican which centered on the problem of overpopulation. With 10 billion people in mind, Cathy and Peter, and many others like them, forsook having children of their own.

"We have nearly seventy million of them already," Cathy mentioned, looking at Mo and Jo. She, too, was becoming more involved in the workings of Solidarity. "Not to mention these two."

It was true. Many members of Solidarity, particularly the new ones, needed nurturing to grow into the best that they could be. It would come, but it needed some effort and attention. Becoming a member was only the first step. When the rat-race was no longer the only motivating factor, many other latent qualities could now be released.

In the meantime, 'these two' were, at the time, trying out their suction cups to climb up the walls and crawl along the ceiling. A new game some genius created to give mothers heart attacks. Their new 'game', if one could call it that, was frequently interrupted by screams of utter delight.

"Sometimes they still act like little children," Peter remarked. It made Winston smile with great satisfaction.

Back in his office, Peter scrolled down the computer files to find the follow-up of the meeting dealing with global overpopulation. Apparently the problem nearly resolved itself by itself. Some time ago, in the Solidarity Monthly Newsletter issued worldwide online, SI Vatican asked its members for input. The problem had been explained, concisely, and left at that. Within four weeks, 87% of the membership replied that they were willing to limit their own offspring to a maximum of two. To assure fair play, 62% proposed genetic manipulation to enforce such a resolution. 42% said that they had already limited their progeny to two or less.

"Not bad for what originated as a trade union organization," Peter mused. He also wondered if the average Solidarity IQ exceeded that of non-members. He was willing to give odds that it did.

That same evening he raised the question with Cathy. "If Winston is right that life-force manifests through us, then it seems that the better hardware we offer it, the more it can achieve through us. Does this make sense?"

"You are becoming computer savvy. I'm impressed."

"No, I'm not. The inner workings are still black magic to me. But don't you think there may be something in it?"

"Well, there is that story about talents, in your Bible..."

"It's not *my* Bible, darling. But you're right," Peter conceded.

"I rather prefer Thomas Aquinas. He said that whatever is received, is received according to the nature of the recipient. That would reinforce your hardware concept."

"Ever assuming we are robots..." Peter mused.

"Or computers?" she asked, a smile playing at the corners of her mouth.

"Don't bring that up again. I love your software just as much."

"Mmmm... I much prefer your hardware..."

They were lucky Winston had taken the children out on the mountain. They had the condo to themselves.

Afterwards, as it so often happened, Peter felt ready to fall soundly asleep. Hardly surprising, since last night he'd left his office after midnight. It was as in the old days, when he was busy trying to be the best physician he could possibly be. By the time he settled into his new responsibilities, he only vaguely recalled his night duties, or his midnight calls to report to the General. It seemed like only yesterday, yet, at the same time, it felt as though that previous existence of his belonged to another man, or, perhaps, to another lifetime. He wondered, if we really are just hardware through which life-force manifests itself, then, perhaps, one could experience a few lifetimes in a single body. After all, it seemed that a body was only a means to an end.

On the other hand, he knew from his days as a physician that a human body is the most magnificent creation in the universe. The physical, material universe, the universe to which he had daily access. A moment later he wondered whatever happened to that world which he and Cathy wrenched out of the matrix of spacetime, and sustained, before it could collapse upon itself, back into its own black hole of birth. The thought that it would take a billion years before its comings and goings might resemble the universe in which he had his being at present, encouraged neither him nor Cathy to pursue their Elohim ambitions any further.

But he couldn't forget that moment of elation they both experienced at the time of creation. Ye are gods, resonated in his ears, even now, when he thought about it.

Are we? Are we really?

How often have I heard that Psalm, he mused, even as his mind and memories were slowly receding into the reality of dreams.

And later, much later, there were those moments of disappointment. As when his self-centered ambitions had been ennobled by JR, who turned the serpent of his anger and fomenting greed upon itself, to save the United States of America from themselves. JR was as far from ambition as a man can be without losing all personality.

Or as when he learned that it had been the children, little Mo and Jo, who took Ruth, their adopted mother, across the Great Divide. He hadn't been ready yet. Nor, he suspected, was he now. He still had to discover what really freed a man, a woman, an entity possessed of human consciousness, to breach the unknown by an act of their will. His exercises aimed at freeing his mind, or his consciousness, from his body were still at a beginner's stage. He could now waggle his phantom limbs, spin within an imaginary cylinder containing his body, examine fleeting images floating behind his closed eyelids, even enter and solidify them, but none of this compared to Winston's Kingdom. What he did were tricks, conjuring acts, worthy of an amateur magician. Not, not nearly, the real thing.

Yet he refused to give up.

At long last, Morpheus took him into his arms and embraced him with the bliss of emptiness.

Peter dreamt of going in and out of a white palace, a castle still empty, waiting to be enriched with people. He knew it was his to populate, to enhance, to fill with friends, to be made a place that is lived in.

He walked in and out, not knowing what to do. He was waiting for someone to show him the way, yet... there was no one. Neither Winston, nor Ruth, nor even his brother Andrew. Not even the children. Cathy? Cathy he didn't even dare hope for. Was she not the epitome of heaven?

He tossed and turned, not happy to rest in Morpheus's arms. Not happy to walk in and out, without rhyme or reason, like walking in circles. Not happy to be so inadequate, so immature.

The images changed.

He saw himself standing on a podium, high enough to dominate the lands all around him. He was there to address his serfs. He was aware of observing himself from both within and without. In a way, he was omnipresent. As he raised his arms, thousands bowed in abject obeisance. He then saw beyond them. His vision reached out past his vassals. There they were. Them. The enemy. With a sneer that distorted his features, he projected his mind and, with a single desire, destroyed hosts of clones and androids and robots who had been marching on his castle. A single wish laid thousands to waste. His power was euphoric. He felt elated, thrilled, enchanted, almighty.

His power was awesome.

We really are gods, his mind told him. Elohim. All-powerful.

And in that instant he fell into a chasm as deep as the podium was high. He fell down, on and on and... his previous lives painted in grotesque, jarring colours on the smooth wall of the bottomless pit. With contorted features, they, his previous faces, were screaming obscenities at him. Wastrel, wastrel, wastrel, wastrel... The words reverberated against the sheer, vertical walls. On and on...

But ye shall die like men...

And then he felt sweetness of balm applied to his heart. The vision receded immediately. It became unreal, as though it had never been. As if he and he alone had seen it, as though he'd created it. For no reason. No reason at all. What folly, he mused, turning on his side, just as Cathy's arm reached out for him and snuggled up against his back.

"It's all right now..." she whispered. "It's all right... Just sleep."

And she held him close as a mother would a crying baby. "Just sleep now..."

And he did.

***

18
Age of Aquarius

"**W**hile the *Prime Cause* expresses itself only through an individual, it is in fact a *Single Source*. Thus, ultimately, all individuals must act as one, without losing their own identities," said the majordomo. As always he sat straight, giving an impression of a man half his years. Peter had never seen him slouch, whether sitting or standing.

In spite of the gravity of the subject matter, Winston and the children were engrossed in a game of chess, with Mo and Jo combining their skills at a subliminal level to match Winston's ability.

"It sounds like a contradiction in terms," Peter's mind, trained in logic, could not quite accept it. "It's either one or individual," he mused aloud.

"Not if you know your Latin." This was as far as Winston went in gentle attempts at humour. "We learned to use the word *individual* indiscriminately."

This time he accentuated the word individual the same way as he previously did with Prime Cause and Single Source.

Peter looked up. Having spent years in medicine, he was as conversant with Latin roots as anybody. "Individual? It's from Latin *individuus*, meaning indivisible or inseparable. Is that what you mean?"

"Precisely. Not something which gives us a personality, which makes us different, but that which joins us into a singular, indivisible whole. It is that which makes us one."

"Like the event horizon of a black hole," Cathy whispered. "It's quite irresistible." Then she smiled, "Sorry, my mind was wandering…"

"Check!" Mo announced, Jo nodding fiercely. Cathy coming back from the fringes of irresistible black holes thought Mo's voice was as proud as a peacock's.

Moira, having detected Cathy's thoughts, started laughing. "Peacocks don't have proud voices. They go google-google-google…"

Jo joined her in the last two google-googles. They sounded like two birds making an impersonation of something between an industrial buzzer and the bray of a donkey, the first syllable being higher and shorter.

Winston instantly responded with his move, which caused the merriment to evaporate into thin air. Having moved his king out of danger, he simultaneously exposed his own queen to attack Mo and Jo's king.

"Check and mate," he said softly.

"I never thought of it this way," Peter murmured. "How did this distortion creep into our language?"

"Over many millennia. The culprit is the ego, which demands recognition." Then he grinned. "Don't forget that we need ego to survive in this reality. And here, the learning process is vastly accelerated."

"So we shouldn't bite the hand that feeds us?"

"Precisely. The religions tell us that we ought to live well enough to go to heaven. That an oxymoron in so many ways. Admittedly, if we don't earn a good position in this life, heaven is nothing to write home about."

This time Cathy looked up.

"Well, briefly, during the last two, two and a half thousand years, we were given all the tips we needed. The whole of the Bible deals exclusively with not so much getting to heaven, but what to do to be able to cope, once we get there."

"And Buddha?"

"Buddha merely discovered the, ah…. Kingdom, as you call it. He discovered that life here is no more than a training ground, so that we might enjoy what heaven is to the full. But Buddha wasn't really a teacher of how to get there. His eight noble truths are designed to help you down here, not up there."

"Now you really have me confused," Peter scratched his head.

"Peter," Winston admonished, "ask Cathy. The world here is not real. It is, well, it is practically empty space. We, with our minds, our needs, our aspirations, give it reality. But it's not really all there, is it?"

"Quite true. We've already discussed it but it bears repeating," Cathy nodded, glad that at last she could contribute to the discussion. "The proportionate distance between an electron spinning around its nucleus is comparable to earth spinning around the sun. The rest is empty space, so to speak."

"So to speak?"

"It is empty of matter, or mass. There are energy fields, forces, that fill the whole matrix of space, but they are very much invisible. At least to our human eyes."

"So why don't I walk through walls?" Peter challenged.

"You could, if you believed you could," Winston offered. He was thinking of great avatars, dead and alive, who seemed to have had no problem in defying what we thought were the laws of nature.

"Well, yes and no." Cathy had more to add. "What makes the matter not solid but impenetrable is the repulsion between electrons' saturated orbits. As you know, two similar forces repel each other. Hence the impenetrability. It is a question of energy, not mass. The negative charge of electrons spinning around atoms in your body are repelled by the negative charge of the electrons in the wall."

"So Winston is right?"

"Well, since in theory Winston is not here, either, he could do anything he would want…"

"Thank you, my dear. For now, I'd rather remain right where I am," Winston said, grabbing the armrests with both hands.

"Seriously, though." Cathy would not give in on her favourite subject. "Neutrinos travel through the very heart of our earth, and don't even slow down. Doesn't that tell you something?"

"You serious?" Peter, in spite of his passion for auras and, at the time, for out-of-body experiences, was still very much a down-to-earth sort of guy. His mind and his emotions seemed to have traveled different paths.

"Well," Cathy continued, "neutrinos are an electrically neutral force, therefore they are not affected by electrical charges. And as the rest of our earth is, as we established, mostly empty space, there is nothing to stop them."

It was ten at night when the children bowed gravely, and then made a wild run for the staircase. For them, this seemed to be the foremost advantage of staying in Westmount. The staircase, with the beautifully carved, rosewood handrail. Peter recalled many a race taking place down its polished surface. When Ruth was still here. Ruth and himself. It felt like ages ago. Right then it seemed to him that not only matter but time wasn't real, either. Perhaps it was all a dream. Perhaps Brahma's. Perhaps our own. One day he hoped to find out.

That night, Winston and the children stayed in the house while Cathy and Peter took a stroll back to the condo. It was no more than a fifteen-minute walk. Just right before retiring. Cathy called it their *Sanbu Yangsheng*, their constitutional walk. According to Chinese tradition, persistence in walking guarantees longer life and a healthier body. They claim that a

relaxed walk makes the *qi* and blood flow smoothly and
provides great benefits. Judging by the way Cathy looked,
they were right.

Even as they left the gate of the property, two shapes
detached themselves from the shadows and followed them at
a discreet distance. Peter smiled. They were his half-human,
extremely powerful guardian angels, provided by JR.

For the last little while, things had been quiet in the office.
The world was unfolding itself as it should. Few people
realized it, but Solidarity International was the first
organization in human history that was not created in order to
compete with other organizations such as political entities,
religions, or industrial and/or commercial concerns. SI
encouraged freedom in all its forms. In a way, it was an
organization not unlike a religious one, with two exceptions.
There was no carrot and no stick. Nothing happened to you—
should you leave it; nor were you rewarded in any special
way—if you remained in its ranks. Everything you were told
at the very beginning, when you first joined, remained true
regardless of external conditions. Industries in which the
majority of employees became members of Solidarity found
it beneficial to join the SI ranks *en masse*, as the Solidarity
members had the reputation of being better workers than
those outside its ranks. The management, of course, almost
invariably had to take pay a cut, if they wanted to remain in
organizations in which the majority of members voted to join
the SI. The vast majority chose to do so. The alternative was
slow erosion of their labour force. There was something
strangely ennobling in doing your best when money was not
the only motivation.

In fact, there were not that many direct benefits. Like all
organizations of even half its size, the SI had the clout to
negotiate the best possible terms for its members in diverse
fields of life. Likewise, the cost of raw materials necessary

for the manufacture of whatever produce, benefited from the same advantage. All parties involved seemed to work for mutual benefit. *E Pluribus Unum* had been at the start, and remained, the SI's preferred motto. The Latin meaning, "out of many one", was a concept taken originally from a poem by Virgil, a Roman poet of the first century BC. Many centuries later, in 1782, it was adopted by an act of Congress to be included in the Seal of the United States.

Later, it found itself first onto gold coins, then silver and, later still, on most ordinary coins in daily use. Recently, the coins substantially lost their value. The motto remained invaluable. For Solidarity it remained its only motto.

Strangely enough, the sentiments originally expressed in the US Constitution were very close to those espoused by the Solidarity. The subsequent countless 'improvements', which the Americans called 'amendments' to the Constitution, left the spirit if not the letter of the original way behind. Many argued that anything that needs 26 or 27 amendments can't be that good. Perhaps they were right.

The SI Constitution drew on the experience of the US, simplified and shortened the principal tenets to make sure that every member could remember them. After all, it was adopted in many languages, and in every one of them it sounded the same. Basically, it said, *E Pluribus Unum.*

In recent years, particularly since the US dollar lost its almighty value, the Americans have begun to rediscover the meaning of the words that originally adorned their official seal. People began rediscovering something familiar, something that brought the memories of better days, of a simpler life, of not being part of the perennial rat race. They were reminded that life does not have to be a constant chase after mammon. They rediscovered the joy of a walk in the park, of a beautiful sunset, of music in the whisper of the wind washing over the vast fields of the Midwest. People remembered why they were alive.

It was time for the Thorntons to host another of their quarterly get-togethers. It seemed to all participants that this event was the source of merging their individual interests with those of others. All of them were, most of their time, so consumed by their professional life that they had little time for contact with other disciplines.

Dr. John Brent, in his late seventies, still put in 50-hour weeks at the Montreal General Hospital. Yet here, at the Thorntons, he led the latest dances, which came from China, and which he had espied the nurses practicing in their rec room at the General. They consisted of doing an impersonation of a snake, winding itself around his wife, Lucy, to which contortions she appeared to be a willing party.

JR looked on with envy, until Cathy pulled him onto the middle of the carpet, looked up at his prodigious height, and said in a very serious tone of voice: "C'mon, Snake, let's wiggle."

And that they did.

Wiggling a six-foot-eight frame, even as lanky as JR's, in circular motion, around a diminutive five-foot-two sylph, who really did contrive to look almost invisible next to his bulk, was a sight to behold. Or not behold, as the case may be. But they continued to wiggle until JR collapsed in a heap at Cathy's feet.

Then came the turn for Cathy's parents. Dr. and Mrs. Bartholomew Mondellay rose to the occasion, but not to the exigencies of wiggling. Instead they gave a distinguished performance of the Northern Lion dance. For a moment they disappeared into the bedroom and came out with an improvised get-up, which impressed all sufficiently to warrant a good round of applause.

Even though Dr. Mondellay had foregone the more contrived acrobatics, they acquitted themselves splendidly. Nevertheless, some of the twists and turns would have tested a much younger man, as Peter soon found out when he attempted to emulate him. Throughout all the performances, Cathy provided the music with the aid of an inverted breadbasket, which served as drums, while the cover from an oversized wok provided the necessary gong.

The most amazing reaction came from Mo and Jo. It seems that to that very day, they had never seen adults, particularly of considerably advanced years, acting like children. They weren't quite sure if they ought to laugh or look serious, until Winston announced that they, Mo and Jo, would perform the next dance.

The children disappeared into the bedroom. While they were changing, Winston explained that, should Miss Walesa ever visit Canada again, it had been their mother's wish that they would welcome the Chief of Solidarity International with an echo of yesterday from her country of origin. He was still explaining Ruth's wishes when a buzzer announced another visitor. Peter clicked open his cell, and both his eyebrows went up. Framed by his tiny screen were three identical ladies, standing at the door to the condo's main entrance. Each one was a spitting image of Lena Walesa.

"Something fishy is going on," he murmured. Nevertheless, out of sheer curiosity, he pressed the admitting button. After all, there were four security guards downstairs who should be able to cope with three women.

Hardly a minute later, the front door opened and Lena Walesa walked into the hall. The other two Lenas vanished into thin air.

"Hello, Peter, how very nice to see you. I understand you are holding a little party tonight. Am I right?"

Peter glanced past her, looking for her doppelgangers.

"Don't worry, my friend. One commandeered an elevator, in case we're in need of a quick getaway, and the other is downstairs. You don't have a heliport here, do you?" Lena delivered all this in a perfectly normal voice as if she was reciting a grocery list.

"Why, Lena, you're very, very welcome."

By then, hearing the exchange, all guests had risen to their feet. Peter still sounded lost. "Don't worry about them." She nodded behind her. "This is what my security people make me do. I think they're a bit paranoid, don't you?"

"Why, yes, a bit, I think…"

"Well, aren't you going to ask me in?"

Peter recovered his senses. He took her arm and, as he led her into the living room, the first notes of *Oberek*, a lively Polish dance, coincided with the bedroom door opening. Jo and Mo, dressed in traditional Polish folk costumes, charged into the living room. The next moment Jo's heels shot up to the ceiling, executed a perfect *holubiec*, or capering, a trick of clicking one's heels when suspended, practically upside down, in the air. Instant applause showed everyone's appreciation. For a while the two youngsters continued to gyrate at a fantastic speed, interrupted only by repeated capering.

Lena stood spellbound.

In spite of a broad smile, two perfect tears formed and rolled slowly down her cheeks. They stayed there, unabashed, till the children finished their dance. Then she walked to them, embraced them both. At long last she let them go.

"Thank you, my darlings," she whispered, "and thank you, Ruth," she added, even more quietly. Only the children could hear, but it was enough for them both to give her another hug.

"It was just for you, Aunt Lena. It was Winston who taught us. He teaches us everything," Jo said.

"Everything," Mo confirmed, nodding her head.

Lena's eyes searched for the majordomo. He wasn't there. Mo and Jo ran to the kitchen and dragged him out. He came unwillingly. "It was all your mother's idea," he explained. "I did nothing."

"So I am told, Winston. Everyone says that you always do nothing, only, by some miracle, everything is always done. I wish you'd join the Solidarity."

"I'm already a member, Ma'am. In my heart."

"Lena," Lena corrected him. "Don't you dare to age me with a title. Why... I'm young enough to be your daughter."

Winston only smiled, but he was caught off guard. Peter and the children could actually read his thoughts, apparently hovering at the very top of his awareness.

"Wow," he thought. "Wow!"

There was nothing spoiled about Winston. Finally he recovered. *If I ever had a daughter, I couldn't imagine anyone more beautiful than you, Lena,* he said. This time, by yet another miracle, no one but Lena could hear him. Then Winston bowed, and minutes later helped Cathy and Peter serve dinner.

When Peter managed to get Lena to himself, he asked her why she didn't call to tell him when she was coming. The meeting had been loosely scheduled for later that month.

"You'll have to ask my security guards. That's right, those, ah, women in the elevator and in the lobby. I suspect my chief of security at home thought that it would be safer if no one knew of my immediate plans."

Peter agreed, but still thought that the Vatican was a bit paranoid. On the other hand, no one could imagine Solidarity International without Lena at its helm.

"Good," he replied instead. "Good thinking."

By eleven, after an extra portion of ice cream, Mo and Jo withdrew to the study. As Cathy checked on them some minutes later, happy snores confirmed that they were both asleep. Or, it could be, that they were visiting the Kingdom. It would explain the smiles on their youthful faces. Cathy closed the door quietly, and, as she joined her guests, she caught Winston's eye. She couldn't be absolutely sure, but for a moment there, she could swear that the majordomo winked at her.

They talked till the early hours. After all, they did this sort of thing only once every three months. And this time, even Lena was there.

Officially, Lena Walesa had flown in for the SI North American Conference on Freedom, which was to be held later that month. They decided to advance the date. As the ranks of Solidarity swelled from millions to billions, it was time to review the constitution.

"Not to change, neither to create amendments, just to review," Lena assured Peter last night. "At most to update it. To make sure it is relevant to today's needs."

Also, Lena had not visited Canada since Peter Thornton took over from his sister-in-law. Lena was probably curious how things were running.

She opened the meeting by welcoming Peter to the position of the Chief of Solidarity International, North American Branch. After a short, almost perfunctory applause, she got straight down to business.

"There are few amongst us who do not recognize freedom as a God-given right. History is brimming with men who preached, beseeched, fought and gave their lives for this most sacred principle of individual freedom. In the American Declaration of Independence, the delegates to the Congress of the United States speak of all men being endowed, by their Creator, with certain unalienable rights, among them Liberty."

She took a small sip of water.

"Liberty ensues from independence—independence from the spirit of liberty."

They were all well aware of the contribution the United States had made to the cause of freedom. The Preamble of the American Constitution spoke of securing "the blessings of liberty to ourselves and our posterity." All the articles that followed are illumined by this preamble. The Bill of Rights declared in force December 15, 1791, defines and further protects these rights with particular accent on freedom of the citizenry. Only later did things go wrong.

Lena continued.

"On June 26, 1945, in the City of San Francisco, a text equally authentic in Chinese, English, French, Russian, and Spanish, reaffirmed faith in, and I quote, the "fundamental human rights, in the dignity and worth of the human person, in the equal rights of men and women..."

Her eyes swept all present at the table.

"So reads the preamble of the Charter of the United Nations," she said softly. "The first text in the history of the human race addressing all people, men and women—the world over. We, the Solidarity, were only the second."

Peter smiled a little sadly. The charter had been affirmed hardly 150 years ago; a long journey indeed since 1215, when King John of England, at Runnymede, signed the *Magna Carta*. An early seed for the charters of freedom to come.

"How few delegates understood the meaning of such noble precepts..." Lena continued, lowering her head. And then she looked up. "But we mustn't give up," she said with a firmness that made everyone sit up.

These were not empty words. There were still many people who shunned freedom. "Freedom from whom, from what?" they said. "Who will take care of us when we're free? Who will tell us what to do, where to work, how to earn our living? Who will tell us what to believe in, what to teach our children, where to send them to school? Who will protect us from the unexpected, the unknown, the unpredictable? What of unemployment? What about our old age? What of...???"

Peter had met those people. Just a few years ago, the wards he paced every morning were filled with them. Lying, side by side, resigned to their fate. Sad, mental derelicts? Or were they still the norm? "How dare they give us freedom?" they would murmur. "We have rights!" they would assert, angrily.

They were not a happy lot. Nor was Peter remembering them.

"Let us never forget," Lena's decisive voice cut into his reveries, "that responsibility is the obverse side of the coin of freedom."

Peter had discussed those matters with Lena before. Her words were mostly for the others. For the able, promising, yet still not always sure of their ground—for the lieutenants and captains of her organization. They needed an occasional pep talk. An emotional shake-up. A reminder of what Solidarity was all about.

Peter sank deeper into his armchair.

Almost eight centuries had elapsed since the signing of the *Magna Carta*. Are we ready to take on the responsibility of being free? Lena thought we were. 220 years have passed since the Declaration of Independence. Are we ready for independence? Are we ready to stand up and walk on our own two feet without the assistance of a king, a prince, church, welfare state looking after us? Are we willing to chart our own direction on the turbulent oceans of life and adventure? Or do we demand our illusory rights without paying the dues of birthright. How could one be sure? How could Lena be so sure? Half of Peter's mind still followed Lena's admonitions; the other half dwelled on reservations, doubts lurking in his turbulent past, perhaps his lingering fears. There was not a shadow of doubt in Lena's words:

"Freedom without responsibility is anarchy."

"Freedom for the select few is oligarchy."

"Freedom imposed on children is irresponsibility."

"Freedom is a privilege to be earned, not given."

With each statement, her eyes peered into each pair of eyes staring at her from around the table.

"Freedom is an idea," she said, and leaned back in her chair.

And ideas are power, Peter mused. Yet to impose one's

ideas on others is equivalent to the practice of the blackest Black Magic. Winston had told him that. Sometimes we infuse others with concepts that are not yet ready to flourish. Is this what Lena was worried about? Was she casting pearls before swine? If so, the swine would remain blameless—we would be the guilty. Great ideas are sacred, and we must cherish that which is holy. We must be careful. Yet to withhold knowledge from one seeking it is paramount to refusing food to a starving child. The greatest teachers always offered, never imposed their knowledge.

In that case, Lena was right. She didn't impose, she offered.

The greater our understanding of freedom, the more responsibility we take on for our brothers. We truly become our brothers' keepers. We begin to perceive that we all are little more than tenants in this world. That we did not create it alone—it has been a joint effort; that we did little to enhance it; that we hardly deserve to be in it. That up to now we were no more than carefree tots in a magic kindergarten, and that it is time to stand up and look over the edge of our playpen. To look at the world that lies outside. A world we have never seen—till now.

It is time to assert the Age of Aquarius.

We have tasted of the tree of knowledge. We became as gods, knowing good and evil. We have learned discrimination. The stage of carefree, irresponsible, wasteful life is over. And as we increase the seeds of our understanding, we begin to take on responsibility for the conditions around us. Our eyes slowly open. We realize that though we cannot be perfect, we can try to do the very best we can. In all walks of life. We make sure that each day, as we retire, we leave the world a slightly better place. Just slightly. Just a little better. Perhaps—a little happier? Perhaps, a little more responsible.

And as we look beyond childhood, we begin to savor the divine, wondrous, intoxicating attribute of freedom. Peter's smile broadened into a wide grin. He just began to understand.

"We have entered the Age of Aquarius," he murmured.

Peter looked up from his reveries. The Age of Aquarius may have begun with the industrial revolution, but only now was it reaching our conscious awareness. Lena stood up. The meeting was almost over. Then, as though on second thought, she raised her hand. For a moment she seemed hesitant, then she closed her eyes and recited from memory.

We the people of the United Nations
Determined to save succeeding generations
from the scourge of war...
and to reaffirm faith in fundamental human rights,
in the dignity and worth of the human person,
in the equal rights of men and women
of nations large and small...
to practice tolerance and live together in peace
with one another as good neighbors...

"These words, ladies and gentlemen, are from The Charter of the United Nations. The document was signed in the City of San Francisco, USA, on the 26th day of June, 1945. Isn't it time we lived up to it?"

Slowly, as if reluctantly, she left the conference room. Her words continued to reverberate in everyone's ears. Isn't it time we lived up to it? To that resolution? And then, in everyone's mind a single thought worked its way to the forefront of his and her awareness.

"Spread the word," it demanded. "Spread the word. The time has come…"

Soon after the meeting, Lena, the two additional Lenas and Peter took an unmarked SI limousine home. Cathy had been waiting for them with a light lunch. As on her past visits, Lena shunned even the most luxurious hotels. She wanted to be in a private house, where people lived like 'normal' people. Where the walls weren't wired for instant messages, the doors controlled by self-closing devices. She wanted to be home.

Within a week or two, Peter would send her the reactions of all people present at the meeting. There was no rush. The Age of Aquarius would last another 2000 years or so.

As Lena came in, Cathy embraced her as she would an older sister. Judging by appearances, not much older. Biologically Lena was almost twenty years Cathy's senior.

As they sat down, Peter asked Lena about her doppelgangers.

"As I told you, the security came up with the idea. It is not new. At the beginning of this century, many world leaders used doubles to protect themselves from attacks. The intention was to confuse the enemy. The identical twins, selected from many applicants, had been enhanced with makeup, sometimes with plastic surgery. Mine are more sophisticated, of course. They were developed with the US artificial intelligence technology, as well as with Indian nanotechnological enhancements. They are soft to the touch, but would crush your hand in theirs if need be. Also they can actually do justice to the Merchant of Venice."

"I beg your pardon?" Cathy's eyes widened.

"If you prick us, do we not bleed? If you tickle us, do we not laugh?" Lena smiled.

"Bleed…?" Peter curiosity was tickled.

"It's a nanotechnological enhancement. The outer skin is cloned, thickened and blood is circulated within its thickness by nanotechnology. Don't ask me how, but I know it is. I tested them."

"You tickled them?"

"No, stupid, she pricked them!" Cathy admonished Peter. Then she lost her confidence. "You did, didn't you?"

"Which?" Lena asked.

Over lunch Lena told them a little of her past.

"I haven't seen my parents for years. I don't think they ever forgave me for, what they call, sitting on the throne of St. Peter. My father, and mother to a lesser degree, were, in a way still are, I suspect, very much practicing Catholics—in the old-fashioned sense of the word. You'd call them fundamentalists, I suppose. Anyway, they think that the dissolution of the Church was all my fault. My father called me the Whore of Babylon. Apparently there is some sort of prophecy that she'd sit on one of the hills of Rome."

Neither Cathy nor Peter had ever seen Lena so sad. She always seemed so strong. So invincible.

"I haven't seen them since the day I moved to the Vatican," she whispered, holding back tears. "They refused to see me. My mother has died since…"

In the end only Vincenzo loved her—more than his own life.

***

Part Four

WINSTON'S KINGDOM

I sit in the light,
The light is me,
I am the light.

Sai Baba
1926—2011

19
Evolution

"**I like to be a master of my domain**," Winston asserted, a gentle smile lightening the gravity of his words.

So much for the inherent humility, thought Peter. He made a conscious effort to block access to his own thoughts. He wanted neither to insult nor to hurt Winston. Not in a billion-billion years.

"That's one with eighteen zeros," Cathy put in.

"Not in a billion-billion, but you can keep trying, if you wish?" Winston was quite unperturbed.

It must have been fifty years since Peter last blushed. So much for shielding my thoughts, he thought, this time making no attempt to hide them. Anyway, he knew that Winston knew how he felt. It wasn't just a question of thoughts, but emotions came into it. And no one would ever question the love Peter felt for the old majordomo.

"There is as much pride in me as in any man," Winston continued. "After all, I am the end product, as you might say, of some fifteen billion years of evolution."

Time may be imaginary, Peter mused, essential only in quantum mechanical calculations, but here, on earth, it went

on inexorably; without rancor or favour, one season
following another. If you didn't pay close attention, then you
might have missed that it just went on and on and on. Thirty
years had passed since Cathy and Peter moved into their 49th
floor condo overlooking the Mount Royal. Now, in his
middle sixties, Peter was in the prime of his years, but thirty
years at the helm of the SI North America was enough for
any man. Cathy, just a few years behind, looked hardly older
than she did 30 years ago.

"Ahhh, the wonders of genetic manipulation." She
glanced at herself in the mirror. "Will you love me when I am
old and gray?" she asked demurely.

"Of course I'll love you when I am old and gray," Peter
replied obediently, and immediately dodged a flying pillow.

Jonathan Thornton was celebrating his first term as the
Chief of Solidarity North America. He went through the
ranks. JR had given him thorough grounding in all matters
pertaining to security. For his part, Peter had opened his eyes
to the skill of delegating matters that can be handled by
others.

"Trust me, Jo, there'll be plenty left for you to do," he
told his successor.

After getting his Ph. D. in political science, mass
psychology and various branches of philosophy, Jonathan
was ready to embark on applying his theories to practice. Last
summer he was elected by 87% of the vote. At the time, he
was devastated.

"How on earth can I serve the remaining 13% if they
don't want me?" he wailed.

"Do you always approve of everything I do?" Peter
asked softly.

"Well, about 87% of the time," he replied, trying hard to
hide his grin. The penny dropped instantly.

Jonathan's problems had increased considerably. What at
the beginning of Peter's mandate amounted to a few million,
now added up to a few *hundred* million members. This

included Canada, the USA, and a large chunk of what used to be called Mexico, which now seemed as much part of the USA as it did of Central America Federation. Since SI had swollen its ranks, national boundaries were progressively losing their meaning. No one would dream of setting one SI group against another on the other side of the border. It would be unconstitutional. Likewise, most federal governments restricted their activities to central planning, economical projections and the collection and maintenance of statistics for everyone's use. They still had the power to levy taxes, but had to account to their voters for the money spent. If unable to do so, the position occupied by the Member of Parliament, the House of Representatives, or the Senate, was automatically declared vacant.

Having shed the exigencies of the office, Peter kept busy by travelling the world and explaining to people the underlying principles of Solidarity International.

"I'm just telling them what the Age of Aquarius is all about," he claimed. When he said that, Winston would pensively nod his agreement.

"Ignorance is no longer bliss," he'd say.

No one could tell how old Winston was. Sometimes he talked of incidents during, what he referred to as, the old days, which would place him in the second half of the previous century. If so, then Winston put in his appearance on this earth of ours at least 150 magnificent years ago.

But they all missed Moira. Little Mo had grown up into an attractive woman while maintaining her girlish charm. Unfortunately, for the last five years, she had resided mostly in the Vatican, warming her way into becoming Lena's right hand. There were those who said that these days Lena was little more than a figurehead, while Moira Thornton made most of the decisions. All who knew Lena personally would never take such stories seriously.

"For years, after Lena is dead and buried, she'll continue to control the SI from beyond," Cathy observed, the last time

Lena Walesa dropped in unexpectedly. "I wish I had her energy!"

But they all really missed Moira, particularly on weekend nights, when they all liked to get together to knock some ideas around.

For mere mortals, time may travel inexorably, but for Lena it was as imaginary as, on occasion, for Cathy. One evening Peter, Winston and Cathy were lingering at the table after dinner, reminiscing about the old days. In all their endeavours there was progress, an unfolding, that took them forward, toward the great, mysterious unknown. Yet neither individual people nor nations develop at the same rate.

"So what of evolution," Peter interjected. "The Hindus say that in this age of Kali, we're going backwards."

"I can't speak for the Hindus," Winston conceded. "But..."

Peter and Cathy relaxed. It was evident, and recently inevitable, that Winston would slip into subliminal communication. He did so more and more often, though only when the three or four of them were alone.

Heaven and earth. Spirit and matter. Possibility and fulfillment. The first dyad refers to the antipodal states of consciousness. The second to that in which the state of consciousness finds its being. The third—to the creative process, which is the substance of evolution.

"The dance of evolution. The going out and the coming in," Peter mused aloud.

Winston nodded.

"We must never forget that there is such a thing as Parallel Evolution. It begins when the conscious mind takes over from the subconscious. In human terms, it occurs when man, a soul, or the light body, having embodied itself in human flesh, gains awareness of its origin. Until that moment the evolutionary movement had been centrifugal, away from the center of origin. As Cathy would say, it started with the Big Bang and it followed the dictates of the expanding universe. This flow, referred to in the Bible as the Law, controls all nature, all aspects of the manifested universe. In metaphysical terms, man's pre-self-realization stage, together with the rest of the animal kingdom, is controlled exclusively by, for the want of a better word, the 'universal subconscious'."

"You are saying that this phase of evolution can be said to be set on automatic?" Peter sounded fascinated. He'd spent years trying to fathom the mysteries of evolution. He also still remembered fragments of the Bible from his seminary days.

"*It is easier for heaven and earth to pass, than one tittle of the law to fail,*" Cathy's memory served her better. "Or... *I came to fulfil the law, not to destroy it.*" She also enjoyed a superb recall. "It is this act of fulfillment of the Law that exonerates the change in the direction of the evolution of man's consciousness, ultimately of the human race. The switch-over from the automatic or subconscious to the willful or conscious mode of being."

"From reactive to proactive," Peter murmured.

Winston looked pleased as Punch. He considered those two as his most advanced children. They were growing up and up, just fine.

He was about to resume his soliloquy when Jo barged in unannounced. He waved hellos to all three and went straight for the bar. He emerged seconds later with a glass of water that looked slightly yellow with age.

"Nothing improves the taste of water as much as Scotch," he announced for the umpteenth time.

"Good day?" Peter inquired hopefully. This was Sunday. He and Cathy had already dragged Winston for a walk on Mount Royal. Usually, Winston's preferred form of exercise was Hatha Yoga.

"Mo called. We got them." Jo replied. "Eleven percent since last month."

"Care to elaborate?"

"We got an eleven percent rise in membership since last

month in Palestine. The best so far," he explained.

"I thought you were looking after North America," Peter said.

"I am, but you know Mo. She calls me every two days just to show off. That's my sister!"

Apparently Mo hadn't changed much.

It was a long story. After a century of struggle, Israel and the adjoining nations became unified into a single state entity. Israel became a semi-autonomous province within a much larger Confederation, which unified most of what had previously been called Arab States. They became unified under a single flag of Palestine. Rather like the Canadian Provinces with their Maple Leaf. Following almost three generations of hatred, people had grown tired. They also seemed to have discovered, belatedly, the similarity of their roots.

"Why fight when you can be friends?"

This simple question had been asked by a number of leaders of adjoining nations, who, until recently, had been feuding as Europe had done around the Middle Ages.

"Why, indeed?" was the simple response from all sides.

Within hardly two years, the rest became history. Of course, both or, rather, all parties agreed to leave religious fundamentalism out of the equation. Those few who did not, remained ostracized, on the fringes of civilized society. A mere three months after the ostracized, on the fringes of civilized society. A mere three months after the unification, the first applications for SI membership began arriving in the Vatican.

"At this rate, soon we shall have one flock under a single shepherd," Peter murmured under his breath.

"The only thing that's missing are the sheep," Cathy added, stifling a giggle.

"Shepherdess. Most of this was Lena's work," Peter added. "I've been there twice, at her request, and accomplished little. Then Lena went…"

Apparently, once they saw Lena, they all decided that Lena Walesa was the reincarnation of the Queen of Sheba, of Tahpenes, of Vashti, Queen Esther and some sixty-odd Queens listed in the Song of Solomon—all rolled into one. All Semites seemed to have agreed on that in tacit unison.

Jo collapsed into one of the armchairs.

'The Condo', as they referred to it, became the place for the sharing of thoughts and ideas. Members of the Solidarity could come and go, and often they did. As did John Brent, Alice and even, though less often, Cathy's parents. They all claimed to drop in just to enjoy the view. Thanks to SI genetic manipulation, old age was virtually a thing of the past. In some ways, one needed assistance to be able to die. Barring accidents, most did, when well over 150. They said they needed a rest.

"There isn't another like it in all of Montreal," each one of them asserted, staring at the Mount Royal. They were right, of course. The view from the 49th floor transcended time.

Westmount remained Jonathan's official residence, with Winston coming and going at will. Of late, this perambulation applied as much to his worldly abodes as it did to his frequent trips to his private, inimitable Kingdom, where all were welcome but few could find their way.

"It will come," he assured them. "When they're ready."

Peter wasn't sure if his patience was getting better or worse with age. When Moira came to town, she also stayed there—in Westmount, not Winston's Kingdom, though there had been moments...

In addition, Jo had fitted two spare rooms for visiting members of Solidarity, who preferred quiet pow-wows at home, rather than in offices or hotels. It was informal, and they felt they could speak more freely. There were the usual security arrangements, though the guards managed to remain fairly inconspicuous. They were 'disguised' as domestic staff. Winston remained the *ex officio* majordomo. As for Mo and

Jo's private life, they enjoyed their freedom. People seldom entered private partnerships before the age of fifty. After all, this corresponded to young thirties in the old days.

After a leisurely lunch, the four of them retired to the armchairs facing the Mount Royal. Cathy put on an old favourite, the Brandenburg Concertos, and picked up the book she was reading. Winston remained in his armchair, though his eyes reached far, far beyond the mountain he was facing. Jo, who seldom stopped working, began running through some data on his laptop.

Peter's attention rested on the mountain slopes. Through little slots in the rich foliage, he could see the path winding up the mountain. Couples, single men and women—perhaps hoping to be couples one day—strolled up and down, were only just visible from this aerie, and then only so when slivers of sunshine pierced the penumbra of their immediate environment. Peter thought of getting his field-glasses, but then he realized that, surely, those people, hiding in the filigree of light and shadow, deserved their privacy, whether happy or lonely, but belonging to their personal, secret world. Each, he thought, each a world unto itself.

Then his mind wandered back to their earlier discussion on evolution.

Man, Peter mused, his new realization contesting the inexorable forces of physical evolution, applied the brakes, and slowly turned the rudder to point in the opposite direction. Until this point in his evolution, man was subject to all the laws that, contrary to the egotistical promulgation of some sacerdotal casts, denied him any expression of free will. Until this point man was subject to the stringent laws of kill or be killed, of survival of the fittest which, till recently, continued to govern the consciousness of the vast majority of the human and all other species. While the rest of nature continued to obey the *dictum* of eat or be eaten, man, some man—but in growing numbers—went on a self-imposed diet.

Many, of course, still remained puppets controlled by the strings of evolutionary forces, the purpose of which was to provide, develop and sustain a vehicle that would initiate Parallel Evolution. This new direction was not regressive, but was characterized by a condition wherein the spiritual content forming the embodied consciousness would be on the increase. The 'vehicle' continued on its way. This new direction did not, in any way, counteract the laws of nature. It was the Spiritual alongside the Material evolution. The centripetal or integrating, as against the centrifugal or dispersing. The Spiritual—leading to Oneness, the Material— to diversity and fragmentation. Apparently, the Source found both necessary to sustain the infinity of life.

Peter looked up to see if anyone would be willing to explore the subject. No such luck, he noticed. He slipped into a semi-waking state. Soon ideas unfolded themselves on the screen of his consciousness. His mind began to explore his accumulated knowledge.

The theory of the oscillating universe is well known, he mused. We, human micro-universes, perform an oscillating dance of binary states of consciousness.

To this end, man is provided with boundless possibilities. Boundless oceans of information. Countless states of consciousness already created, ready for man to enter, to become one with, at his leisure. In this alone man retained his free will. He could not deny his destiny, but he could choose his time. *There is no time in eternity*, Peter recalled Winston's words. But man needn't have worried about having a suitable vehicle—his future had been assured. Darwin, Peter recalled, asserted that *Hence we may look with some confidence to a secure future of great length. And as natural selection works solely by and for the good of each being, all corporeal and mental endowments will tend to progress towards perfection.* Peter was amazed that he remembered the quote word for word. Darwin had chosen not to mention that intellectual endowments are an integral part of the material universe.

At some stage during his meanderings, Peter's eyes closed, his breathing became slower, more regular. Moments later he saw Winston in his usual white, flowing toga, evidently his preferred apparel in his own realm. As usual, he was giving a lecture. Peter was surprised to see Ruth and Andrew sitting a few rows back from the front, in rapt attention. He sat himself on a flat stone, some distance away, unwilling to disturb anyone already listening.

"…and at the point when the change in the evolutionary direction takes place, man becomes aware of the Ocean of Endless Possibilities. He becomes aware and is awed by the sudden awareness of order, harmony, balance—Divine Laws resulting unavoidably in prolific Beauty. This nascent realization grows, matures, gradually sublimates all previous views of the universe. Until this moment, the embodied consciousness was not capable of recognizing the wonder of creation. It may be unwise to assume that the return trip, the Parallel Evolution, would be much shorter than that which brought us from Eden to this point in our awareness."

The silence was spellbinding. It seemed that no one stirred, no one breathed, unwilling to miss a single syllable.

"Knowledge is that which keeps evolution on an even keel. Love is that which binds it together; it is the gathering—the centripetal Force. It draws, with ever increasing intensity, until all is gathered, all is brought back to its point of origin. Like a universal Black Hole. Only… once the Hole absorbs infinity, it is no longer black. It is replete with light."

Winston looked around. Peter followed his eyes. Indeed! There she was, hardly an arm-length from where he was sitting. Why do we always look far for what is often so very close? She also smiled recognition.

"Nothing escapes from its overpowering attraction," Winston continued. The reference to black hole must have been addressed to Cathy.

"As men, we cannot know what happens at its enigmatic

center. What happens in the Heart of God? Not even Light escapes It, not even ultimate divine Knowledge. The best we can hope for is to meet and observe the rare souls that approach the end of their return journeys. We must always remain aware that theirs was not a journey in time, nor in space, but a journey within an ocean of consciousness. We can bask in the reflected light of their knowledge, be drawn by the love emanating from their core. They are the Beacons, the Way-showers, the Paragons of Evolution."

Peter sensed Cathy's arm on his shoulder.

"Is this the essence of Parallel Evolution? The evolution in Life itself?" He felt her emotive thoughts prodding his mind.

"Where they lead, we must follow. It is the nature of our being," Winston added, as if stating the obvious.

The wind bloweth where it listeth...

"And what then? What of the Light at the Heart of a Black Hole?" This was Cathy again.

Winston turned and instantly Cathy felt his eyes fall in her.

"At some fleeting instant of yet another eternity, when all is gathered, bathed in the bliss of Oneness, saturated with such Love as to be no longer confinable within the affluence of Singularity of Being.... That which is ONE shall, once more, effloresce into infinite diversity."

For a moment the word ONE continued to reverberate as though repeated by echoes of the surrounding mountains. Then Winston spoke again, this time subliminally, as though not to disturb the oneness that seemed to engulf them.

"And time will start again, expand into new space, and foster new evolution. Billions of years later Adam will reach the stage when his subconscious, his animal soul, will add substance to his being. And then a new, a fragile infant shall be born in his heart, a new awareness, that of a child longing to return home."

The echoes retreated into the infinity of space. Total

silence prevailed.

"And he will spin the web of an ascending spiral, the eternal dance of Love, in search of the essence of Being."

Peter opened his eyes. Cathy's book was lying on her lap, her face bathed in blissful happiness. I wasn't hallucinating. Yes, he mused, she really was there.

Thank you, Winston.

It was a warm evening. One of the problems with the 49th floor was that there were no opening windows. Something to do with wind traveling upwards, along the surface of the facades, and creating a negative pressure many times stronger that the velocity of wind itself. You could be sucked right out.

Peter and Cathy decided to go for a stroll on Mount Royal. The balmy summer day seemed to be asking for it. Most of the heat had already dissipated, the green foliage absorbing the rest of it.

Winston, in spite of protests from his hosts, decided to stay behind and clean up after dinner. He refused to give in. Just as Peter and Cathy were leaving the building, a vertical stick insect joined them.

"You're too late for dinner, JR. Join us for a walk and a drink later," said Peter.

JR nodded. "I've eaten already."

There was no harm. JR was in the habit of dropping in, unannounced, just for a chat, or a beer, which he invariably brought himself. Now he spun on his heel and headed for the mountain. Every twenty steps or so, he waited for the rest of them to catch up.

"Why don't you go ahead and we'll meet at the terrace in front of the Chalet," Peter suggested.

The Chalet, known as *Chalet du Mont-Royal*, was inaugurated in 1932. Its walls trace the history of Montreal, and the Kondiaronk front offers unparalleled views of the downtown area and the Saint Lawrence River.

A half-hour later Peter and Cathy were standing at the steps of the Chalet. Below them, myriad street-lamps, some twinkling, some steadfast, immovable, defined the extremities of the city. The dark mysterious ribbon of the Saint Laurence River, winding itself from west to east, was cut, in a few places, by the ever-moving white and red lights of cars traveling to and fro across the near-invisible bridges. Peter and Cathy had seen this view a thousand times, yet Cathy, once again, sighed. Over the years, they'd shared many a silent moment here, just looking.

Then they looked around. JR was nowhere to be seen.

Usually, visitors were not allowed in the park after nine p.m. This July the hours had been extended and the number of mounted police doubled to assure public safety. Peter ran up the steps of the Chalet and peeked inside. No JR. Nor was there any sight of him on the paved terrace outside. There were only about thirty or forty people around; it would have been impossible not to see a man of his height.

Alas, no JR.

Peter pulled out his electronic spotter. The top brass in SI had been issued devices capable of detecting the presence of a Solidarity member up to 25 feet away. The purpose was to check if a particular person wearing SI insignia was a *bona fide* member, or, possibly, an impostor.

Peter scanned the immediate area. He then asked Cathy to stay put, in case JR misjudged the time of their arrival at the top of the mountain while taking a more circuitous route. Himself, Peter went in a wider circle, pointing the device into the bushes adjoining the extensive terrace. Still no results.

He went back to Cathy and told her that he'd like to check the inside of the Chalet. After some ten minutes of peeking in various corners, under the tables and display stands, he descended the staircase to the public washrooms. If JR had an upset stomach, this would be a preferred place to find him. All stalls were empty, the door swinging in a half-open position. Peter was about to go back to Cathy when he heard a moan.

He spun back, this time getting down on his hands and knees. The place was empty, he confirmed. No feet protruded from under any of the stalls.

"I must have imagined it," he thought, making for the stairs, when he heard another vague sound.

It came from the direction of the cleaner's cupboard.

The door was locked. He knocked.

"JR?" he said in a loud whisper. "JR?" Peter repeated louder.

"God, I'm stupid!" Peter exclaimed, drawing the electronic spotter from his pocket and clicking it open. A definite pulse registered in his hand. There was a member of Solidarity very nearby.

Peter run up the stairs, vaulted the service counter of the fast-food cafe, and moments later was running back downstairs, with forks, knives and some other implements he had found behind the counter. It never crossed his mind to call the police.

Cleaning cupboards are not equipped with complex security locks. Peter remembered picking such locks when still an intern at the General, to find privacy with a pretty nurse. Within seconds he had the door open.

JR sat bent in half, propped against the far wall, his head between his knees. Peter touched his shoulder. JR remained still. Peter touched his aorta. Nothing. But the neck was still warm.

Peter got to his knees and, without thinking, embraced JR's gaunt body. He stayed that way for a while, expecting to feel a sign of weakness in his own body, as he always had in the past.

Nothing.

Have I lost it? *Oh, God, surely You will not withdraw Your power when I need it for my friend?*

This was the first time Peter had prayed since he'd walked out of the seminary. He had no idea what God he was addressing. Just a power outside himself. Greater than himself. Omnipresent. The force of life Itself?

Finally, as he continued to feel nothing, he let go and lowered himself against the wall. So it is gone, he mused. It ruined my career and now, when I really need it, it is gone.

"You need what, Peter?"

Peter opened his eyes. Sitting next to him, his back also against the wall, was the smiling face of his friend. In the relative darkness, JR's eyes seemed suspended in the air. His eyes were shining like two little torches.

"JR?"

"Help me to get out of here, Peter, I'm so cramped I can't even get to my feet."

Peter moved out of the way, JR lay down on his side, and pushed away from the wall, thus straightening out his legs. Then he turned onto his stomach, drew the legs under him, and got to a kneeling position.

"Well? I'm not here to pray. Help me up!"

Peter, still disbelieving what had happed, helped JR to his feet. In the past, when the pulse was weak and Peter managed to restore it, his own body was near collapse with exhaustion. Today—nothing. It was as if nothing had happened. Just surprise. In the past, he recalled, he always thought that he'd accomplished something. Not that he had any edifying experience of the esoteric, but he felt that the 'patient' was going to get better. Today he knew nothing of the sort. It was as if he'd left his own body behind and allowed some external agency to use it for its own ends.

"How did you find me?" JR asked.

Peter shook his head. He wasn't sure JR knew about his healing 'gift'. Or scourge, as he used to call it. And now? And now it had saved the life of his friend. Peter showed JR his sensor.

"It was easy," he said. "I just clicked it on."

"Oh…" JR was not quite himself. It was apparent that he had no idea what had happened to him.

"Cathy's waiting outside."

With Peter pulling and JR pushing, JR rose to his feet. He leaned against the wall for support.

"Where am I?" he asked.

"You went ahead quickly and lost your way," Peter offered.

"Oh…" JR was unusually agreeable.

Cathy saw them coming from below through the glass door. She breathed a sigh of relief.

"This must have been the longest bout with constipation I've ever witnessed," she whispered to Peter.

"You don't know the half of it," he assured her.

At least for now, Peter didn't want to discuss it. He wasn't sure what had happened either. He definitely hadn't lost his 'touch', but the healing process was different from whatever it had been before. He was anxious to speak to Winston.

For now Peter decided not to let JR out of his sight. Whoever had attacked him might still be in the vicinity. He didn't suspect international participation. Rather, JR, particularly if sitting on a toilet in a public washroom, might have presented a skinny subject, easy to rob. The attacker must have been surprised when he laid JR out and, probably, couldn't fit him back into the stall. If the cleaning cupboard had been open, he might have decided to hide the body before anyone would find the two of them still downstairs.

Unless it was the cleaner, or some other member of the maintenance personnel, and he had the key. JR would look into it tomorrow. For now, Peter decided to enjoy the walk, the view, and the wonderful smell of nature all around them. It is a rare gift that the Montrealers have preserved for their children. The 100-hectare park rises to the highest point in the city, some 234 meters above sea level. It was the jewel of

Montreal since 1876 and still the favourite spot for lovers and just strollers alike.

As if nothing had happened, the three of them continued their walk to the very top of the mountain, and then, easily, allowing for *qi* to flow gently, they strolled down, Peter making sure that JR didn't stray ahead of them.

Soon they were back at home. JR didn't bring his own beer, and, with a most comically miserable face, sipped tea with the rest of them.

"It ain't got no suds," he complained.

On the other hand, he did justice to the night-snacks Winston had prepared in their absence. Peter never understood how a man could eat as much as JR and remain a spindly skeleton.

There was a tacit agreement that, on such nightly sessions, they'd never talk business. Usually, Winston would recount some stories from his rich past, or Cathy might describe the latest innovations in the field of experimental physics. What thirty years ago was called theoretical was moving into the experimental phase. Peter felt sure that any moment now, they'd create a black hole that would swallow them all.

"Don't worry, darling," she assured him. "It would probably spit us out on the other side. The theoreticians now hold that what goes in must come out. Somewhere."

Winston watched them with a nondescript smile playing about his lips. Recently, on special occasions, he would agree to stay the night at the condo. Unless Jo needed him, of course. Whenever he stayed in the study, Peter had the best dreams imaginable. He assumed it was Winston's way of saying thank you. Peter only wished he'd agree to stay the night more often.

***

20

Winston's Kingdom

"**Healing, even at a distance,** occurs when your vibrations are synchronized with those of the patient, provided you and your light body become one. Like Cathy's strings, which vibrate in unison. If such synchronicity occurs, healing takes place. Why? Because your light body is always perfect. It is the expression of an idea, built up by mind."

What Winston didn't tell Peter at the time was that this congruence must occur between the subconscious and the unconscious. Conscious awareness of this equivalence takes place much later.

After JR left, Peter told Winston what had taken place at the Chalet. He described, as best he could, how he found JR, his pulse rate, and what he attempted to do to bring him back to life. At the same time, he tried to explain the absence of tiredness that, in the past, had always accompanied such ministrations.

Winston seldom, if ever, gave a straight answer. His contention was that all answers lie within us, only we, for whatever reason, block them from our awareness. "That is why each event might have a different answer for each and every person," he claimed. But this was some time ago.

"How does one come alive?" Peter asked, thinking of JR coming back from what looked like the very edge of death.

But he was too late. Winston sighed and closes his eyes. Only later did Peter realize that Winston had given him the answer before he'd asked for it. *Healing, even at a distance, occurs when your vibrations are synchronized,* he'd said. Vibrations that are perfect. The vibrations of your real self. Your true self. Where there is perfection there is no death. There is only life.

More and more often, Winston appeared to momentarily leave the earthly environs for what he called the true reality. While he was 'in transit', discussions with him took place in a different timeframe. In fact, they seemed divorced from our concept of time altogether. They were no longer sequential. His answers would come before being asked, as it happened with the JR problem. It was up to the recipient of the answers to make head and tail of them. As for Winston, he would come back, refreshed, though not for long. It seemed that gradually he was leaving the earth behind. He still served, did his job—it was his nature—but he was less persistent at it.

A few days ago Peter had asked him about the Kingdom. Winston's Kingdom. The old man insisted that it was not his. Or, at least, not his alone.

"We all start as an idea. Then the universal mind, you can call it the creative force, differentiates this idea into countless components and builds them out of light. Cathy would call them the quanta of photons. Only light, in the true realm, is replete with knowledge. Or intelligence. Also, each component is endowed with consciousness. Not self-consciousness, but consciousness nevertheless. Some become manifest at a rudimentary level, such as trees or grass, some at more advanced, as we are. But in material reality, we are all mere projections of the primary differentiation."

He talked long into the night. As he did, Peter saw, perhaps just imagined, the shimmering contours of Ruth and Andrew, and Cathy, of course, and the children, now fully grown, sitting around and listening. Long into the night...

There were moments when Peter wasn't sure if he was dreaming the whole thing or even... hallucinating. His medical training was a lasting barrier between himself and his visions. Perhaps that was why Winston had stepped in. Perhaps that was why he had to accept the gift of healing—to see the invisible light flowing through his hands. Peter thought he was getting closer to understanding. But coming back to that particular evening, or night, his vision was still confused. The next day Cathy asked him how he had enjoyed the lecture Winston had given.

"You heard?"

"I was sitting next you, darling. Why do you not believe the evidence of your heart?"

The evidence of my heart? He still didn't recognize his heart, his emotions, as one of his senses. Had that been his problem all along?

"I thought he gave lectures only in, you know, that place..."

"His Kingdom? Peter, Kingdom is within you—and without you. Kingdom is where you decide it is."

"And in it we are all one?" Winston had told him that.

"Ultimately. The Kingdom is where the first differentiation takes place. You are where your attention is. We all come from a single source, and there, in the Kingdom, we find our individual expressions, though never apart from each other."

"How can that be?"

"Look at your motto. *E pluribus Unum.* Remember? That says it all. In a way, as I understand it, that's what Solidarity is all about."

"I never thought of it that way. You mean the Solidarity is... is... all part of it?"

"We are all part of it. This realm, here, on earth, is imaginary. In a way, so is it there. Up there, if you like. But essentially, it is all one. One reality is the extension of the other. Every differentiation is no more than a transient projection of the whole."

Later that day, in the office, Jonathan called a conference. As soon as the departmental heads sat down, the faces of Lena and Moira appeared on the wall screen. Behind them there were two rows of people, the Solidarity's senior staff in the Vatican. For a moment or two the two ladies looked at each other, and then Lena spoke.

"I asked Moira Thornton to advise you about the problem we are facing. We do not seem to have the expertise to tackle it on our own."

For the first time ever, Lena's tone of voice was showing a sharp edge. She seemed ready to take drastic action, and was being held back by whatever the balancing factors were.

"Thank you, Ma'am," Moira started formally, as did Lena before her. "We have reached the level at which we must establish our relationship with the whole world."

She appeared to scan the faces of all present. In the Vatican, she and Lena were facing a similar wall screen, which displayed the faces of North American SI leaders. Her eyes showed unusual maturity for one so young. Even from the screen, at around forty, she radiated the wisdom of the ages.

"We are no longer an organization helping those who were too weak to help themselves. We are certainly no longer a glorified trade union. Far from it. Various governments of the world are now calling upon the Solidarity International to make decisions that affect the whole of humanity. We, Lena Walesa and I, are not sure the Solidarity should get involved in politics at that level."

She sat back. The silence was stunning. People, brought up in the philosophy of non-interference, were flabbergasted. Nobody expected such a statement from the Vatican. What does she mean 'not sure'? How can she not be sure? We are all sure…

"Are you suggesting that Solidarity is called upon to create a world government?" Jonathan took the bull by the horns. Others followed.

"A new United Nations?"

"An international authority?"

"A police force?"

There were a number of other questions. Each enunciated with a degree of rancor and incredulity.

"Has it to do with international justice?" Peter asked.

Lena and Moira remained silent. They seemed to be waiting for others to have their say before they would reveal their own thinking.

For reasons Peter couldn't explain, at this particular moment he recalled Cathy's recent words, *the kingdom is within you and without you.* Is this what it was all about? Are we to begin reflecting, globally, Winston's Kingdom down here? Down here on earth? But we hardly know what Winston's Kingdom is!

Peter noticed that all eyes were centered on him. Since he'd asked his question no one had spoken.

Innocence. The Garden of Eden. Watering your own garden? Isn't that what the Age of Aquarius is supposed to be? The age of individuality? Ideas available to all, without judgment. Only you remained the judge. Judgment is left to the Son. The Son is the individualized consciousness.

"Can you elaborate, Peter?" This was Lena.

"No. I can't, really. What I meant had not so much to do with justice, only with arbitration. But even that could infringe on individual rights."

"Not if both parties agree to it in advance," someone offered.

The Kingdom is created by consciousness, sustained by thought, and when you withdraw attention from it, it…

dissolves? It takes a long time to imbue it with sufficient density to remain extant for any length of time on its own.

When you learn that, it becomes your Kingdom, and you are its absolute ruler. Unless... unless you give your creation some autonomy...

"Aristotle said that Justice consists of giving people their dues," Peter said, just to take a stab at the answer expected from him. "What Aristotle failed to tell us was who is to decide who and what they deserve. His statement was meaningless..." he concluded lamely.

On the other hand... all judgment is left to the Son... are we not all children of the most high?

So we can't avoid passing judgment?

Yet if you judge, so you will be judged. By whom?

Back to square one.

"It seems that we have no choice. We must become immortal," he almost said it aloud. But even in his subliminal whisper he lacked conviction.

"It would seem like the right thing to do," he heard Cathy's voice in his head. Or had it been Winston's?

Am I going mad?

"We must create conditions in which people of the world can find justice without compulsion. It seems to me that consented arbitration is the only possible solution," Peter took up his cause again.

"Who would be the arbitrator?" Moira asked after murmur on both sides of the Atlantic had died down.

"Solidarity International," Lena answered. It appeared that she invoked the answer she wanted to hear all along. She glanced at Peter gratefully. She knew she could count on him. She was that clever.

"All those in favour raise your arm, please," Moira commanded from across the Atlantic. Raising one's arm was just a traditional response to an open vote. In reality, each member present, on 'both' sides of the 'table', pressed a

button built into the arm of each chair. The fingerprint
identified the author of the vote. The buttons were only
operational at voting time. Moira's request activated them. It
would be active for ten seconds only. Lena had learned long
ago that if you give people enough time, they would find
many reasons to counter their own convictions. The
subconscious rejects new concepts. It relies exclusively on
the tried and true. The inspiration, the thought that emanated
from their unconscious, would be questioned and most
probably discarded. For years now, all voting in the SI had
been guided by the principles of spontaneity.

Moments later, the wall screen went opaque. The
meeting was over. Apparently, they were not to see the
results of the vote at this time.

"Congrats, Peter, you've done it again!" JR was
stretching out his hand.

"Again?"

"What? You forgot the Ponzis?"

Surely, Peter mused, he's not still giving me credit for
that? He smiled weakly. "Oh, that..." By then JR was
shaking his hand. For a man as skinny as he was, he had an
amazingly firm grip.

Well, in a way, it was my idea, Peter thought. And a
moment later he was embarrassed by his own pigheadedness.
Why is it so hard to grow up, he mused, not for the first time.

"We spend years in Kindergarten," Winston said, his voice
much too young for a man his age. He looked around, his
benevolent smile embracing each of them individually.

On this occasion, the usual group of friends gathered in
Westmount, around the fireplace. It was much too early for a
real, roaring fire, but Jo, the host, insisted on at least a small
hearth. It would be the first of the season. Soon the colours
would adorn the mountain, again, with a crown of gold and
rubies. So repetitive, so perennial, yet never less beautiful. It

seemed that ugliness was always transient; beauty—even if interrupted by seasons—eternal.

"Evolution of consciousness as an individual entity, or self, advances through three distinct phases: the Kindergarten, the School and the University. Progressively, these phases serve to assert individuality, expand its range of awareness and, ultimately, pass beyond the inherently assumed limitations. And Kindergarten is where we all start."

The crackle of the fire, which Jo had set for the occasion, added mystery to Winston's words.

"It begins when the rudimentary consciousness asserts its will to survive as an individual unit. An amoeba, a virus, a bacterium. The mono-cellular entity becomes aware of the inside and the immediate outside of itself. It defines its territory, its boundaries. The primitive consciousness learns the laws of survival by re-embodying itself within ever more complex physical forms. Each re-embodiment is designed to increase the scope of its operations. The Sanskrit scriptures place the number of transmigrations of each individualization of consciousness at eight million four hundred thousand. Hopefully this number includes the second phase of our evolution, though I doubt it. Suffice to say that the primary stage of our existence consists exclusively of assuring physical survival and wellbeing."

Winston looked around. He held everyone's attention.

"The learning process in this phase relies on repetitive conditioning," he resumed. "The method is that of trial and error. The repetitions serve to develop the subconscious—a storehouse of information—on which the primitive individualization can draw to survive within its embodiment in ever-changing environments. Its responses to challenges are reactive, i.e., automatic or instinctive. There is little evidence of free will or deductive reasoning, although the acquired experience is carefully stored in the genetic code of the biological constructs the entity produces to advance its evolution. At this stage, the individualized consciousness is subject to the indomitable laws of nature. A mistake costs it its life. Its biological life."

Winston stopped, leaned back, seemingly gathering his thoughts. Cathy rose quietly and disappeared into the kitchen. She came back with a large carafe of water, with ice cubes jingling like Christmas bells. A few slices of lemon added zest and aroma. She never served wine when Winston was talking.

She placed the tray on the sideboard, and Jonathan busied himself with distribution of glasses. JR sniffed at his, with mild hope of detecting the smell of beer. He smiled when he saw Peter's expression, who caught himself reading JR's mind.

"Well, I like it," JR said defensively.

"I know, imported." They both grinned.

Winston took a sip from his glass, then looked at Peter. "The next phase is the School," he said. "I rather think that Peter has great expertise in this stage of our development." He raised his glass in encouragement.

Peter sighed but did not refuse the invitation to continue.

"During this phase," Peter said, vainly trying to match Winston's *gravitas*, "the entity develops advanced communication skills," he pointed to himself, grinning, "and becomes susceptible to the influences of theoretical knowledge. It learns to be selective in its relationship to the universal laws governing its environment. In the School," he capitalized the letter S with a large sweep of his arm, "the teachers are responsible for the efficacy of imparting knowledge to their pupils. During this evolutionary phase, the units of consciousness are organized within a variety of classrooms. The purpose of this tendency towards aggregations is to extend the awareness of the self beyond its space/time confines, i.e.: beyond its physical limitations. The classrooms consist of groups within which the self reaches out to include the allegiance to families, clans, villages, towns, religious congregations and national formations—with which the Self can identify. In order to facilitate control over the nascent units of consciousness, the teachers, or those in authority, endeavour to maintain them in abject ignorance. We are taught that obedience—to those in power—is a virtue. Regrettably, with few exceptions, the teachers are also ignorant of the true reality, but their very ignorance aids the entities to free themselves from the imposed rigours. The rare Avatars, invariably non-conformists, thus in direct opposition to the prevailing *status quo*, cast seeds of wisdom on the developing states of consciousness. Also, regrettably, the seeds seldom strike fertile soil. More often than not they meet an inflexible mindset, bent on protecting rather than improving acquired knowledge. Other seeds reach receptive minds, but are stifled by the orthodox establishment in control. The few who break with traditions are ridiculed, often persecuted, sometimes killed. Those wielding power strongly discourage free thought and individuality. The School is tough," he concluded with a lopsided grin.

This was the first time that Peter had been asked to share his non-professional knowledge with anyone. He took a sip of water and looked, shyly, at his audience. He wondered if they all knew that what he'd described was essentially his own experience. He felt considerable relief that no one laughed, or even sniggered. Encouraged, he resumed.

"The last segment of this phase is characterized by rebellion." How well I know it, he mused. "We gradually lose faith in our teachers. We observe countless contradictions between their teaching and their pattern of behaviour. This dichotomy is particularly in evidence within the sacerdotal and political ranks, the two groups most concerned with controlling our minds and... our material wealth. We still obey, mostly due to inbred fear, but simultaneously begin to strike out on our own. This invariably leads to a period of apostasy that results in achieving a degree of freedom from previous conditioning. When we feel secure, we begin to compare the various teachings, each claiming absolute exclusivity over truth. We discover that if we eliminate ninety-nine percent of the miasma that our teachers, that is to say, including our leaders, politicians, preachers, priests, parents, or elders, have imposed on the *original* teachings, the residual essence is virtually the same. We begin to suspect that if all the great Avatars taught the same *a priori* knowledge, then there must be an original source from which they, the Avatars, drew their wisdom."

Peter took a deep breath.

"We begin searching for the Source."

He said the last words as though exhaling them from his lungs. Like Winston before him, he sank back against the armchair.

Winston looked pleased. Peter couldn't be sure how much of what he'd said in the last part of his resume came from his own experience, and how much of it was simply conveying, or putting into words, Winston's own thoughts invading his mind. Whichever it was, he was pleased that his portion of the evolutionary phase analysis was over.

For a little while only the crackling of the fire interrupted the pensive silence. Jo poked the grate with an iron, added two logs, and sat back to listen.

"And now, my friends, we arrive at the gates of the University," Winston announced, once more gathering everyone's attention.

"We become students," he continued. "We discover that our newly found freedom is commensurate with our acceptance of responsibility. We no longer hold teachers, preachers, priests, confessors, psychologists, politicians, our parents, or even circumstances, responsible for our survival. In fact, our definition of survival is undergoing a fundamental change. The extension of our physical life is no longer our priority. Quality takes preference over quantity. We begin to suspect—then know—that we are entities with an unimaginable potential. We learn from every quarter, from the past and the present, from nature, from the positive and negative traits still integral to our mental, emotional and physical embodiments. We learn the difference between reactive and causative action. We refuse to conform for the sake of the illusion of security we used to derive from the concept of belonging. We become individuals."

He stopped once more to take another sip of water.

"It is never easy. But one day, each one of us must step beyond conformity."

Every member of this little gathering had already done so, but no one had ever put it into words. They stopped practicing the dictates of a particular sacerdotal group, rejected impositions of political parties, or organizations, which attempted to impose their thinking on them as individuals.

"The university deals with that which has neither beginning nor end. It finds its reality outside the constraints of the spacetime continuum. This realization empowers us to step outside our material limitations. Outside our physical bodies. From this new vantage ground we observe the forces controlling our environment. We observe the rich becoming richer, the poor—poorer. The happy—increasing in their joy, the miserable sinking into depression. *Regardless of external circumstances.*"

Winston stressed his last four words, piercing each one of them with his eyes that seemed to hide mysteries still untold.

"We became aware of the universal rule that, although heretofore unwittingly, controlled us from the moment we became enwrapped in material reality."

His voice rose a few decibels.

"We become aware that our thoughts create reality; that we are the product of our contemplation."

Winston closed his eyes. The silence stretched till it became ponderous. Everyone had questions; no one wanted to be the first to ask.

Cathy stirred first. "I'm sorry, Winston, but I never had

much success with contemplation," she said, sounding both
shy and disappointed.

"I rather thought that you've done a beautiful job, young
lady," Winston replied smiling, his eyes still closed.

"Have done? I don't understand."

"Cathy, you didn't listen. You *are* the product of your
contemplation. We all are. We cannot be anything else,"
Winston explained. Now he was staring at her with
admiration.

"You mean... you..."

"Of course, you are the product of the contemplation of
your true self. What else could you be?"

Cathy let out a deep sigh of relief. They were all
beginning to understand what Winston was talking about.

Winston delivered the rest of the discourse directly, to
each one individually.

*We note that every thought we entertain influences our
environment. Every thought we energize with emotion defines
our future. We learn to control our thoughts. We become
selective in the use of, and learn to control, our emotions. We
learn that to realize a dream, we must have a dream. To
reach a goal, we must have a goal. To realize the impossible,
we must believe that everything is possible. We become the
conscious effect of the creative power of our beliefs. We
perceive that at every instant of existence, we are the
consequence of our past, the forerunners of our futures.*

We take control.

*Growing we grow, maturing we mature, ever reaching
for the eternally receding horizon. Slowly, so very slowly, it
dawns on us that there are no horizons. We realize that we,
ourselves, define the characteristics and the scope of our
reality. We realize that we create the universe in which we
find our being.*

Then he spoke aloud again, in his normal sonorous voice,
yet everyone heard it as approaching thunder.

"The lightning strikes. Time stops. We begin living in the present."

During the week following the transatlantic conference, Solidarity International made an announcement on the international airways. In essence, the statement read through the satellite hookup by Lena Walesa said that Solidarity International welcomes proposals from individuals, regardless of their affiliation to any groups, organizations or nations, which would lead to the creation of a World Court of Arbitration. The decision of the Court, she said, would be binding on all parties.

Peter thought she could have saved herself the trouble by just asking Winston what to do. Of course, he wasn't serious. In this particular Age, the whole purpose was to empower the individual. If people registered to be bound by the court's decision, this would enable individual people to take national governments to court. Such freedom of action could create endless backlogs. Every Tom, Dick or Harry, not to mention Henrietta, could, in theory, take the UK or the USA to court and demand retribution for real or imagined wrongs.

To overcome this, Lena proposed a stratification of jurisprudence, based on the existing judicial systems. There would be seven steps one would have to take to reach the Supreme Court of Arbitration. The system would be run exclusively by the present members of the judiciary, provided they were members of Solidarity International. Any lawyer, advocate or solicitor could apply for the job.

"Rome wasn't built in a day," Moira said, when she called Peter that evening. "But it's a start." And then she added softly, "I don't suppose you could bounce it off Winston?"

Peter smiled. That same evening he closed his eyes and listened. He knew that Moira could have done exactly the same herself. Just listen. The infinite source of all knowledge was equally accessible to us all. Not that Winston ever claimed to be that source. Nevertheless, for the little group that gathered periodically at the condo, or at Jo's Westmount home, he was certainly its most formidable transformer.

After a while, Peter saw Winston's face hovering a few feet in front of his closed eyes. The majordomo didn't say anything. He only smiled. For Peter that was enough.

***

21
Ego

The next day, on Monday, JR knocked on Peter's office door. It was unusual for JR to come without calling first. The secretary showed him in.

"This may be nothing," he said, "but I think you ought to know."

Peter looked up from his computer. "Sit down, JR. What is it?"

"I thought I'd tell you what happened last night."

"On the mountain?"

"Yes." JR stretched his legs. "It hit me around eight last night. I finished tying up some odds and ends in the office, yes, I know it was Sunday, but it had to be done. Anyway, I was ready to go home, and decided to drop in on you guys just to stretch my legs."

Peter leaned forward and peeked over the edge of his desk. They were stretched all right. JR waved him back to his seat. "I felt a sting on my neck and thought nothing much of it. The days are still warm and, since the environmentalists had their way, there's an occasional mosquito even downtown. By the time I got to your place I felt a bit woozy. When you suggested a walk, I thought it was a great idea to clear my head. If I recall, I nodded and went ahead. You with me?"

"So far..." Peter nodded.

"By the time I got to the top of the mountain, my wooziness got worse. I began to suspect some sort of foul play. I went down to the washroom to splash some water on my face. When that didn't help, I locked myself in the cleaner's cupboard."

"You did what?"

"Well, it wouldn't do to be found by the Yankees while I was still feeling groggy," he explained. By now in JR's vocabulary 'Yankees' stood for the ungodly of all shapes and sizes.

Peter sat back. "You locked yourself..."

JR nodded. "Anyway, last night I subjected myself to spectral analysis. I don't mean the ghostly apparition type spectral, only, well..." He began studying the ceiling. "All Nanotechs have a specific spectrogram. It is not a one-nano-fits-all affair. All nano-injections are fitted to a specific blood type and a number of other biological traits. It results in minuscule radiation emitted by the nano-injections, which in turn affect the functioning of your synapses. Your brain. The brain of a Nanotech."

JR sank deeper into his armchair. Peter waited, having only a vague idea of what JR was talking about.

"Well, my new spectrogram doesn't match the original. I've been tampered with." JR concluded.

Peter didn't even know what questions to ask. It was evident that JR was concerned, but not scared out of his wits.

"Do you know how to correct the, ah, the..."

"Spectrogram? Yes and no. The simplest way is to have a complete blood change, a hundred percent transfusion, but that would revert me to my old self."

Peter smiled. "Would that be so bad?"

JR regarded his friend for a little while, then sighed. "You know how you felt when you got your gift?" He looked up at Peter, who was obviously surprised that JR knew so much about it. "Winston and I talk, you know..." JR pointed upwards with his thumb.

Peter nodded. Of course, he thought, up there, Winston mentioned, we are all one—whatever that means...

"Well, losing my nano-abilities would be like you getting your gift, only in reverse. That's not very clear, but it's the best I can do." He could hardly tell Peter that reverting to being 'normal' would be like suddenly becoming a moron.

Peter sat back. "Do you feel you're in danger?"

"I don't feel any different. What bothers me is that whatever they've done to me is well beyond the abilities of our American friends. This is strictly nano, i.e. Sino or possibly Indian. Although the Indians wouldn't interfere with their own product. It seems that the dragon is flexing his muscles."

"What can we do?"

"I want to fly to Mumbai."

As Chief of Canada, JR needed Jonathan's OK, but Peter was his friend. He felt more comfortable talking to him about it. After all, this wasn't strictly business; it was at least semi-private.

"Of course," was Peter's answer. "I'll talk to Jo."

JR nodded his thanks, but continued to fidget, looking a bit miserable. He fiddled with the position of his endless lower limbs for sometime before coming to the point.

"It seems to me," he said, "that there must be a falling out in the Sino-Indian bloc. I think they're entering a phase of direct competition. It could be dangerous for the rest of us."

Peter knew that by the "rest of us" JR was thinking of the rest of the world in general and of SI in particular. It certainly looked as though JR may have been right. It was one thing to counteract robots—who reacted adversely to specific magnetic waves, or even androids—with their absence of auras, but Nanotechs were indistinguishable from other humans, except that they were ten times smarter. Ten times smarter than the smartest among us. The only unknown was if the nano-conversions would, in time, kill the recipients. It could take decades, perhaps generations before anyone could be sure. For the present, all beneficiaries of the technology were glorified guinea pigs.

They never discussed that aspect of it.

Peter was alone that evening. Cathy flew to CERN, Winston stayed in Westmount, having a pow-wow with Jo. Peter wondered if a time would come when one would never feel lonely, unwanted. As 'up there', he supposed. It was one of those rare evening when he missed company. He helped himself to a Scotch and sank into an armchair. Even the view of the mountain did not relieve his mounting nostalgia.

Life is a search for happiness, he mused. We spend lifetimes chasing the elusive rainbow. Paradoxically, the proponents of various religions unanimously issued a guarantee on achieving such a blessed state. After death, of course—in heaven. After they liberated us from our worldly ties. Midas, like his sacerdotal successors, attempted to find happiness this side of the Great Divide. To no avail.

And yet...

And yet, among all the false prophets there was one Man who promised happiness here and now. Happiness for the *living*. He also said that the truth will set us free. *Will*, he'd said. Not would nor might. And that the truth, and knowledge, and even happiness, all lay within us.

Within us? Here and now?

We don't have to die to be happy?

He, that Man, was the reason why Peter had entered the seminary. Long, long ago. When he still had faith.

When Peter opened his eyes, Winston was sitting next to him. His, even as Peter's, eyes, as though in unison, unseeing, wandered aimlessly over the treetops. Lately he and Winston had spent more and more time in, often silent, communion—their minds in total sync. They were thinking as one. As lovers sometimes do, only Winston and Peter loved each other in a manner few lovers can. It was like father and son, best friend and mentor, all rolled into one.

The modern gurus, Peter heard unspoken words, *manage to generate considerable confusion in the area of the pursuit*

*of happiness. Some admonish us to identify with our true self,
never explaining what this enigmatic entity is. Others talk of
sanctifying our lower self until it is 'saved'. The first group is
predominant among the adherents of eastern philosophies,
the second finds its base in the western religious systems,
what used to be known as Christianity. Yet to a student of
both myths, ranging from the Sanskrit Vedas to the Bible,
neither of the assertions seems accurate.*

Peter smiled. That had always been his problem. From
the moment he began thinking for himself.

"Why the dichotomy between the higher and lower
selves?" he muttered.

"The reason lies in oversimplification of the thesis."

Winston spoke hardly above a whisper, often missing
whole sentences, expecting Peter to sense the meaning
directly from his mind.

"A closer study indicates that there are not two but three
aspects to the human condition. The first two are subjects of
scientific study and can be defined in psychoanalytical terms
as the ego and the id, or the conscious and the subconscious
selves. We talked about it before. To recap, the Bible
identifies these by the first two syllables of the name Israel,
though in reverse order. *Is* represents the passive or the
subconscious, while *Ra*, the active or conscious aspect. *Is*
also symbolizes the animal soul, or the sum-total of physical
or material acquired knowledge. The modern science could
endow the DNA with the repository of this trait."

The rest he communicated at a subliminal level.

*Next comes the most histrionic jump in our spiritual
evolution. The knowledge lies dormant within our
unconscious, ever ready to be brought into conscious
awareness. The moment we are ready.*

"A conscious search for True Self. You, Peter, began in
the seminary, though you were not aware of it, at the time."
This last was, again, spoken aloud. "In fact, you got further in
medicine…"

Peter remembered it well.

But it's not all fun and games. While, say, 20 years of schooling and midnight oil might have made him a reasonably competent physician, there were no such guarantees on his spiritual journey. Many charlatans had told him that if only he were 'good', he would be saved. Not so! He soon learned that if he were saved, then, and only then, he might be good. Not before.

That was really when his struggle began in earnest. This, and later his healing gift, were both only the beginning.

At this realization Winston looked Peter in the eyes.

"The journey towards a greater awareness of our true self is characterized by progressively identifying with the whole, at the expense of the particular," he said, in the stentorian voice he reserved for occasions when he was sharing the arcane. "The illusory separation between 'you' and 'I' loses its intensity. As the ego weakens, so does the polarization; so does what the Orientals call *maya*. Our reality becomes homogeneous. We discover the singularity of the source, of our origin. And then another strange thing happens. We begin to regard our physical body as no more than a shadow cast by our true self. Our priorities change."

Peter nodded. He was well aware of how very much his priorities had changed. Lately, after some 30 years of trial and error, he no longer spent hours feeling sorry for himself, nor even practicing any of his more esoteric exercises. He was too busy trying to be of service to others. Surprisingly, it came to him quite naturally.

Still, it was not an easy journey.

He'd learned long ago that the tepid, the halfhearted, were the greatest losers. They lost the illusion of physical reality and gained nothing in exchange. They were the lost, the undecided, uncommitted. They were straddling the fence. They tried to serve two masters. It couldn't be done.

But most of all, Peter had learned that the journey of self-discovery was a journey of love. At the same time, it was a false journey if we didn't enjoy it. Ultimately, our joy might be full. Full—here and now.

Thanks to Winston.

Peter shook his head. He heard a quiet knock on the door. He sighed, got up, walked up to the Judas hole and bent down to see who it might be. It had to be a friend or the security guards in the entrance lobby wouldn't have let him in. Or her?

He smiled, hardly believing his eyes.

"Hi, Peter," Winston said, still waiting outside to be allowed in, "I thought you might like a chat."

Peter nodded. "Yes, my friend. Yes, I might." Peter was past being surprised at anything Winston did or seemed to do.

They talked till the early hours. And then Winston took him where he'd never been before. "This can be all yours," he said, showing him beauty beyond words. "Yet... no one can give it to you."

The next moment Peter found himself sitting on the sofa, facing the mountain. Later, Cathy joined them. Peter didn't even try to check if she was real. Almost immediately, a strange dreaminess seemed to engulf him.

He saw himself sitting in a rowboat, facing an old man. He knew that man was a monk, from a nearby monastery. His head was hidden under a cowl pulled well over his face. At long last, he was being taken across the river to Shangri La. A lazy, winding river, in which the currents seemed to come and go at will. Only the old monk knew the way to the other side. Only he knew how to avoid whirls and eddies which would threaten the life of an inexperienced oarsman.

"At last," Peter thought, "at long last I shall find my way to the other side..."

Even as he thought that, he saw a body floating alongside the boat. It was inert, as only a corpse can be.

"Poor bastard," Peter thought, "he wasn't lucky enough to find an experienced oarsman."

The body seemed to keep pace with the boat. At last

Peter asked the old monk, "Who was that?"

"Look closer," the monk replied. This time the old man's voice sounded familiar.

As Peter peered at the body, he felt a strange distaste. Almost at once he drew back in horror. The body was his own.

"I thought you wouldn't need it any more," said the old monk, as he continued to dip his oar in the dark waters, slowly approaching the distant shore.

For a while, Peter continued to feel the current pulling him across the river. Then his eyes saw the mountain looming outside his window. At least Mount Royal was real.

"The body was my ego," he said, taking a deep breath. "It's not easy, is it?"

"It is not supposed to be," replied Winston. "But, it's worth it. Life is not defined by biological activity, nor even by the presence of an intellect. There is life in trees, in a single blade of grass. The presence of life demands that that in which it is present, does not impede its free will."

"You mean that we all have unlimited free will? What of the will of God? Tell that to the fundamentalists…"

He stopped short. There were no more fundamentalists. No more priests, rabbis, nor imams. We were on our own. We watered our own gardens. We drifted, ever so slowly, across the dark waters of the Great Divide.

"No, I do not mean that. What I said was that life does not tolerate the infringement on its free will, not that the object through which it manifests can display free will with impunity. Surely, Peter, you of all people know that we, humans, are little more than biologically structured robots, made capable of moving around in search of food to feed our genes."

"Wow! I wouldn't have expected that from you. I could have said that, or Cathy, but you?"

"You have said that. I'm merely repeating your words."

Peter remembered. "I like to call a spade a spade."

"And a robot a robot."

"The difference lies in free will," Winston continued. "Robots are programmed to act in a certain way. Nature is not. Nature has a predisposition to act this way or that, but if you were to subtract the concept of free will, you would eliminate mutations and thus erase evolution."

Peter nodded. "Mutations are little more than nature's evolutionary mistakes. The church would call them sins. Luckily for us, nature is the greatest sinner of all."

Cathy hardly moved a muscle during this discussion. Perhaps she wasn't real after all. Perhaps it was only Peter's loneliness that materialized her presence. She usually kept quiet unless the subject matter touched on her particular expertise. Even at this time, she couldn't resist.

"You know…" she began tentatively, her mind still wrestling with the previous subject, "what fascinates me the most? It is the very concept of life. Not esoteric, or in its spiritual sense, but down here. Under our eyes. I was watching a tiny bug. It could move from place to place, it didn't trip over its own six legs, it knew how to ferret out food, eat it, digest it. It could lower its temperature and metabolism in order to sleep, recharge its batteries so to speak, and finally, it could procreate. And all this astounding knowledge was contained in a being measuring less than two millimeters in length, and half that in height."

"Yet life was manifested in it or, as Winston would say, through it. Hey, maybe Winston's right?" Peter murmured. Was there any difference between life here and 'there'?

And as he lowered his eyes to the moonlight-washed mountain, he also realized that he was completely alone.

Next morning Peter found JR waiting outside the door of his office. It was no longer the hub controlling Solidarity North America, but his old office he'd vacated, three decades ago, when he'd been appointed to serve as the boss. For a while JR stood motionless, lost in thought. In such moments one could speak to him and he wouldn't react. At least, not immediately. This time he saw Peter approaching from the bank of elevators.

Peter was also early, and his secretary wasn't in yet. That explained why JR stood outside. It must have been pressing. He began talking before they entered.

"We have six of them. Of us, I mean. Six Nanotechs. We were all enhanced in Mumbai, about six months apart. Officially, we are still under observation. Ours was the latest model, or technique, which was to be implemented in the market, following two years with no adverse effects. So far there have been no negative reactions. In fact, there still might not be any..."

"Sit down, JR. You look haggard. Did you sleep last night?"

JR ignored Peter's question.

"One of my men, John Ravitz, managed to take a photo of the man injecting him from a distance. He used the modern version of an Amazonian blowpipe, a compressed air discharge. The fellow used it because it is practically silent."

"JR, sit down!"

JR spun on Peter as if stung. Obviously his mind was working at a speed most human minds don't usually work at all.

"What!?" he almost shouted. It seemed that only now did he become fully aware of Peter's presence. "Sorry, I've been thinking..."

"I've noticed," Peter murmured.

"Sorry. I was trying to work it all out and have it ready for you. I seem to have slowed down."

"You are not alone, JR. We may not think as fast as you do, but we do have our moments," Peter spoke calmly. Calm, right then, was what JR needed most.

"The problem is," JR said, hanging his head down, "that when I'm agitated, I can't think at all... it doesn't make sense, does it?" And with that admission he finally stretched his legs under Peter's desk. "Sorry," he repeated, looking a bit like a very overgrown, skinny puppy.

"Just relax," Peter said, and dialed for coffee. Almost immediately two cups came out of a little machine beside his desk. It was the only addition he had requested when he moved back.

"Did your problem with excitement and cogitation happen only just now?"

"Good Lord, no. It happens every time. Emotions cause an overload with which the neurons cannot cope. They are already working at roughly ten times the usual capacity."

That made sense. One would have to be a very balanced personality to become a Nanotech. One would have to have nerves of steel.

JR smiled. "Thanks," he said softly. "I'm all right now." He sipped but didn't down his coffee.

After a while, he told Peter what had happened. Last night he told the other five Nanotechs to put themselves through the spectrogram test. His suspicions were confirmed. First he thought that, just perhaps, it was a malfunctioning of the original infusion. He called Mumbai.

"Nothing of the sort, they said. All subjects function perfectly well, they insisted. It had to be the popgun," JR concluded.

His mind worked just fine, Peter thought. He was sure they'd get to the bottom of this. As long as JR kept his cool.

"That made me think. Why would some no good SOB want to do harm to Nanotechs, who are miles away from Mumbai, and are not doing anyone any harm?"

Peter decided to wait and see. If JR couldn't figure it out, nor would he.

"I told you that Ravitz managed to get a photo of the no-good... well, anyway. I put my men on bus and railway stations and the airports, both Dorval and Mirabel. Obviously we have contacts with the security people there, who are members of SI. One hand washes another. They picked up the fellow early this morning. He was trying to take a night flight to New Delhi. It's the only direct flight to India. They kept him on ice for me. I got there at four a.m., and by five they released him on my recognizance. By seven this morning I had the story."

"I do hope you didn't use..."

"Don't be silly, Peter. We have sophisticated means of interrogation. Mostly hypnosis under a chemically induced state." He looked at Peter as if seeking approval.

"Go on..."

"It's almost a funny story. The guy is a traditional Hindu, who believes that nanotechnology is running counter to the dictates of the goddess Kali. You see, according to the Hindus, we are now in the last phase of Brahma's sleep, under the auspices of Kali, which will result in the dissolution of the world. According to him, nanotechnology might interfere with the gradual deterioration of the human race, and thus should be destroyed."

"So he did threaten your life?"

"He injected us with a substance which he hoped would adversely affect our nano-abilities. He meant us no harm, as such. He was hoping that the substance would oxidize the metal components of the enhancement, which are now part and parcel of my blood. In Mumbai they don't think that would be possible, but the sample of my blood is already there and they are making tests on it."

"It all sounds a little bit childish," Peter said.

"It wouldn't if it had worked. Anyway, I have to fly to Mumbai to undergo further tests. They want to give me a thorough going over. Also, this fellow confessed, in his trance, that there is a whole group of them in India, who want to put the nano-business out of business. It takes all types."

"So when are you leaving?"

JR glanced at his watch. "At ten-thirty this morning. That's why I've been waiting for you, to brief you before I go."

"And what about sleep?"

"I'll sleep on the plane. They are keeping a seat for me next to the emergency exit. It's the only place where my legs can fit." For the first time since he came in, JR smiled.

"So what made you so nervous, when you first came in?" Peter asked.

"I'll tell you when I get back. It has to do with ego. A large expanding ego." JR said, and the next moment he was closing the door behind him.

He had a plane to catch. And, knowing him, he probably had to change, pack, eat and shower before going to Dorval Airport. Not necessarily in that order.

"Good luck, my friend," Peter said, to the chair JR had just vacated. JR was already in the elevator.

That evening, in the condo, Winston made it all quite clear. "We are here not to enhance our bodies, only our souls," he said. "Our states of consciousness. Nanotechnology does not really help with that."

"Surely it is no worse than genetic manipulation, is it?"

"Yes and no. Genetic manipulation enhances your biological system in a biological way. You might say that it cooperates with nature, which is the reflection of... of higher realms. Nanotechnology introduces foreign materials into the body. In a way, it is on a par with drugs, and drugs, as you know, reduce your control over your domain."

"I gather," Peter put in, "that we are not here to improve the environment. We are here to learn to improve ourselves within the environment."

"Precisely," Winston nodded. "As you know, up there," he winked, "it's only our control that matters. Everything is the result of our imagination, so to speak. It is up to our ability to visualize things."

Peter remembered previous chats as well as his medical studies. Our eyes are sensitive to photons, he affirmed in his own mind. Then Cathy joined him.

"Photons are quanta of electromagnetic energy. The vast range of the electromagnetic waves includes, *inter alia,* X rays, gamma rays, radio and television waves as well as what we know as light. The waves range from lengths greater than the diameter of the earth to others so short that a billion strung together would barely span the width of your fingernail. To this day, the vast majority of these photons remain invisible to the naked eye."

Peter wasn't sure if Cathy had just conveyed all of this aloud, or directly to his receptive mind. He nodded just the same.

"There is a good reason for this," he put in. And when no one spoke, he continued. "Many of us think that human vision operates on principles similar to a camera: we take a picture and store it in memory for later use. This is true only in part. The human retina is not a uniform surface. Only an area about one-third of a millimeter in diameter can absorb information in great detail. This area contains special light-sensitive cells. The rest of the retina transmits impressions of whole groups of cells, and this offers much less detail. Only about one-hundredth of the visual field can absorb an image with any precision. Thus, though a single glance offers us an *impression,* thousands of coordinated eye movements, up and down and sidewise, are required to scan a landscape or a large painting in any detail."

He was about to continue when Winston raised his hand.

"And yet," the majordomo said quietly, "the saints, the mystics, the spiritual masters, report of such beauty as to be completely beyond the perception of mere mortals. Is there a different way of looking altogether? Do the spiritual masters know something we don't? Or perhaps there is something akin to spiritual eyes, spiritual vision, which reaches far and beyond the one million fibers of our visual nerve, beyond the one-third of a millimeter of our ultra-sensitive retina."

All three smiled. Cathy and Peter were well aware of the diversity of colour they witnessed in Winston's Kingdom.

"Or…" Winston added slowly, "or is it a matter of mescaline, peyote, jimsonweed or hallucinogenic mushrooms?"

Peter and Cathy had both read the old classics of Aldous Huxley as well as the teachings of Don Juan offered by Carlos Castaneda. They remained silent.

"Or even…" and this time Winston hardly whispered, "by the latest version of nanotechnology?"

So that was where he was going with this… Peter smiled his understanding. Nor is it the result of having your right parietal cortex stimulated with an electrode, he mused, remembering his own mistakes. But surely, JR was above such things. The tall, lanky figure of his friend shimmered before their eyes. Could a man of such generosity of mind, of spirit, be influenced adversely by the new technology?

"JR is a wonderful man," Winston was quick to add. "But you must remember that our origin lies in a single source. When we began our journey back, we were aware of nothing but our own self. After billions of years, we reached our present consciousness. JR is as developed as anyone who has access to, ah… our kingdom. Yet, when there, he remains apart."

Peter remembered the magnificent eagle soaring over his head, disappearing beyond the clouds, and alighting at the inaccessible aerie. "It is what keeps him apart," Winston said, "that seems to be the problem. But, he must realize it himself."

Peter nodded. He recalled JR's words. *…losing my nano-abilities would be like you getting your gift, only in reverse.* Poor JR. Such a wonderful gift…

***

22
Life

"**How important is life?**" Cathy asked. Her questions had a tendency to come out of nowhere. Sometimes she was on a completely different tangent of whatever was being discussed.

"Why do you ask?"

"I've been reading," she replied. "In the West, actually this includes the Middle East, great ecclesiastic dignitaries assured us that human life is the most sacred of all. Our leaders, or at least the leaders of our recent history, in an effort to guide people who are at the stage of development that requires guidance, added such prerequisites as dignity, equality, well-being, and an adequate level of financial security."

Peter thought of the Constitution of the USA.

"Apparently we all have an inalienable right to employment, education, free medical care, pensions, a roof over our heads and enough to eat to make us at least reasonably unhealthy. All to enhance our life," he put in.

"Most sacred life, of course," Cathy insisted.

There was a slight sneer in her tone. When Peter didn't comment, she went on.

"What is life, Peter? Can you define it?"

Peter put his computer away. China and their nano-tricks will have to wait. He saw that Cathy wouldn't give in until she'd drawn him into the discussion. At least his medical background gave him some claim to expertise.

"Some claim that life begins at the moment of conception. Sperm winds its murky way toward an unsuspecting egg, a tiny puncture, and bingo, we have life. Others say that life is only manifest when the cranium appears in the outside world and the baby takes its first breath. But how did the baby get there? That's an easy one. There was a cell, which divided into two cells, which divided into two cells each, which... rather like a single bacterium which in a mere eight hours can divide to produce a billion bacteria. That's right, one billion. All in a day's work. Of course, according to some religious authorities this life doesn't matter. It is not sacred; it is not human."

"Convenient," Cathy said. She still sounded frustrated. Were these unrequited maternal instincts stirring in her breast?

"The baby eats, defecates, sleeps, crawls, walks, and grows," Peter continued, pretending not to notice her tone. "It, the grown up baby, walks *on* and *in* its own offal. No, it no longer needs the security of diapers; he or she is trained now—rather like a kitten—only it took a lot longer. Nevertheless, it does walk in its own biological waste."

"How?" Cathy asked, this time seemingly interested.

"How, you ask? Well, as the baby walks, every hour it sheds around one point five million dead skin flakes. We recognize them as dust on our floors. But do not worry. A veritable army of insatiable mites spends their entire existence eating up bits and pieces of our dead, dried-up pieces of skin. Epidermal delight. The more we shed, the more they eat... and multiply. Our loss is their gain. But although they save us from eventual drowning in the dead cells of our own bodies, their life is not sacred, either." This time Peter sounded vaguely annoyed at his early conditioning.

"Are you saying that life is a biological infestation? That there is life in our organs, brain, heart, blood, cells? Are we impregnated with it? Are we alone imbued with this *sacred* cycle of life that so diligently omits all other biological forms?"

She looked at the mountain crawling with people.

"Are we alone?" she added after a minute or two.

Peter decided to keep this unemotional. "Certainly not physically," her replied. "We live in great togetherness. Not with other people. With them—we fight. We live in relative harmony with some hundred thousand billion microbes. For your mathematically minded brain, this figure looks like this," he scribbled 100,000,000,000,000 on a paper napkin. "Or 10^{14}," he also wrote it down.

She nodded. "I know what ten to the fourteenth looks like."

He ignored that.

"We are permanent hosts to this congregation," he continued. "Without them we would die. That is to say, our biological functions would cease. We are at the mercy of vermin. But they are not sacred, either. And worse. We are also hosts to hosts of viruses—pieces of genetic material surrounded by protein. Some time ago, and this was long before nanotechnology came into the picture, the scientists have added prions, pieces of protein which, contrary to bacteria, viruses, and protozoa, do not even need DNA to divide and multiply."

"Do they all *want* to live?" Cathy's eyes were filled with wonder. "They don't teach us such things in physics," she admitted.

"And then there are parasites," Peter was on a roll. It had been at least ten years since he discussed biology with anyone in any detail. "They seem to attack the sacred humans and the unholy animals alike. No preferential treatment is accorded. Parasites are responsible for more death than any other organism."

"Do they all want to live?" Cathy repeated. For a brief moment she pictured the countless parasites crawling all over her body. Both inside and out. It was a disgusting image, to say the least. She was close to feeling sick.

"What? Well, no. I don't think they can oppose the dictates of nature. They are reactive, not proactive." Peter stopped, but his mind continued in the same vein. "Rather like most people I know," he murmured.

So what makes us, humans, so sacred, he mused? We are a battlefield on which the viruses, the bacteria, and our immune system are engaged in a combat to the death. Eat or be eaten. There is no mercy in this world of which we seem to be such an integral part. We—until recently—were the sacred cows of religious powerhouses. To my knowledge, most religions acclaim us to be superior to whatever we come in contact with. Even if we can't even see it. Even if it kills us with the ease of a microscopic virus.

Is this really life?

He sensed Cathy probing his mind.

Or is life something which has nothing to do with any of the above?

Winston must be right. Life is not at all a biological infestation, be it of viral, bacterial, parasitic, or human variety. At the biological level, we all eat, defecate, multiply, kill with no mercy. All of us—including the sacred cows. Perhaps more so. We, humans, kill even when we are not hungry. Just for pleasure. For sport.

Is this what makes us superior? Complete disregard of physiological life born of a deeper knowledge that such is not the real thing? Cathy and Peter exchanged sad smiles. They needed Winston to set the record straight.

Washington was up in lights. The steps of the US Capitol had been scrubbed clean. For the last two days Pennsylvania Avenue was kept clear of traffic. US Marine uniforms could be seen everywhere. One simply didn't know whom one could trust.

This would be the first inauguration that would take place in early autumn, forsaking the date of January 20th, as ratified by the 20th Amendment. People were tired of amendments. Tired of robots, androids, clones and other artificial or semi-artificial creations, even though they did make life a lot easier. They also made life a lot duller. Americans were, essentially, innovative people. Innovation is usually bred by necessity. Innovation had been taken out of their hands.

Also, there was little choice for the change of date. The outgoing president, together with his four vice presidents, had long been suspected, and now had been certified, to be androids. Their original human counterparts, who lent their genes for the doppelgangers, had all been arrested in the Caribbean. They had been hopping islands every few months to avoid detection. Yet even this idea hadn't been their own. They got their inspiration from a number of European senior officials of various governments, who invested public money to created their own doppelgangers to carry out their duties, while they sunned themselves in the Balearic Islands of Mallorca, Menorca, Ibiza and more recently Formentera. It appeared that all of them had been having the time of their life. Until now. The European bunch had been nabbed in a joint effort inspired by the SI.

Meanwhile, in the USA, a quick election called for by the Senate House Leader resulted in Francisco Gomez's being appointed to serve, *pro tempore*, as the 52nd President of the United States. Or to serve until a more formal review could be conducted by both Houses. Until then, the new president would have to improvise as best he could. He had one advantage. He was a long-time member of Solidarity International.

This was why Moira Thornton flew in from the Vatican. Lena felt that the Solidarity ought to be represented to give instant support to the new president, if need be.

The President expressed his gratitude by inviting Moira

to the State Reception. Peter thought that his adopted niece did Solidarity International justice. In her clinging, simple yet elegant gown, she looked gorgeous. The rest of the Thornton clan, together with Winston and JR, spent their time glued to the large office TV screen. Jo couldn't believe his sister looked that good. Strangely enough, this was the first time that Winston had visited the SI Headquarters. Jo acted as perfect host. He even organized a carafe of Sangria, in honour of the new president's ethnic origin. It was appreciated by all. Even Winston. When the camera centered on Moira, Jo couldn't resist making his feelings known.

"It can't be she," he asserted gravely. "Obviously, it is some phony doppelganger pretending to be my sister."

He was wrong.

On the other hand, Peter knew that look on Jo's face. He was proud as a peacock of his sister. Of her position, her looks, and generally of the way she conducted herself. One could almost say that she breathed new life into Washington. It was high time for a change at the top.

Later that week, towards the evening, Winston, surrounded by 'boys and girls', was holding court in Westmount. It was one of those rare occasions when they were all together. Peter had just come back from Sao Paulo, and Moira, who had flown in from Rome for the inauguration, lingered a few days in Montreal. She and Cathy spent most of the time catching up on old memories. Winston still loved this Westmount place, especially when both 'children' were home. This time Winston initiated the discussion. It sounded as though he'd been eavesdropping, in his own inimitable way, on the conversation Peter and Cathy had had earlier that week on the subject of life.

"According to the remnants of the so-called Christian religion, not ideology, just the religion, we are our bodies, and as such we are sacred. This is why, for years, the religionists forbade abortion, in direct opposition to mother nature. They accused all who disagreed with them to be indulging in an annual or, better still, a perennial blood bath."

"Why so-called?"

"All religions have missed the point. Those who organized religions completely misunderstood the teachings of the Great Masters." It sounded as though he'd capitalized the last two words.

"Surely, not all religions. I still think the teaching of Lao Tsu brought to the world great wisdom." Cathy's tone sounded defensive.

"Of course it did. As did Moses, most of the prophets, Jesus, before him Buddha, Krishna—they all did. I'm not talking about their message. I'm talking about what people did with it. With the message."

"I understand."

Peter smiled sadly, recalling the conversation he and Cathy had had earlier that week. "I remember the fights over abortion, less than a half-century ago. Even during my medical studies, there had been people who called the few abortions that took place at the time 'mass slaughter'. No, not the slaughter of the millions of cows and calves, pigs and piglets, fowl and fish and whatever else served to distend our obese paunches, but of 'pre-born' children." He drew inverted comas in the air with his fingers. "Until that time, the adjectives 'pre-born' or 'unborn', or 'undead' had been reserved for ghouls, the living dead adorning our Halloween horror films. Later we were told that children have joined those grotesque ranks. Albeit, thankfully, only the pre-born variety. It seemed, at the time, that a faction calling itself 'pro-lifers', or religious fundamentalists, would have liked to make abortion illegal, probably under the penalty of death."

"The same cannot be said for Mother Nature," Winston put in quietly. "Did you ever wonder what exactly is a fundamentalist?"

Everyone looked at Winston. The term had almost disappeared from everyday use. Winston smiled with paternal indulgence.

"In the past, people believed that the human body has, or owns, its own soul. Not that the soul owns the body, which it has built to its own specifications. A sort of inversion of truth."

"That's it?" Peter sounded dubious.

"The consequences of this assumption were stunning. People treated the Bible as a historical account of the Jewish tribes, gallivanting all over the Middle East, killing everything and pretty much everyone in their path."

"And in fact...?" someone put in.

"In fact the Bible is a compendium of knowledge, what can only be described as spiritual knowledge, or that which enables us to cope in the, let us say, upper realms, or realities."

Finally everyone knew what he meant. Peter nodded several times and returned to his own past.

"When I was still a medical student, extensive studies had shown that most newly conceived human embryos harbor colossal genetic defects that are incompatible with life. Furthermore, we learned that most pregnancies—whether naturally occurring or the result of test-tube fertilization—quietly fail within days or a few weeks after conception. It seemed, at the time, that we had no choice but to make Mother Nature illegal."

Cathy looked up at Peter with admiration. There still were moments when she missed the authority he once held as a physician.

"Moreover," Peter was on a roll, "it is quite apparent that the vast majority of 'pro-lifers' were men, and thus had not been recently pregnant. They knew nothing of multiple spontaneous abortions, even though such contributed to a blood-bath infinitely greater than the one to which they were referring."

Happily, with the upsurge of Solidarity, people's individual freedoms had been raised to new heights. No one would dare to tell a woman what she might or might not do with her own body. The fact that the world was rapidly nearing the capacity to feed itself also tended to calm down the hysterical cries of the remaining few misguided fundamentalists.

No one in their right mind questioned the thesis that life begins at conception. It was taken for granted, however, that one referred to *biological life*. There was no mention of 'soul' or any other intangible concept. Colloquially, one referred to life such as is abundantly manifested in *all* animals, fowl and fish, which the human race had no qualms in slaughtering in order to masticate them in vastly excessive quantities. The problem resided in the excess, not in the fact *per se*.

Peter nodded to himself. "It would seem that Jesus of Nazareth is said to have eaten meat, while Hitler was a vegetarian," he muttered. "I wonder if Adolf was also a 'pro-lifer'?" Peter sensed that both Cathy and Winston had been following his train of thought.

They both nodded.

"I believe so was Pol Pot and the minor but picturesque murderer Charles Manson," JR added. "Vegans all."

"Ah, the pro-lifers..." Even Winston found them hard to swallow.

"All the same, I have always been fascinated by biological manifestation." Peter seemed taken back to his early days. "Sausage-shaped globs of DNA, known as chromosomes, carry practically all the genes inside a cell. Most human cells contain forty-six chromosomes, of which only twenty-three from each parent are passed on at impregnation. Has life already begun? Are the residual chromosomes murdered? There are *millions* of them."

"The slaughter gets worse?" This was Cathy.

"Compared to the other mammals, and in spite of gross overpopulation of our globe, humans are very inefficient reproducers," Peter continued. "Only about one-in-four of natural monthly attempts results in pregnancy. Are the

products of unsuccessful attempts murdered? The eggs have
been impregnated, but sensitive hormone tests have also
shown that a high percentage of early pregnancies end, as
mentioned earlier, within a few days, weeks at best. Nature is
very selective. Whatever she doesn't like, she aborts. For a
time, the human embryos hover on the brink of molecular
self-destruction. Then, after a perilous beginning, some
achieve genetic stability and continue their growth. Some, in
time, become babies. *Born* babies."

"You worry too much, Peter," Winston put it. "I'm sure
in another few million years evolution will improve her
batting average. Perhaps we can help nature in her quest. But
for now, let's not make nature illegal just because she
protects our biological integrity by an ongoing, continuous
'blood-bath'."

This was as close as Winston ever got to humour tinged
with irony.

"Nevertheless, speaking as an ex-physician," evidently
Peter needed to unburden himself, "we still haven't defined if,
and if so when, human life becomes different from the rest of
fauna. If we claim a different status from the rest of the
animal kingdom, if we do not abide by the kill-or-be-killed
dictum for food, for territory, for power, then I see little or no
evidence of it. We certainly murder a great many more of our
own species than any other mammal. And we kill not just our
'pre-born', but the well and truly and very selectively born
children, as well as our adults and our hapless elderly. We
murder them indiscriminately, individually and *en masse*,
often without rancor. We then adorn the chests of our most
successful murderers with colorful ribbons, elevate them to
the ranks of heroes, build statues for them, put their
unaffected faces on postage stamps. We are really proud of
them. We forget that the genes in those murdered do not
differ in any way from the genes which our parents passed on
to us. We murder because we like murdering. It is in our
blood. It is carried in our genes."

"Except in those few who kill no more," Cathy whispered.

Towards the end of his little dissertation, Peter was gazing down at the headline of the bulletin on his computer pad. Below the headline, the article stated that "by this date, Sudan has been at war with its neighbours for 74 years". The article was headed by a title in large letters:

THOUSANDS DIE IN TERRITORIAL DISPUTES IN CENTRAL SUDAN

Peter pointed to the screen for all to see. Each looked and passed the tiny screen to the next person.

"Amen," Peter whispered, thinking of Cathy's last words.

"Amen," repeated Mo and Jo, in perfect unison, as though they were still children.

"Amen," said Cathy.

JR's eyes drifted to some place to which only he had access. Peter remembered when JR had refused to swat a mosquito.

"She must be thirsty…" he'd said at the time.

Winston smiled. "It is amazing how people managed to confuse spirit and matter. One could argue that they are the same. That if you slow down the vibrations sufficiently, then ultimately all spirit would be expressed as matter. After all, isn't spirit ubiquitous?"

Moira was leaving tomorrow, and this was their last evening together. Just family, which always included Winston. This time they met at the condo. Unfortunately, Jo had to be away in Toronto, on business.

"On the other hand, it is hard to imagine that people would confuse water with ice, not to mention steam," Cathy put in.

"Precisely," said Winston. Then he looked out through the window at the park below him. It was obvious that, in spite of his esoteric proclivities, he loved nature. "Animals do communicate," he resumed. "But if they could talk our language, then the moment a carnivore catches a herbivore, the latter would leave its outer casing, its outer body, and most probably say with its best French accent, *Bon appétit.*"

"You mean the *real* animal, the spirit of the herbivore, would no longer be inside the body which was about to be masticated by the carnivore."

"As I was saying, precisely; although I prefer the word consciousness to spirit. All living creatures, in both fauna and flora, which manifest life as defined by ongoing change, are one with the manifestation of life, until the two are set apart by life's withdrawal."

"It seems that you cannot kill life. Only the form it incorporates at any particular time," Peter nodded. "Anymore than you don't kill the artist when you destroy his or her painting."

"Something like that," Winston agreed.

"The Big Guy in the sky is quite an artist," Cathy mused, her eyes also drifting to the treetops. "Quite an artist..."

"And now imagine the life-force being omnipresent, intelligent, willing to share its wealth."

"All-knowing?" Peter offered.

"Only in its potential form, not in its manifestation. After all, progress is only achieved by preserving successful mistakes, which is an attribute of our intelligence, not knowledge." When Peter looked up, he added, "mutations."

"How would you define this life-force?" Cathy, like her idol Einstein, wanted to know the thoughts of God. "You can't define it. To define means to set limits. There are no limits to life. Its potential is infinite."

This took Peter back to his days in the seminary. He recalled reading about Georg Hegel, who claimed that modern philosophers were either Spinozists, who refused to define god, or not philosophers at all. That statement, too, survived to this day.

"And what do you think, little one?" Winston turned to Moira, who throughout the exchange had remained silent.

"Frankly, I don't know why you bother with such things. Isn't today more exciting than yesterday?"

They all agreed that it was. The next discussion centered on the spectacular growth in the ranks of the Solidarity movement. All of a sudden, Little Moira couldn't stop talking. She didn't stop until seven, when she had to run to catch a plane to the Vatican.

"No peace for the guilty," she whispered. "Perhaps one day I'll join in your discussions."

She didn't have to. After all, she'd had Winston teaching her since she was little more than a baby. For her, his teaching was the only way to look at reality. The only natural way. She was a very lucky woman.

Peter and Cathy offered to drive Moira to Dorval Airport, but she preferred to say good-byes in private. Anyway, a limousine waited for her, down below, with two doppelganger guards. Not really needed any more, but Lena had insisted. They all rose to their feet. Cathy held Moira in her arms for a little while. She was as close to a daughter as Cathy had ever had.

After she left, silence descended over the room like a blanket of invisible fog. Although she hardly spoke, her presence made the whole place younger. More alive? Sometime later, for some reason, Moira's visit brought the subject of evolution to the forefront of Peter's mind. He was thinking of Moira's visit down south.

"Why is evolution so slow?" he was thinking of the mistakes the Americans had made prior to the recent inauguration.

"It's us," Cathy replied. "There is so little time..." Her voice was dreamy, as it always turned when her mind hovered in no-man's-land—between physics and metaphysics.

Peter gave her a questioning look.

"In physics it is called phase transition." When Peter's expression didn't change, she continued. "Think of water. In the liquid form its molecules are spread evenly, and it looks the same from whichever side you look at it."

Peter nodded. He still had no idea what she was talking about.

"When, at zero degrees Celsius, it turns to ice, it assumes crystalline form. As with all crystals, it looks different from every side. Also, it cannot flow, change location, change anything unless pushed by an external force. But..." she gazed triumphantly at Peter, "it does expand!"

"Your point being?"

"Peter, think. Expansion of water is equivalent to evolution. It can only expand in its solid form, and it can expand only within clearly defined parameters."

Peter's eyes narrowed. "We, in our 'solid' form, are limited to the amount of evolutionary expansion we can produce... but..."

"But that means that solid form is not our 'normal' condition."

"Exactly!"

"I'll need Winston to come in on this," Peter went back to thinking aloud. His lips didn't move, but his face assumed a series of expressions changing between concentration, puzzlement and hesitant Eurekas.

"If we are ice, and water is our natural habitat," he continued, "then what of gas?"

"We are not water, well, little more than sixty percent, Peter. I'm only using the parallel between us and the universal laws. After all, we can't elude them."

"So gas is like spirit?" Peter went on on his own.

"I have no idea. But if you want to draw parallels, then our physical bodies would correspond to ice, our thoughts to water, and spirit to... gas, I suppose."

Peter's face grew tense. He was struggling.

"That's not it. Our natural habitat is not physical, nor is it conceptual, as we would be if it were thought. There must be something in-between."

"Like emotions? Imagination...?" Cathy offered.

"Yes, something between creative thought and final manifestation. The in-between state, which has access to all of the past but which, apparently, cannot advance the evolution."

"And spirit?" Cathy whispered, as though afraid to interfere with Peter's thoughts.

"And spirit is the Source. The Idea. Logos."

"To make logos become solid, we need..."

"To develop it with our thought processes and to give it life with our emotions."

After a little while, as though triggered by shared desire, the three of them merged their minds.

This is not our natural habitat... but necessary to advance evolution... but we spend here, on earth, only a small fraction of our existence... and the rest of the time... at the next step... the subconscious... the out-of-body experience...

Cathy went back to speech. "At what some call the astral reality, we can draw on spirit and thought, and we are not limited to three-dimensional constraints... I suspect our bodies, there, are made up of photons. Photons only. No mass."

"You sound like a scientist again," Peter smiled.

He loved the way Cathy was always practical, her feet firmly planted on the ground, even if the ground might have changed its porosity and raised her to realms they'd visited, together, on special occasions.

Neither Cathy nor Peter had noticed that Winston was standing, silently, by the door. As immobile as ever, now seemingly also invisible at will. Peter wondered if Winston was really there. He contemplated throwing something, anything, at the old majordomo, just to make sure he was not imagining things himself. In the same instant he felt embarrassed at his juvenile notion. Whatever Winston's intentions might be, he certainly was there, or here, for no reason other than to help them. It seemed to be his nature.

Evidently Winston became aware of Peter's thoughts. Before Peter could hide them, the tall man smiled with an expression of a permissive father regarding his son.

"Science is a good place to start," he said, looking at Cathy. "Metaphysics are nothing more than physics we do not yet understand."

"As yet...?" Cathy smiled.

"Yes, young lady, as yet." The same feeling that his voice conveyed moments ago towards Peter now embraced Cathy. "Perhaps we should think of reality in terms of matter, photons, thought waves, and... spirit?" It was as much a statement as a question.

"Or ideas, mind, emotions and the result?" Cathy just loved being referred to as a young lady.

"This, too, is acceptable," Winston nodded.

"Gas, liquid and solid, but only gas has perfect symmetry?" When she noticed raised eyebrows, she added, "Symmetry is the property of a physical system that does not change when the system is transformed in some manner."

"Which proves...?"

Cathy looked confused, as though having lost her train of thought.

"What *Doctor* Mondellay thinks is," Winston came to her aid in a most formal manner, as though stressing that one ought to always start an argument from one's strength, "that spirit is omnipresent regardless of what form it takes."

Peter looked somewhere between annoyed and jealous. Cathy was taking over in his relationship with Winston. There were moments when Peter was more juvenile than Mo or Jo had been some 30 years ago. His ego was a terrible anchor. He couldn't explain his emotional quirks even to himself.

"No, Peter." Winston's voice was soothing. "We are all one."

"Now that makes everything clear!" Peter sighed, but the annoyance was now directed at himself. He was getting lost in this discussion.

"Peter, darling. Winston is saying that gas, liquid and solid matter are one and the same thing, only they went through a process known as phase transition, and..."

"...we, humans, are spirit which went through the transition of thought, then emotions or imagination, and finally into solid or material form," Peter concluded, feeling both smug and pleased with himself.

He turned to see if Winston's face would show confirmation. Too late. The majordomo had melted into the woodwork. Only there was no woodwork. Winston just disappeared. With others present, the old majordomo behaved as any other human being would. Not so when Peter and Cathy were alone.

Peter shrugged. It wasn't the first time that Winston arrived and left without any explanation. At least none that he could think of. Again, Cathy read Peter's mind.

"Perhaps he's right," she said softly. "Perhaps we are all one."

Peter leaned back and stretched his legs. Then he took a few deep breaths and became quite still.

It is as she says... It's all to do with vibrations. At a higher level of consciousness, the vibrations become more similar. Or perhaps, more attuned to each other. Ultimately, at the level the ancients perceived as God, they are all identical. However, even at the astral level it is quite difficult to set us apart. It takes a conscious effort. That is why we all try hard to maintain our physical appearance.

Individualization begins the moment a black hole is sustained as an independent entity...

Peter heard the words in his head. The subject was Cathy's, but it sounded like Winston. Actually it sounded like Winston imitating Cathy's voice?

Peter grinned when he felt an emotional chuckle. The voice continued.

You might think of it as its own, seemingly microscopic little bang. I say seemingly, because while its material manifestation is tiny, within its heart lies infinite power. The power we call spirit. Or that which lies beyond the confines of time, and space, and imagination, and even thought.

Even as the voice ceased, Winston's figure once again loomed before Peter. As solid as the wall through which he apparently walked in.

"I don't walk through walls, Peter." Winston said, again. He'd explained it before.

***

23
Love

JR's jet from Mumbai landed at 4:00 p.m. At 5:00 p.m. he dismissed his two security guards, and moments later knocked on Peter's door. Not waiting for an invitation, he strode in, charging like a hungry lion. Perhaps a giant stick insect would be a better metaphor. His face indicated that his news couldn't wait.

"I can deliver to you India," he said. "I really should be saying it to Lena, but..." he looked around, "you will do."

At that he collapsed into the armchair, performing the usual leg acrobatics in the process.

"Welcome back, JR. Had a nice trip?"

"I can deliver..."

"...India on a silver platter," Peter finished for him. Then he leaned back and studied his friend. JR looked exactly the same, yet there was something intangible about him that he couldn't put his finger on. And then Peter heard his voice in his head.

I did it... I got rid of it... I needed to...

He couldn't say it out loud.

So he was no longer a Nanotech. Even as Peter studied his friend, he felt desperately sorry for him. He knew how much the additional mental capacity had meant to him. Further, JR would never abuse it. He couldn't. Within his gaunt body there lived a most noble soul.

Thanks...

You're very welcome. And welcome to...

So that was what JR had to tell him. Not the Solidarity successes on the Subcontinent of India, but his personal sacrifice to become one with his friends. The silver platter was just an excuse.

"Welcome," he repeated, practically in a daze himself.

Peter wasn't sure what he was welcoming JR to, but it felt as if suddenly JR had become part of him. An inseparable part. It was both a wondrous and an inexplicable feeling. He felt like getting up and embracing him. That's what people do when they love each other. Peter thought this could only happen between a man and a woman. This… well, this was different, but it was just as deep.

For but an instant, he wondered if JR's sacrifice would diminish his usefulness to the Solidarity. The next moment he was ashamed of his suspicions. What if? Solidarity was billions, JR was one. Unique.

"So, what happened, JR?"

Suddenly the need for a rapid-fire report, which JR had exhibited only minutes ago, evaporated into thin air. Simultaneously, JR appeared more relaxed than he'd been for years.

"It was interesting. The fellow who got to me did me an enormous favour. He'd explained to me the consequences of employing outside agencies to accentuate the differences between people. You won't believe this, Peter, but at times he sounded exactly like Winston!"

"He sounds like a friend of yours…"

"Well, let me tell you. He seemed quite different before and after they'd given me the transfusion. I can't explain it, but…"

"Don't bother. From now on you'll find many things you will not be able to explain."

"You mean the Nanotech made such a difference?"

"Yes, but not in the way you think. You are now open to a reality from which you shielded yourself."

"You don't say…" he sat up.

It was time to ask him about his original news. JR seemed to have relegated them to a lesser priority.

"And what about the silver platter?" Peter brought him back to earthly reality.

"Oh, that. Well, that seems to be very good news. I didn't report it officially yet. But that group of people, who were, well... against nanotechnological brain manipulation, they thought that Solidarity embodies all the fundamental prerequisites for the Age of Aquarius. Anyway... those people are big. Millions of them. They claim they have hundreds of millions. The Swami sounded pretty knowledgeable, too."

"I thought they ascribed to the Age of Kali," Peter said.

"That's the funny part of it. They now claim that... you're not quite up to scratch with that, are you?" JR sensed Peter's unease. "Well, there are four Ages, or Yugas, in the Hindu calendar. Kali, that's the last age, began around 3102 BCE. On February 18th, if you want to be exact. Around midnight. A while back..." JR smiled like a 70-year-old mischievous boy. "Nevertheless, traditionally, it is said to last 432,000 years. That's only a quarter of Satya Yuga, The Golden Age, but still, no rush to pack your bags."

This was classic, pre-nano JR. He was mixing fact with humour with an ease that made Peter smile. Once again, he welcomed him back. Once again, JR read his mind.

"Thanks again," he murmured. This time he looked serious.

"Anyway, the Swami Sri Yogoda, that's the guy who zapped me, and yes, he does have a title. Anyway, he said that each Yuga is subdivided into four sub-ages, i.e. golden, silver and so on, and there is absolutely no need to be miserable all the time, biting your nails and all that, until the final dissolution."

"So on or about February 18th, four hundred thirty-five thousand plus whatever, we shall all go kaput?" Peter did his best to look worried.

"Well, the Swami wasn't insistent, but he did say, there was a chance that the Surya Siddanta may be right."

"That's the astrological dissertation, I presume?"

"Got it in one."

"Well," Peter said judiciously, "I'm glad we don't have to rush."

"And what about that tattoo?" Peter remembered.

"That was a cover. In India there are so many believers in so many things that you should cover all your bases, if you know what I mean."

Peter didn't play, watch, or listen to baseball, but he had heard about bases.

"You'd better get back to your base. People might be looking for you. You only have some 435,100 years, give or take a dozen, to get there. As for the Solidarity aspect, I think we ought to pass it on to Moira, in writing."

"Of course," JR said and was gone before the proverbial dust settled.

It was a tradition now. Four of five times a week, after work, Peter, Cathy and JR would drop in on Winston, in Westmount, although Jo tended to disappear on his own, probably with friends his own age. They would chat about what friends chat about, but sometimes Winston would plunge into one of his enlightening lectures. So it was the day after JR got back from India. JR got there first, and we can only assume that Winston welcomed him like a lost sheep. Or was it the prodigal son? Anyway, by the time the rest of them got there, JR's eyes were already shining. Perhaps that was why Winston launched into his next discussion.

"Heaven, for the want of a better word," he said, "is where consciousness is still undifferentiated. We can think of it as a field of infinite possibilities. It is, you might say, unaware of itself. Here, or there," his thumb pointed upwards, then sidewise, then hovered all over the place, "we have self-awareness. In the mental realm we are the mental interpretations of an idea. We see our differentiated consciousness in terms of what Cathy calls strings. You might call them 'vibrating quanta of nothing,' or, at most, of nothing much."

"Actually strings and other subatomic particles with a potential for combining," Cathy couldn't resist butting in.

Winston nodded. "In fact, everything in the manifested, that is to say, differentiated universes, consists of vibration. Starting with Cathy's strings, all the way to planets, suns and galaxies."

He looked around, sweeping them all with his arms.

"But however we express ourselves, we never stop being one. That is our essential nature. We really are one."

Coming from Winston, it sounded like immutable truth.

"And hell?" Peter murmured. After all, he had been raised in the Christian tradition.

"There is, of course, no such thing as hell." Winston dismissed the question as of no consequence. "Heaven, as undifferentiated consciousness, seems imbued with a predisposition for order and harmony, but also it cannot shed its fundamental nature, which is love. Love is manifested in many ways, in different realities, but essentially it is that which makes us one. Hell, if there were such a thing, would be a state of consciousness of total alienation. It happens, sometimes. When it does, people go mad. They cannot reconcile with the idea of being completely apart. Which, in true reality, cannot happen, of course. It is only imaginary, or limited to the material reality, or to the physical realm."

Peter was still struggling with more fundamental questions. Such as... what am I doing here? If there is heaven but not hell, what has God to do with anything? Finally he came out with it.

"When talking of heaven and hell, can we separate them from the concept of God?"

He sounded slightly embarrassed. It had been years, but in Peter the remnants of old conditioning still lingered on. Or, perhaps, he was getting old.

"God, or the idea behind the omnipresent creative force, through the process of evolution, or its inherent predisposition towards order and harmony latent in chaos, created man, for the purpose of experiencing self-awareness."

"*Moi?*" Peter tried to lessen his ignorance with lightness.

"You, Peter. But not alone. The sum total of all creatures, including plants, microbes, bugs, fish, birds and all the fauna and flora exhibiting even the most primitive forms of self-awareness, all together they add up to the self-awareness of God. And this God I spell with a capital G." The next sentence came directly to Peter's mind.

That part of you which is the individualization of divine self-awareness is indestructible, immortal, and thus also divine.

JR, who until now had sat still and in silence, suddenly looked up. It was apparent that Winston's last words had also reached him. He looked as though something had opened the gate to his understanding.

"Until we, humanity, realize that we are immortal, we shall continue to walk around in circles. Hence, the Wheel of Awagawan. Of course, to be immortal one must stop being dead," JR said, his eyes shining again as they did when Peter first came in. Apparently, in the dim and murky past, JR had also benefited from Christian upbringing.

For a brief moment they all felt as one. Then the euphoria was dispelled as quickly as it came. But the memory remained.

It was also at that precise moment that Peter realized that when Winston addressed him, he addressed his, Peter's, true self.

"If I'm in tune with my own essence, I can hear him at the subliminal level. By the same token I can read his mind. In a way, it is like reading my own..."

Peter also realized that countless avatars, saints and mystics, from time immemorial, had taught the same philosophy which Winston was trying to impart to this small group of his friends and family. For years, it seemed to have fallen on deaf ears. Perhaps our ears were not deaf, but dead… still dead.

On November 4ᵗʰ, Lena officially welcomed the Prime Minister of India to the Vatican. The PM came to sign an official declaration that henceforth every citizen of India is free and encouraged to join the Solidarity International. As of this day, all members of the Government of India will limit their salaries to the maximum allowed in the Solidarity Constitution. Montreal's top echelons gathered together to listen in to the SI international broadcast.

"Solidarity unites people," the elderly gentleman said.

He spoke of the relative merits of various religious systems and then praised Solidarity, once again, for its lack of coercion. "You unite by attraction, not by building walls to keep people in or out."

Peter wondered. Was this attraction also built into our genes? It was evident that some mysterious force tied parents to their progeny. An adopted son or daughter, at some stage of their life, seemed to long to meet his or her biological parents. Was that love built into their genes? Love as a fatal attraction that became overpowering?

Later the Prime Minister couldn't resist a dig at China. He spoke slowly, with measured words.

> The age of the walls is over. The East Germans had built it to keep people in. The Israelis, to keep people out. The Americans followed their example along their southern border. But they all learned from a wall that took twenty-one centuries to build: the Great Wall of China. All walls are signs of

national cowardice. India is afraid of no one. It welcomes everyone. India believes in sharing, in Solidarity.

This statement, he claimed later, had been necessary as a politically motivated ploy. Until that day, the Government of the People's Republic of China had actively discouraged their citizens from joining the SI. They held that their own "communist" party had as much if not more to offer. There were few people alive who knew what the historical concept of communism stood for. By the end of this century, China would probably be a more capitalistic country than the USA ever was. Or at least, their capitalism was already more spread around. However, old habits of holding on to power die hard.

Although a number of prime ministers of European countries had individually joined Solidarity International, and thus subscribed to the official postulates, they had never spoken out, at least not *ex officio*, that all their citizens should follow in their footsteps. Following the example of India, of the 44 European nations, 37 countries, all members of the European Union, made declarations similar to that of the PM of India.

"Solidarity was always a grass roots movement," Peter explained. "It never encouraged governmental sponsorships, and certainly would refuse to grant membership to any but individual applicants. Some 50 years ago this would have been technically impossible, but these days, with computers having long passed multiple Turing Tests, the processing of individual requests became possible."

"Turing Test?" someone asked.

"For years," JR stepped in with the explanation, "the late Alan Turing had been harassed for his supposition that machines can think. Finally, when the USA had proven that a machine could emulate every known human mental function, the Test had been accepted by all who were not lumbered with philosophical definitions of the word 'thinking'."

"Nevertheless," Peter took over, "all countries, with the noted exception of USA, have discouraged androids designed to emulate human appearance. Now that President Gomez was an open supporter of SI, this, too, may soon come to pass."

If the growth of Solidarity International were to continue at the present rate, within the next twenty years or so the world would be united under its banner.

"And what then?" asked Peter, still more interested in the future than in the present.

"Who can tell," JR mused aloud. "The Age of Aquarius has hardly began. We still have almost two thousand years to go."

It was then that Peter realized the full benefit of being immortal.

"No, Cathy, love exists throughout the universe," Winston asserted. His voice allowed for no shadow of doubt. "Look around you. Do things fly off into outer space? Does the moon lose its shine? Is the sun no longer warming our bones with its blissful embrace? Do the buds not open at the first sign of spring?"

"Why, no, Sir."

Cathy wasn't sure why Winston had directed his words at her, but preferred not to argue with him. Lately, quite unwittingly, usually against his strong objections, she began to throw in an occasional 'Sir', when addressing the old majordomo. Yes. Winston was getting old. His body was. He's almost done his job. Finished his mission.

Cathy and Peter, with Jonathan and JR on the other side and Winston at the head of the table, were just finishing their monthly Sunday dinner. Only Moira was missing. They remembered her every time they sat together at the table.

Facing Winston, at the other end of the table, there was an empty plate. Just in case she dropped in. With Winston around, all things were possible.

"To discuss love, you must first know what love really is," Winston admonished again.

Just before he made this statement, Cathy had compared human love-making to that of other animals. She claimed there was hardly any difference, and if non-humans didn't enjoy it as much, then it was their problem.

Peter got up and switched off the lights. The reflection in the windows disappeared, and below them, almost at the same height, the mountain loomed as though waiting to be invited to share their thoughts. For a while Peter stared, fascinated, and then turned his eyes upwards. There was relative darkness over the mountain, which made the sky visible. Here and there a star caught his attention.

Stars... galaxies... dreamy wisps of nebulas...

Were they also but states of consciousness created in somebody's mind and then manifested, solidified into particles of matter, of burning hydrogen atoms?

He felt drawn into the coldness of space embracing the fires of the suns.

Yet all is one, he mused. Held together by centripetal forces that Winston called love. Will they, too, one day, develop self-awareness? I did, he smiled. Yet once I was an amoeba. Then... perhaps a thousand amoebas? A million? How many cells does my body imbue with self-awareness? How many cells does my soul hold together with love? Isn't that what Winston is saying? Isn't love the force that stops us from falling apart? Disintegrating into countless strings so dear to Cathy's heart? How many stars are held, lovingly, by the consciousness of the whole universe?

One single Consciousness that seems bent on sharing Its attributes with Its own creation, with all that are capable, or willing, to accept Its gifts. It created countless milliards of hypothetical states into which we, the nascent units of awareness, can enter, learn and advance. But we are not independent. We are as reliant on the One as a babe-in-arms is reliant upon the unconditional love of its mother. Without it, the babe dies. With it—it prospers. In time, hardly understanding the process, the babe grows up and asserts its own individuality. Sadly, it often forgets whence it came...

Is that what true love is all about?

As though awakening, Peter realized that everyone was following his silent musings. They didn't intrude. Just gently regarded, as though from afar, yet closer than the most intimate embrace. They all loved each other. In so many ways...

Let me count the ways...

How do I love thee? How do I love the lord, my soul, my true self. He never thought of loving his true self. It seemed unnatural. Loving one's own self?

Even as you love your neighbour...

Not more—just as much. The neighbour and the lord were also one. Loving your neighbour was also like loving yourself. How strange, he thought. The knowledge was there all along. For ages. Millennia? Why didn't we listen? It was there all the time. Why are we so blind?

...as those that have eyes yet do not see?

He felt a touch on his arm. Cathy moved over and put her hand on his arm. She stroked him gently. There was no need for words. At moments such as these they were one.

This seemed to Peter to be the greatest mystery.

No matter how we fragment our way of thinking, our perceptions will ultimately flow together again. Echoing the Middle Path, the Yin and the Yang are neither good nor bad; they are the general terms for the opposite forces which work at all times to remain in balance. We are what they have in common.

Cathy smiled. "In *Tao Te Ching*, Lao-Tzu admonishes us to give up all striving. This state of consciousness, devoid of strife, of anger or envy, where no wars or struggles upset the divine state of balance, the Bible calls Jerusalem. The city of Peace. A state of mind beyond human understanding. Rumi, the great Sufi poet, said that it is necessary to note that opposite things work together, even though nominally opposed."

Her words resonated in Peter's mind as though they were his own. Dear Cathy. Some thirty years ago those had been other people's words. Today, they were part of his awareness.

Once more, Peter and Cathy's eyes drifted to the stars, so distant, inaccessible, yet so much part of the beauty of Earth, the planet that, according to Winston, they'd created in their dreams.

"It is not my Kingdom that is the dream. It is the here and now that is not real," he had said only last week. "Only there true balance exists, untrammeled by egotistical emotions."

And now, as he continued, his words, like music, reverberated within their hearts.

All that we refer to as good or evil is unreal. Such states of consciousness lack reality because they, like all that is diluted, are relative. The very same thought, action, or event can serve as a whole spectrum of moral discrimination. A speeding ambulance can save someone's life, kill a stray dog, child, an elderly person reacting too slowly to its mission of mercy. A knife in the hands of a discontented neurotic kills; in the hands of a surgeon extends our embodiment. Same thoughts, same actions, same objects—different effects. None are good, none evil. There is nothing intrinsically good about prolonging a stagnating life, nothing intrinsically bad about assisting in its termination. Nothing is useless if it serves to teach us something.

"Teach whom? Who is us?" This sounded like JR. He'd only just rediscovered his freedom.

We are all individualized states of consciousness. Though matter is transient—the consciousness goes on.

Biological matter soon disintegrates, emotions last longer, ideas hold sway over generations. Consciousness lasts forever. You can kill a man's body; you cannot kill his soul.

Peter knew this to be true. Man cannot even destroy it himself. He'd tried, hard enough. What man can do, however, is to lose track of it. That he was an expert at. Whatever we believe in becomes our reality. If we don't believe in immortality, we are not immortal. The soul, however, for whom the disbeliever provided a temporary home—is. None of us have a soul; though, for a short while, Soul tries hard to have us. One at a time. Aren't we lucky?

"It seems to me..." Cathy obviously needed to hear the sound of a human voice. She spoke softly, with a certain reverence. "It seems to me soul is that which restores a state of balance. When we accept this condition of being, we become one with the soul."

No one argued.

A State of Balance.

Buddha called it the Middle Path. Not the good or the bad, the saintly or the profane. The *Middle* path. The path that is non-judgmental. The path which recognizes that all is One.

"Surely, that must be the greatest realization of love," this occurred to all simultaneously.

Then Cathy spoke again. "It seems futile to discuss, let alone insist, which is better: the gravitational pull of the sun or the centrifugal force inherent in the movement of the planets. Is one good—the other evil? What nonsense! Too much of one, and we plunge into the nuclear inferno. Too much of the other, and we destroy all biological and zoological life by freezing them in the black void of space. Both forces are equally destructive if one takes pre-eminence over the other."

For every opinion we hold, an equal and opposite opinion will manifest itself.

This last felt like Winston. And then he added, "Goodnight all," and everyone got up and embraced. They always did that lately. It seemed so natural. Almost necessary.

Yet the moment Cathy and Peter retired, watching the usual interplay of light and shadow reflected on the ceiling from the polished marble windowsill, Winston's presence was back.

"Go to sleep," he said. They did, almost instantly.

Winston took them both on a strange journey. He showed Peter and Cathy the inside of human minds. He picked people at random, at a distance.

"Mo and Jo cannot do this yet, but soon you both will," he said as clearly as if he were standing next to them. "But not yet…"

"But why? Wouldn't it be fascinating?"

"It would, but your love is not strong enough. This ability would give you ultimate power over your adversary, or rival. Such power is bound to corrupt. Neither you nor they are quite ready yet."

"When," Peter asked, "when will I be ready?"

"When you no longer have a single adversary in the whole wide world."

Next morning, Peter and Cathy lay still for a long time, remembering the dream.

"Imagine, darling, not a single enemy…"

"Isn't that what heaven is all about?"

"Perhaps. Many think that life, in the Kingdom, is too easy. After a little while—a thousand or two of earthly years—they feel the need for greater challenge. The dualistic reality provides that. Also, the penalties for mistakes are much greater, if by true reality's standards very short-lived. But they do provide the stimulus to try harder, to push the boundaries of the unknown. That is why the Americans did so well. They are truly a great nation."

"Americans, the Yankees?"

"Americans, the Yankees. They worked harder than most people, kept trying new things, new experiences, crossed new boundaries, took risks. Sure they made thousands, millions of mistakes. It's as Einstein said, 'Anyone who has never made a mistake has never tried anything new,' Albert was one clever dude, as JR would say."

"Einstein?"

"Einstein. And not because he tried to understand the dualistic reality. It can't be done. Not really. It's a question of balance. Every great wisdom is balanced with great stupidity. That's the nature of this reality. It's, sort of, not real…"

Peter felt the closeness not just of Cathy's body; her whole being seemed to merge with his.

"Aye," Peter nodded. "I sure made plenty," thinking of the plethora of mistakes he'd made in his life. "They used to call them sins…"

They both sensed Winston smiling. They also both knew that he was not there, not physically with them; yet his presence was palpable. The mind can play strange tricks, if you let it.

"That's the problems with religions," Winston's smile said, "they always try to make physical reality real. As for you, my boy, I can only say—well done. Didn't you know? Heaven has to be earned."

"By making mistakes?" Peter was still thinking of mistakes being sins.

"If we were perfect, we wouldn't have to go down there," Winston smiled. "Perfection is elusive. Each time you think you hold it in your grasp, it recedes beyond the next horizon."

It struck Peter that, for the most part, Winston was speaking from 'up there', from non-physical reality.

"Do religions do more harm than good?" Peter had been tortured by this question for years.

"At least," Winston smiled broadly, "we can't accuse any of the religions of not making their share of mistakes, can we?"

In some ways, this satisfied Peter's qualms, though not in the way he'd expected.

"I guess that's why we have to be immortal," Peter concluded. And, somehow, this realization made him feel better. He hoped that, in a billion years or so, he might improve somewhat.

"In a billion years you will have reached the first day of the following billion... but, don't worry about it. Time doesn't really exist. We just use it for convenience."

And what of heaven on earth?

Winston smiled at Peter's thoughts.

"You must accept, Peter, that we experience life in a dualistic reality. It relies exclusively on a state of balance. Nothing else matters. This law applies to every one of us. Our positive deeds are automatically balanced by their opposites."

"You are not implying that every good deed must be balanced by one that is evil?" Cathy didn't like the idea.

"In the fullness of time, Cathy, in the fullness of time," Winston's thoughts continued to formulate in both their minds. "And, can you define what is good and what is evil?"

"Why, of course..." she began and then pulled up.

"There is no evil, Cathy. Evil is only the absence of good. When good is restored, evil evaporates like a wisp of steam on a cold day..."

Winston's disembodied arm gestured towards the snow-covered mountain. Their condo seemed to be the only place in Montreal where winter contrived to look more beautiful than any other season.

Cathy still looked dubious.

"I think, darling, I'm beginning to understand. Life-force, or consciousness, or spirit, or whatever you wish to call it, is omnipresent. This fact alone precludes the reality of evil. You know from physics that two elements cannot occupy the same space. And," Peter thought of Winston, "I strongly suspect that what is true of elements is true of other constituents of our physical reality."

Cathy's eyes opened wide, then she pouted her lips. But her thoughts conveyed a different message. *I love you, darling,* her silent emotion flooded Peter's awareness. *Me too*, he replied, as silently. *Me too*. It seemed that their love was still at a personal level.

And Winston nodded his understanding.

So much for heaven on earth, thought Peter. And then he saw a surreptitious smile on Winston's kind features. It looked more real than when he was physically present. Even as Peter looked, the smile dissolved into a warm feeling.

Remember Peter and you, too, Cathy. You are neither your ego, nor are you your body. You are the life force that manifests as a body of light in the glorious Kingdom that is our true home. Here, on earth, this life-force that people call spirit manifests as love.

***

24
Majordomo

O foolish mind,
why do you go here and there in search of Lord Vishnu,
when He is very much present in you?

Teluga poem

A man asked a superb violinist, which of his great recordings is his favourite. The one I'm working on, replied the virtuoso. So it is with the creative force. It lives in the present, in the moment of creation. Neither past nor future exists in its nature. The spirit, as some call it, generates ideas. The mind—executes them. By the time an idea is manifest, the only interest in it is how to maintain it, or improve it, or put a better one in its place. Keeping what's there is outside the terms of reference."

For what might prove to be the last time, they all met, high up in the condo, suspended halfway between the lustrous sheen of the Saint Laurence River and the low-lying clouds. Winston looked at the little group gathered around him. He alone was sitting down, yet he seemed to dominate the room with his presence. Particularly surprising since Lena was there also.

They were all there.

The Mondellays, the Brents, Jonathan and Moira, Lena Walesa, who flew from the Vatican with Mo just for this occasion, JR, and, of course, Cathy and Peter. The occasion? Winston had said that he was about to retire. The very idea seemed preposterous. Wasn't Winston eternal? He seemed to be part of the air they all breathed. He was integral to everyone's nature. When asked where he was going, he wouldn't say.

"I'm no longer needed here," he'd assure everyone who asked. "My job is done."

Nobody could get anymore out of him. Perhaps he'd visit his beloved India, Cathy whispered to Peter. He used to talk a great deal about it. Though at his age…?

Winston sat back. His countenance relaxed, seemingly passive, detached. Silence ruled supreme, yet each person present heard his words as clearly as if he were speaking aloud.

The life force invades anything and everything the mind creates without judgment or discrimination. Imagination is the action of the life force, the inspiration for the various phases of creativity. Ultimately all phases function under the auspices of free will, constrained only by universal laws sustaining the particular reality.

"We are the channels through which the creative process takes place. The entities of light. That's us," he said, this time his sonorous basso bouncing off the walls.

"We are the entities of light?" Peter repeated.

"Yes. Our true nature is manifest in our light body. Don't look so smug, my boy. It is only one phase higher than physical." Winston allowed himself a knowing grin. "The transition body you encounter in your dream can and does solidify in the… Kingdom. In the true reality. To your real senses, photons appear as solid as atoms do here, but laws controlling objects that have mass do not confine them."

Knowingly, Winston glanced at Cathy.

"You mentioned phases?" Her voice sounded a little timid. Somehow Winston knew she had a question to ask. Also, on that day, perhaps for the first time ever, Winston's tone sounded intimidating.

"Solid, liquid, gas, and photons. All well known to you, Cathy. The transient body we experience when dreaming can solidify to enter the next phase. With practice, the light body is available to you at all times. It has been proven, affirmed and displayed, by virtually all avatars, as well as a number of living and transitioned saints."

"You mean dead?"

"No. There is no death. Remember, our physical body is not real. Atoms, as we discussed before, are mostly empty space. The body consisting of photons is more real than anything you can detect here with your physical senses, although those quanta of light are rarely detectable to physical eyes."

Again silence filled the room, yet Winston continued to hold everyone's attention.

There are many phases in the lower universes, and the life force, left on its own, becomes subject to the same laws as all physical energies. But the force, as such, is the only force that is indestructible. Light, as Cathy will tell you, travels at its optimum velocity only in a vacuum. You and I can quicken that force, to allow it to behave in its natural fashion.

Winston closed his eyes. For a while, only the white noise of air-conditioning, set at its minimum, was heard. No one dared to speak. No one wanted to. This was Winston's day.

It was the time of transition. It was that time of the year when Mount Royal received its first gentle sprinkling of light, quick-melting caress of snow. Here and there, one could still see residual shades of red and gold, though the conifers were already rising in prominence.

For some reason, everyone expected something momentous to take place. Everyone looked relaxed, yet an undercurrent of an inexplicable sense of unease hovered in the air. Like a scent of roses that were not in bloom yet, though the buds were already breaking. Perhaps it was the scent of the unknown.

Finally Peter broke the silence. "So the creative force has no interest in keeping me alive?"

"Not as you are. Don't forget that everything in this reality is transient. While you, its individuation, occupy the physical body created by the mind, life-force's only interest lies in your body's continuous rebuilding, possible improvement, in repairing its foibles so that ultimately the next body the mind creates will be better." Winston spoke slowly, as if talking were becoming difficult for him.

"Like improving the immune system..." Peter mused aloud.

"Exactly. To sustain anything for any duration in this reality takes an enormous effort of the mind."

"Mind, the builder."

Winston nodded.

Only now did the guests stir. Before sitting down, a little tentatively, they had all pulled their chairs and armchairs to face Winston. Cathy served light refreshments, then settled on the carpet at Winston's feet.

Even as they all sat down, Dr. and Mrs. Brent, as well as Cathy's parents, evidently thought that silence was the better part of valour. They did not ask any questions, nor did they contribute their own opinions. Yet their eyes indicated an unprecedented degree of attention. Perhaps at their age, matters discussed were not easy to follow. For his part, JR confined himself to crossing and uncrossing his legs, with silent flourish. Once or twice he opened his mouth, only to think better of it, nodding to himself.

Lena, well, Lena looked different. She wasn't used to not being the center of attention. Now she wasn't; yet it seemed obvious that she liked it. That she liked it a lot. She also looked as though she knew Winston better than anyone else.

Cathy looked up at the old man's face.

"My biggest remaining problem," she said, "is how to reconcile the concept of omnipresent goodness with the carnivores masticating herbivores with total impunity. When I see an animal suffering, or when I see, even on TV, a lion catching an antelope in its jaws, my heart turns to putty. I have to turn my head..."

Peter nodded. He didn't think it macho, but he felt pretty much the same.

"It's always the same problem," Winston sighed. "Your mind accepts that this reality is not real, but your heart refuses to let it go. For as long as your emotions are attached to the false premise, you will continue to suffer."

For the first time since Peter had met him, Winston looked sad. Even when Ruth died, he had shown no sorrow. Now, his eyelids drooped, hiding the fires smouldering in his eyes; his brow creased deeply in the middle of his forehead.

"I wish I could help you with that," he added. "I can offer you wine, but you have to drink it yourself."

Wine, Cathy knew, always symbolized spiritual knowledge or, in this case, simply... the truth. Spiritual? Winston had never spoken of spirits. For him there was only the truth or illusion.

"Only the degree of self-awareness defines the difference between man and beast. Nothing else. The nature of consciousness residing in both is the same. The most I can assure you is that in the instant that the jaws of the lion close on the physical body of the antelope, the antelope's consciousness has already left it, even as yours does when your attention shifts to the true reality. All consciousness, not just human, is indestructible."

In the silence that followed, Cathy formulated the question everyone wanted to ask, yet no one dared. Finally she spoke out.

"Who are you?"

Her thought reached Winston before she uttered the question. Her eyes continued to study Winston's face. It was time for words to dissolve into silence. For some reason they all heard him, though he expounded his thoughts as though thinking of someone else.

It took him many, many years. Many lifetimes. He never stopped trying. Never stop trying. After all, you have plenty of time. Eternity?

Who is he, you ask?

Who are you? I guess you've already guessed it.

Cosmic man exists beyond time. He is both, the beginning and the final goal of creation. He is Purusha, Adam Kadmon, Anthropos, Insan-i Kamil, elsewhere known as Pangu, or Bagua. In simpler words, it is that part of the individual which is immortal.

Then his lips began moving again.

"Yes. Immortal. You all, as differentiated units of consciousness, are immortal. So, don't worry about the time factor. It doesn't really exist. Think, instead, about chaos. That is where most of us find our being. But chaos is a misleading term. There is an underlying order and harmony hiding within it. In its potential form. Our job is to unravel it, bring it to the fore."

Perhaps, that's our only job?

He began musing again.

It is likewise with time. All events coexist simultaneously. The past and future are only a way of arranging them in a sequential order. Your past might be someone else's future. And vice versa.

I suppose, it is time to tell you the truth. I gathered you all here, because I hope you can absorb it. Some people cannot. With them, one has to start again. Often from the very beginning. Still, there's no hurry. Time... well, you'll soon know.

It has been ages since I imagined a house on the slopes of Westmount. In it, I felt there should be two young minds, ready to absorb the true reality. The real world. Anyway, I promised... There had been details I had to arrange to make that possible. I had to be many things to many people. As I grow, develop, I hope to become more things to more people.

"Does any of this make sense to you?" His voice sounded distant. "It does to me."

The greatest fun was becoming Peter. He was such a challenging subject. I first imbued his character with religion, then denied it all with science and finally exposed him to the true reality. I must have... I suffered all his agonies, but, let's face it, I'm the richer for it. And, in truth, I haven't suffered his dance at all...

"I still have no idea at which point my imagination became reality." He smiled a self-deprecatory smile. "It was a little like writing a book. A novel. You know what you want it to be about, where you are going with it, but you often have little idea how to get there. In time, the creations of your mind, your imagination, take over. They come alive with a life of their own."

"Do they ever!" This was Moira; she couldn't resist voicing her agreement on hearing Winston's story unfold.

Winston nodded. "In time you can hardly control them. In fact, after a while, you let them have free rein. Think of it as granting someone free will. They are still part of you, but they do their own thing. It's wonderful watching them, seeing them develop." He glanced at Cathy's parents. "You get the feeling of it when you watch your own children."

Winston was beginning to look tired. His exemplary straight back, for years seemingly cast in bronze, now sagged, almost imperceptibly, perhaps under the weight of the years he'd spent in this world. His head leaned back, his hair spread in a fan of gray atop the high back of the armchair. Cathy offered him a glass of water. He took a sip, then another. For a while he rested.

"But let us start at the beginning." He spoke again, with a clearer voice. "You know from your scriptures that you've spent some time gallivanting in paradise in a state of abject irresponsibility. Your forefathers called it Eden. All you needed had been provided for you. As a matter of fact, it still is, only now you have to stretch your arm to get it. Also, today, most people want so much more than they need. At the time, all you had to do was to have fun. As best you could. You had been innocent, carefree, a little bit as I am—even now. In my case it's because I don't worry. I know that only order and harmony, and the resulting love and goodness and beauty, are permanent. All else—all imperfection—is transient. In terms of eternity—ephemeral."

His voice weakened even as he spoke.

How do I know?

I think you've already guessed it. If not, let it remain a mystery. Most people love mysteries.

He cleared his throat.

"Anyway, fun went on for quite a while, and then I realized that you were getting nowhere very fast. I had to help you. I know some of you won't believe me, but it is for you that I created the material world. Until then, until the Big Bang, as Cathy would call it, all was perfect. All was Whole. And then, and please remember, it was just for you, I had to create an artificial state of duality. At the time, I didn't fully realize—or better said, the full impact had not reached my attention—that concomitant with duality is also space and time."

Oh, yes! We, too, make mistakes. Only the Source is perfect.

He took a deep, halting breath.

"The instant I realized it, I tried to reduce it to a minimum. I made time as flexible as I could. I didn't want any of you to remain away from perfect reality any longer than was necessary. I made the physical life as short as possible—just enough for you to learn your lesson, and return. Of course... you had other ideas..." He smiled, once again, sadly. "That creative spark in you came from me," he whispered. Obviously... Where else?

For a while everyone closed their eyes, wondering at the sage's words. Not all of them made sense. They each met Winston individually; each cherished their personal contact, often thinking it imaginary. They seldom believed, fully, what they'd heard, at night, in their dreams, sometimes in lucid moments with eyes closed, listening to their hearts. It had been Winston, always, trying to help yet not to interfere. Not to infringe upon gods endowed with free will.

For a time it looked as if Winston were sleeping. Motionless, his breathing slow and regular, his face relaxed. Yet they continued to hear his voice, though sometimes he spoke as though of someone else.

Now it is time for me to move on. Of course Winston will remain in true reality, in case you need him. My children, all of you, will cope on your own. For a while. I know, from personal experience, that you learn best from your mistakes. I should know. Many of you are my mistakes.

"Does he mean us?" Cathy heard Peter's emotive thought.

"Shhhh..." she replied in kind.

But don't worry, you'll never be completely apart from me. Till the end of time, at some level of perception, we shall remain one. Indivisible. I within you, you all—an integral part of me. You probably don't know it, but it is wonderful to be seen through your eyes. You seem to have always imagined your creator, the author of your being, to be some sort of old man with a long beard. Really, many of you used to think that. I thought, when I painted the Sistine Chapel ceiling, it wasn't a bad likeness. Adam was a bit overweight, but I was still learning. I'll continue to learn. For ever, I guess...

"You follow what I am saying?" he asked aloud. His eyes remained closed.

Our job, that is to say, my job, is to seed souls, or the individualized units of consciousness, with subliminal awareness of true reality. It cannot be done while you are going about your business. Your attention is tied up in your actions. It's tied up with space and time. With change. There is an old saying, "you are, where your attention is." That is true. That is also where your heart is.

With visible effort, Winston sat up straighter.

"Most people are at whatever and wherever they are doing something—even if it's nothing at all. Perhaps that is the worst of all. I gave you so many opportunities, and many of you chose to do nothing at all. You may not realize this, but my words, even now, reverberate in the dark corners of humanity's unconscious. Some of them, not you, my friends, are actively preoccupied with being vegetables. Others get so tied up in their work that they forget why they are living on Earth." This time his eyes opened and glanced steadily at every one present. "That's not very good, either. But most say, I'm a doctor, or a physician, or an actor, or a bus driver, or... whatever. In fact you are all actors. As I once said, the world is but a stage. Remember? It was in Stratford, a small market town in south Warwickshire. The Old Country." A smile lit up his tired features.

"Ah, yes, those were strange days..." And then, for just an instant, he looked at each face turned toward him. "Now you must think I'm omnipresent, right?"

There was some quiet throat-clearing.

"At least when you're asleep," he spoke again, "we get some sort of access to their subconscious. We. Oh, yes, I am not alone. Never have been. On the other hand, I often think that I am one, only I imagine there are many of me. You know... like Elohim. Or three in one, that famed trinity. Why trinity? Why not an infinite number? Everything else is infinite?"

His eyes drifted towards the mountain.

Sometimes I think that it's not easy being me. On the other hand, I've got you. Many, many of you. Countless. And animals and birds, and fish and trees, and flowers. I really love flowers. They are my, sort of, baksheesh. A free gift.

It's fun.

"And then I have Winstons. Not that many, but the few are worth a million. All right—a great, great number. They in turn are a still greater number. And so on, and so forth. Some would call them the chosen ones. Well, you are all chosen, every one of you, only most of you don't know it. You are all chosen to become Winstons. That's what evolution is all about. That and the expanding universe, right, Cathy? I promise to make enough room for you. For ever and ever, worlds without end... Haven't I heard that one before?"

Ahhh, you're all such kidders. You must have gotten it from me. Ha, ha.

"I think that the sense of humour is probably one of my better ideas. It also helps to cover up the unsuccessful attempts. Sure there are many. The Universe is a large place. And Infinity is a very large number. Nobody's perfect."

Strike that last one.

About then time seemed to stop, to be suspended in abeyance. Yet they all continued to hear his voice. Only no one was sure, any more, who was really speaking. Aren't we all one?

One of the bigger problems I faced was how to provide the environment in which my ideas could flourish.

Though Winston's eyes remained closed, his head turned towards Lena.

She is the one who ultimately created an even playing field for many. I've been struggling with this for ages.

*Literally. Then I had it. I inspired a wise man to institute the
Zodiac. The Procession of Equinoxes. I don't mean the circle
of animals, but the Ages. In each Age humanity was given
specific opportunities to acquire particular traits individuals
would need to function well in the following Age, or phase.*

And so on...

Minute by minute, his thoughts seemed to reach them
from farther away.

*...these had been designed to advance the creative
process itself. Solidarity is a vehicle through which all are
given the same opportunities... the Zodiac Ages are just bats
of an eyelid.*

A smile widened his lips.

*...for you, they each span more than 2000 of your years.
Enough to learn to control your thoughts, or to learn to love
your enemy...*

Suddenly Winston sat up. His voice came over as
strongly as ever.

"Now, you must learn to fend for yourselves.
Kindergarten is over and you just graduated to School. You
have a long way to go, but it's a start." His arms embraced
the little gathering. "At least for some of you." Then his face
saddened. "So few among so many..."

Then his voice gathered strength again.

"Tell them. Tell them all. Free will is the most powerful
force in the universe. Not love. Love is omnipresent, it is
what makes us one, it cannot be negated; it is invincible, like
life. But free will can be lost. It can also be used to set us
apart."

For a while there was silence. Although everyone had a
thousand questions, no one dared to interrupt it.

"And now just for the few of you," Winston resumed.
"Your *nephesh*, your animal soul, your subconscious, is your
contribution to the whole. It carries billions of years of
knowledge. It is really worth saving."

All eyes looked up.

"It is worth saving," he repeated. "True reality is virtually static. Those who abide in it don't advance much. They are like children in Paradise. That is why even those who don't have to, any more, choose to enmesh themselves, periodically, in dualistic reality. To progress still further. Yes, here, on Earth. And other Earths. They are the people you call geniuses, or avatars, or even saviours."

When silence stretched for an undetermined time that felt like ages, Peter couldn't resist asking a question close to his heart.

"And what of dreams, Sir?" Peter had never before addressed Winston as Sir. He heard the answer in his head. They all did.

...treat them with care. I use dreams to help you. For many of you they are your first introduction to the true reality. When dreams become conscious, you have taken your first step to my Kingdom.

"There, I said it!" Suddenly he sounded young. "My Kingdom. And Winston's Kingdom. And your Kingdom. They are all one, yet all slightly different... yet, again, all indivisible from the Whole."

"Countless   Kingdoms?"   Peter   couldn't   resist interrupting. He was like a schoolboy hungry for knowledge.

"Yes," came a surprising answer. "Countless Kingdoms. There are many gods, yet only one Source. Sometimes I dream of being a star, surrounded by my own solar system. Such beauty... Or I spread my thoughts across a galactic cloud, swirling with a multitude of hues... I'm sure others dream of new universes..."

They all found the concept of infinity hard to grasp.

"But we all live in the here and now," Cathy murmured.

One day you'll wake up and realize that the life that you took so seriously was, after all, just a dream. That it was a dance of life, a performance, a gift freely given, for your edification.

"Yes, my children. We create the worlds we live in. Gods have gods, have gods, have gods... ad infinitum. All the way to the Source from which all creation flows."

I am within the Source, because the Source is omnipresent. The Source is within me, because the Source is omnipresent. You are where your attention is. When you place your attention on the Source, we become one. When you take your attention away, you create transient realities, until you return to the Source. That is as it is.

"Gods...? Many gods?" this was Peter again.

"Which gods?" Others joined him. "It took millennia for religions to create monotheism and now..."

Winston's tone of voice hardened.

"You are all gods," he commanded with great authority. "Gods are individualizations of the Source who can say no; who can oppose, if briefly, the attributes of the Source. Sometimes this ability is called free will. As I told you, your will, exercised correctly, is the most powerful force in the Universe. You can draw on creative force as much as you know how. Then, you are rewarded royally by your great acts, punished by their absence or by your ignorance."

You and you alone wield the power of right and wrong. The Source is always impartial.

There were moments when Winston spoke and seemed to transfer thoughts directly at the same time.

"Oh, yes," Peter mused. He was unaware that his thoughts were accessible to everyone present. He looked at Cathy. "We are all gods. We just die like men. Haven't you ever noticed how beautiful most children are, and how unsightly so many of us become with age? Why do you think that is so? Could it be that we are all doing something wrong? Ignorance is not bliss."

"Look for perfection but don't look for gods." Winston spoke aloud. "Look for divine attributes. There are countless gods, in countless universes. And they all draw on the Source."

The air surrounding Winston's armchair shimmered, grew brighter, then slowly, as though with reluctance, returned to normal. The last words they all heard came from an empty chair.

Goodbye, for now. Always remember, we are one. You won't see me for a little while, neither as Winston, nor as Peter, nor Cathy, nor as any of my favourite children. I am all—yet none of them. If you need me, look within. I may be invisible, but I'm always there.
Waiting.

***

If you enjoyed this story,
please write a brief review on Amazon.
Thanks.

So long...

Acknowledgments

As always, my thanks to my friends for their perceptive comments and to my wife, Bozena Happach, for inspiring my life and offering comments during and after the completion of the first draft. Also, my very special thanks go to Kate Jones, whose diligent editing as well as subsequent proofreading raised this effort of mine to acceptable literary standards.

Some of the subjects mentioned in this novel are discussed in greater details in my essays published as ebooks by Inhousepress. Among them: *The Carrot and the Stick,* Essay #28; *Power,* Essay #5; *Parallel Evolution,* Essay #46; *Freedom,* essay #8; *Self,* Essay #19; *Life,* Essay #4; and *Beyond Religion,* Essay #52, can be found in *Beyond Religion,* Volume I (Collection of Essays by Stanislaw Kapuscinski).

Balance, Essay #4, originates in *Beyond Religion* Volume II, while *Blood Bath,* Essay # 10, *Green Eyed Monster,* essay #32, and *Visual Perception,* essay #12, are further discussed in *Beyond Religion* Volume III (also by Stanislaw Kapuscinski). My research also drew on *The Emerging Mind,* by Vilayanur Ramachandran, particularly pgs. 114—115. I am grateful to INHOUSEPRESS and the BBC for providing me with such excellent sources.

Sincerely,
Stan I.S. Law